DEAR DOTTY

DEAR DOTTY

A Novel

Jaclyn Westlake

AVON

An Imprint of HarperCollins*Publishers*

DEAR DOTTY. Copyright © 2024 by Jaclyn Raggio-Westlake. All rights reserved. Printed in the United States of America. No part of this book may be used or reproduced in any manner whatsoever without written permission except in the case of brief quotations embodied in critical articles and reviews. For information, address HarperCollins Publishers, 195 Broadway, New York, NY 10007.

HarperCollins books may be purchased for educational, business, or sales promotional use. For information, please email the Special Markets Department at SPsales@harpercollins.com.

FIRST EDITION

Designed by Diahann Sturge

Pug dog illustration © Igillustrator / Shutterstock

Library of Congress Cataloging-in-Publication Data has been applied for.

ISBN 978-0-06-334071-8

24 25 26 27 28 LBC 5 4 3 2 1

For Brian, who always believed that I could do this (even when I wasn't so sure). Thank you for your love, support, and all that iced coffee.

And for Indy, who remained steadfastly by my side (or in my lap or on my keyboard), softly snoring, as I typed every word of this story.

DEAR DOTTY

PROLOGUE

MAY

I was halfway through making a mental list of everything I wanted to tell Dotty about when I remembered that she was dead. I kept forgetting. Remembering felt like waking up from a pleasant dream only to find that my home had been incinerated in a firenado.

I would gladly *live* in a firenado if it would bring Dotty back.

My hands trailed along the thinning upholstery of my chair. It was rough and scratchy beneath my fingertips. My best friend, Marcia, had taught me to focus on whatever I could see, feel, hear, or smell whenever I needed to be more present. It usually helped, but now that I think about it, I probably shouldn't call Marcia my best friend anymore. Not after what she did.

"How did you know her again?" My brother, Tommy, was talking to Dotty's lawyer, a tall, sandy-haired man who insisted we call him Peter. I'd never be able to do that, though, because his full name was Peter Simpson, Esquire, and that was the kind of name that begged to be said in its entirety.

Peter Simpson, Esquire sat behind a comically large desk with ornately carved legs. His office was small—no bigger than my living room, which wasn't saying much—so his desk took up more than half the space. The rest of us—my parents, my brother, and his poor, pregnant wife, Lily—sat on a mismatched collection of stools and chairs that Peter had dragged from disparate corners of the room upon our arrival.

Tommy was telling Peter about how Mom had suddenly decided to leave Dad for no discernible reason. My brother was leaning forward, eyes narrowed with suspicion as he spoke. He was weirdly territorial around other lawyers. It was one of his many annoying traits.

I'd never admit this to Tommy's face, but I was starting to think that maybe caring too much about your job wasn't such a bad thing. Maybe if I cared more I wouldn't have gotten fired. (Stealing all the best snacks from the office pantry probably didn't help, either. But in my defense, the siren call of a cheese puff is all but impossible to resist.)

Peter Simpson, Esquire waited patiently for my brother to finish talking. Then he nodded. "Dotty told me. And we've accounted for that in the will."

Dad forced out a barking huff of a laugh, startling Dotty's pug from her catatonic state. Bug sat upright in my lap and sighed. I wrapped my arms protectively around her pudgy little tummy.

"How long have you been planning this divorce, Claire?" Dad had swiveled on his stool to face Mom, who stared straight ahead and refused to respond.

Dad raked his hands through his graying curls. "I can't believe this. It's in the goddamned will? My aunt knew before I did?" He was talking to Peter Simpson, Esquire, now.

"Let's try to get through this without dragging Mr. Simpson into our family drama," Mom said through her teeth. This must have been killing her.

Dad looked back and forth between Mom and Peter before giving up and sinking back into his chair. "Fine by me."

If Dotty were here, she'd be leaning over to whisper a crack about my family's ridiculous behavior in my ear. I could almost feel her wrinkled hand resting on my wrist, the cool metal band of her turquoise ring pressing against my skin.

Dotty was the only one who could make me feel calm in the midst of my family's chaos. She made being a misfit look easy. Fun, even. But now she was gone. Right when I needed her the most. The shoddy patchwork that was my life had ripped at the seams and I had no clue how to stitch it all back together. I needed Dotty to tell me where I'd gone wrong. She was never shy about that sort of thing.

I hated that I'd never get to talk to her again. Hated that I'd have to face my twenty-fifth birthday without her. Hated that I'd only learned her real name was Eugenia this morning. *Where did "Dotty" come from?* I'd asked. No one bothered to give me a straight answer.

I used the hood of Bug's knit sweater to dab at my eyes, unsure if my tears were from sadness or shame. Either way, she didn't seem to mind.

Now Mom was saying something about my current state of unemployment as Tommy nodded in agreement. They were talking about me as if I weren't even there, as if I were the ghost.

My shoulders sagged with grief. I was exhausted. I hadn't slept at all last night. Or the night before, for that matter. But that had been for a very different reason. My one-night stand with Donovan felt distant and foggy, almost like it had happened to someone else. That was probably for the best, since I wasn't supposed to be talking to him. Let alone sleeping with him.

I mentally retraced my steps, analyzing all the mistakes that had led me here. Had I gone to the wrong college? Accepted the wrong job? Been born into the wrong family? Probably, to all three. But, if I had to single out a fateful moment, one specific turning point, there was only one that came to mind.

As I sat there in that cramped little office, my thoughts clouded by despair, one thing was crystal clear: I never should have gone to the beach with Marcia that day.

CHAPTER ONE

MARCH

Six Weeks Earlier

Y ou can't go to work today." It was a Thursday morning and still dark outside. Marcia stood in the doorway of my bedroom, light from the hall illuminating the tight curls of her hair.

"Five more minutes," I said, pulling the covers over my head. I was always grumpy in the mornings. Especially on weekdays. I didn't exactly hate my job, but I definitely didn't like it, either. Driftwood was the type of start-up everyone wanted to work at after they graduated from college—the office boasted rows of Ping-Pong tables, a dedicated barista, and views of the Bay Bridge. And the people were nice enough. But selling software was not nearly as glamorous as my manager, Raj, made it sound when I'd interviewed with him. Every cold call was just another opportunity to embarrass myself. That wears on you after a while.

Marcia flipped on the bedroom light with a dramatic sigh and stalked over to my bed. "It's going to be eighty-five degrees this afternoon."

"Go away."

She tugged my bedspread off in one fluid motion. "Don't you know what this means?"

I grabbed Bob, my stuffed frog, and used him to shield my eyes from the blinding light, his gangly limbs dangling by my ears. Marcia tried to pitch me on harebrained schemes like this every few months. She'd decide that we needed to take a road trip back to our old college town because she was craving a slice of pizza from our favorite restaurant, or she'd say we needed to dress up as Santa Claus and run around the city with flasks of peppermint schnapps in our boots. And once she got an idea like that in her head, she was relentless. "I think this means you're dead to me."

She yanked Bob off my head. "Rosie," she said before pausing dramatically. I half expected her to announce that she'd been nominated for an Oscar. "Today is a beach day."

Real, true, bona fide beach days were a rarity in San Francisco. So when the weather gods graced the city with a heat wave, half the population would drop what they were doing and run to Baker Beach or Chrissy Field.

"Come on, Ro," Marcia was full-on whining now. "Didn't you hear me? We're going to the beach." She picked up my limp arm and started tugging. "You need to text your boss that you had a family emergency or something and then come help me in the kitchen. I'm making frozen vodka watermelon pops."

"The sun isn't even out yet," I said, still trying to process everything Marcia was saying. I was not a morning person. "And I can't miss work." She dropped my arm and stomped to the other side of the room, her footsteps echoing on the bare hardwood, and began rummaging around in my closet. I listened as she tossed shoes and purses and dirty laundry aside in search of god knows what.

Marcia and I had been friends since the first day of third grade, when we'd walked into Ms. Noor's class, both clutching identical Hannah Montana lunch boxes. But we didn't become best friends until two weeks later, when we discovered that we preferred the contents of each other's lunch boxes. Mom always sent me to school with a bland peanut butter and jelly sandwich and a bag of celery sticks while Marcia's dad would pack her plantain and bean porridge with crackers or rice stew and bananas. When I told Marcia that her dad's cooking was the most delicious thing I'd ever tasted, she would roll her eyes and say, "My parents make me eat Nigerian food all the time. Sometimes I just want something boring."

It was the perfect metaphor for our relationship: I found Marcia to be endlessly fascinating (her dad had moved to California from an entirely different country! I wasn't even sure if mine had ever left the state), and she knew I was boring-as-could-be but loved me anyway. When our moms realized that they'd graduated from the same high school (albeit a few years apart), it sealed the deal. We were the perfect combination of similar and different, destined to be friends forever.

Giving in to the inevitable, I rolled onto my side, propping myself up on an elbow. "What are you looking for?"

She didn't look up. "Where do you keep your backpack?"

"What do you need a backpack for?"

Marcia turned to face me; her brown eyes were narrowed, lips pursed. "For beer," she said, like it was the most obvious thing in the world.

I flopped back down on the bed. "I'll find it for you. Just get out of my room."

"Fine. But I want to see your beautiful face in the kitchen in ten minutes or less."

I lobbed my pillow in her direction. It landed at her feet with a feeble thud. "Make it fifteen," I said, half pouting, half smiling.

* * *

I tucked the straps of my bathing suit under my armpits and lay back on the towel, reveling in the delightful warmth of the sun on my chest. Marcia was right. There was no way I could have gone to work on a day like this. After years of working under the harsh glow of fluorescent office lighting, I was in desperate need of a tan.

"Another beer?" Marcia asked, rummaging around in my old college backpack. She'd lined it with a plastic garbage bag and filled it with ice.

"Why not?" I stretched out a hand.

"What did your boss say?"

I shoved a rolled towel behind my shoulders and took a sip of beer, feeling myself sink further into sheer bliss. There was something wickedly luxurious about drinking before noon on a workday.

"He didn't respond to my text."

Marcia looked at her own phone. "Maybe he's taking the day off, too."

"Maybe," I said. But I doubted it. If Driftwood were a cult, Raj would be its most loyal member. He seemed to genuinely enjoy being at work.

I would have given anything to genuinely enjoy being at work.

"You're not missing anything major today, right?"

I shook my head. "Just a cold-calling workshop. Raj wants us to try out some new scripts, but I'll just practice by myself tomorrow." I did my best to keep my tone light and breezy. It was *probably* fine that I was missing today's training, but Raj had specifically mentioned that it would be helpful if I came, as part of the per-formance improvement plan he'd made for me. He made them for everyone on the team anytime they didn't hit quota for the previous quarter. It was just a formality—some strategy he'd picked up during one of his many seminars for "up-and-coming leaders"—but still. He'd definitely notice I wasn't there. And I'd definitely hear something about it tomorrow.

But that was tomorrow's problem.

Marcia took a long pull of beer and then looked around as if surveying her kingdom. She wore her favorite bathing suit, a vibrant green one-piece, and oversize Ray-Ban sunglasses that made her look like she could be an influencer. Her dewy, deep brown complexion and obnoxiously high cheekbones didn't hurt, either.

Marcia sighed. "I needed this."

Marcia was a publicist at Drip, one of the largest PR firms in San Francisco. She'd started as an intern two years ago and had been promoted twice since then. She now had her own assistant and was a full-fledged workaholic. There were moments when I'd start to feel jealous of how quickly her career had taken off, but then I'd remind myself of how she was always out the door before the sun rose and sometimes wouldn't return home until around the time I was getting ready for bed.

There was also the gray hair incident.

Just three weeks after Marcia took on her newest client—a young, rich, and terribly handsome entrepreneur named Donovan Ng—I found Marcia sitting alone in the bathroom, clutching a pair of tweezers in one hand and a compact in the other. "Are you okay?" I asked, squatting down so we were at eye level. "You look like you swallowed a goldfish."

"It's much worse than that," she said, her voice sounding distant, hollow. "I found a gray hair . . . down *there*."

She'd been trying to work up the courage to pluck it out but was paralyzed by the threat of more growing back in its place. I happily volunteered after she swore me to secrecy. We never spoke of it again. But I'd concluded that as glamorous as Marcia's job seemed, it probably wasn't worth all the stress.

"How are things going with Donovan Ng?" I asked.

"Annoying," Marcia said. "He's so picky. If I didn't know any better, I'd think he would have preferred to plan this party himself."

Donovan had hired Marcia's agency to handle the grand opening of his new venture capital firm. She'd spent an inordinate number of hours planning what sounded like an incredible launch party (a bar buyout complete with branded swag, signature cocktails, and a surprise musical guest), and from what I'd gathered, Donovan had been overly involved every step of the way. He made Marcia send him daily updates and texted her constantly.

"When's the party?"

"The first Friday in May. I can't wait for it to be over."

I moved my sunglasses to the top of my head and swiveled my neck to face her. "But won't you miss working with Donovan?"

"Not even a little bit."

I'd visited Donovan Ng's LinkedIn profile precisely four times since Marcia had told me about him. He was gorgeous, as advertised, with dark, stylish hair and the kind of smile that made you wish you could afford to get your teeth professionally whitened. "He can't be *that* bad."

"You're just saying that because you think he's hot. But his looks have no effect on me." She tossed her hair dramatically. "Guys like Donovan aren't my type—he's way too high maintenance."

The idea of Marcia having "a type" was a bit of a stretch. She'd brought home all kinds of guys over the years: veiny CrossFit fanatics, skinny hipsters with thick glasses, frat guys in polo shirts. The one thing they'd all had in common was that they were not relationship material. Marcia was too restless to commit to anyone for more than a few weeks.

"Well, I think the party sounds fun," I said.

"Want to come?"

I bolted upright, sending my sunglasses flying into the sand. "Do I want to go to an exclusive party where I could breathe the same air as Donovan Ng? Is that even a question?"

Marcia laughed. "Wow, okay. It'll be nice to have you there for moral support, just try to play it cool." She moved her hand in a circular motion. "Because this is a lot."

I returned my sunglasses to the bridge of my nose and brushed stray grains of sand from my cheeks. "I'm always cool."

"Uh-huh," Marcia said. She was wearing her *my best friend is ridiculous but I love her anyway* smile. "We can go out afterward, too. To celebrate my freedom."

I wriggled my shoulders, not bothering to hide my excitement. "Thank you, Marshmallow!"

"We'd agreed you wouldn't call me that in public."

"You may be Marcia Adebayo, PR superstar to the rest of the world, but you'll always be my Marshmallow. Even in public." I held up a finger. "Especially in public."

"You're so annoying." She shook her head before picking up her phone and waving it in my direction. "Selfie time."

And here was the fundamental difference between Marcia and me. I would have been perfectly content to lie flat on my beach towel all day, and she couldn't sit still for more than six minutes. I'd timed her. "Don't you have enough pictures of yourself already?"

Marcia peered at me over the top of her sunglasses. "We've been through this, Rosie," she said, feigning annoyance. "Someday we're going to be old and tired and boring and all we'll have to look back on are the images of our youth."

I'd heard the "Images of Our Youth" speech before. Marcia had been fine-tuning it ever since our senior year of high school when she'd tried to convince me to start a crowdfunding campaign so we could hire a film crew to document prom night. It's no wonder she'd ended up working in public relations. It was scary how persuasive she could be.

"Whatever," I said as Marcia stretched her arm above her head. She alternated between snapping photos, squinting at the screen, and rotating on her towel to capture the best lighting.

"That's the one," she finally said, declaring victory.

"If you post anything, don't tag me," I said, thinking of Raj. I'd stupidly accepted his follow request on Instagram when I started at Driftwood and had regretted it ever since. If I had to pity like one more of Raj's lame hiking photos, my thumbs might fall off in protest.

Marcia's eyes remained fixed on her phone. "I'm not going to post these. They're just for the guy I'm talking to."

I ran through the names Marcia had mentioned over the past few weeks, but only one came to mind. "Kickball guy?"

"Maybe," she said coyly, biting her lip.

"Is he an Elephant?" I asked, referring to Marcia's team, the Enyimba Kickball Club, which was named after the most famous soccer team in Nigeria. Their mascot was an elephant, which I, of course, loved. Elephants were one of my favorite animals. After apes and pigs, of course. Marcia had been really into kickball for the past few weeks and had even taken to dragging herself out of bed to practice on Saturday mornings, which was wildly out of character. She usually loved sleeping in on weekends. But maybe she'd been motivated by more than honing her recreational sports skills.

Marcia shook her head. "No. He's on another team" was all she said. She finished her text, then turned to me. "Should we go take a picture by the bridge?"

It was an inartful dodge, but I decided to let it slide for now.

Baker Beach sat at the foot of the Golden Gate Bridge, encircled by rocky cliffsides and tree-lined hiking trails. People were always going out of their way to take family photos or engagement pictures there. It was a little cliché, but I couldn't blame them—it was stunning, especially on a clear sunny day like today. The bridge's rust-colored towers complemented the blue sky and green cliffs so perfectly that you could almost convince yourself it had been there all along, a natural outgrowth that had risen from the swirling waters below.

The sun had only grown brighter since we'd arrived that morning, the temperature creeping from warm to hot. "Can we dip our feet in the water first? I can feel my insides starting to sizzle."

"With lines like that, how are you still single?"

"It's a mystery," I said with an exaggerated shrug.

It wasn't a mystery. While I certainly wasn't above a drunken bar makeout or a one-night stand here and there, I also wasn't looking for a boyfriend. The idea sounded nice, but not nice enough to troll dating apps or accept Marcia's attempts to fix me up with guys from her kickball league. She was the boy-obsessed one. I figured I'd find my person when the time was right. My sister-in-law, Lily, said that was because I was secretly a romantic, but I wasn't so sure.

Marcia and I threw our wallets and phones into her macramé bag before picking our way down the beach, past a group of guys in thigh-high swim trunks drinking canned rosé and a row of identical-looking blond girls with matching SoulCycle towels. I think I heard one of them giggling about a group of elderly nudists sunbathing by the foot of the bridge.

The buzz of activity faded behind us as the sound of crashing waves grew louder. I breathed in the briny ocean air as we neared the water's edge. I needed to do stuff like this more often. I liked the way I was feeling—relaxed and free. That part of myself had been slipping away over the past couple of years. It's surprisingly difficult to be carefree when you have responsibilities.

It dawned on me that maybe Marcia needed more days like this, too. I promised myself I'd be better about helping her blow off steam.

"Oh my god." Marcia's voice broke into my thoughts. "Isn't that your aunt?"

I followed her gaze down the beach, my breath catching at the sight of a gaggle of naked senior citizens strutting along the shoreline, their assorted private parts bouncing limply as they walked. At the center was a pale, wrinkled old woman with a familiar silver bob and a puff of gray hair in a spot I'd never be able to unsee. She wore a radiant smile and had a purple fanny pack fastened around her waist.

It was my great-aunt Dotty.

I spun instinctively in the other direction and grabbed Marcia's hand. "We have to get out of here."

Marcia giggled as I began pulling her down the beach. "Was that Dotty?"

"Unfortunately."

Marcia glanced over her shoulder and then stopped in her tracks. "Too late. She's coming this way. Actually she's . . . jogging this way."

I refused to turn around. I didn't need another look at my naked aunt. The image was already burned into my retinas.

"Hey there, kiddo!" Dotty's voice sounded closer than I'd expected. "Almost didn't recognize you in your skivvies." Before I knew it, she had one hand on either of my shoulders and was planting a kiss on each of my cheeks. Then she did the same thing to Marcia, who smirked with delight.

"Beautiful day, isn't it?" Dotty said, taking a step back. It took everything in me to keep my eyes glued to her face.

"Dotty, you're naked."

"I know. Isn't it great?" She struck a pose. "You two should try it sometime. Enjoy those young bodies while you have 'em. You'll look like the rest of us soon enough."

"You look great," Marcia said, her eyes sweeping up and down Dotty's wrinkled frame.

Dotty leaned in as if she were about to share a secret. "It's all the sex."

That sent Marcia into a laughing fit.

Dotty glanced back at her naked friends, who'd stopped to enjoy the waves lapping at their ankles. They seemed oblivious to the stares of the crowd. A part of me admired their total absence of shame. But the other part was utterly horrified.

"I should probably get back to the group. But I'm so glad you girls are playing hooky," she said. "Your generation takes work way too seriously. There's so much more to life."

Dotty eyed me pointedly. Marcia nodded her agreement. I guess it takes one to know one.

"Say," Dotty said, "want me to snap a picture of you two before I head out?"

"Really?" Marcia asked, bouncing on her heels. "That would be great." She went to hand Dotty her phone, but my aunt waved her off before reaching into her fanny pack and producing a small digital camera.

"How about a real picture?" Dotty said, holding the camera up like a trophy.

Marcia tucked her phone back into her bag before dragging me into the water. She wrapped her arms around me and pressed her cheek to mine. She smelled like sunscreen. "Smile like your eighty-year-old aunt's vagina isn't on display," she said through her teeth. That got me to laugh.

"Got it," Dotty declared, holding the screen away from her face to review her work. "I'll email this over to you when I get home. Sound good, kiddo?"

I nodded dumbly, still shell-shocked from seeing my aunt in the buff. Dotty gave a final wave before rejoining her naked friends.

"Your aunt's so cool," Marcia said with genuine admiration in her voice. "I think I want to be her when I grow up. Only less naked."

I rubbed my temples in a futile attempt to erase the events of the past five minutes from my memory. "Definitely less naked."

Marcia draped her arm over my shoulder. "What a day," she said dreamily. "Totally worth missing work, right?"

"Totally," I agreed, turning to face the sparkling waters of the Pacific. Familial nudity aside, today had been pretty great. With any luck, seeing Dotty naked would be the worst—and only—consequence of calling out sick.

From: Dotty Polk
To: Rosie Benson
Subject: Bathing Beauties!
Date: March 24

Dear Rosie,

Great running into you at the beach yesterday! We should meet up there more often. Baker Beach is one of my all-time favorite spots. Bug loves it, too. Anyway, I've attached the photo I took of you and Marcia to this email. It's frame-worthy if you ask me. You were glowing yesterday—haven't seen that side of you in months.

Will I be seeing you at your parents' place for dinner tonight? I want to tell you about my trip to Peru. I'm working on an article about my entomologist friend, Dr. Burmeister. He's counting tiger moths in the Amazon. It's fascinating work!

Love,
Dotty

CHAPTER TWO

I sat, only mildly sunburnt, at my desk snacking on a bag of cheese puffs and admiring the picture Dotty had taken of Marcia and me. It looked candid, like Dotty had snapped it when we thought no one was looking. Marcia and I were wrapped in the kind of hug you save for your best friend, beaming at each other, both midlaugh, with shimmering green-blue water swirling around our calves. Dotty was right—it was frameworthy.

"Rosie, will you be joining us?"

I tried not to flinch at Raj's sudden appearance above my desk, his fingers curling around the frosted glass wall. I glanced at the time. It was 3:34 P.M. and I was late.

"I'll be right there," I said. "Sorry."

"Great." He knocked his knuckle on the glass. "We're in the Redwood Room." He disappeared down the hall without waiting for a response.

I minimized the photo and sent up a silent prayer that Raj hadn't seen my screen. He would have said something if he had, wouldn't he? I pushed the thought from my mind and snuck a final cheese puff before tucking the bag into my desk drawer.

* * *

"Ready?" Raj asked, flashing an alarmingly white, toothy smile.

"Ready," I lied. I hoped no one could tell that my eyelids were sweating. I'd been dreading this moment all week, ever since Raj returned from his leadership seminar and announced that we'd be trying out a new training exercise: cold-calling as a team! He'd said it as if we'd all won a trip to Disneyland. I'd planned on practicing the new call scripts yesterday, but then I called out sick instead and went to the beach. Most of my day today had been consumed by attending to my neglected inbox. So this was going to be interesting.

I drew a deep breath, pulled up my customer profile, and dialed the number, doing my best not to wince when the line started to ring. I could feel my coworkers' eyes on me, waiting for me to implode. Performing well under pressure wasn't really my thing. Maybe I'd get lucky and no one would pick up.

"This is Jan," an authoritative voice answered, making the room feel suddenly cramped. I could have sworn the glass walls had inched their way closer to the conference table when I wasn't looking.

"Hi, Jan," I said, sounding froggier than I would have liked, "this is Rosie with Driftwood Technologies." Raj flashed me an encouraging thumbs-up. Getting praise for introducing yourself over the phone was like being awarded a participation trophy, but at least I was off to a decent start.

"Okay . . ."

I cleared my throat. "I was on LinkedIn earlier today, and I wanted to tell you that I enjoyed your post about integrating technology into human resources." Jan didn't reply. Raj made an exaggerated circular motion with his hand, a signal for me to keep going. "I also noticed that you're a cat person. So am I. Well, I like dogs, too. And frogs. All animals, really." Raj dropped his face into his hands.

"Who is this again?"

"Sorry—" I stopped myself. Raj had told me a million times not to apologize during sales calls. "This is Rosie with Driftwood Technologies."

"How do I know you?"

"You don't," I said, speaking with increased urgency. "But I think I can help you. I know you're a PlainStaff customer and I think our software could save you money, give you a smoother user experience, and make you better at your job." I cast a glance around the room, but not a single person would meet my eye. Still, I soldiered on. "Jan, how about we schedule some time for a demonstration next week? I can come to your office. I know exactly where it is. I walk by the Transamerica building every day. It's right next to my bus stop."

There was a long, excruciating pause. "That won't be necessary." Another pause. "Please don't call me again." Then the line went dead.

I don't know how much time passed before Raj spoke, but I could feel the seconds scraping by, slow and painful. I tugged at the sleeves of my sweater, bringing them down around my thumbs, and used the soft fabric to dab at my eyelids. I was sure all my eye makeup had melted off, carried away by a nervous sweat.

"How do you think that went, Rosie?"

"Not great."

"What would you do differently next time?"

"Everything."

Raj leaned back in his ergonomic chair, tapping a pen on the reclaimed wood table. It was acacia, I think. Dotty would know. She was like an encyclopedia of useless facts. "Chad, Gemma, do either of you have any feedback for Rosie?"

Gemma twisted the end of one of her braids between her manicured fingers before attempting to make a thoughtful facial expression. "I thought you sounded pretty confident in the beginning."

Raj nodded as if Gemma had said something profoundly helpful. "Chad?"

Chad smirked. "Where did all the cat stuff come from?"

My cheeks warmed. "Her profile said she volunteers at a cat shelter."

"You sounded like a stalker," Chad said, not bothering to suppress a laugh. "Especially when you were all 'I can come to your office.' You were giving off a serious I-want-to-wear-your-skin vibe."

I couldn't believe I'd ever had a crush on him. Dotty had always warned me never to trust a man with perfect hair.

"It wasn't *that* bad," Gemma said, giving Chad's shoulder a playful shove.

Raj leaned forward, the zipper of his Driftwood Technologies fleece dangling over the table. I was almost two years into this job, and I still couldn't tell whether he owned five identical vests or if he wore the same one every day. And I wasn't sure which would be worse. "I think what Chad is trying to say is that when we look for relevant information about our potential customers, it's best to keep it specific to work."

I nodded, doing my best to look like I was taking it all in stride. Cold calls were by far the worst part of my job. I didn't even like sales. But it paid pretty well, even when I didn't make my numbers, which was every quarter. On the bright side, most of the business development representatives got promoted to either account executives or account managers after two years. I wanted to be an account manager because they didn't have to make cold calls. I was so close I could taste it.

"Thanks for the feedback, guys. I'll keep at it," I said. I was always saying stuff like that: *I'll keep at it, let's do this, let's crush it.*

I'd become fluent in meaningless phrases designed to make people feel pumped.

"Excellent," Raj said, seemingly satisfied. "Let's give someone else a shot, shall we? Gemma?"

I settled back into my chair and flattened my shaking hands on my thighs. That was a disaster, but at least the room was back to its original size again.

Chad's and Gemma's calls went much better than mine had. Gemma struck up a lively conversation with a human resources director about the benefits of running payroll and paid time off on the same system. Chad got his prospective customer howling with laughter over some lame story about PlainStaff's recent data breach. I had to make a concerted effort not to roll my eyes as Raj beamed with pride. If this became our new Friday afternoon team-building activity, I might have to join the Witness Protection Program.

"Great job today, everyone," Raj said, shutting his laptop. "Hope you all have an epic weekend."

We said our goodbyes and I made my way back toward my workstation, past the Ping-Pong tables that no one ever used, past the always-busy kombucha tap, and past the massive, reclaimed wood reception desk, but I stopped short at the community pantry. Driftwood had the best snack selection I had ever seen, and it was impossible to resist. I ducked inside and stuffed bags of jalapeño chips, peanut butter pretzels, and cheese puffs into my Driftwood tote bag. The good snacks always ran out first, so I'd taken to stockpiling a personal stash at my desk. Junk food was one of my few sources of comfort, and at a place like Driftwood, where my boss seemed to relish putting me in the hot seat in front of my obnoxiously perfect coworkers, I needed all the comfort I could get.

I dumped my haul into my secret snack drawer and turned

the lock before flipping off the strand of twinkle lights I'd strung up my first week on the job. I was unplugging my laptop when Raj's head appeared over the frosted half wall of my cubicle. "Hey, Rosie." He said it like he was a sympathetic doctor checking on a terminally ill patient.

"Hey, Raj."

"Any big plans tonight?"

"I'm having dinner with my family. Same as every Friday," I said. I couldn't wait to get to my parents' house. I needed to see Dotty. She always made me feel better after a bad day. But I wasn't going to tell Raj any of that. He was only capable of communicating in toxic positivity.

"That's great," he said, bobbing his head enthusiastically. Raj was only a few years older than me—maybe twenty-seven?—but the benevolent boss vibe he'd carefully cultivated made him seem ancient.

"Yep."

"Hey, let's sync up on Monday. Can you put something on my calendar?"

This wasn't good. Sync-ups usually amounted to Raj bending over backward to list all the things I was doing wrong in the most diplomatic way possible. But pretending that I valued his attempts at mentorship was part of this twisted little game we'd been playing. I summoned my most bubbly voice. "Sure!"

"Excellent." He tapped his fingers on the shiny white glass. "I'll see you Monday."

"See you then," I said, trying to ignore a familiar feeling of dread. Monday was going to be rough. But I had the whole weekend ahead of me and I wasn't going to let one of Raj's feedback sessions get me down now.

CHAPTER THREE

Is that a new jacket?" Mom asked, pulling me into a too-tight hug, her freshly highlighted hair tickling my cheek. "It looks new."

Mom had been horrified when I'd decided to move to San Francisco with Marcia after college. "Don't you want to live at home for a while? Save up some money?" she'd said, eyebrows raised. Questioning me about my spending habits was now her form of revenge.

"It's good to see you too, Mom." I patted her back and wriggled out of her embrace. Then I hung my suspiciously new-looking jacket on one of the hooks by the front door and beelined for the kitchen. I knew I'd find Dad there, at his usual post behind the bar whipping up a fresh batch of margaritas for cocktail hour. He didn't disappoint, pressing an icy, salt-rimmed glass into my hand and kissing the top of my head. "How's my little CEO in the making?"

I was hardly a CEO in the making (I considered myself more of a reluctant saleswoman with a hopeful lottery win in the making), but I liked the idea of Dad thinking I was capable of climbing the corporate ladder.

I held up the drink. "I'm better now." He beamed with pride, broadening his slight chest and revealing a gap-toothed grin. Dad might have been a great accountant, but wine and spirits were his real passion. He'd once spent an hour explaining the agave harvesting process to me in excruciating detail. That had been a very long night.

"Well, if it isn't my favorite niece," a familiar voice rasped. I turned to see Dotty standing at the entrance to the kitchen, a martini in one hand and a tubby little pug tucked under her other arm. I was relieved to see that she wore the same outfit she always did: black slacks, black turtleneck, vibrantly hued pashmina (tonight it was fuchsia), and matching cat-eye glasses. "Life is short," she'd once told me, "I don't have time to worry about clothes." Dad said that was because Dotty was a part-time nudist. I'd hoped that was a joke, but unfortunately, I now knew it to be true.

I smiled, maybe my first real smile all day. "If it isn't my favorite aunt," I said, the beginnings of a dull stress headache melting away.

Dotty winked in response to our usual greeting as her dog, Bug, began kicking her legs as if she were paddling through water. Dotty set her on the floor and I knelt just in time for her to scramble into my lap. "Hi, Love Bug," I said, scratching behind her stubby ears. She grunted a reply as any lingering worries about my Monday meeting with Raj evaporated. Bug, with her smooshy little face, bulging eyes, crooked tail, and cable-knit sweater that didn't quite fit over her tummy, was like antianxiety medication.

Dotty strode to her favorite barstool and set her glass on top of a coaster that read *World's Greatest Aunt*. I scooped Bug into my arms and joined her at the counter. Dotty kissed me on either cheek. "How are you, kiddo? Quit that job yet?" she asked before licking her thumb and dabbing at the plum-colored lipstick marks I was sure she'd left on my face.

Dotty was shameless about telling everyone what she thought about their lives, and she made no secret of her disdain for my choice in employers. She'd warned me hundreds of times not to work at companies that offered free food, insisting it was a trap. I would have chalked Dotty's bluntness up to her old age, but Dad said she'd been like this for as long as he could remember. The key to dealing with Dotty's unsolicited advice was to get her talking about something else. The woman loved the sound of her own voice and was full of wild stories. My personal favorites were the time she followed a politician into the bathroom just to tell him she hated his tie, the time she smashed a car window to rescue a trapped dog, and the time she accidentally ended up on *The Price Is Right*. She claimed it was because Bob Barker had the hots for her.

I passed Bug back to Dotty and tied one of Mom's floral aprons around my waist. "How was Peru?" I asked, hoping to change the subject.

"I see right through you, kiddo," she said, narrowing her eyes. But she didn't protest.

We slipped into a familiar rhythm: me chopping vegetables, sipping my drink, and passing pieces of carrot to Bug; Dotty talking about her latest adventure in international travel (this time it was counting tiger moths in the Amazonian rainforest); and my parents bickering over the proper technique for marinating a chicken. Soon enough, the house smelled of sizzling garlic. Then Dad put on his go-to Frank Sinatra playlist. I savored every moment of our well-worn Friday-night routine. Until my brother arrived.

"Look what the cat dragged in," Dotty cracked as Tommy and his wife, Lily, walked through the door. I did my best to hide a smirk. It's not that I hated Tommy. I loved him, just like I was supposed to. But we were different in every way: he was tall and lean and graceful like Mom, with golden hair and symmetrical features. I took after Dad: brown hair, brown eyes, neither tall nor short, and always a little rumpled.

Tommy was my parents' favorite, and everyone knew it. He was the reason my parents got married in the first place, a souvenir of their young love. There was no competing with that. No matter how hard I tried to keep up with Tommy, I never could. He was on the partner track at a fancy law firm. He intentionally creased his pants. We were worlds apart. Especially now that he was married with a baby on the way.

The most grating thing about my brother was that he always happened to be doing something remarkable right around the time I was accomplishing something mediocre. Like in seventh grade, when I decided to try out for the school play. I'd practiced for weeks, singing "The Sun Will Come Out Tomorrow" in the shower, rehearsing choreography in my bedroom mirror, and reciting my monologue to Twizzlers, our family cat. The morning the cast list was posted, I made Marcia walk to school with me an hour earlier than usual because I couldn't stand waiting.

When we got to the auditorium, there was a white piece of paper taped to the door. I elbowed past the other kids and ran my finger down the list, feeling increasingly crestfallen as it became apparent that I hadn't gotten any of the lead roles. But there at the bottom, under "Ensemble" was my name: Rosie Benson. I'd made it. I couldn't wait to tell my family.

Marcia and I ended up getting detention for talking in history class (we were simply agreeing that learning about the Great Depression was, in fact, depressing), so I'd gotten home late that day. When I walked through the door, I found Mom and Tommy sitting at the dining room table. Mom had tears streaming down her face as she said, "Rosie, your brother was just offered a scholarship to play baseball at UCLA!"

I didn't bother telling my parents about the play until a week later.

"Hey, sis," Tommy called from across the room, tugging my attention away from the pepper I was dicing. I held up the knife and waved it in response. I didn't mean it as an act of hostility, but the thought that he might take it that way was quite satisfying.

"What can I help with?" my sister-in-law asked, her rounded belly pressing against the marble countertop. Lily was one of those women who made pregnancy look like a trip to the spa. She was literally glowing. The only time my skin had ever looked that good was when Marcia had talked me into buying a Groupon for a couple's mud bath.

"I've got it covered," I said, trying to sound confident. I'm not sure if it was because Lily was almost ten years older than me, or because she was Liliana Lopez: Realtor to the Richie Riches of Silicon Valley, or because her dark hair always seemed to be luminously shiny, but I never quite felt like we were on equal footing.

Lily eased herself onto a stool next to Dotty, watching as I sliced a fat red tomato. "Can I show you a trick?" She didn't wait for me to respond. "Dicing the tomato this way will keep all the juice from squirting everywhere." She mimed a cutting motion with her hands, her gigantic diamond ring winking at me from under the bright kitchen lights.

"On second thought, you can help Tommy set the table," I said, pretending not to notice Dotty's wry, knowing smirk out of the corner of my eye.

* * *

"No meat for me," Dotty said, adjusting Bug on her lap as we passed plates around the dining room table.

"We know, Dotty," everyone replied in unison.

"You can never be too careful," she said, sounding gravely serious. Dotty never missed an opportunity to remind us of her dietary preferences. Maybe she didn't trust Mom not to sneak a stray splash of chicken broth into her pasta sauce. "Your mother doesn't seem to understand that veganism is practically a religion," she'd once told me.

I had stopped eating meat after an unfortunate experience with my high school's 4H club. (I didn't know that they were raising animals to be auctioned off for *slaughter* when I signed up. I naively believed we were just taking care of them for the enriching experience. I cried for weeks when they took my piglet, Poppy, away.) But I didn't want to make a big show of my eating habits like Dotty did. Mostly because I didn't want to deal with Mom's disapproval. Sometimes I think she even forgot, which was the way I liked it.

I don't know what it was about Mom and Dotty, but they'd never fully warmed to each other. Maybe it was because Dotty was Dad's favorite (and only) aunt, and he was her precious nephew. There wasn't a lot of space for Mom when Dotty was around. And Dad had only grown closer to Dotty since my grandma Ruth, Dotty's sister, had died.

I think Mom and Dotty were just too different to get along. Mom was traditional and polished and cared about what other people thought. She stayed home to raise Tommy and me and loved watching home renovation shows and looked great in pearls. Dotty was single and independent and decidedly unpolished. She traveled incessantly and collected troll dolls and cared about endangered beetles. And she wouldn't be caught dead wearing pearls. The only thing they had in common was us. At least that was enough to keep the peace.

Once we'd finished passing serving dishes and filling our plates, Dad rose from his seat at the head of the table and held up a bottle of wine as if he were a sommelier at a fine restaurant. "Tonight, we'll be enjoying a 2015 bottle of Châteauneuf-du-Pape from France's Rhône region," he said. That meant nothing to me, but 2015 was a while ago, so I assumed I should be impressed. I made a point of jutting out my bottom lip and nodding slowly, hoping to appear both sophisticated and appreciative.

"How much did you spend on that bottle, David?" Mom asked. I could tell she was annoyed because she was talking out of the left side of her mouth.

"You won't care once you taste it," Dad said as he expertly wrapped a cloth napkin around the base of the bottle. "This vintage is exceptional."

Dad filled everyone's glasses (Lily's with water) before raising his, signaling the rest of us to do the same. "To my dear family," he said, "thank you, as always, for giving me the greatest gift of all—the gift of your presence." He didn't seem to notice Mom rolling her eyes. Mom and I didn't agree on many things, but when it came to Dad's cheesiness, we were a united front.

Dinner progressed the same way all our family dinners did: Dad talked about tax season, Mom grilled Lily about her upcoming baby shower (wouldn't peonies make lovely centerpieces?), Tommy jabbered on about intellectual property or something, and Dotty interjected comments about the bee population, frequent flier programs, nondairy ice cream, pumas (the cat not the shoe), and microplastics wherever she saw fit. I nodded along blandly, hoping no one would ask me about my job or my bank account or my nonexistent love life.

"Can you pass the wine?" I whispered to Lily.

"Only if you let me smell your glass."

"Deal."

I topped off my glass and passed it to Lily, who closed her eyes and took a long, deep breath. "God, I miss wine."

"The doctor said you could drink a glass every once in a while," Tommy said.

"I don't care what the doctor said," Lily replied through gritted teeth. "I'm not taking any chances."

Mom said Lily's doctor told her that her pregnancy was borderline geriatric, which didn't make any sense to me because Lily was hardly old. Still, it must have shaken her. I'd often wondered if it bothered her that she was a few years older than Tommy. I certainly wouldn't be excited to date a twenty-year-old. But I know age matters less the older you get. At least that's what Dotty told me.

"Pregnant women booze it up in France, you know," Dotty said. Lily shot her a look. I took the glass out of her hand.

"How's work going, Rosie?" Mom asked. The way she was sitting, with her elbows resting on the table, hands folded under her chin, made me feel inexplicably guilty, like I'd been caught doing something wrong.

"It's great."

"Care to elaborate?"

"Well"—I took a big gulp of wine before returning my glass to the table—"I'm still learning a lot. My boss is really into employee development, so that's cool." I paused, hoping that had satisfied Mom, but her arched eyebrow suggested that I should continue. "Plus, my coworkers are great. Supersupportive." I tried to push Chad's smug face from my mind.

"Aren't you due for a promotion soon?" Tommy asked, glancing up from the roll he'd just finished slathering with butter. I think he was trying to help, but he sounded suspicious, maybe even accusatory.

I bobbed my head. "Yep. They promote everyone in my role after two years."

"Everyone?" Mom asked. Her eyebrow looked like it was caught in a fishhook.

"Yes, Mom. Everyone. Even me."

"And is that what you truly want?" I turned to face Dotty, who squinted at me through oversize glasses. "You don't have to turn yourself into a corporate clone just because everyone else is, you know."

I'd wanted to be a primatologist—just like Jane Goodall—since I was five. At first, I just liked the idea of living in the jungle and making friends with apes (who wouldn't?), but over time, my dreams became more about wanting to take care of animals—wild and domesticated. By the time I was in high school, I'd decided that I was going to become a veterinarian.

But making the jump from high school science classes to preveterinary college courses was a lot harder than I'd anticipated. And dorm life proved to be detrimental to my study habits. I'll never forget the look on Mom's face when I'd told her I'd failed both my college biology and organic chemistry classes. "Totally unacceptable," she'd said. It hadn't helped that my perfect older brother had been on track to graduate magna cum laude that summer.

So I'd changed my major to business (Mom's suggestion), scrapped my plans to apply to veterinary school after graduation, and took a job at the most reputable start-up I could find. And it was all working out just fine so far. Probably because it had to. If it didn't, I'd be a total and complete failure in the eyes of my family, washed up before I even turned twenty-five.

I know everyone in my generation was supposed to have goals and passions, or whatever. And I knew that someday, I would find mine. Maybe I'd open my own animal shelter or invent the next Beanie Baby or suddenly discover a burning desire to raise children. But until I figured it out, I needed a job, and it might as well be one at a cool company.

I turned to look Dotty square in the eye. She wouldn't buy it otherwise. "I'm hardly a clone, Dotty," I said, mostly believing it. "And yes. This is what I want."

Dotty licked a stray breadcrumb from the corner of her mouth. I could tell she wasn't convinced, but the rest of my family seemed to approve.

"That's wonderful, sweetheart," Dad said. "Soon enough you'll be running the place. We'll take you out for a nice dinner to celebrate when it's official."

I nodded uneasily, feigning confidence. From what I could tell so far, that's what adulthood was mostly all about: pretending.

Tommy cleared his throat and eyed Lily meaningfully. "Speaking of celebrations, Lily and I have some exciting news." I reached for my wine, relieved for the change of subject, yet weary of Tommy and Lily's news. Leave it to my brother to rescue me from an interrogation by announcing yet another accomplishment.

Dad leaned forward. "Well, don't leave us hanging."

Tommy grinned. "We're buying the house down the street!"

Of course they were. It only took moments for my parents to erupt into a flurry of congratulations. I believe the term "dream come true" was thrown around.

"That house was listed for almost two million dollars," Dotty said. Tommy beamed, appearing to mistake Dotty's judgment for approval. "Waste of money if you ask me," she said under her breath.

"That's great news," I said, flashing the *I'm a proud sister who isn't at all jealous* smile I'd spent years perfecting. "Congratulations."

Something pointy jabbed at my shin. I lifted the lace tablecloth just in time to see Dotty kick me again. "Ouch," I said, dropping the cloth.

"Don't feel bad, kiddo," she whispered, a conspiratorial glint in her eyes, "you wouldn't want to live in a neighborhood like this anyway. You're too much of a free spirit. Just like your old aunt Dotty." She reached a skinny arm across the table to squeeze my elbow.

I patted her leathery hand. She was probably right. I loved my life in the city. And I had no interest in moving back to my old neighborhood. I just wished my family was a little more supportive of me. Or, better yet, a little less enthusiastic about their support for Tommy.

But at least I had Dotty.

CHAPTER FOUR

O n Monday morning, I was greeted by an urgent meeting invitation from Raj. He'd checked the "mandatory" box to drive the point home. I'd nearly, blissfully forgotten over the weekend about his request for a sync-up today. But now that I was back in the office, the familiar tension between my shoulders had returned.

I found Raj sitting next to Kara Chen, our team's "People Operations Liaison." She moved a neat stack of papers from the top of the table to her lap as I walked through the door. It didn't take long for me to realize that this didn't bode well. I was in for another performance coaching session. These meetings were happening with increasing frequency. "Have a seat," Raj said in the tone he usually reserved for client meetings. "Anywhere you'd like is fine."

I rolled a blue chair out from under the rugged wood table, leaving one seat between myself and Raj. Kara looked on silently, an inscrutable statue with impeccable posture. She'd always struck me as the type of person who went to bed at the exact same time every night and ate white toast with a thin swipe of margarine for breakfast. But if Dotty had taught me anything, it was that you could never be sure what people were up to when they weren't at work. For all I knew, Kara wrote bigfoot erotica and dropped ecstasy at Burning Man every year. I was suddenly desperately curious about whether she had any interesting pets.

Raj made a show of rubbing his hands up and down his face as if he were washing it with soap and water. Then he said, "Rosie, I was disappointed by your performance on Friday. You would have benefited from attending our practice session the day before."

I willed my cheeks not to glow red. "I know, I'm sorry. I was . . . sick."

His face twisted into a frown. "Look, it's your right to use your PTO however you'd like, but given your performance issues, I would have hoped that you'd prioritize work over a day at the beach with friends."

I gulped audibly. Had Raj seen the picture on my monitor? No, he would have come out and said it. "How did you—"

"It doesn't matter how I know," Raj said.

I pressed my palms into either side of the chair and decided to change tack. "You're right, Raj. I should have come in. I'm sorry."

"I hope it was worth it."

Kara, who I'd almost forgotten was in the room, cleared her throat loudly, a subtle signal for Raj to stop talking. "Rosie," she said, her tone even, "I'd like to hear from your perspective how you're feeling about this job."

How on earth was I supposed to answer that? I didn't love my job, that was for sure. But that's what working in the corporate world was, right? Slogging through your daily responsibilities with the hope that someday it would all pay off.

"Well, I'm obviously pumped to be here," I said, the words feeling plastic and ridiculous in my mouth. "I know I'm not great at cold calls, but I'm better when no one is watching me." My eyes darted to Raj. "And I like working with existing customers a lot. That's why I want to try the account management track."

A pained look crossed Raj's face, like he'd just noticed a spot of dirt on his maniacally white sneakers. He looked over at Kara, who gave him a tight nod. "So, the most critical part of this job is bringing in new business . . . and you haven't sourced any in almost three months."

That was technically true. But I had grown my existing accounts by 30 percent that quarter. And that was way over quota. I pointed this out to Raj.

"But that's only part of your job, Rosie."

My stomach did a nauseating flip. "You don't think I'm doing a good job?"

That appeared to throw both Kara and Raj off-balance. They turned to face each other, engaging in what seemed to be a silent negotiation about who would answer my question.

Kara lost. "Rosie, what Raj is trying to say is that you haven't been meeting *all* the requirements of your role. And he's discussed this with you"—she glanced down at her paperwork—"three times over the past nine months during your performance coaching sessions. Do you recall these conversations?"

Of course I recalled those conversations. Raj was hyperfocused on employee development and constructive criticism. He'd even gone to a seminar titled "How to Turn Feedback into Fuel." I nodded.

"Okay, good." Kara pulled her glossless lips into a tight line that almost resembled a smile. "Now we're all on the same page. So, Driftwood company policy dictates that employment is subject to review after three formal warnings . . ."

Formal warnings? Is that what those meetings had been? Raj pushed everyone on the team, always insisting that we had more in us, that we could be better than the day before. I considered his constant reminders to keep practicing, try out different call scripts, and work on my networking skills to be a nuisance, sure, but none of our meetings had ever seemed like warnings.

". . . and while we do appreciate your hard work, we've decided that we need to reevaluate your role here."

The pit in my stomach yawned out in every direction as I fell back against my chair, the posture-correcting curve jabbing into my spine. I shook my head, trying to clear away the fog that had started accumulating in my brain. "Reevaluate my role? What does that even mean?"

Raj, who'd been alternating between fiddling with the zipper of his vest, tapping his index fingers on the table, and feigning fascination with the ceiling, suddenly decided to rejoin the conversation. "What Kara means is that we're letting you go."

* * *

When I was six and Tommy was twelve, we got in a bad car accident with Dotty. I don't have any specific memories from that day, just fragments. The sun in my eyes. Dotty adjusting the volume on the manual dial. Tommy folding a paper airplane. What I do remember clearly is the feeling. One minute we were cruising down the highway, and the next, we weren't. I can still feel the slam of the other car as it T-boned Dotty's yellow Volkswagen Beetle. I can still hear the sizzle of shattering glass. I can still remember the way the world suddenly stopped making sense.

That's kind of how getting fired felt. At least this time I wasn't going to end up with six stitches over my eye. Come to think of it, I might have preferred the stitches.

I know I choked back tears. I know I asked for another chance. I know Raj said he was so sorry, but this decision was final.

Then Kara was pushing a stack of papers across the table, using a ballpoint pen to point out where I needed to sign. I was handed two envelopes: the first containing my final paycheck and another with two weeks' severance.

At some point, I was informed that Driftwood would no longer be assisting me with my student loan payments.

I think Raj shook my hand. I know he stood over my shoulder, watching as I boxed up the personal items in my desk—a strand of lights; a framed picture of Marcia and me from last Halloween, both of us rendered unrecognizable by our bushy Mario and Luigi mustaches; a mug that read *SMASH THE PATRIARCHY* in big, bold letters (a gift from Dotty, of course). And then Raj walked me out.

He didn't let me take my snacks.

*　*　*

"Damn, Ro. What are you going to do?" Marcia sat beside me on our sagging IKEA couch, clutching a mugful of wine. She'd uncorked a bottle of red when she found me crying on the kitchen floor, poured herself a glass, and then dropped a comically long aluminum straw into the bottle for me.

I took a long sip and stared at the *Starry Knight* knockoff on our wall. Were the swirling stars making me dizzy or had getting fired given me vertigo? "Start looking for another job, I guess."

"Obviously. But what do you *want* to do?"

I shrugged. "Sales?"

"Why would you look for another job that you hate on purpose?"

"I didn't hate my job. I hated *Raj*."

Marcia made a *hmm* sound as she turned to face me. She tucked her legs off to one side and draped an arm on the back of the couch. "You honestly didn't know you were on probation?"

"I never even heard the word 'probation.'"

"Not even a warning?"

"Apparently my performance improvement meetings were supposed to be warnings."

"Wait a sec," Marcia said, holding up her hands, palms out. "Were you on a performance improvement plan?"

I shrugged again.

"Like a PIP?"

"I guess so."

"Rosie." There was a tinge of exasperation in her tone. "Managers use those to build a case for firing their employees. We did that with one of my interns at work a few months back. Remember?"

I vaguely remembered Marcia complaining about an intern who never showed up to work on time and consistently forgot to proofread press releases. Marcia had spent the better part of a Saturday afternoon fielding calls from angry executives at Bobble when their company name appeared as "Booble" in three separate articles on three very important websites.

I pressed the heels of my hands against my eyes. "I'm such an idiot."

Marcia dropped her hand onto my knee. "No, you're not."

"I never should have taken a day off."

"What does taking a sick day have to do with getting fired?"

I lowered my hands, defeated. "Raj knew I wasn't sick. He said it was the last straw."

Marcia perked up at that, her posture stiffening. "How did he know?"

"No idea," I said. "I think he might have seen Dotty's picture of us on my computer. Or maybe Chad overheard me talking to Gemma and told him."

She let out a long breath. "Wow."

"I know. Unbelievable, right?"

Marcia nodded, her eyes fixed on the corner of the room.

I shook my head, lost in my growing sense of indignation. "I think I hate Raj. Like legitimately hate him."

"I don't blame you," Marcia said. She scooted closer to me on the couch. I leaned my head on her shoulder. We sat there for a long while before she spoke again.

"This probably isn't the best time to tell you this, but George called me today. He's raising our rent by two hundred dollars next month."

A flutter of panic rose in my chest. Despite what had been a stable paycheck and a competitive salary, I'd been living paycheck to paycheck ever since Marcia and I had moved to the city. Between rent, utilities, and the credit card debt I'd racked up on new furniture and clothes to suit my postgraduation lifestyle, my finances were stretched thin.

Marcia grabbed my wrist. "Rosie, don't stress. We'll figure it out."

"Okay," I said, feeling anything but. I knew we'd have to have a serious talk about rent. And groceries. And the garbage bill. But not yet. I needed a night to wallow. I needed my best friend to split a bottle of wine with me and pretend my life wasn't falling apart.

Because, in reality, I was screwed.

* * *

At the end of the week, late Friday night, my phone buzzed in urgent, rapid succession, startling me out of my *Fresh Prince of Bel-Air* marathon. I hit pause and reached for my nightstand, nearly knocking a days-old cup of coffee over in the process.

After a thoroughly depressing review of my finances (which

included $16,000 in outstanding student loan debt, a $7,200 credit card bill, and a looming rent increase), I'd spent the last few days in bed, vacillating between bookmarking job postings, writing, deleting, and rewriting my résumé, and crying into Bob the Frog. I hadn't changed out of my pajamas since Wednesday. I couldn't stop turning my meeting with Raj and Kara over and over in my mind. What if I hadn't gone to the beach with Marcia that day? What if I'd practiced my call scripts like Raj had asked? What if, what if, what if.

I pressed the home button on my cell phone, illuminating a string of messages. Every member of my family had texted me within minutes of each other.

Tommy: Have you talked to Mom?

Mom: Call me when you can.

Lily: You missed a crazy dinner.

Dad: We love you, sweetie. No matter what.

Dotty: Still up for lunch Sunday?

My heart raced with panic. Did my family know I'd gotten fired? I hadn't told a soul besides Marcia. And I'd lied about having to go to some team-building event to get out of family dinner that night. I wasn't ready to face them.

I figured Dotty would be the safest person to text back, but I didn't want to commit to lunch. I didn't want to see anyone ever again for the rest of my life.

But I probably wasn't in any position to be turning down free meals.

Dotty it was.

> **Me:** Sure. What happened tonight?

Dotty: I'll see you at my place at noon on Sunday.

> **Me:** Ok. What happened tonight?

Dotty: Do you like Mediterranean food?

> **Me:** That's fine. But what happened tonight?

Dotty: I'll make dolmas.

> **Me:** Dotty, for the love of god. What the hell happened tonight?

Dotty: Your parents are splitting up. See you Sunday!

I must have screamed because Marcia burst into my room, wild-eyed and wielding a coat hanger. "Everything okay?" she asked, looking around my messy but empty room.

"Dotty said my parents are getting a divorce."

My best friend's face instantly dropped. "Oh my god. What? Why?"

It occurred to me that I couldn't feel my body. Everything was numb. "I don't know. I guess I should call my family."

Marcia took a step closer to my bed. "Do you want me to stay here with you?"

I nodded, throwing the covers back so she could climb into bed with me. She slid off her heels and settled in beside me. She was wearing her favorite jeans and a pair of gold hoop earrings. "Are you going out tonight?"

She threw the comforter over her legs. "Not anymore."

I don't know what I would have done without Marcia. She'd been holding me together all week, and now she was giving up another night to help me pick up the pieces of my rapidly shattering life.

CHAPTER FIVE

APRIL

Dotty's front door was unlocked as usual. She lived in an artsy waterfront town just over the Golden Gate Bridge in a simple, shingled house that was built into a rocky hillside across the street from a harbor filled with old boats in various states of decay. Dotty's house didn't have a driveway and you had to walk up forty-seven steps to get to her front door. She'd assured me on multiple occasions that the stairs were enough deterrent for would-be intruders, declaring, "If they make the climb, they can have whatever they want."

I called out to let Dotty know I'd arrived as I stepped inside. It was common knowledge in our family that you should always announce yourself when you entered Dotty's house because Dad had once walked in on her making love to a woman named Paula, who then decided to stay for tea. "I can't believe she takes lovers at her age," Mom had said disapprovingly after Dad told us the story through fits of laughter.

"In here, kiddo!" Dotty called from the kitchen.

I found her standing over a mortar and pestle, Bug sitting on the counter beside her, watching patiently. Dotty's glasses sat on top of her head, and the sleeves of her black turtleneck were rolled up to her elbows. I set my forearms on the counter, leaning forward so I could peer into the bowl. "What are you making?"

She didn't look up. "I'm muddling mint for muddled mint lemonade. There's nothing like the fresh stuff. Don't ever forget that." This was one of my favorite things about going to Dotty's house. She didn't just have you over for lunch. She hosted you. There was a difference.

"Can I help?"

Dotty lifted her gaze to meet mine, her mouth drooping as she took me in. "You look like hell."

"Thank you," I said, tugging on my limp ponytail.

"Don't take the divorce so hard, kiddo. It could be a good thing. From the sound of it, your mom hasn't been happy for years."

So she'd said. Apparently, Mom had been considering divorce for some time now, which was news to the rest of us. Including Dad. And despite Mom's tearful attempt at an explanation, I still didn't understand where this was coming from. I'd spent the better part of yesterday trying to piece together the events of the night before, and all I'd come away with was that Mom had decided to ask Dad for a divorce right in the middle of dinner. *Can you pass the rolls? Also, I'd like to end our thirty-year marriage.* According to Lily, all hell had broken loose from there.

The headlines were: Mom wanted out, Dad was blindsided, Lily couldn't stop crying, and Tommy didn't know any more than I did.

I'd come to Dotty's hoping for clarity, but it was evident that she hadn't thought through what my parents' split would mean for the rest of the family. I'd only had one day to consider the ramifications of Mom's decision and I already had a long, long list of reasons why this was an awful idea.

Dotty looked back down at the bowl and gave the pestle one final twist. "Have you talked to your mother?"

"Yes."

"And?"

I sighed dramatically. "She said no one cheated, no one did anything wrong, and that she's sure this is what she wants."

Dotty gave a tight nod of approval. "And your dad?"

"He's a wreck. Completely shocked. He said that Mom had asked him to go to couples' therapy a few years ago, but then she dropped it. He thought they were happy," I said, my voice cracking as tears welled up in the corners of my eyes.

Dotty shook her head as she set the pestle on top of a towel shaped like a lemon. "Your father is a wonderful man, but he can be a bit oblivious."

I dabbed at my eyes with the backs of my hands. "I can't believe Mom is doing this."

Dotty shot me a look. "It takes two to tango, kiddo. The older you get, the more you'll learn that sometimes things fall apart, and it's not anyone's fault." Then she passed me a platter piled high with dolmas, hummus, and cucumber salad and said, "We'll be eating outside."

I carried Dotty's spread out onto the wooden deck off the kitchen and set it on a rusty patio table. Dotty had already laid out plates, napkins, and glasses—none of them matching. Bug followed close behind, turning in three tight circles before settling on a cushion near my feet.

When Dotty emerged from the house, she was holding a pitcher of lemonade in one hand and a small, vintage radio in the other. "Ambiance," she said, setting the radio next to Bug. I could just make out the sound of classical music floating from the speakers.

Dotty reached for my glass, eyeing me as she filled it. I pretended not to notice, turning my face toward the sun.

"Your mother is following her heart, you know." She handed me the glass. "And that's unimaginably difficult for someone like her."

"Following her heart? More like losing her mind," I muttered, taking the glass. Dotty narrowed her eyes in disapproval, but I could tell she was trying not to laugh. She always pressed her lips together when she didn't want me to know that she thought I was being funny. "So what exactly happened Friday night?"

Dotty took a bite of cucumber salad and held up an index finger as she chewed. I snuck Bug a scrap of pita bread while I waited. "Something must have transpired right before dinner," she said, leaning toward me. "Whatever it was, it was the last straw for your mother. They were barely speaking to each other when I got there. The whole night was"—she turned her gaze toward the sky, wafting her hand as she searched for the right word—"frosty."

I raised my eyebrows. "Frosty?"

She jabbed a purple fingernail in my direction. "Frosty."

Dotty took a swig from her glass. "Anyway, I'm sure your mother has her reasons. And we'll hear them soon enough."

I didn't want an explanation. I wanted an intervention. But arguing with Dotty was an exercise in futility.

"Something else is bothering you," Dotty said, squinting an eye. I attempted a casual shrug, but she wasn't buying it. "Spill."

A flick of shame pinged against my temples, like a pebble hitting a windshield. Saying the words out loud would make it all the more real. But hiding from reality wouldn't do me any good, either. I braced my hands on either side of the chair, took a deep breath, and said, "I got fired."

Dotty balled her fists and began shaking them in the air as if her team had just scored a winning basket. "That's wonderful!"

My embarrassment rearranged itself into irritation. "Can you at least pretend to feel sorry for me?"

"I've been feeling sorry for you for months! Why do you think I've been telling you to quit for so long? That job's never been right for you."

"What do you want me to say, Dotty? That I was bad at my job? That I have no idea what to do with myself? That I'm a total failure?"

"Yes. Doesn't it feel good to say it out loud?"

I dropped my face into my hands. "I need the money."

She blew out a forceful huff of breath. "You and everyone else, kiddo. But that doesn't mean you have to sell your soul. This'll end up being one of the best things that ever happened to you. You'll see."

My lips tightened into an involuntary pout. Dotty relishing my demise was not what I needed right now.

"Say," Dotty said, dropping her fork with a clatter, "that reminds me. I have something I want to show you." With that, she rose from her chair and disappeared into the house. When she returned, she was clutching a thin stack of papers. She handed them to me without explanation.

I flipped through the pages as recognition crept in. They were printouts of emails Dotty and I had exchanged when I was in college, the contents mainly consisting of me gushing about how excited I was to be off on my own, taking the first step toward pursuing my dream. I'd been so naive.

Dotty and I had been pen pals for as long as I could remember— exchanging postcards from Dotty's travels, amateur watercolor paintings from my elementary-school art class, books Dotty thought I would like (she was incredibly supportive of my *Goosebumps* phase, claiming it was healthy to give yourself a scare every now and again), and, once I was old enough to have my own account, emails. By the time I was in high school, I would write to Dotty every time I had a problem. Even if I didn't always take her advice, I knew she'd never judge me.

"Remember how excited you were about working with animals?" Dotty asked. I stopped flipping through the pages and looked up at her. "You'd light up whenever you talked about it."

I pulled out the last page of the pile. It was my final email on the subject, the one where I'd told Dotty I'd failed my classes. I'd poured my heart out about how embarrassed and devastated I was. I passed the sheet to her. "Remember how it ended?"

She waved me off. "A temporary setback."

Dotty had been the only person in my family who hadn't openly celebrated when I'd decided to abandon my foolish Jane Goodall fantasy. When I'd told her that I'd changed my major, she shook her head and asked why I didn't just hire a tutor and try again. "Because Rosie's parents can only afford four years of tuition," Mom had responded for me through gritted teeth.

"I have a friend who runs an animal shelter just outside of town," Dotty said now, her whole face lighting up. "She's got a bunch of goats and pigs and chickens, even a cow called Barb. Want me to ask if she's hiring?"

My heart warmed at the thought of a cow named Barb, but I knew what Dotty was doing. "Thanks for the offer," I said, "but I don't think so."

Dotty crossed her arms over her chest. "You know something, kiddo? You're acting like your life is over, like everything's already been decided. And that couldn't be further from the truth."

"I'm not like you, Dotty."

She leaned forward and rested her hand on my forearm. She wore a quarter-size turquoise ring on her middle finger. "You don't need to be like me," she said, her eyes boring into mine. "You need to be like you."

"This *is* me, Dotty."

She shook her head. "No, it isn't."

And with that, I started crying. Sobbing, actually, my shoulders convulsing, my breath ragged and gasping, fat tears rolling down my face. Dotty rose from her chair to wrap me in a hug, my head pressed against her chest.

"Get it out," she said, her voice firm, but gentle. "You've had a rough week."

Dotty let me cry for what felt like hours, and when I was done, she took my chin in her hand and said, "All you need to do now is figure out what comes next. That's your only job."

I blinked, my eyes puffy. "How?"

Dotty released my chin and turned to pick up my old emails. "Same as always: write it out and then send it my way."

I nodded, too tired and grateful to protest. "Okay. I will."

"Atta girl," Dotty said. "Now, I think this calls for something a little stronger than lemonade. How about I make us a couple of filthy martinis?"

I wiped my nose with my sleeve. "I thought you'd never ask."

She grinned. And somehow, that made everything better.

At least for a little while.

CHAPTER SIX

offee?" Marcia asked, jiggling the steel carafe in my direction. It was Wednesday, not that days of the week mattered to me anymore. Unemployment will do that to you.

"Yes, please," I said, putting the finishing touches on Marcia's peanut butter and jelly sandwich. I'd taken to packing her lunches every day since I'd lost my job. "Big day ahead."

It was barely even light outside, and Marcia was already dressed in burgundy yoga pants and a matching crop top, her hair pulled into two identical buns on the top of her head. She stood on her toes to reach a small cabinet above the microwave and pulled out a ceramic mug.

"Any interviews today?" she asked. Her tone indicated that she already knew the answer.

I shook my head.

Marcia set the mug on the counter and filled it to the brim, tendrils of heat curling upward. "You'll find something soon," she said before handing the mug to me. I wrapped both hands around it, reveling in the warmth.

"Definitely," I said. It felt like a lie.

It had been nearly a month since I'd lost my job, and all I had to show for it was a string of failed first-round interviews.

I'd told Javier, a recruiter at DingDong, that my greatest weakness was sales.

I'd choked when Renata, the sales manager at Splash, asked where I saw myself in five years. "Hopefully with a pet," I'd said gamely. She hadn't been amused.

When Sam, a monotoned recruiter at iCloud, had asked me to sell him a banana, I'd told him—after an excruciatingly long pause—that I didn't really like bananas, I preferred plantains, so I wasn't sure if I could sell one.

It's not that I was purposely sabotaging myself. I really was trying. But, with every meandering answer or slip of the tongue, my confidence waned. And when my confidence waned, my rambling got worse. It was a vicious cycle.

On the bright side, I'd gotten my first unemployment check. It wasn't much, but it was something. I'd pulled together just enough to cover my rent for the next month, but I had almost nothing left for food. Let alone my student loans.

I needed to talk with Marcia. Between the two of us, I was sure we could figure this out. And yet, I was terrified to bring it up. "Are you going to yoga this morning?" I asked, instead, eyeing her outfit.

She shook her head.

"A run?"

She jutted out her bottom lip. "Nah."

I took a sip of coffee and watched her do the same. She was avoiding eye contact. Something was up. "Are you working from home today?"

"I wasn't planning to."

Now that I thought about it, I hadn't heard Marcia come home last night. She'd texted something about going to happy hour with her kickball team after the game, but I'd fallen asleep in the middle of watching *Office Space*, a very old but very relatable movie. "Where were you last night?"

She cocked her head, the hint of a smile dancing around the corners of her mouth. "What do you mean?"

I set my coffee down and crossed my arms over my chest. "Are those your kickball clothes?"

"They're not *not* my kickball clothes."

"Marcia!"

"What?"

"Who is he?"

She slapped her hand over her eyes. "It's the same guy. The one from my kickball league."

"How long has this been going on?"

She parted her fingers, revealing one brown eye. "Awhile."

"How could you not tell me?" She usually told me everything in excruciating detail. Down to the curve of a guy's— "Oh my god. You like him."

Marcia dropped her hand. "I might." She was blushing. "I don't know. He's . . . different."

"When can I meet him?"

She shook her head. "Oh no. It's way too soon."

"Please?" I whined.

She continued shaking her head more vigorously now. "Nope."

"But if you loooove him," I said, shimmying my shoulders, "wouldn't you want your best friend to love him, too?"

Marcia tilted her head to the side. "Of course."

"So what's the problem?"

She hesitated, searching for the right words. "I'm pretty sure you're not going to like him. Positive actually." She hesitated, her forehead rippling. "Ro, I—"

Her phone buzzed loudly on the counter, its vibrations echoing off the yellowing tiles. Marcia grabbed it, squinting at the screen. "I need to take this." She feigned annoyance at the disruption, but I could have sworn I saw relief wash across her face as she answered. It was gone by the time she'd turned on her heel and headed down the hall toward her room.

She was avoiding me. And I was pretty sure I knew why. It was time to address the rent-check-size elephant in the room.

* * *

That night, when I heard the scrape of Marcia's key in the front door, I ran to the hallway to greet her. "How was your day?" I asked, with an overabundance of cheer as I shoved a wineglass into her hand.

"Fine," she said, eyeing me suspiciously. "Why are you being weird?"

"I cooked!"

Marcia sweetly pretended that the soggy pasta and overly steamed broccoli I'd made her was delicious. At least she didn't have to pretend to like the wine. I'd decided to open one of the bottles Dad had given me for Christmas. I had been hoping to save it for a special occasion (like getting a new job), but I figured getting back on Marcia's good side was as noble a reason as any.

"That David Benson sure does know his wine," Marcia said. "He should open a winery or work in a tasting room or something."

"He'd never quit his job," I said. "He's way too square for that."

Marcia shrugged. "People can change. Look at your mom."

"Don't remind me." I waved my hand in front of my face like I was shooing away a fly. "I can't think about that right now. Let's talk about literally anything else. Like work! Tell me about work," I said, leaning forward. "I'm starting to forget what it's like."

She responded with what was probably meant to be a good-natured eye roll, but her irritation was palpable. My jokes about unemployment were wearing thin, but she obliged all the same, telling me about the last-minute details she had to iron out for Donovan's launch party and how excited she was to move on to her next project.

"I can't believe it's next Friday," I said, mustering as much enthusiasm as I could. I'd been looking forward to this party for weeks, but my misadventures in job searching had blunted my excitement. Hanging out with the gainfully employed probably wouldn't do much for my waning confidence.

"It can't be over soon enough," Marcia said.

"It's going to be amazing."

Marcia picked up her glass and took another sip. "Thanks," she paused, seeming to brace herself. "How's the job search going?"

I dropped my eyes to my plate and pushed a mushy piece of broccoli around with my fork. "I've been meaning to talk to you about that . . ."

"Rosie . . ." She said my name like I was a kid who broke a vase but refused to come clean about it. "What's going on?"

I told her everything. She listened patiently, letting me get it all out. When I finished, I drew a huge breath, realizing that I hadn't been breathing at all. "I'm doing everything I can, but it's not working," I said as my chin began to wobble.

Marcia set her fork down and wiped her hands with the paper towel I'd laid out as a napkin. "You aren't doing everything you can," she said quietly.

"What are you talking about?"

"Doing everything would mean borrowing money from your

parents, selling your old clothes for extra cash, driving for Uber."
She held out a new finger for every item on her list and kept going.
"Getting a temp job, or—god forbid—being open to something
that isn't at a fancy tech company." She hit me with a look. "You
haven't done *any* of it. You just keep banging your head against the
same wall over and over again and hoping for the best. That's literally the definition of insanity."

"You don't think I can get another sales job?"

"I don't think *you* think you can get another sales job."

My nostrils flared involuntarily. "So what if that's true? Should
I just give up on having any semblance of a respectable career? You
want me to drive an Uber for the rest of my life?"

"What I'm trying to say is you need to be more adaptable,
broaden your perspective."

"You wouldn't understand. You have it so easy."

"What's that supposed to mean?"

"You've been promoted like three times already."

She huffed, exasperated. "Ah, yes. Being the only Black woman
on my team made that incredibly easy, what with racism being
solved and all."

I was an idiot. Marcia was so good at everything she did that
sometimes I forgot about all of the crap she dealt with. But that
was no excuse. Marcia didn't have the luxury of forgetting. "You're
right," I said. "I'm sorry. That came out totally wrong. I know how
hard you work."

"At least ten times as hard as the Chads of the world. I just make
it *look* easy," she corrected me. "And that's because I'm actually
good at my job."

"I was good at my job," I said half-heartedly.

"Then why did you get fired?" Marcia's eyes flashed with pent-
up resentment. "You were on a performance plan for *months*,

Rosie. You're not going to move past this until you own your mistakes!"

"Mistakes?" I asked, feeling my cheeks grow hotter with every passing second. "Like going to the beach with you that day?"

Marcia made a show of rolling her eyes. "Come *on*. That's not why you got fired. If you were doing what you were supposed to be doing and not slacking off and ignoring half your responsibilities, no one would have cared that you took the day off."

Her words struck me like a shot from a sniper, right between the eyes. I knew she was right. "Well, I guess I'm just an irresponsible idiot who's too dumb to notice that they're terrible at their job."

Marcia shook her head. "Don't pull that."

"Pull what?"

"That woe-is-me crap. I'm sorry this happened, but I don't feel sorry for you. You need to get it together."

We sat in tense silence, her fuming, me sulking. "I don't want to have to move out," I said finally, my voice quiet. Moving back home wasn't an option. Lily had told me during one of her near daily text sessions (I was almost positive that my family had put her in charge of Rosie-watch) that Mom and Dad could barely stand to be in the same room together, and there was no way I was going to be the third wheel on that dysfunctional wagon. And I certainly couldn't ask them for money, not after Mom had called to yell at me about getting fired and I'd sworn up and down that I had plenty of money in savings to get her off my back.

Marcia took a long breath, apparently gathering her patience. "I don't want you to have to move out, either."

"I'm going to run out of money soon."

"Okay."

"This is all Raj's fault."

"We both know that isn't true." She rose from her seat and started clearing our plates. "Just think about what I said."

I listened as she stalked down the hall, set our dishes in the kitchen sink, and turned on the faucet. "Great talk," I muttered. I pushed myself back from the table as my dirty napkin floated to the floor. I didn't bother to pick it up.

* * *

I had trouble falling asleep that night. Marcia and I had only gotten into a handful of fights over the years, usually over stupid things, like when she lost my favorite sweater or the time I accidentally let it slip to her mom that she'd gotten a tattoo. This was much more real.

When I woke up the next morning, Marcia had already left for work. And she'd done all the dishes—even the silverware. I felt like a monster.

I'd been wallowing in self-pity for too long. It was time to accept that the only thing I was a victim of was my own shortcomings. I needed to do better.

I wanted to do better.

I didn't hear from Marcia all day. But by the time she got home that night I'd applied to seven new sales jobs, dropped off an application at the coffee shop down the street, cleaned out my entire closet, dragged a garbage bag full of clothes to a fancy thrift shop, and returned with two hundred and forty-six dollars in cash.

From: Rosie Benson
To: Dotty Polk
Subject: Should I go?
Date: May 5

Dear Dotty,

I got into a fight with Marcia the other night. Well, Marcia got into a fight with me might be a better way to put it. I'd never seen her so angry. She said I haven't been trying hard enough to get a new job. And that it was my fault that I got fired.

I think what hurts the most is that I know she's right. But whenever I think I've worked up the courage to tell her that, I can't quite bring myself to say it out loud.

So we still haven't made up. But I had an idea: Marcia invited me to her work party a few weeks ago—for moral support. The party is tonight. Do you think I should go? To support her?

It would probably be a good networking opportunity for me, too. There will be lots of important tech people there. And she did say I needed to be trying harder.

Thanks for listening, Dotty. Miss you!

XO Rosie

To: Rosie Benson
From: Dotty Polk
Subject: Re: Should I go?
Date: May 5

Dear Rosie,

It's been my experience that those closest to us tend to hold up the harshest mirrors. And when they do, we usually don't like what we see. I know it stings, but Marcia's honesty is a gift. A friend who is willing to be brutally honest with you is hard to come by. You're very lucky.

If I were you, I'd swallow my pride and apologize right away.

As for that party, I think you should check to make sure you're still invited before you get all dolled up. Marcia might need some space to cool off.

Anyway, I'm hitting the hay early tonight, kiddo. I'm beat. I had a long day at the shelter with Barb the cow. I'd really love for you to meet her. Maybe we can go for a visit next week? I'll call you.

XO Dotty

CHAPTER SEVEN

MAY

I attempted to get the bartender's attention, elongating my neck and standing on my toes as if growing an inch or two would yield faster service. It didn't. The bar was packed with thirsty-looking hipsters in skinny jeans and dark-rimmed glasses, branded tote bags swinging from their shoulders. I was amazed at how many people Marcia had gotten to show up to Donovan's launch party.

Now if only I could get a drink.

I'd ignored Dotty's advice about coming. Marcia and I had been avoiding each other all week, but she also hadn't rescinded the invitation, so I was pretty sure she'd see my showing up to celebrate with her as a grand gesture.

"What are you doing here?" Marcia hissed, appearing at my side. Her hair was pulled into a tight bun on top of her head. A lanyard with a plastic VIP pass dangled from her neck.

"You invited me."

She shot me a look. "I didn't think you'd still come after the other night."

"I wanted to support you."

Marcia caught the bartender's eye and gave him a wave. He nodded in acknowledgment.

"I've been trying to get a drink for the better part of an hour," I said, my tone a mix of awe and annoyance. She didn't respond, so I tried a different tack. "You said I should do everything in my power to get a new job. I figured this could be a good networking opportunity. Maybe Donovan's company is hiring."

Marcia moved her head from side to side, like she was working out a kink in her neck.

"What'll it be?" the bartender asked, resting a beefy fist on the counter. He had a unicorn tattoo on his forearm and a pink stud in his nose.

"One vodka soda with lime," Marcia said, before adding, "and make it good vodka. I can't afford a hangover."

"I'll have the same," I piped in. This would be the first time in my life that I didn't drink the well stuff. Marcia was moving up in the world.

"You got it," the bartender said, his voice gruff but warm. I liked him.

Marcia pulled out her phone, the screen casting her face in a bluish glow. "I don't have time for this," she said.

"What do you mean?"

She set her phone on the counter, screen facing up. "I mean that I can't babysit you tonight." Her words felt like a slap. I blinked back tears. "Sorry," she said, shaking her head. "That was harsh. I'm just under a lot of stress and I don't have the bandwidth to do this right now."

"I get it," I said. "I just wanted to apologize. You were right. About everything. And I know I haven't been easy to live with lately."

"That's an understatement."

Marcia's phone buzzed, causing it to rattle against the stone countertop. She picked it up and frowned. "Great." She turned to look at me. "I have to go." Marcia started toward the back of the bar before turning back to me. "You can have my drink. And you can stay, I guess. Just don't talk to anyone who looks important, okay?"

I nodded, unsure whether I should feel relieved that Marcia appeared to be thawing or devastated that she thought I would be capable of ruining this night for her.

"Thanks," she said, clutching her phone to her chest as she backed away. "Have fun." I watched as Marcia speed walked over to the VIP section where a ridiculously good-looking man in a dark blazer was standing behind a velvet rope. It was Donovan Ng. I recognized him from his picture on LinkedIn. Marcia hadn't exaggerated how hot he was.

Donovan's brow furrowed as Marcia approached. He immediately began pointing at a screen that appeared to have stopped working. Marcia put her hands up, palms out, and nodded. I knew that posture well. She used it on me when I was being irrational.

"Two vodka sodas with lime," the bartender said to the back of my head. I turned to face him. "I used the good stuff. But, if you really want to avoid a hangover, you should try gin. It's botanical."

"Thanks." I smiled and reached for my drink.

He gestured to the empty space beside me. "Scare her away?"

"Something like that."

"You don't look so scary to me," he said with a wink. "If you need anything else, the name's Bart."

If middle-aged bartenders with fanciful tattoos were my type, Bart would have been a real keeper.

* * *

I downed my vodka soda and then Marcia's, only to be rewarded with a much-needed buzz and a very full bladder.

Marcia hadn't returned since running off to deal with Donovan, and it didn't look like she would. I'd caught a glimpse of her while the promotional video played on a huge screen suspended above the crowd. She'd been standing off to the side, furiously typing a message into her phone. I'd turned my attention back to the video when Donovan appeared. I think he was talking about changing the world through ethical investing, or something. But I was far more interested in his beautiful mouth than the words that were coming out of it. When I finally tore my eyes away from the screen, Marcia was gone.

It was time to admit defeat. I ordered an Uber before asking Bart for directions to the bathroom. All I wanted to do, after peeing, of course, was pull on a pair of sweatpants and cozy up on the couch with a frozen pizza and a *Friends* marathon. Alone.

I pushed my way through the crowd, my bladder swelling with every step. Thankfully, there was no line for the gender-neutral bathrooms. I burst through a swinging door and took three steps across the penny-tiled floor but stopped short of the stalls. There was someone else in the bathroom. A man. Standing next to a urinal.

"Oh— Sorry," I said, squeezing my eyes shut.

"You're not a reporter, are you?" a deep voice asked. "If you are, this is off the record." I cracked one eye open to see the man waving his hands in front of him, a silver flask glinting in the dim lighting.

"I just had to pee . . ." I said, drawing out the word *pee* as I took in the dark, perfectly coiffed hair, the politician-white teeth. "You're Donovan Ng."

He surrendered a smile. "I am. And you are?"

"Rosie Benson."

"Hi, Rosie Benson."

It was a lot to process. Donovan was practically a celebrity. I couldn't quite reconcile the charismatic entrepreneur I'd just watched on a massive screen with the guy standing next to the urinal. "Why are you drinking alone in the bathroom at your own party?"

He leaned against the wall, his hair almost blending in with the inky black tiles. He wore a burgundy blazer over a crisp white shirt unbuttoned by one too many. I could just make out a tuft of dark chest hair. "It's all a bit much sometimes," he said, his eyes looking at something distant. "Do you ever feel like everyone wants a piece of you?"

"No."

He laughed, his Adam's apple bobbing. "Lucky."

"My roommate planned this party for you."

"Marcia Adebayo?"

I nodded. "She's been falling asleep sitting up every night for the past week. I found her phone in the refrigerator the other day, and I think she walked into the shower holding her laptop this morning." I crossed my arms over my chest. It occurred to me that vodka made me more blunt than usual. This must have been what it felt like to be Dotty.

Donovan took a swig from the flask and grimaced. "I know I've been getting on her nerves. I don't mean to. Marcia's been great— I'll be sure to give her boss a glowing review as long as you promise not to tell her where I'm hiding."

I eyed him, feeling my defenses crumble. Maybe being the reason Marcia got yet another promotion would get her to forgive me. Plus, Donovan was . . . charming. And so much nicer than I'd expected. Normal, even. "Deal."

"Excellent." He held out the flask. "Fireball?"

"Sure."

He pushed off the wall and strode across the room. I pried my saucer-size eyes off his gorgeous face and took the flask. The Fireball went down with surprising ease.

"Good, right?" Donovan said as I handed the flask back to him.

"It tastes like cinnamon gummy bears."

He let out a small laugh. I couldn't make out a single pore on his face. "Yeah, it does."

"Do you do this a lot?"

"Drink Fireball?"

"Hide from everyone at your own party."

He took another swig from the flask, seeming to consider his answer. "This part is a necessary evil. I have to show up to these things if I want to do the stuff I really care about."

"Which is?"

He cracked a smirk. "Didn't you see the video? I want to change the world."

My eyes rolled involuntarily. "Do you really?"

"Yes, I really do. My family has more money than they'll ever be able to spend, and I think we should be investing it in causes that actually matter. Even if they'll never turn a profit."

Admiration bloomed in my chest. Or was it my bladder? "That's amazing," I said, shifting my weight from one foot to the other. "I don't mean to be rude, but I really have to pee."

Surprise, then understanding danced across Donovan's face. He stepped to the side and gestured toward the stalls. "Be my guest."

"I don't want you to hear me."

"I'll run the water."

"Can't you just step outside for a second?"

"I'll get mobbed."

"Donovan."

"Rosie."

I frowned. He pouted. "Fine," I said. I couldn't waste another second arguing. "But I want you to close your eyes and plug your ears."

"I'll even sing."

"Whatever." I brushed past him and stepped into the stall at the far side of the room. Donovan kept his promise. I heard the faucet turn on and then he started to sing "Waterfalls." And he didn't stop until I reemerged, feeling about twenty pounds lighter.

"TLC, huh?" I asked while I washed my hands.

He handed me a paper towel. "It seemed appropriate. Given the circumstances."

I couldn't argue with that logic. "Nice choice," I said, tossing the paper towel into the garbage can by the door. I wasn't sure what to do next. I wanted to stay here, talking to Donovan, but I didn't want to overstay my welcome. My phone buzzed in my purse. I pulled it out and peered at the screen, my vision slightly blurred. My Uber had arrived.

"Do you have any plans after this?" Donovan asked. The way the spot between his eyebrows creased made my legs feel wobbly.

I don't know if it was the Fireball or the TLC soundtrack playing on a loop in my head or the way it felt to have Donovan's eyes on me, but I was emboldened. I held up my phone, proof that I had a getaway car at the ready. "Wanna get out of here?"

"My hero," Donovan said, grinning. "I thought you'd never ask."

I started to turn toward the door, but something—maybe a guilty conscience or an allegiance to Marcia—gave me pause. "Don't you have to, like, schmooze the crowd or give a speech or something?"

Donovan's face lit up with amusement. "Schmooze?"

I rolled my eyes, pretending to be exasperated when really I was charmed. "Don't you have to *network* or something?"

He shook his head. "Nah. I already made the rounds with all the big investors before the video presentation. At this point everyone is going to be more focused on getting drunk for free than wondering where I am. You'd be saving me from having to talk to inebriated tech bros who won't remember a thing I said by the morning."

I bit my lip, weighing my options. I definitely wanted to keep hanging out with Donovan, but I didn't want to ruin anything for Marcia, either.

Donovan took my hand, making the decision for me. "It's my party and I can leave when I want to," he said, intertwining his fingers with mine. "I'll even text my business partner to tell her I'm not feeling well. She'll cover for me."

And with that, he led me out of the bathroom and toward my patiently waiting Uber driver.

I didn't see Marcia on the way out. If she saw me and Donovan, she didn't do anything to try to stop us.

CHAPTER EIGHT

I woke up in Donovan's bed. My last clear memory of the night before was Bart flashing me a thumbs-up as I left the bar and hopped into an Uber with Donovan. The rest of our evening was a whirlwind of Fireball and late-night pizza and kissing. So much kissing.

I blinked my eyes open, my gaze slowly sweeping across the room. Gauzy sunlight streamed through the floor-to-ceiling windows, casting a warm glow across the hardwood floors, which were spotless. The walls were white, but an expensive-looking white, with huge silver frames, each bearing an artsy photo of San Francisco landmarks: Sutro Tower, the Bay Bridge, Alcatraz. My clothes from last night had been neatly folded and placed on a gray armchair in the corner. I looked down, relieved to see that I was wearing one of Donovan's T-shirts.

"Good morning," Donovan said softly. He was shirtless, with wet hair and a thick white towel draped around his neck. He held a glass of water in his hand. "Sorry to wake you so early. I have an investor brunch down the peninsula this morning." He arranged his face into a look that said, *you know how it is.* Even though I had no idea how it was. Brunch in my world consisted of bottomless mimosas at Dotty's favorite drag bar, but I nodded all the same.

He set the glass on the nightstand. I breathed in his scent—an involuntary reflex. "You smell like an expensive Christmas tree," I said. Apparently, I was still drunk.

He laughed, revealing a dimple that made my heart feel like Jell-O. "Thank you?"

"You're welcome," I mumbled, digging my face into a pillow. "What time is it?"

"Seven thirty."

"Ungodly."

"Tell me about it. What about you? Any big plans today?"

I threw my arm over my eyes. "More sleep," I grumbled.

"Lucky."

He crossed the expansive bedroom and slid his closet door open, revealing a seemingly endless row of starched button-down shirts. They were arranged by color, from light to dark. He dropped the towel into a leather hamper and selected a blue-and-white-checkered shirt. I couldn't help watching as the muscles in his taut stomach rippled with every movement. My cheeks warmed as I flashed on another fragmented memory: running my fingers down that bare chest, down his stomach, down, down, down. "What are you staring at?" Donovan said, a mischievous glint in his dark eyes.

I racked my brain for a cover story. "That shirt doesn't go with those pants." It was the best I could come up with on the fly.

Donovan stopped midbutton, his face falling as he looked at his dark jeans. I willed myself to sit up, wary of a looming hangover, but my head felt surprisingly clear. My mouth, on the other hand, was dry and grimy. I reached for the water on the glossy white nightstand.

"Doesn't everything go with jeans?"

I took a long drink of water, swishing it around in my mouth before swallowing. "Pretty much," I said, "I was just messing with you."

Donovan cocked his head, eyebrows raised. "Funny." I raised my glass in response before taking another drink. I didn't normally do this, wake up in strange men's apartments. But I felt surprisingly comfortable around Donovan. It was like we'd been friends in a past life or something.

"Can I use your bathroom?"

He gestured toward a frosted glass door that probably cost more than my car. "Be my guest."

I swung my feet onto the floor, surprised by its warmth. "Do you have heated floors?"

He tucked his shirt into his pants with a smooth shove. "Yep."

"You're rich," I said.

"You're drunk," he countered. We were both right.

Donovan's bathroom was covered in wall-to-wall marble. All gray and white and glass. Dotty would have hated it. I beelined over to the mirror, my nose practically touching the glass. My mascara was clumped around the corners of my eyes and my hair was a tangled mess. I ran my fingers through my hair and scrubbed my face, feeling vaguely guilty about the dark smears I left on Donovan's white towel. "Do you have any mouthwash?" I called, carefully folding the towel and placing it in a small hamper under the sink.

"Cabinet on the left!" he called through the door.

I padded over to the other vanity and tugged it open. And that's when I realized that Donovan might be a psychopath. It wasn't just his closet that was fanatically organized. Each shelf of the vanity was dedicated to a different hygienic need: neatly stacked containers of floss, electric toothbrush heads, tubes of toothpaste, and bottles of mouthwash lined the top shelf. Below that were containers of hair products, ranging from gel to mousse to hair spray—all organized by brand (none of which I'd heard of). The lowest shelf boasted more face creams than a drugstore. But that wasn't the craziest part. He'd used a label maker for every section, as if he might forget what went where.

I pushed thoughts of *Dexter* from my mind and dumped a capful of mouthwash into my mouth. It was no substitute for brushing, but the minty freshness would be enough for now. I pulled on my clothes from the night before, pushing away memories about how they came off (frantically, haphazardly, piece by piece in a drunken blur), and put Donovan's T-shirt in the hamper. Feeling more or less human again, I reemerged to find Donovan sitting on his neatly made bed, lost in his phone.

"So," I said, doing my best to sound casual. "You're a neat freak?"

His head snapped up, eyes softening as he took me in. He flashed me a sheepish smile.

"I have a mild case of obsessive-compulsive disorder. It's a side effect of growing up as the only son of an overbearing politician. At least that's what my therapist says."

"It's charming, in a creepy serial killer way."

"Just don't look in my freezer."

"I won't as long as you don't look in my closet."

He arched an eyebrow. "Are you inviting me into your bedroom?"

I gave him a coy look. "Maybe. As long as you promise not to murder me."

"I think that can be arranged."

"No one has ever promised not to murder me before."

He wriggled his eyebrows. "There's a first time for everything."

It was official: I had a monster crush on Donovan Ng.

As my Uber pulled away from Donovan's building (which had a doorman and a seating area in the lobby that was nicer than my parents' living room), I felt like I was moving between two worlds.

Donovan's was sleek and cool and full of possibility. Mine was dull and small and bland. The thought of getting another glimpse into Donovan's lifestyle was thrilling. Almost as thrilling as the prospect of doing what we did last night again.

* * *

I eased the door to our apartment open, kicked off my boots, and tiptoed into the kitchen, feeling increasingly guilty with every step. I'd texted Marcia last night to let her know I wouldn't be coming home, but I hadn't told her who I was with. She'd made me promise not to talk to anyone important, and I'd gone *way* further than that with Donovan.

The kitchen was unusually tidy, save for a cardboard pizza box and a pair of wineglasses on the counter, a film of red wine crusted along their base. My stomach growled at the thought of pizza, but as the sound of Marcia's snoring floated down the hallway, I decided I'd rather go back to sleep. Food could wait.

But brushing my teeth could not.

I poured myself a glass of water before creeping past Marcia's bedroom, the door only open a crack, and into the bathroom. I was almost through humming the second verse of "Waterfalls," rhythmically swishing the bristles of my toothbrush across my teeth, when something tugged at my attention. It was a forest-green tech vest dangling from the towel hook on the back of the door. I took a step closer as the familiar logo snapped into focus. What was my old Driftwood vest doing in our bathroom? I could have sworn I'd cleared out all my Driftwood crap after I'd gotten fired.

That thing belonged in the garbage. I reached my hand toward the vest, fingers splayed, toothbrush dangling from my mouth, and yanked it off the hook, pulling the door ajar in the process. It was larger than I remembered and the fleece was soft beneath my fingers, well-worn. A shadow of realization crept across my mind as footsteps thudded down the hallway. I jerked my head back toward the door as it creaked open, revealing the last person I ever expected to see in my apartment.

"Raj?" I said through a mouthful of toothpaste.

"Fuuuuck." He was shirtless and barefoot, wearing just a pair of boxer shorts.

I spat into the sink and turned back to face him. "What are you doing here?"

My former boss moved his hands to cover his crotch before flashing a nervous smile. It was way too early for those teeth. "We didn't think you'd be home this early."

We. Not I. *We.*

And that's when it hit me. Raj was Marcia's secret boyfriend. "Oh my god," I spat, throwing Raj's vest at his head. I rubbed my eyes, as if that would make it all go away.

"I'm so sorry," Raj said, coming unglued from his spot in the doorway. He backed away, turning his head toward Marcia's bedroom. "I'll get Marcia."

I braced myself against the pedestal sink in our tiny bathroom as the room began to spin, my hangover and shock twisting into a nasty cocktail. I stared down into the drain and tried to steady myself.

"Rosie?" Marcia's voice was groggy with sleep. She stood in the doorway, eyes puffy, ponytail askew. Her eyes welled with tears as she took a step toward me. "I'm so sorry—"

I held up a hand to stop her. "How long?"

"I can explain—"

"How long?" It came out strangled, not quite a cry but almost. Her shoulders slumped. "Three months."

I nodded. "So you were screwing him when he fired me, then?"

"I didn't know. Not at first." She dropped her gaze to the floor. "And we aren't just hooking up. It's . . . serious."

"Serious enough to lie to me?"

She lifted her chin, meeting my eyes. "Rosie. I'm so, so sorry."

Something about the sincerity in her voice, the pain on her face, made the neurons in my brain flash red. This wasn't a conversation I could have. Not right now. "Don't," I said, gritting my teeth, "just don't."

"But—"

"I want him and his stupid vest gone," I said. It was almost a growl. "*Now.*"

She crossed her arms across her stomach and took a step back. "Okay. Can I—"

"Now," I said, more quietly this time. I lowered my eyes to the drain as Marcia shut the door, leaving me alone inside that cold little bathroom.

* * *

I stomped down the hall and into my room, intent on packing a bag. I needed to get out of that apartment. I was sure Dotty would let me stay over for the weekend. Worst case, I could go see Tommy and Lily. Although that felt like an extreme option.

I yanked open my purse and pulled out my phone. It vibrated with several missed calls and text notifications, all from Dad. I called him back without listening to any of his voice mails.

He answered on the third ring. His voice sounded strange. "Rosie?"

"Dad? What's up?"

There was a long pause. I heard a rumble of noise in the background. He was in the car. "Have you heard from Dotty?"

My hands tightened around the phone. "She emailed me last night. Why?"

I sensed Dad's heavy sigh through the phone. "We were supposed to meet for breakfast this morning, but she never showed . . . and she hasn't been answering her phone. I'm just getting off at her exit now."

A trickle of nausea crept up my throat. Dotty had been known to blow off the occasional family dinner, but she wasn't the type to ignore Dad. "I can be there in half an hour," I said.

He sighed again. This time I think it was from relief. "Thanks, sweetie."

I changed as quickly as I could, tugging on yoga pants and an old college sweatshirt before running out the door. By the time I got to my car, my hands were shaking—from fear or anger or a hangover, I didn't know. All I knew was that I needed to get to Dotty.

That drive to her house was the longest drive of my life.

CHAPTER NINE

The first thing I noticed as I turned onto Dotty's street was the police car. Then the ambulance. Then Dad, standing at the bottom of Dotty's obnoxiously steep stairs, hand over his mouth, nodding slowly in response to something an officer was saying. I pulled into a neighboring driveway and burst out of the car, tears already clouding my eyes as I ran to Dad's side. I'll never forget the look on his face. It was like he'd seen a ghost.

He pulled me into a crushing hug and let out a deep, guttural sob. "She's gone, Rosie. She's gone. She's gone." He said it over and over. More times than I could count.

I knew exactly what he was saying, but my brain, maybe in an effort to protect me from the awful, unthinkable truth, couldn't quite process his words. "What do you mean?"

Dad took a step back, squeezing my shoulders. He looked thinner than the last time I'd seen him, his cheeks slightly sunken. "She's passed away, sweetheart."

I sank to the ground. The world swirled around me as I fought the urge to throw up. Dad knelt beside me, rubbing my back, just as he had so many times when I'd skinned a knee or scraped an elbow as a kid. "I know, sweetie, I know. I know," he said. This couldn't be happening. It was impossible. A world without Dotty was impossible.

I couldn't catch my breath. I couldn't stop crying. Dad was crying too. None of it seemed real.

I don't know how long we sat on the grass outside of Dotty's house before I asked, my voice wooden and distant, what happened.

Dad pulled his knees up to his chest and rocked gently from side to side. "I'm not sure. She looked like she was sleeping, but when I stepped closer"—he dipped his head—"I could tell she wasn't breathing. I called for help, but it was too late. She was already gone."

Gone.

That's how life worked. Things could be snatched away in a cruel, cold instant. Things you took for granted. Things you didn't know you needed. Relied on.

What was I going to do without her?

What was Bug going to do without her? My stomach turned to cement. "Dad, where's Bug?" I was on my feet, starting toward Dotty's steps before he had a chance to answer.

"She's inside!" he called, his voice fading as I moved away. "I couldn't get her to leave Dotty's side."

I swore under my breath and broke into a run. I arrived at the top of Dotty's steps, panting and shaking. The front door hung wide open, soft yellow light spilling from inside. I hesitated, worried about what I'd find.

A mournful howl, the most tragic sound I'd ever heard, beckoned me inside. I stepped into the living room, my jaw relaxing at the sight. The space looked just like it always had—cluttered and kitschy. There was a half-assembled puzzle on the coffee table, an empty glass of wine on the kitchen counter, a smattering of books and magazines spread out on one end of the couch. I could feel Dotty in the room, like she'd only just stepped into the kitchen.

The bedroom was different, heavier. I found Bug at the foot of the bed, where Dotty lay, motionless but peaceful. I understood how Dad might have thought she was asleep. A stretcher stood in the corner, left behind by the paramedics I'd passed in the hallway. Bug tilted her head toward the ceiling and let out another sorrowful howl as I walked into the room. I swear my heart splintered into a dozen pieces at the sight of her. She looked so small, so helpless.

How long had she been here mourning her best friend?

I fought back tears, desperately wanting to be strong. "Hey, Love Bug," I said gently as I eased my way toward the bed. She thumped her tail at the familiar nickname. I knelt beside the bed and extended my hand. She gave my thumb a single lick before lying down. I heard her loud and clear: she didn't want to leave. "I'm so sorry about Dotty," I said. "But do you think you can come with me just for a little bit? We can go for a walk. Maybe get some treats?" Bug cocked her head at the T-word, but she didn't budge.

I hazarded a look at Dotty, unable to shake the feeling that she might wake up at any moment. I wished she would. I looked back at Bug, who was shivering. "Sweet girl," I said, scratching the top of her head. "This is the worst thing that's ever happened to either of us." Bug turned her big brown eyes back to Dotty. "Maybe we can say goodbye to her together." I rose from my crouched position and sat down at the edge of the bed. This was the closest I'd ever been to a dead person. I'd been so much younger when my grandparents had died and too afraid to go anywhere near their caskets.

Bug crept gingerly toward me and climbed into my lap. I wrapped my arms around her shivering body and kissed the top of her head. Her fur was soft beneath my lips. I steeled my nerves, willing myself to be brave. "Dotty," I said, turning my gaze toward my aunt, a woman who'd been so full of fire that it had never oc-curred to me that her flame wouldn't burn forever, "Bug wants you to know that she loves you so much. More than anything, right, Bug?" I looked down at Bug, who appeared to be listening intently, her stubby ears perked. I turned back to Dotty. "And Bug wants to tell you that she wouldn't have wanted anyone else in the whole world to adopt her. You gave her the best home and the happiest life she could have hoped for." I paused, reflecting on how sweet Dotty and Bug were together. They'd been inseparable. "And . . . I want you to know that I'm going to take care of Bug. She's going to be safe with me. I'll protect her for you." A heavy tear rolled down my cheek and landed on top of Bug's head. She didn't seem to notice. "I'll take care of you from now on, Bug. I promise."

Bug pressed her warm little body into mine. She wasn't shaking anymore.

CHAPTER TEN

Dotty had once told me that grief was love with nowhere to go—that was why it hurt so bad. Now I knew what she'd meant.

In the hours after Dotty died, grief had taken up residence in the fiber of my muscles, nestled in between tendons and bones. If I didn't know any better, I would've thought I was coming down with the flu. I ached for Dotty.

I spent the rest of the day on Mom and Dad's couch with Bug curled up by my side. I didn't want to think about jobs. Or Marcia and Raj. Or how weird my parents were acting, not so subtly keeping to their separate rooms. I didn't care. I barely had the strength to lift my own arms.

Tommy and Lily came by that afternoon. They'd been busy moving into their new house down the street. Tommy was all business, talking about funeral arrangements with Dad in the kitchen. Lily and her belly found me on the couch. "Can I sit?" she asked.

I gestured to the open space by my feet. "Be my guest."

Lily sank into the cushions with a sigh, but she didn't say anything for a long time. When she finally did, it was more to herself than to me. "I was just over for lunch a few days ago. She was fine . . . as energetic as ever."

I squeezed Bug a little tighter. "The paramedics said they think it was a stroke."

Lily nodded, her eyes fixed on the wall across the room. "I'd always wondered if it would be easier this way. Fast, no suffering, no long goodbyes . . ." She wiped a tear from her cheek. "Now I know this is so much worse."

Lily's mom, Lucía, had died when she was twelve after a long battle with lung cancer. She didn't talk about it a lot, but I'd once heard Tommy telling Mom that Lily still cried herself to sleep about it twice a year—on her mom's birthday and the anniversary of her death.

I wanted to comfort Lily, but I didn't know how. "Dotty really loved you," I offered. "More than she loved Tommy."

She cracked a small smile before swiping away another tear. "I know." She laughed. "She said that to his face. Multiple times."

"I wish I'd been there to see that." The thought brought me the first moment of joy I'd felt since my world came crashing down that morning.

"You were her favorite, though."

"She was mine, too."

"I know."

"She emailed me last night and said she was going to bed early. That she was exhausted. I never got a chance to write back. I went to a dumb party instead."

Lily placed a firm hand on my socked foot and gave it a squeeze. "I was at the movies when my mom died. She was having a good day, so she'd practically thrown me out of the house, insisting that I go do something fun . . . it took me a long time to forgive myself."

"You didn't do anything wrong," I said.

"Neither did you."

Sitting with Lily made me feel a little better. Bug, too. She crawled into Lily's lap as best she could so Lily could scratch behind her ears. But the reprieve was only temporary. When Lily left to run to the grocery store, Bug returned to my side. The look she gave me said it all: Lily was great, but she was no Dotty.

No one ever could be.

* * *

We drifted through the hours, picking at a bowl of grapes that Mom set out on the kitchen counter, mindlessly staring at our phones, blowing our noses. Every so often, someone would start talking about Dotty. *Remember that time she smuggled those baby chicks out of a petting zoo? Didn't she go through a phase where she wouldn't eat anything orange? I already miss her perfume.* At some point, the TV clicked on. Dad might have been watching the news. I wasn't paying attention.

Eventually, pizza boxes appeared, sending the smell of cheese and olives and bell peppers wafting into the living room. I forced myself off the couch as Bug grunted her disapproval. "Do you want any pizza?" I asked her. She just sighed.

When I made my way into the dining room, I was struck by the lack of warmth. It wasn't that the temperature was cold, but that feeling, the ease and familiarity I was so accustomed to, just wasn't there. The table wasn't set. Dad wasn't at his usual post behind the bar. Mom wasn't sautéing garlic and onions over the stove. Dotty wasn't perched on her barstool, sipping a martini as she regaled us with tales of her recent adventures. In fact, the room was entirely empty. This was the first time I'd been home since Mom had decided she wanted a divorce. Was it always like this now? Or was the shadowy cloud that now loomed over my childhood home a result of Dotty's death? I wondered if the darkness would ever pass.

The phone rang somewhere in the back of the house. "Benson residence," Mom trilled, as if all was right with the world.

I flipped open a pizza box and eyed the pepperoni suspiciously. I'd only tried pepperoni once in my life, at Tommy's tenth birthday party. I took a bite, wanting to fit in with the other kids, but promptly spat it out, disgusted by the rubbery, greasy texture. "Tastes like death, huh, kiddo?" Dotty had said, rubbing my back. "Want me to get you a piece of cheese instead?" I scraped my tongue along the top of my teeth, desperate to get the nasty taste out of my mouth. "That's a yes." She'd laughed. "Be right back." I'd avoided pepperoni ever since.

Dad emerged from the dark hallway, looking ten years older than he had that morning. His brown curls were tinged with fresh flecks of gray, and his usually golden skin looked pale. I tried not to stare at the shadows under his eyes.

"Hey, sweetie," he said. His upbeat tone felt forced, but the hug was real. I squeezed him back. I felt awful for Dad. Dotty had been like a second mother to him. He must have been devastated. As terrible as today had been, I was glad I was there with him, that he didn't have to go through it alone.

Eventually, Dad pulled out of our hug and made a show of eyeing the pizza boxes. "Let's eat," he said tiredly. "I'm starving."

I'd just placed a slice on a paper plate when Mom appeared in the doorway. She was clutching the phone to her chest. "That was Dotty's attorney," she said quietly. "He wants to go over Dotty's will with us on Monday morning."

"So soon?" Dad asked.

Mom shot him a look. "Honestly, David, I think we should just be happy that Dotty had a will at all. She wasn't exactly organized."

"You're a real piece of work, Claire."

"I'm just being honest, *David*."

Then my parents began to argue. About everything: Dotty, the house, their respective wills, the divorce. I stopped paying attention when they started in on the pizza toppings (Mom had neglected to hold the onion on Dad's Hawaiian Special).

I tried to take a bite of pizza, but it tasted like salt and cardboard. I spit it into a napkin and pushed my plate across the counter, no longer hungry.

CHAPTER ELEVEN

On Monday morning, we piled into the cramped office of Peter Simpson, Esquire, encircling his imposing, aggressively polished wood desk on an assortment of wingback chairs, wobbly stools, and a ratty old ottoman. Bug greeted Peter with a muted tail wag and half-hearted lick before retreating to the safety of my lap. She now sat upright and unusually still, as though she understood the importance of the moment.

Peter Simpson, Esquire was tall, tan, and blond, with striking hazel eyes and a smile that transformed his face into an attractive collage of well-worn wrinkles. He looked more like a retired surfer than an attorney. I don't know why I'd expected him to be gray-haired and covered in tweed, with a collection of dragonflies mounted on the wall.

Peter scooped a stack of papers into a pile using his big, gruff hands as he cleared his throat. He paused, flashing a somber smile to no one in particular. "I was so sorry to learn of Dotty's passing," he said. "I considered her a close friend."

Dad shifted in his chair. Tommy eyed Peter suspiciously. I could feel a standoff brewing. Tommy hated other lawyers.

"That's lovely, Peter. Thank you," Mom said. I could have sworn she batted her eyelashes. If Dad noticed, he didn't let on. He sat still, unmoving, one hand tucked under his chin.

"How did you know her again?" Tommy asked, his harsh tone a sharp contrast to Mom's sugary-sweet one. Peter didn't seem to care.

"She found me in the phone book if that gives you any idea of how long ago we met. She'd just taken an assignment in Indonesia, if I remember correctly. Wherever it was, it prompted Dotty to get her affairs in order. Something about Komodo dragons . . ." Peter's voice trailed off as he disappeared into the old memory, nostalgia dancing across his face. "Anyway, she said she liked my name, so she called me up, and we hit it off. We've been friends ever since."

Tommy huffed. He'd once told me that lawyers who write wills were barely a step above ambulance chasers. I was sure he had an opinion about attorneys who considered their clients friends, too. Lily jabbed him in the ribs.

"Well," Peter said, plucking a thin green folder off the desk, "no sense in postponing the inevitable. Unless there's anything I need to know first?" He cast a glance around the room, his middle finger hovering along the edge of the file.

Tommy straightened his back, sitting taller on the barstool Peter had dragged out of a tiny closet when we'd arrived. "My parents, David and Claire"—he gestured toward Mom and Dad, respectively—"are in the process of filing for divorce."

Peter nodded. "Dotty told me. And we've accounted for that in the will."

That snapped Dad out of his catatonic state. He dropped his hand from beneath his chin and turned to Mom. "How long have you been planning this divorce, Claire?" I wrapped my arms more tightly around Bug.

Mom didn't reply. Dad raked his hands through his graying curls. "I can't believe this. It's in the goddamned will? My aunt knew before I did?" He was talking to Peter now.

Peter raised his hands. "I think you're misunderstanding, David," he said gently. "Dotty and I spoke regularly about all sorts of things. Including our families. When she told me about your plans to divorce, I advised her that we could edit the will if she wished."

"Advised her?" Tommy jumped in. "It sounds more like you tricked an old woman into letting you rack up your chargeable hours." Lily placed a hand on Tommy's forearm.

Peter shook his head. "I haven't issued Dotty an invoice in over a decade. We were friends."

"Let's try to get through this without dragging Mr. Simpson into our family drama," Mom said through her teeth. This must have been killing her.

Dad sat back in his chair. "Fine by me."

"Good," Peter said, flipping open the file. "And for what it's worth, Claire, this office has seen much worse. I once had an elderly client punch her sister square in the nose." Tommy looked like that's what he wanted to do to Peter. "All right then," Peter said, running a finger down the page. "Here we go. The last will and testament of Eugenia Mae Polk—"

"Who the hell is Eugenia?" It was out of my mouth before I even realized it was a thought in my head. Peter stared back at me blankly, mouth slightly ajar.

"That's Dotty's real name, sweetheart," Mom said.

"You didn't think Dotty was her actual name, did you?" Tommy asked.

I'd honestly never given it any thought. She'd always been Dotty to me. "Where did 'Dotty' come from?"

"An old nickname, I think," Mom said, turning to Dad for confirmation.

He nodded but refused to meet Mom's gaze. "I think she got it back in college. Or maybe high school."

"She never told you the story?" Peter asked.

"Can we just get on with it?" Tommy grumbled.

Peter obliged, pressing on. "I'll send all of you copies in case you're interested in doing a full read-through." He shot a glance at Tommy. "But for now, I'll give you the highlights. Dotty is leaving her house to each of you in equal parts. One quarter to David, one to Claire, one to Tommy and Lily, and one to Rosie. You can do whatever you'd like with it—move in, sell it, rent it out." The thought of someone else living in Dotty's house made my stomach flip. "She wants David to have all her family photos and heirlooms," Peter said, turning the page. "I've got a comprehensive list here, mostly fine china and a handful of paintings. She'd like Claire to have her jewelry and has indicated that she can help herself to any of the furniture, presumably to furnish a new place, whenever she decides to procure one."

Dad tensed, swiveling in his chair to look at Mom, who refused to pry her eyes away from Peter. "Now you're moving out? Have you already bought a house I don't know about? Started a new family?" He said it to the side of her face.

"Not now, David," Mom said, her lips barely moving.

He dragged his hands down his face, his fingertips curled into miniature claws.

"Peter, please continue," Mom said, through tightened lips.

Peter looked to Dad, who wasn't taking his eyes off Mom. We sat in heavy silence for too long, Bug's steady heartbeat thrumming against my arms. Finally, Peter drew a breath and read on. "Dotty is leaving all her books to Tommy and Lily and their future children." He looked up at Lily and wriggled his eyebrows. "It's quite a collection. Volumes and volumes on history and anthropology, even astrophysics." Lily smiled politely. "And Rosie," he said, drawing out my name. "Dotty would like you to have Bug."

The energy in Peter's cramped office shifted as five sets of eyes landed on me. My throat constricted with emotion. My breath came in shallow stabs. No one said anything. Were they waiting for me to react? I didn't know how to.

Mom spoke first. "Are we sure that's the right choice?" she asked. "Wouldn't it be better for Tommy and Lily to take her? Or David?"

"Where, exactly, do you plan on living when you move out, Claire?" Dad asked Mom, his voice rising.

"Let me have a look at that," Tommy said, reaching for the will.

"Relax, Tommy," Lily hissed.

The room blurred as the chaos of my normally reserved family spun out of control. But I hardly noticed. Because Dotty had trusted me with the most precious thing in her life. Bug was mine. I pressed my chin against the top of her furry little head as fat tears rolled down my face.

"I'm keeping her," I said, my voice louder, stronger than I'd ever heard it. My words sliced through the room, bringing about an abrupt silence, save for the creak of a rickety chair.

Mom leaned forward, peering past a seething Dad. "Sweetheart, I know how much you love Bug, but owning a dog is a huge responsibility . . ." She didn't need to finish the thought. I knew what she meant. We all did.

I stuck out my chin in defiance and stated again, "I'm keeping her." End of conversation. Dotty had cast the ultimate vote of confidence in me. That was all that mattered.

"We can talk about this later," Mom said. She'd sooner die than argue in front of a stranger. Especially a handsome one like Peter Simpson, Esquire.

"Did Dotty leave Rosie any money for Bug's care?" Tommy asked. His question sounded more like an accusation. But it got my attention. Bug and I leaned forward, awaiting Peter's response.

"Not exactly," he said. "You all stand to earn some money from Dotty's house, however you decide to manage it, but Dotty left her remaining monetary assets to charity."

Tommy jerked forward. Lily grabbed his shoulder. He settled back onto his seat. "What does that mean, exactly?" she asked.

"Well," Peter said, leaning back in his chair. I half expected him to tuck his hands behind his head and kick his feet up onto the desk. "It's pretty simple, really. She's directed that the balances of her accounts be gifted to a handful of nonprofit organizations—all charitable causes that she's long supported. After her remaining debts have been paid, of course."

"How much money are we talking about here?" Tommy asked.

Peter spun a pen between his long fingers. "Dotty wanted the value of her donations to remain anonymous," he said, pausing to stare at the pen. "But let's put it this way: she lived a modest life. So it would make sense for you to assume that her savings were modest as well."

If anyone were to ask me about my own savings account, I'd probably describe it as "modest," too. And by modest, I'd mean nonexistent. "Are you saying she was broke?" I asked.

Peter dropped the pen onto his desk and leaned forward. "I can't betray Dotty's confidence by answering that question," he said, before turning to Tommy. "Attorney-client privilege and all that." He winked. I couldn't help but smile as Tommy's head took on the appearance of a tomato.

"But she took so many trips . . ." Mom said, her voice trailing off.

"Those were for work," Lily said.

Dad scraped his hands against the rough stubble on his face. "I wish I would have known if she needed money. I would have helped her."

"She never even got to retire," Tommy said. He almost sounded sad.

We sat there, in Peter's cramped office, absorbing this revelation, all the pieces falling into place. Dotty working well into her golden years. Peter providing his services pro bono. Dotty's old, outdated house. She was just getting by. I'd always assumed that Dotty had had enough money to live on her own terms. I never thought to question why she hadn't retired.

"Should we talk about the funeral?" Lily asked.

Peter shook his head. "I'm afraid not." He picked up Dotty's file and flipped through several pages before apparently finding the one he was looking for. "She wants to be cremated. And she doesn't want any kind of service."

Lily gasped. "But we've already started making arrangements . . ."

Peter arranged his face into a sympathetic expression but didn't respond.

Tommy turned to Dad. "Did you know about any of this?"

Dad scoffed. "I don't know anything about my own family, apparently."

"Honestly, David," Mom said.

Maybe it was my newfound confidence, or the fact that I was Bug's person now, but I was suddenly emboldened, confident that I had a more stable foothold among the adults in the room. "In case you've forgotten, Dotty is *dead*. Can you please not make this about yourselves?"

Mom pinched the bridge of her nose with her thumb and pointer finger, her eyes squeezed shut. Dad slumped in his chair.

"What are you smiling about?" Tommy spat at Peter, who sat grinning behind his comically huge desk.

Peter attempted to suppress his smile but failed miserably. "It's just that . . . Rosie, you're the spitting image of your aunt."

* * *

We wrapped up with Peter and stepped outside, everyone appearing relieved to be back in the sunlight and fresh air. Dad offered to take me to Dotty's house to pick up my car and a few more of Bug's belongings. Tommy and Lily agreed to give Mom a ride back to my parents' house, not that she planned to live there for much longer. We said our goodbyes, some frostier than others, and went our separate ways.

"There's something I don't trust about that guy," I heard Tommy mutter to Lily on the way to their car. "I'm going to go through that will with a fine-tooth comb."

Lily took his hand, intertwining her fingers between his. "I'm sad, too," she said.

CHAPTER TWELVE

Being back in Dotty's house felt wrong. The air was stale and the floorboards creaked more loudly than I remembered. The fog outside cast a gloomy gray light through the living room. Dad flipped on a lamp in the corner, but it did little to dissipate the darkness.

Bug, still traumatized from the last time she was here, cowered in my arms. Her soft whimpers threatened to break off yet another piece of my heart.

"Okay," Dad said tiredly. "We'll just gather up a few of Bug's things and be on our way." He looked old in this light. Or maybe splitting with Mom had aged him. I'd tried to ask him about it on the car ride over, but he'd insisted that I knew as much as he did. "I thought we were happy," he'd said, shrugging his shoulders, hands gripping the steering wheel. "She had everything she ever needed. Everything she ever wanted."

I'd long ago given up on trying to understand Mom. Vaguely unhappy seemed to be her default setting. Still, I worried about Dad.

I looked around the lifeless living room. The cluttered shelves and stacks of magazines and endless array of tchotchkes that had once imbued Dotty's home with personality now made it feel sad and messy. It was as if Dotty had taken the house's soul with her. Dad pulled a cloth grocery bag off the hook by the door and shook it open. He began picking up Bug's toys from the floor and stuffing them into the bag. I started toward the kitchen to look for her food but stopped at a wall of photos in the hall. There were pictures of Dotty with our family: at Mom and Dad's wedding, Tommy's first birthday party, my high school graduation. But I didn't recognize most of the people in the rest of her photos. Dotty was always talking about her friends who lived all over the world. They all had exotic professions like entomologist or flamenco dancer. Now I'd never know who any of them were.

Bug whined, twisting in my arms. I set her on the floor, and she darted toward Dad, curious about why he was bagging up her most prized possessions. The sooner we could get out of there, the better.

I found Bug's kibble in a cabinet and set it on the counter. Then I grabbed her food and water bowls off the floor and gave them a quick rinse in the sink. Dad appeared at the other side of the counter, where I used to stand while Dotty made me lunch. "I got her leash and toys," he said. "Is there anything else?"

"Just her bed. She had one in Dotty's room, but . . ." I let my voice trail off. I didn't need to say it. There was no way I was going back into that room. "I'll get the one in her office."

Dad nodded in approval. "I'll dry these off," he said, gesturing to the steel bowls.

Dotty's office was less depressing than the living room. Maybe because she and I never spent much time back there. It was overly full, just like the rest of her house, with dark, emerald walls, a large wood desk, and an inordinate amount of brightly colored poufs littering the floor. The shelves were lined with what had to be hundreds of books, and the walls bore more photos of smiling strangers in mismatched frames. Were these people the reason

Dotty hadn't had any money when she died? Had she spent it all on plane flights and train tickets to visit them?

And where were they now?

I pictured them wondering why Dotty hadn't returned their calls. Or worrying when she didn't show up to a long-standing brunch date. Would they stop by the house, only to find it empty and cold, her knickknacks gathering dust?

My grandma Ruth used to read the obituaries in her spare time, occasionally commenting when someone she knew had died. Dad said it was normal for older people to do that, although I couldn't for the life of me understand why. It was too sad to imagine Dotty's friends finding out from the paper. I had to tell them. But I didn't even know their names.

I looked around the room, searching for what, exactly, I didn't know. An old-fashioned address book, maybe? But the clutter was overwhelming.

I heard Bug's little footsteps echoing down the hallway, slow and hesitant. "In here," I called, kneeling to greet her as she appeared in the doorway. She looked worried. Her forehead was more wrinkled than usual. As I reached for her, a black charging cable caught my eye. It snaked from an outlet in the corner of the room across the floor and under Dotty's desk, leading to an old laptop.

I gave Bug an absent-minded scratch behind her ear before crawling over to the laptop. She whined as I pulled away but was in my lap before I even had a chance to open Dotty's computer. "We're almost done," I assured her. "I just have to do something first."

I opened the laptop, my heart skipping a beat as it glowed to life. I clicked on the internet browser, silently praying that Dotty hadn't logged out of her email account.

She hadn't. I sighed loudly, surprised to feel my heart thumping in my chest. I rested my chin on top of Bug's head as I began to type, my fingers picking up speed as the message crystallized in my mind.

I wasn't writing just to let Dotty's friends know that she'd died. I was seizing an opportunity. A chance to get to know her better, to feel close to her again. I wanted to know who she was to them. I wanted to hear their stories. I wanted more Dotty.

Bug's panting turned into a steady cry. "Just a minute," I said uselessly.

"Rosie?" Dad's voice floated down the hallway, making me jump. "Are you okay?"

"Fine," I called back. "Be right there."

I checked to make sure I'd copied all Dotty's contacts into the address bar. I wanted to proofread what I'd written, but Bug was starting to shake. I settled for a cursory scan before hitting send, feeling a thrill of relief zip across my rib cage.

At least they would know now.

I closed the laptop and slid it back under the desk. Then I picked up Bug, tucking her under one arm and her bed under the other. I switched off the lights and pulled the door shut.

It felt like another goodbye.

* * *

I didn't tell Marcia about Dotty. Or about Bug, for that matter. But somehow, she knew. She had taken to sending alternating text messages—apologies, condolences, offers to help. Lather, rinse, repeat.

My shock and sadness over Dotty's death had blunted my anger, taken the venom out of it. What had been a hot, bubbling fury was now gone, replaced by cool, hollow indifference. I was hurt

and nowhere near ready to forgive Marcia. I still had so many un-
answered questions swirling around in my head. How many times
had Marcia lied to me about where she was going and who she was
with? Had Raj known that he was dating my best friend when he
fired me?

Was that *why* he'd fired me?

I couldn't bear the thought of Marcia having had something to
do with my professional demise, but a nagging feeling in my gut
knew that it was a possibility. The thought of my performance at
work being fodder for their pillow talk should have filled me with
rage.

But I had no energy for rage.

Not right now.

I took Bug back to our apartment because there wasn't really
anywhere else to go. I couldn't stand another night at home with
my parents, with Dad drinking until his eyelids hung heavy and
Mom making thinly veiled jabs about my myriad failures. Marcia
greeted me with a cup of hot chocolate and treats for Bug. I allowed her to hug me, but left my arms hanging limply by my sides.
Bug eagerly accepted Marcia's bribe, rolling onto her back for a
belly rub. We'd need to have a talk about that later.

"Rosie, I'm so sorry," she said. "About everything. But especially
Dotty."

I nodded, my face blank.

"Can I bring you anything to eat?"

"Can Bug and I have the couch for the night?"

A wounded look crossed her face. I was pushing her away, re-
jecting her attempts to comfort me. But I wasn't trying to be cruel.
Just honest.

"Yeah, of course," she said, clearing her throat. "I'll be in my
room. Text me if you need anything?"

"Sure," I said. Marcia gave Bug a final pat before grabbing her glass of wine and starting down the hall toward her room. "Thanks, Marcia," I said. "For"—I made a sweeping gesture—"all this."

She attempted a smile, but it didn't stick. "Of course," she said quietly before disappearing behind her bedroom door.

I dragged my bag to my bedroom, where I found a bouquet of sunflowers (Dotty's favorite) on my nightstand and a variety of my favorite snacks—cheese puffs and pretzels and M&Ms—arranged into the shape of a heart on the bed. At the center, there was a stack of *National Geographic* magazines with a card on top. She'd signed it *Marshmallow*.

I couldn't help but feel like this was all for someone else. Like Marcia was trying to comfort the old Rosie.

But after everything that had happened over the last two days, the old Rosie was gone.

Hi Everyone,

My name is Rosie Benson. I'm Dotty's niece. Her great-niece, actually.

In case you haven't heard, Dotty passed away this past Saturday. They think it was a stroke. I'm told it was peaceful. She looked peaceful.

I know this might sound strange, but I'm here at Dotty's house gathering up a few of her things, and I guess I'm realizing that as close as I thought we were, there was a lot I didn't know. I'm starting to wonder if I ever really knew her at all.

I want to learn more about her life. Not just the parts I saw. I want to know the real stuff. Was she happy? Did she have any regrets? If she could go back in time and live life all over again, would she change anything?

I'd give almost anything to ask her myself. The truth is, I could really use her advice right now. But since that isn't possible, I'm hoping you can help me.

Can you tell me about her? I want to know who she was to you.

Sincerely,
Rosie

P.S. Please send your responses to me directly. I've copied myself on this email.

From: Sonia Fernández
To: Rosie Benson
Subject: Re: Dotty
Date: May 14

Dear Rosie,

I'm so terribly sorry to hear about your great-aunt Dotty. Please forgive me, as I'm still processing this news. I just saw Dotty last weekend, and she was as fit as ever.

I run a small sanctuary for farmed animals—cows, pigs, chickens, goats. We're a lean operation and we rely on volunteers to keep things running smoothly. Dotty has been my most loyal and reliable volunteer. She's been coming here since the day our barn doors opened. It's not every day that spunky old gals show up to muck stalls. I was so impressed by the way she rolled up her sleeves, grabbed a shovel, and got right to work.

Our animals adored Dotty. I swear they'd memorized the sound of her car's engine. She was the only person (besides myself) I ever saw them line up along the fence to greet. It was the cutest thing.

Is Bug holding up okay? She must be devastated. If there's anything I can do to assist with her care, please let me know. She's always welcome here. And so are you, Rosie. Dotty was always saying how much she wanted to bring you along for a visit. She was sure you'd love it here.

Take your time, of course. But I'd really love to meet you.

I'm sure you have some great stories about your aunt. And I'd be happy to share some of my favorites with you, too. She and I grew pretty close over the years. Kind of like family.

Sending love and condolences to you and yours,
Sonia Fernández
Founder
Happy Hooves Animal Sanctuary

Sonia was the first person to respond to my email about Dotty. It took me two whole days to write her back. Not because I didn't want to, but because in those forty-eight hours, I barely got out of bed. When I wasn't sleeping, I was reading through my old email exchanges with Dotty. I'd written to her about everything—my parents, my brother, crushes on boys, my first period, the time Marcia and I got caught trying to steal a musty pair of bowling shoes from Lucky Strike. And Dotty had always taken the time to write a thoughtful response, regardless of the size or severity of my problems. She'd served as my de facto advice columnist since I was a kid. My own personal Dear Abby.

And now I was all on my own.

By day three, I knew I needed to pull myself out of this fog. If not for me, then for Bug.

When Dotty had invited me to join her at Happy Hooves, I'd turned her down. I didn't know it at the time, but I was going to spend the rest of my life regretting it. She'd wanted to share this piece of her life with me, and I'd batted it away, too wrapped up in my own self-pity to see it for the opportunity it was.

Dotty was a huge part of my life. But I now realized that I'd only seen tiny slivers of hers. And they always revolved around the two of us: hikes through the Marin Headlands, brunch in the city, martini-fueled cocktail hours at her place, Dotty imploring me to shake with my wrist, not my whole arm. And then there were the family dinners, Dotty and I getting lost in the shuffle of Tommy's bragging or Mom's meddling.

But I'd never met any of Dotty's friends. I'd never seen her holding court at a party or out on a date or mucking a stall.

And I never would.

I hoped Sonia would be the next best thing.

* * *

As I turned down a winding dirt road and pulled up to the front of an iron gate with a hand-carved wooden sign that read WELCOME TO HAPPY HOOVES ANIMAL SANCTUARY, my breath caught in my throat. Just beyond a simple fence was what looked like a real-life version of *Charlotte's Web*. Cows and pigs, sheep, goats, and even a donkey milled about a small paddock, chewing on straw, drinking from a large metal trough, and making an assortment of moos and oinks and bleats that were so adorable my heart felt like it might explode. Bug, who'd been uncharacteristically subdued since Dotty's death, leapt from my lap, placing her paws on the side of my door so she could see out the window. When I opened my door, she scrambled out, practically tripping over herself as she sprinted toward the paddock, clouds of dirt kicking up in her wake.

A short, muscular woman who looked to be in her midfifties emerged from the barn, carrying a speckled rooster under her arm. She had tan, corded forearms and a spiked pixie cut, her bangs fastened to the side by a bright red ladybug clip. "Rosie. I'm Sonia," she said, her demeanor decidedly no-nonsense, but then she held out her free arm for a hug. It was an effort not to cry when she said, "Dotty would be so happy that you're here."

Sonia took a step back and jerked her head toward the barn. Then she said, "Let's get you suited up."

"Suited up?"

She squinted into the sun. "I need help mucking these stalls. Besides, working with your hands can do wonders for a broken heart."

I don't know what I'd expected from this visit, but it wasn't work boots and a shovel. Although I didn't hate the idea, either. I nodded before following Sonia toward a row of stalls.

* * *

"Watch the horns!" Sonia's voice called from the other side of the barn. "Barb's a real sweet gal, but she thinks she's Bug's size." Barb was a thousand-pound cow who'd taken to following me around the paddock, her big, soulful brown eyes carefully watching my every move. I leaned my shovel against the faded wood siding and swept my gaze around the stall. It was a simple, square room with wood walls, an aluminum roof, concrete floors, and a long water trough that stretched along the far wall.

I gave Barb's nose a pat before returning to my shovel. I hadn't mucked a stall since my first summer home from college, after I'd failed most of my classes but before I'd come to terms with the consequences. I'd taken a job at a horse stable, reasoning that any animal experience was better than nothing. I'd almost forgotten how much I missed it. Not that shoveling dirty hay and clumps of poop was especially fun, but it felt good to work outside, under the sun. Plus, there were adorable animals everywhere I looked. I'd already met a pig named Arthur, a family of goats, each named after a *Flintstones* character, and a skittish donkey called Pickles. Each had taken a turn peering past Barb and into the stall where

I worked, curious about this strange new person who'd come to clean their rooms.

I placed my shovel at the edge of the stall and pushed forward, the metal scraping against the concrete pad below. Then I dropped a full scoop of yellowing hay peppered with what looked like chocolate pellets into a waiting wheelbarrow. I could feel Barb's eyes on me the entire time. I'd hated it when Raj looked over my shoulder, but Barb was a much better supervisor than he had ever been. "Let's go, Barb," I said, pushing the wheelbarrow around the back of the barn. She obliged, lumbering slowly behind me.

"You've made a friend," Sonia said as we rounded the corner. She was crouched down next to the black-and-white-speckled rooster. "Barb doesn't normally warm up to strangers this quickly."

My heart fluttered. I firmly believed there was no greater compliment than an animal deeming you fit for friendship. "I think I'm going to have to take her home with me."

"I bet your roommate would love that." Sonia stood, smiling.

I laughed, thinking of Marcia trying to squeeze past Barb in our narrow hallway.

The speckled rooster puffed his chest up, tipped his head back, and opened his beak to let out a robust cock-a-doodle-doo, the sound echoing off the barn and surrounding hills. Satisfied with his performance, he flapped his wings and returned to pecking at the dirt.

"Looks like Rocket's feeling better," Sonia said, smiling gently at the bird.

"What was wrong with him?"

"Coccidiosis," she replied, without taking her eyes off the rooster. "It's a—"

"Parasitic infection," I said, my face twisting with concern. "Poor guy."

Sonia turned her gaze toward me, looking impressed. "You know your chickens."

I explained, "I thought I was going to work with animals when I was younger."

"You're still young."

I suppose that was technically true, but I felt like I'd aged a decade in the past few weeks. Something strong nudged my back, causing me to take an exaggerated step forward, startling Rocket. I turned to see Barb, who'd grown impatient with all the chitchat. Her big brown eyes implored me to get back to work. "I guess I should get moving," I said.

"Barb's the boss."

The rest of the morning went on like that. Shoveling hay, making trips to the compost pile, keeping pace with Barb. Sonia was right; there was something comforting about working with my hands, being able to see my progress.

I finished ripping open another bag of hay and stood, resting my gloved hands on my hips. Barb's massive head hovered above the trough along the far wall, a somber expression on her face.

"How do you like it here?" Sonia asked as she carefully side-stepped Barb.

I paused, listening to the sound of Bug barking and grunting in the paddock beyond the stall. She was playing a game that looked a lot like tag with Arthur the pig. "It's paradise," I said.

Sonia beamed. "I think so, too. Mind if I help you finish up?"

We went to work spreading hay across the freshly swept concrete. I had cleaned six enclosures that morning and could feel exhaustion seeping in. But it wasn't the heavy, oppressive, never-ending exhaustion of grief. It was more like contented, satisfied exhaustion that came from good, hard, honest work.

"I want you to know that you're welcome back anytime," Sonia

said, as she smoothed out the last of the hay. "There's no shortage
of work to do around the stalls. You wouldn't believe how messy
goats can be." She shook her head in mock disapproval but wore a
wide grin on her face.

"I would love that."

Sonia's grin widened. "Excellent," she said, as if we'd just settled
an important business deal. "Well, I think our work for the day is
done." She wriggled her eyebrows. "Ready for a proper tour?"

* * *

"We rescued this one from a veal crate," Sonia said, patting Barb's
side as she munched on a patch of grass. We were walking the
grounds outside the paddock with Barb in tow. "She was a tiny
little thing back then. We used to be able to let her in the house."

"No wonder she thinks she's the size of a dog," I said.

Sonia chuckled. "It's hard not to spoil them. Especially when
they're new."

She'd opened Happy Hooves four years ago. Her first resident
had been a sickly chicken that had gotten stuck in a fence on a
neighbor's farm. Since then Sonia had taken in or rehomed almost a hundred animals. Happy Hooves was now home to about
thirty—a mix of goats, sheep, cows, donkeys, and pigs, all rescued
from a variety of harrowing circumstances. Pickles was saved from
a hoarder. Arthur was pulled off a truck bound for the slaughter-
house. The Flintstones were surrendered by an elderly farmer. The
ranch also housed sixteen chickens, three roosters, and a family of
wild ducks that had taken up residence in the pond at the center
of the sanctuary. "The pigs don't seem to mind sharing," Sonia
said. "As long as the ducks don't bother them while they nap in
the mud."

"Do you have any spiders?" I asked, thinking again of *Charlotte's Web*.

"Plenty!" Sonia laughed. "But as far as I know, none of them can spell."

"Too bad."

We wandered the property line, our boots sticking in the mud near the pond, flies buzzing by, the sun on our faces. I could feel my cheeks starting to burn, but I didn't care. "What did you do before this?" I asked Sonia. I had a million more questions for her—about the animals, and her relationship with Dotty, and whether any of the goats had ever tried to eat her clothes.

Sonia walked on slowly, not breaking her pace. "I was an investment banker. I made a bunch of money, but I was miserable, so . . ." She let the answer trail off, deciding to gesture around the property instead. "This place didn't spring up overnight, obviously. And I had help. My husband takes care of the animals on the weekend, and our son helps out with fundraising in his spare time. He works in tech." She said *tech* like it was a bad word.

"How did Dotty find this place?"

Sonia furrowed her brow. "I never thought to ask. She sort of just showed up and then it was like she'd always been here."

I nodded. That sounded like Dotty.

"She used to get through that whole row of stalls in half the time it took you," she continued, shaking her head. "I called her Super Dotty."

Most people would probably be mortified that their eighty-year-old aunt had outpaced them in manual labor, but I was just plain impressed.

"We're really going to miss her around here," Sonia said, more to herself than to me. I liked knowing that I wasn't the only one who was grieving Dotty, that other people were going to miss her, too.

The tour ended with Sonia forcing a stack of homemade granola bars wrapped in wax paper into my hands before pulling me into a crushing hug. She made me promise to come back as soon as I could. Then she stood in the dusty driveway, her hand held in a fixed wave as Bug and I drove off. Bug cried a little as we turned the corner. I felt like I might cry, too.

When I climbed into bed that night, tired and sore and thoroughly worn out, I felt completely and wholly content.

It was the best I'd slept in weeks.

CHAPTER FOURTEEN

The next morning, I was startled awake by the ringer on my phone. I'd taken to answering every call I received just in case it was a recruiter—even though those calls had been steadily dwindling. I did my best to mask the sleep in my voice but was unsuccessful. "This is Rosie Benson," I croaked.

"Hi, Rosie Benson," said a voice on the other end.

"Hi," I said, my tone tentative.

"Did I wake you?"

"No," I lied.

"Shit. Is it weird that I called? Should I have played it cool and texted instead? I waited a week. That must count for something, right?"

It was Donovan Ng. Somehow, it had only been a week since I'd woken up in his glossy white condo, but it seemed like a lifetime. I'd almost forgotten about him.

"Have I completely scared you off?" Donovan's question prodded me back to reality.

"No," I said, shaking my head, hoping to clear away the cobwebs. "Not at all. I'm glad you called. It's just been a really weird week."

"Weird how?"

"It's a very long story."

"Want to try to explain it to me over dinner next week? I swear I'm a good listener. And I'm not nearly as shallow as I look."

I wasn't sure what the protocol was for dating after your life had imploded. Do you wait a week? A month? My chest tightened at the realization that aside from Bug, I didn't really have anyone else to talk to. I wasn't ready to deal with Marcia yet. And my family was wrapped up in their own issues. I was all alone without Dotty.

And it had been a long time since I'd had a nice dinner. I could use the distraction.

So I said yes.

* * *

I swirled the rich burgundy liquid around the bulbous wineglass, pretending to care about the streaks that unfurled like ticker tape. "Good legs," I said before taking a sip.

A wide grin spread across Donovan's chiseled face. "You don't know anything about wine, do you?"

"Nope." I took another sip.

"You're so normal," he marveled.

I set my glass on the table. "I'm not sure how to take that."

"As a compliment. I like normal—it's grossly underrated."

"You don't hang out with normal people?"

Donovan drummed his fingers on the base of his wineglass. "Not enough," he said and shook his head. His dark, coiffed hair didn't budge. "I was the mayor's kid growing up, so everyone was always either making fun of me or kissing my ass. That definitely wasn't normal. Then I went to an Ivy League school with a bunch of other spawn of the successful, and then I started my company . . ."

I narrowed my eyes. "So it's nice to hang out with a commoner for a change?"

He furrowed his brow playfully. "You know what I mean. I feel like I can breathe around you is all."

I knew exactly what he meant. Lately there were fewer and fewer people whom I felt I could breathe around.

My eyes drifted to the spread of delicious Spanish-style tapas that littered the table: papas bravas, pan con tomate, empanadas, and shishito peppers. This was going to be the best meal I'd had in . . . maybe ever. "Do you have any normal friends?"

He bit into a charred pepper, eyeing me as he chewed. "A few. And we do all the things you're supposed to do at our age. We go on hikes and eat brunch and hang around ironic dive bars and plan trips to South America."

"Do you eat avocado toast?"

"All the time."

"I can't believe I'm about to say this, but, Donovan, I think you might be normal."

"That's the nicest thing anyone's ever said to me."

"I aim to please."

Donovan picked up the bottle of wine and jiggled it in my direction. I nodded.

"So now that I've revealed my normalness," he said, refilling my glass, "are you ready to tell me about your very unnormal week?"

Was I really going to pop the hood on the mess that was my life, revealing every frayed edge and crossed wire to this gorgeous, impossibly grown-up stranger? I blew out a long breath, my lips sputtering. "It's more like very unnormal *months*," I said.

He dipped his chin in a sympathetic nod, sending my heart into a backflip. "Go on."

So I did. I told Donovan Ng everything. I told him about my job and my parents and Dotty and Marcia and Raj. Turned out he really was a great listener. He didn't interrupt me once, just sat there, nodding with understanding, his dark eyes swimming with sympathy. At some point, he reached across the table to hold my hand. He was still holding it when I finally finished.

"I'm so sorry," Donovan said. "Any one of those things would be enough to drive a person into a deep depression. And you're dealing with it all at once."

I hadn't thought of it that way. Donovan saying it out loud felt like pressing on a bruise. "Thank you," I said. "I haven't really talked to anyone about any of it . . ." My voice trailed off. I couldn't bring myself to say the rest. That I'd lost my two best friends in the span of a day.

Donovan furrowed his brow in concern. "Are you and Marcia going to be okay?"

My mouth twitched involuntarily. I honestly wasn't sure. We'd barely spoken since the truth about her and Raj had come out. She'd been spending most of her time at his place. And when she was home, she'd tiptoe around me, as if I was the one who'd become totally unhinged. "I hope so," I said.

His voice dropped to a new whisper. "Do you think she might be the reason that Raj knew you went to the beach that day?"

"I really, really hope not."

"Me too," he said. I believed him.

"I don't know how I'd ever get past that. I'm still trying to wrap my head around the rest of it."

Donovan eyed me with sympathy. "I've seen people recover from worse."

"Yeah?"

"Yeah." He slid the last shishito pepper in my direction. "Can I share something with you?"

I nodded, staring at the pepper.

"Growing up, my parents were this perfect couple. My mom

was San Francisco's first woman mayor and my dad was the CEO of the family shipping business. We lived in this big old house in the heart of the city where my parents hosted important people from all over the world. And they were wild about each other. I used to catch them making out in the butler's pantry." He shuddered playfully. "But when I was in high school, my dad had a massive heart attack. The doctor said he'd died almost instantly. He wasn't even fifty yet."

"I'm so sorry," I said. The words felt flat and pointless.

He shrugged. "It's okay. It was a while ago now."

"Still."

"Yeah. Anyway, a few weeks after Dad died, we found out that he had a whole other family. Like another wife and two kids."

It was an effort not to spit out my wine. "What?"

"Crazy, right? It was this huge scandal and so hard on my mom. But, very long story short, we all got through it."

"How?"

Donovan looked at the ceiling, weighing how to respond. "Therapy, time, and forgiveness, I guess," he said.

"Do you have a relationship with your half siblings?"

He smiled. "That's the thing. Not only did I get a new brother and sister, but my mom got a new best friend. We're this weird little blended family now. Thanks to my dad."

Donovan's dad made my mom sound like a saint. I almost wished she had a secret family. Then at least we would have an explanation for her behavior.

"That is . . . wild. I can't even wrap my mind around it."

"I know," he said, amusement dancing across his face. "I don't talk about it very much. But I wanted to tell you because I mean it when I say that I've seen people get over some pretty terrible betrayals."

I nodded. It was a small comfort, but a comfort nonetheless.

"It takes time, obviously," Donovan continued. "And you have to get mad first. My therapist says you have to allow yourself to feel your feelings before you can move on."

"Thank you for telling me," I said. "It makes me feel better to know I'm not the only one with messed-up parents."

Donovan's smile broadened. "Glad my twisted little family can do some good." He reached for the wine and topped off our glasses, draining the bottle. "Now that we've established that we both have familial issues worthy of therapy, what else can I do to cheer you up?"

I forced myself to smile so I wouldn't start to cry. Donovan was so sweet. "Well, I'd ask you to resurrect my aunt, but I'm pretty sure that technology doesn't exist yet."

Donovan gave a solemn shake of the head. "We're a few years out from that, I'm afraid."

"Figures. I guess I'll just settle for help finding a job then," I cracked.

But this time Donovan didn't laugh. "I can definitely help you with that."

"Oh no—" I held out my hands, waving him off. "I was just joking—"

"I know this woman," Donovan pressed on. "Her name is Nadine Lyons-Shaw. She owns a recruiting agency in the city. I'll call her tomorrow, ask her to set you up with some temp work."

I could feel my cheeks growing hot. I didn't want Donovan to think I was using him for his connections, but I *was* getting desperate. "You really don't have to do that."

"It's nothing. And I'm happy to help." His voice was casual but insistent. "Nadine's always looking for new people to send out on jobs around the city—mostly administrative stuff. She's helped me out with a few of my hires and I've paid her some pretty big commissions. She owes me."

"Wow. I don't know what to say. Thank you."

"Don't thank me too much yet. Nadine is . . . tough."

"Tough how?"

"She's just really particular. Which I respect—don't get me wrong. But she can be a little intimidating. You'll be fine, though. I'm sure you two will get along great."

Our server, a lanky string bean of a man with dark, slicked-back hair, approached our table before I could respond. "Good to see you again, Donovan," he said, placing the check on the edge of the table. Donovan smiled in acknowledgment as he reached for the bill.

"Any objection to me buying your dinner tonight?" he asked.

"Why don't we split it?" I replied, hoping he'd turn me down. I was all for equality and independence and all that, but I was also unemployed.

Donovan shook his head, sliding his card into the folder and setting it back on the edge of the table. "You can get the next one. After Nadine gets you a job."

"Deal," I said. "Thank you. For everything."

"I really like hanging out with you," he said. "How do you feel about a nightcap back at my place?"

The thought of another night at Donovan's sent a thrill of excitement zipping across my stomach. "Only if it involves a flask of Fireball."

His crisp white shirt strained against his broad shoulders as he leaned forward. "That can be arranged."

I leaned forward, too. "Then I'm in."

"Excellent," he said, grinning.

We never got around to the Fireball.

From: Tommy Benson
To: Rosie Benson
Subject: Re: Dotty
Date: May 30

Hi Ro,

Did you hack into our dead aunt's email account? The legality of that is questionable, but I know you're going through a lot, so I guess I'll let it slide.

(That was a joke. I know you think I'm boring as hell, but I do, in fact, have a sense of humor.)

You know what I'll never forget about Dotty? Nothing got by that woman. I used to watch her watching the rest of the family. She'd stare at Dad, then Mom, then you, then me, keeping her eyes on each of us for minutes at a time. And she wouldn't say a word. Then, almost out of nowhere, she would blurt out the most blunt, uncomfortable truths. When I was twelve, she told me I should become a lawyer because I was "stubborn as hell and too smart for my own good." She called me out for smoking way too much weed when I was a junior in high school. She said if I didn't get my shit together, I'd never become the person I wanted to be. She even told me I should marry Lily.

I always thought Dotty went too easy on you. She'd get pissed at me whenever I started to slack off, but when you got put on academic probation, she defended you. She was all for my settling down with Lily, but she'd shoot Mom death glares whenever she wondered why you hadn't found a boyfriend yet. I never understood it. It must have had something to do with the way she read us. Maybe she knew what each of us needed. Maybe she knew us better than we knew ourselves.

I don't know why she was always watching. I never thought to ask her.

This probably hasn't answered any of your questions. I think I'm grappling with those same questions myself. Maybe one of these days we can grab a coffee and talk it through? We've never done that, have we?

For what it's worth, I'm really proud of you for how you're handling all this. I know things have been hard for you lately. I'm here if you need me. I always have been. Even if I don't know how to show it.

Love,
Tommy

CHAPTER FIFTEEN

JUNE

Donovan moved quickly. By the first Friday in June, I found myself sitting in the front lobby of Le Agency, wearing an ill-fitting blazer and a pair of trousers that were just a bit too tight. I'd been so proud of the profit I'd turned when I sold most of my wardrobe, until I realized that I had nothing left to wear. Luckily, Marcia and I were about the same size. She'd insisted I raid her closet before she left for work that morning. I wasn't sure if she actually wanted to help me or just wanted me to get a job—any job—so that she could start bringing Raj around the apartment more often. Whatever her reasons, I wasn't in a position to turn her down.

The blazer was overkill, though. I knew it would be, but Donovan had advised me to overdress. "Nadine is something of a fashionista. I think her mom is from France or something," he'd said. "So dress chic."

I didn't feel chic. I felt like a fraud.

I pulled out my phone and reread Tommy's email. He was *proud* of me. I didn't know that I needed to hear that from my brother until he'd said it. Maybe Dotty wasn't the only person in my family who believed in me. The thought gave me a much-needed burst of confidence.

"Rosie?" My head snapped up as my hand flew to my purse, also on loan from Marcia. "Nadine is ready for you." I flashed the office manager a tight smile as I stood. "Follow me," he said, beckoning me forward with an enthusiastic-looking hand motion reminiscent of spirit fingers.

"I'm Evan, by the way," he said over his shoulder as he started toward the back of the office. I noticed he wore tiny diamond studs in each ear. His coiffed blond hair was unreasonably shiny.

"I'm Rosie," I replied. "But you already know that." The back of the office looked like a natural extension of the lobby: decidedly feminine, with white marble, pink orchids, and glimmering gold accents everywhere I looked. It wasn't a terribly large space, but it felt open and airy, almost like a spa. An olive-skinned woman in severe-looking black glasses with a tight purple ponytail sat at a glass-topped desk, staring intently at a monitor. There were two desks on either side of her, both empty.

"That's Pilar," Evan said, jerking his head toward the woman. "And Kate's meeting with another candidate." He pointed toward two small glass-walled conference rooms at the back of the office. "You might get to meet her on your way out. She's great," he said. I couldn't tell if he was being sarcastic.

"Cool," I replied, adjusting Marcia's blazer.

"We'll just be back here," Evan said, pushing on an imposing frosted glass door. We stepped inside a private office that looked more like a lounge at a fancy downtown hotel, with thick floor-to-ceiling drapes, powder-blue upholstered armchairs, and a vintage wood desk. The picture frames, hardcover books, and decorative gold accent items that filled the bookshelf along the wall looked like they'd been staged for a photo shoot. I was sure I smelled jasmine but couldn't figure out where it was coming from. "Go ahead and have a seat," Evan said, gesturing to the overly stuffed chairs. "Nadine is just making herself an espresso. Can I get you anything while you wait?"

I shook my head, feeling dazed. I'd never seen an office like this before.

"Okay," Evan said, turning to leave. "Good lu—"

"Water would be great," I blurted, coming to my senses. My mouth always dried up when I was uncomfortable.

"You got it."

He disappeared behind the frosted door as I did my best to settle into the overly stuffed chair, trying not to get swallowed by the cushions.

I'd just gotten settled when I heard the door creaking open behind me. I turned to see a tall, striking woman gliding into the office. She wore emerald-green pumps and a white pantsuit. Her dark hair was deeply parted to the side and pulled into a low bun. Her lipstick was the color of rubies. "Rosie," she said, her voice much huskier than I'd anticipated, "I'm Nadine Lyons-Shaw." She extended her hand.

I stood, feeling small and frumpy as I took it. "It's so nice to meet you," I said, suddenly wishing I was wearing something more sophisticated than strawberry Chapstick on my lips.

Nadine took a step back, eyeing me from head to toe, and smiled, revealing a row of catlike teeth, her canines sitting slightly forward. "What a fabulous blazer," she practically purred.

"Thanks," I said, feeling positively dazzled. "It's my roommate's."

She let out a breathy laugh as my cheeks warmed. "You're honest. I like that." She flashed me a Cheshire grin and gestured for me to have a seat. I couldn't help staring as Nadine circled around her desk before setting a small mug full of espresso on a waiting saucer. Her movements were liquid, graceful. Like a ballerina.

"So," Nadine said as she settled into her chair. "Donovan says you're interested in temp work."

I wasn't sure if it was a question or a statement. "Yes? I—"

The door creaked open again and Evan appeared, holding a glass of ice water. He set it on top of a heavy-looking gold coaster and turned to leave without saying a word. "Thank you, Evan," Nadine called after him. She waited for the door to click shut before returning her gaze to me. "Isn't he wonderful?"

"Really wonderful," I agreed.

"Can I see your résumé?"

"Oh. Right! Of course," I said, feeling flustered. I reached into Marcia's purse and dug out a copy of my résumé. "Here you go." I passed it across the desk to Nadine. "Sorry."

"Don't apologize. Women apologize too much. Do you ever hear men saying they're sorry?"

"I don't—"

"Driftwood, huh?" she said, pinching my résumé between her thumb and index finger, as if being careful not to smudge fresh ink.

"Yep."

Nadine looked up. Her eyes were more amber than brown. "Donovan didn't mention Driftwood. What happened there?"

"Driftwood was great," I said, slipping into my practiced script, "but I'm ready for a change—"

She held up a hand for me to stop. My mouth snapped shut as my heart began to race. Nadine dropped my résumé, letting it fall onto the desk. She folded her hands and leaned forward. "Rosie, it's my job to be an advocate for my candidates. I'm on your side, so you can give it to me straight. No need to dance around the truth."

I sighed, deciding that I might as well come clean. "I got fired," I said, feeling my shoulders drop. "Two months ago."

Nadine made a sympathetic clucking sound with her tongue. "They're ruthless over there," she said with a shake of her head. "That's why we don't—*won't*—work with them."

"But—"

"I've seen them cast too many talented, promising people aside for the most ridiculous reasons," she said with a dismissive wave of her hand. "I can't work with clients like that. It's not what Le Agency is about." She tilted her head to the side and arranged her mouth into a pout. "Why'd they let you go? Didn't make your unrealistic sales goals?" I fought the urge to let my mouth drop open, settling for a nod instead. Nadine rolled her eyes. "The problem with Driftwood is that they don't invest enough time in developing their staff. And they promote their managers way too soon. Who was your boss? Some twenty-six-year-old with a hard-on for synergy?"

Maybe it was Nadine's use of the term "hard-on" that kicked something loose in my mind, but I suddenly felt like I could be myself. "Are you psychic or something?"

"Don't I wish," she said wryly. "If that were the case, I would have caught my first husband cheating with the babysitter much sooner." I couldn't tell if she was joking, but she moved on before I could ask. "Well, let me tell you a little about what we do here, and then we can talk about some potential assignments. Sound good?"

"That sounds great," I said, as my entire body relaxed. Nadine's unexpected warmth made me feel like maybe things really were going to be okay.

"Fabulous," Nadine said, falling into what sounded like a wellworn pitch. "What we do is akin to sales, except our products are jobs and people. The way we see it, we're like professional matchmakers. Our clients tell us what they're looking for in an employee, and our candidates tell us what they're looking for in a job. It's on us to make the right connection." She knitted her fingers together for effect. "Simple enough, right?" I nodded. "Good. So as opportunities come across my desk that I think you might be a strong fit for, I'll reach out to you to see if you're interested. If you are, we'll schedule an interview. And I'll coach you every step of the way, of course. You won't be in this alone." My heart rate finally slowed. I couldn't feel my pulse in my ears anymore. "You look relieved."

"I am," I said. "I've blown all my interviews so far. I get so nervous."

"Interviewing can be incredibly nerve-racking," Nadine said sympathetically. Talking with her was like confiding in a friend's cool older sister. "We can help you get more comfortable. Maybe do a few practice rounds before we throw you in the deep end." She winked. "In that vein, why don't you tell me a bit about your role with Driftwood?"

Talking honestly about Driftwood was like letting out a breath I didn't know I was holding. I readily owned up to my shortcomings, but I told Nadine about my accomplishments, too. Like the account I'd grown by 26 percent in my first year or the HR manager I'd talked out of ending his contract. It felt good to remember that I hadn't been terrible at *every* aspect of my job. Nadine listened intently, occasionally flicking her eyes to my résumé and jotting notes in the margins.

When I finished, she leaned back in her chair, her wrist dangling over the arm as she played with the emerald bauble on her finger. "Do you have any questions for me?"

Her amber eyes held my gaze. I had the odd sensation of feeling hypnotized. I forced my mouth to form words. "Yes," I said, regaining my confidence. "I noticed that there was an empty desk when I walked in."

"Is that a question?"

Dotty had once told me that I was good at noticing people's strengths, seeing them for who they really were. And it sounded like that was a lot of what being a Le Agency recruiter entailed. I decided to take my shot. "Are you hiring? For another recruiter?"

The side of Nadine's mouth quirked up into a half smile. "One of my recruiters just left last week. I was going to hold off on replacing her, but now that you mention it, I think you could be really successful here, with some mentoring, of course. Would you be interested?"

I interlaced my fingers and squeezed my hands together under the desk, forcing myself to play it cool. "I would be very interested."

"All right then," Nadine said, still playing with her ring. "I'll have Evan draw up an offer for you this afternoon, and we can reconnect in a few days, say, early next week?"

"That sounds great. Thank you," I said, surprised by the emotion in my voice. It was a relief to feel wanted, even if this wasn't exactly what I'd envisioned for myself. Maybe this would be even better.

"Excellent," Nadine said, rising from her chair and extending her hand. "It was a pleasure, Rosie."

I leapt up from my seat too quickly, feeling inexplicably rushed. As I reached my arm across the desk, my elbow knocked against the untouched glass of water. To my horror, water quickly spread across Nadine's desk, under her keyboard, and onto her planner before puddling on the floor.

"Oh my god. I'm so sorry," I said as I began frantically picking up Nadine's neatly arranged belongings, heroically rescuing a soaked notepad and an engraved stapler. My facade of composure had evaporated, a distant memory.

"It's fine," Nadine said, stepping around a growing puddle, "I'll have Evan clean this up."

I paused, realizing how ridiculous I must have looked clutching soaked papers to my chest. "This is so embarrassing."

Nadine waved me off. "You're not the first, believe me. I'll just take the cost of the damage out of your first paycheck." She winked, but I wasn't sure if she was kidding.

* * *

By the time I got home that afternoon, feeling a mix of elation (I got a job offer!) and embarrassment (I almost drowned my future boss!), all I wanted to do was melt into the couch with Bug, left-over Thai food, and my old pal Jerry Seinfeld. But I knew something was off the moment I set foot in our apartment. It smelled good. Really, really good. "Marcia?" I called out, bewilderment lingering in my voice. "Are you . . . cooking?"

"Hey, Ro," Marcia called tentatively from the kitchen, like she was surprised that I lived there. I made my way down the long, narrow hall, following the delicious smell and unmistakable sound of a sizzling skillet. My heart swelled at the thought that Marcia had cooked for me.

But when I stepped into the kitchen, there was Raj, vest and all, standing over a simmering pot, wielding a wooden spoon, a black-and-white-checkered apron tied around his waist. Marcia sat on the counter, sipping a glass of red wine, still in her work clothes. It was the kind of picture-perfect image that would garner a thousand likes on Instagram. Bug rushed to greet me, panting and wiggling with excitement while the rest of us stood in silent, suspended animation.

Raj, as overconfident as ever, spoke first. "Hi, Rosie. It's really good to see you again."

I'd been so distracted by my grief over Dotty, my anxiety about work, and my budding relationship with Donovan that I'd almost forgotten how much I hated Raj. Almost. I did my best to summon actual daggers from my eyes. "I wish I could say the same."

Raj laughed. Actually laughed. "Come on. You can't possibly hate me that much."

"Oh, you'd be surprised," Marcia muttered under her breath, keeping her eyes on the faded linoleum floor.

"Hey, I'm really sorry about your aunt," Raj said. "Marcia told me how close you two were. You must be devastated."

I turned my gaze to Marcia, who looked like she wanted to climb into her wineglass. How could she do this to me? It was one thing to keep sneaking around with Raj but throwing him in my face like this was next level. I wanted to scream. To cry. To shake her and ask why *him*?

But more than anything, I wanted my best friend back.

This was so out of character for her. A part of me wondered if Marcia had been replaced by an evil twin. Having a secret twin seemed entirely plausible when we were growing up. As kids, we'd spent hours watching *Sister Sister* and *Parent Trap* and laughing about all the tricks we'd play on the unsuspecting people in our lives when our doppelgängers inevitably showed up.

If only the explanation for Marcia's behavior were that simple.

"I made enough for all three of us," Raj said, his voice hopeful.

My stomach betrayed me, growling loudly at the idea of eating whatever Raj was cooking. I hated how good it smelled. I could feel Marcia watching me, willing me to cave, to figure out a way to be okay with this. But I wasn't. I balled my hands into fists and straightened my spine. "I already have plans," I said, an idea forming as I spoke, ". . . with *Donovan Ng*." I shot a pointed look at Marcia, whose mouth had fallen open. I pressed on, not bothering to suppress a smug, triumphant smile. "Do you mind watching Bug tonight?"

* * *

I skulked off to my room to text Donovan. And to pretend I was getting ready for a nonexistent date. I didn't know where I would go if he wasn't around, but anywhere Raj *wasn't* would do.

To my surprise, Donovan texted me back right away.

> On my way to an underground whiskey tasting with some clients. Want to join?

I had to be at my parents' house bright and early tomorrow morning for Lily's baby shower. I'd been dreading it ever since I got the invitation, but even more so recently. Getting tipsy on brown liquor the night before probably wasn't the best idea.

And yet.

I *did* get a job offer today. And it *was* all because of Donovan.

And, perhaps most importantly, this might be my one and only chance to go to an underground whiskey tasting. I didn't even know that was a thing.

I shimmied into my tightest jeans and a low-cut sweater before brushing my teeth and spritzing my hair with Marcia's dry shampoo. By the time I left, she and Raj were sitting at the little bistro table in the living room. I bid a quiet goodbye to Bug, who whined softly as I shut the front door. I promised myself that I'd ask if I could bring her along next time.

From: Lily Lopez-Benson
To: Rosie Benson
Subject: Re: Dotty
Date: May 22

Hi Rosie,

This is such a lovely idea. Maybe you can put all the responses you get into a memory book. That would be a nice Christmas present for your dad. I'd love a copy, too.

Dotty was so many things to me over the years. She was the first person to make me feel truly welcome in this family, the one I could always turn to for unflinchingly honest advice, and hands down, the strongest woman I ever met. (For the record, she was stronger than every man I've ever met, too.)

I don't know if you remember this, but at your parents' anniversary party two years ago, I was feeling positively miserable but doing my best to hide it. Dotty was elbowing your dad out of the way, trying to get him to make space for her seitan kabobs when she noticed me sneaking off to the bathroom. I was crying on the edge of the tub when I heard a knock on the door and a voice say, "What's going on in there, Lilypad?"

Tommy and I had agreed not to tell anyone that our IVF cycle hadn't worked. I was sure telling the rest of the family would only throw salt in a very fresh wound. So I had told myself that I could put on a brave face and get through it. It wasn't like I'd lost a baby. I hadn't even been pregnant.

"Not so fast, missy," Dotty had said, handing me a balled-up wad of toilet paper. "You've suffered an unspeakable loss. You need to grieve." And then she sat there with me while I cried, her on the toilet, me on the tub. It was just what I needed.

And do you know what got me through the next failed round? Dotty. I had always known I wanted to have a baby of my own. But when it looked like that might not happen for us, I realized that, eventually, I'd be okay. Dotty had lived such a vibrant life, and she was so important to our family. She showed me that there are lots of different ways to find fulfillment.

So was she happy? Absolutely. Dotty was the happiest person I've ever known.

Love,
Lily

P.S. Looking forward to seeing you at the shower. I have something to ask you.

CHAPTER SIXTEEN

I arrived at my parents' house in an aggressively floral sundress, clutching an unwrapped package of onesies and a box of diapers, single malt whiskey vapors rippling out of every pore. My brother's lips curled into an amused grin as I stepped through a wall of streamers. Mom had decorated the house to within an inch of its life. Cotton-candy pink balloons, flowers, and tiny rubber pacifiers choked the living room. "Look at you, all ready for high tea," Tommy cracked.

I shoved the box of diapers into his chest. "Happy baby shower."

He grinned. "You smell like a bar."

I shot him a look.

"A *classy* bar."

"I need to wrap your present."

"I'll do it for you if you tell me what you did last night."

"I don't know what you're talking about."

"Please?" He looked over his shoulder and back to me, lowering his voice. "I never get to do anything fun anymore."

I gave my brother a once-over. He wore his usual outfit: pressed khakis and a button-down shirt (today it was pink in honor of the baby). His golden hair was freshly cut; his loafers were spotless. He looked like a grown-up. So I took pity on him. "Fine," I said with a sigh, setting the onesies on top of the diaper box. "I'm sort of seeing someone." Tommy raised his eyebrows, looking impressed. "I was on a date."

"At a whiskey factory?"

"It was a whiskey tasting, actually."

Tommy blew out a sharp breath, his lips sputtering. "Who is this guy?"

"He runs a VC firm."

"How'd you manage that?"

I held up my hands to frame my face. "I'm actually quite charming. In case you hadn't noticed."

He nudged me with his elbow. "Of course I noticed." Something about the drop of kindness in my brother's voice was enough to send tears to the corners of my eyes. I blinked and looked away. "Hey," Tommy said, putting a hand on my shoulder. "You okay?"

"I'm fine," I said, not sure if it was true. "These past few weeks have just been . . . a lot."

"Did you get my email?"

I hadn't written back to Tommy yet. Or Lily, for that matter. But their emails had surprised me for vastly different reasons. I didn't know Lily had struggled to get pregnant. Or that Tommy had such a good read on Dotty.

But I was most surprised by the idea that my older brother would want to meet me for coffee.

"Hey," Tommy said, pulling me into a hug. "I meant what I said, okay? I'm here if you want to talk."

I surprised myself by hugging him back. "Thank you."

He squeezed me tighter, squishing my face against his shirt. It smelled like the laundry detergent Mom used when we were growing up. "I know you miss her. I miss her, too."

Bug whined at my feet. It was like she knew we were talking about Dotty.

Tommy turned to Bug. "Hey, girl, how could I forget about you?" He bent to pat her on the head and was rewarded with three thumps of her tail.

"I figured Bug could hang out with you and Dad during the party," I said. "She's been through enough trauma already. No need to put her through more."

Tommy smirked. "I thought all girls loved baby showers."

I gestured to myself and Bug. "Not these girls."

"Fair enough. Don't mention anything to Mom, but Lily's kind of been dreading today."

"Has Mom been getting on her nerves?"

Tommy moved the big box of diapers from one hand to the other. "Actually, no. Not lately." He glanced over his shoulder. "Mom's been kind of MIA. She just signed a lease on a new apartment."

I hadn't heard from Mom in weeks, but that wasn't out of the ordinary. Especially when I'd figured she was all up in Tommy and Lily's business. But the fact that she hadn't bothered to tell me she was officially moving out stung.

A woman in head-to-toe pastel breezed through the front door, sending streamers flapping. She gave Tommy an enthusiastic wave and he nodded in response. "Lily's outside," he said, pointing toward the yard. She thanked him before disappearing behind a wall of balloons.

"Well, at least Mom didn't skimp on the decorations."

"Yeah," Tommy said, a note of appreciation in his voice. "She was here bright and early this morning, acting like everything was normal, so I guess the old Mom is somewhere in there."

He adjusted the diaper box against his hip. "C'mon, let's go get Bug settled. Dad will be excited to see you two. Wait until you see what he's done with your old room since Mom decided to move out."

I followed Tommy down the hallway toward the back of the house. He stopped outside the door that used to be my room and knocked, stepping inside without waiting for a response. Dad sat on a brown leather couch where my bed used to be. He lit up when the three of us walked in, pausing to set his wineglass on a small end table before wrapping me in a long hug. "There's my favorite girl," he said, his whiskers scratching my cheek.

I got a better look at him when he pulled away: his curly hair was unkempt, his five o'clock shadow was on the verge of becoming a full-blown beard. His eyes looked tired behind his glasses. "How are you, sweetheart?"

I summoned a smile. "Good," I said, feeling closer to meaning it than I had in a while.

Dad gave me a good-natured slap on the shoulder before bending to pick up Bug. She responded with an enthusiastic grunt.

"I like what you've done with the place," I said, taking in the full extent of Dad's redecorating efforts.

"Thanks," Dad said, looking around the room as if he was seeing it for the first time. It was predominantly brown, but in a cozy way. He'd replaced my gauzy blue curtains with heavy-looking drapes, mounted a large flat-screen TV in the corner where my desk used to be, and installed rich cherrywood shelves on either side of my old closet. Bottles of wine filled almost every level, white tags bearing Dad's scratchy handwriting hanging from their necks. An avocado-green urn sat in the top corner. It held Dotty's ashes, I knew. She'd been cremated without fanfare and delivered to my parents' house via FedEx. I looked away. Dad grinned. "Now I can finally display my wine."

I ignored the pang of sadness that echoed through my rib cage.

"Tommy and I are doing a tasting while you girls take over the rest of the house," Dad said. He sank back into the sofa, Bug still cradled in his arms. "We'll save you a bottle."

"Thanks," I said, sensing that I'd avoided my sisterly responsibilities for as long as was polite. "I'd better get out there."

"Oh," Dad said, jumping up off the couch. "I have something for you." He plucked a piece of paper off the printer. "My response to your email, as requested." I took the paper from his hands. It was an entire page, single-spaced. "I can forward it to you if that would be better," Dad said, his earnest smile threatening to break my heart.

I looked down at Dad's letter. "No," I replied. "This is perfect."

* * *

"Did you save your placenta?" Lily's coworker asked, pushing cake around her plate.

"Of course," Lily's college friend replied. "The umbilical cord, too." Everyone at the table nodded in approval.

I studied my cake, suddenly nauseated by the red raspberry filling. I slid the plate across the table and reached for the champagne, wishing for something stronger. I filled my glass to the brim as one of Lily's friends droned on about something called a mucus plug. I'd already endured enough baby talk to last a lifetime and Lily had yet to open a single present. The women at my table—mostly Lily's sorority sisters—had discussed everything from nipple cream and breast pumps to changing tables and diaper blowouts with breathtaking seriousness.

I cast a longing glance across the yard to Lily's family table. A group of her cousins had flown up from San Diego and her aunt Luna had even traveled all the way from Mexico City. I would have done just about anything to be sitting with them instead. The waves of laughter rising from their table were a clear sign that they definitely weren't discussing bodily functions. I wanted to ask Luna about the Templo Mayor ruins in the center of Mexico City that Dotty had told me about. She'd visited just a few years ago.

Dotty had hated baby showers. "They're like going away parties for the poor woman's life," she'd always quipped. Somewhere between a rousing round of baby bingo and a game of guess-what's-in-the-diaper, I realized she might have been right. Mom seemed to relish every minute, the huge smile never once slipping from her face.

She'd greeted me with her usual too-tight hug before recommending that I should check the medicine cabinet for some eye drops. "Late night?" she'd asked, her eyebrow spiking.

"I'm fine, Mom. I've just been really busy."

"Did you get a new job that I don't know about?"

"Actually, yes," I said, surprising myself. I hadn't technically accepted Nadine's offer yet, but I knew I was going to. I didn't have any other options. Plus, Donovan had seemed genuinely impressed that I'd landed a job with Nadine herself. So I told Mom about Le Agency and left out the part about all the strings Donovan had to pull to get me a meeting with Nadine.

"Well, I hope you take *this* opportunity seriously."

I chose to ignore Mom's dig. "So," I said, not bothering to mask the annoyance in my voice. "I hear you've found a new apartment?"

To my surprise, Mom's face softened, the fine lines around her eyes easing. "I've been meaning to call you about that."

It was probably as close to an apology as I'd ever get from her. Mom said her new place was a "cute as a button" one-bedroom in the heart of downtown Santa Clara. She'd been moderately horrified when Marcia and I chose our tiny apartment because of its proximity to the best bars and restaurants in the city, and now here she was going on and on about how excited she was to be able to walk to dinner. But that was Mom. Consistently unaware of her own hypocrisy.

"Rosie," one of Lily's sorority sisters said, bringing me back to my present hellish reality, "does all this make you want to settle down?"

I took a long gulp of champagne as everyone at the table turned their gaze to me. "Not really."

The woman looked like she'd been slapped but recovered quickly. "That's okay," she said sweetly, "you have time."

"How old are you?" another blonde asked.

"I'll be twenty-five in February."

A chorus of "oohs" escaped the table. "You're so young," the first one said. "I bet once you hold Lily's baby, you'll feel it."

"Feel what?"

"The itch," another said, as if that explained everything.

"Baby fever is real," a woman with a newborn glued to her chest said dreamily. "I just had a baby, and I already want another!"

A collective "mmm" rippled across the table. "There's just nothing like it," one of the blondes said.

"I know," agreed the breastfeeding woman. "I just feel so bad for women who never have children. Can you imagine? Missing out on all this?" She looked down at the pink infant in her arms.

I could imagine it.

"My aunt Dotty never had kids."

"Lily told us," Blonde Number Two said, her voice dripping with pity. "How sad." Everyone nodded. I reached for the bottle of champagne.

I'd never considered Dotty not having children to be sad. And I couldn't picture her having been happy as a mother, either. I said a silent prayer that Lily, who'd recently proved herself to be cooler than I'd thought, wouldn't turn into one of these Stepford zombie-moms.

"What's Lily's birth plan?" someone asked as a thrill of energy raced through the group. Childbirth was an evergreen topic with this crowd, apparently. I sighed, leaning back into my chair, relieved to let their attention shift away from me and my reproductive prospects.

* * *

Lily opened presents like a pro, cooing over every package as if it were the most precious, thoughtful gift she'd ever received. I watched, smiling and nodding politely along with the rest of the women as my mind wandered to Dad's letter. It took everything in me not to pull it out of my purse and read it at the table.

I begrudgingly let Mom rope me into cleaning up the mountain of pastel pink wrapping paper as the party was finally winding down.

"Did you see your father's wine cellar?"

"Yep," I said. "It's nice. Very Dad."

"Mmm . . ." Mom replied as she stuffed a wad of paper into an enormous garbage bag.

"What do you care? You're moving out."

"Why are you always so short with me?"

I wrestled with a piece of ribbon that had somehow become tangled around my arm. "Shouldn't I be asking you that?"

"Rosie," Mom said, her shoulders drooping, "all I ever want to do is support you."

It was as if we were living in alternate dimensions. In my world, Mom was overbearing, nitpicky, and impossible to please. In her world, she was Super Mom: loving, supportive, and encouraging. I didn't dare imagine what the version of me that lived in Mom's world was like.

"Why haven't you written back to my email about Dotty?"

Mom balked. "I didn't think you wanted me to."

"Why would you think that?" I said, more loudly than I intended. "God, Mom. Do you even miss her?"

"How could you say that? I loved Dotty."

"You weren't very nice to her when she was alive."

Mom looked around the party, clearly worried that one of Lily's insufferable friends might have picked up on our argument. "Let's not do this now."

This was Mom's go-to trick. She'd always insist on decorum as soon as a conversation got too real. "Whatever. I should probably get Bug home anyway." I handed Mom the mangled gift bag I'd been holding and stalked off without saying goodbye.

* * *

"Thank you so much for coming, Auntie Rosie," Lily said sweetly as I shrugged on my sweater.

"Of course," I said, pouring every last ounce of energy into sounding genuine. "I can't wait to meet the baby."

Lily ran her hand over her belly. "Not long to go. Can you believe it?"

I shook my head.

"There's actually something I wanted to talk to you about," Lily said, her voice dipping. She gestured to the streamer-filled living room. "Do you want to sit for a minute?"

"Okay . . ."

Lily eased herself onto the couch as I plopped down beside her.

She kicked off her shoes (a very tall pair of bright pink heels) and sighed with relief. "I swear to god, I'm not wearing heels again until after this baby is born."

"At least you look cute."

"You're nice. I feel monstrous." I started to protest, but she shook her head. "It's true. I'm huge. Anyway, I wanted to talk to you about my birth plan." I bristled involuntarily. I'd had enough childbirth talk for one millennium, but Lily didn't seem to notice. "Not to pull the dead mom card, but as you know, my mom is dead." She forced out a laugh, but it sounded put on. I moved my hand onto Lily's knee. She covered it with hers. "And my dad lives on the other side of the country. So, since my parents can't be with me when the baby is born, I was hoping that you might want to. Be there, I mean. In the delivery room."

I didn't know what to say. I didn't know what to do, what to think.

I must have made a face because Lily's expression crumpled. "I didn't mean to upset you. It's just that—"

"I'd be honored," I said.

"Really?"

I nodded.

Lily sprang across the couch, pulling me into a hug. "That means so much to me."

I squeezed her back. "Are you sure you don't want my mom?"

Lily sat back, wiping a tear away with the heel of her hand. "I love your mom," she said, "but having her there would feel like I was replacing my mom, somehow." She squeezed my hand. "But with you, it would be like having a sister there. And I always wanted a sister."

It was the nicest thing anyone had ever said to me.

Dear Rosie,

Did Dotty ever tell you about her history with your grandpa Archie? I don't remember all the details, but I've done my best to recall them below. Your mom may know more. Grandma Ruth might have shared some with her. Claire was always closer to my mom than I was. Although Grandma Ruth was pretty private. Nothing like Dotty. It's a marvel that sisters raised in the same household can turn out so differently.

When Dotty was in her early twenties, she took a secretary job at a travel agency. On Fridays, the office would order lunch from a deli down the street, and Dotty would volunteer to pick it up. She said she hated being trapped in the office all day.

Your great-grandpa—Archie's father—happened to be the owner of that deli. And Archie worked there on his summers home from college. That's where they met. It didn't take long for Archie to ask Dotty out on a date.

Dotty said she was drawn to Archie because he was unique. He didn't act like a lot of young men at the time. He admired Dotty's intelligence and offbeat view of the world. He gladly told her stories about what it was like to go to college—and even encouraged her to do so! Which was incredibly uncommon back then. It sounds like they had some wild times together, too—smoking weed, going to secret concerts in friends' basements, the kind of things young people get up to. I'm sure you can imagine.

Soon enough, Archie proposed and Dotty turned him down. On some level, she must have known that she didn't want the kind of life Archie wanted to give her. The life he ultimately ended up building with her little sister.

Dotty fled the continent shortly after breaking things off with Archie. I'm not sure how or why she ended up in Hawaii, but she lived there for some time.

When Dotty returned home, Ruth insisted on talking to Dotty right away. She dragged her into the bedroom they'd shared as children and begged her not to be angry. Then, through tears, she explained that she and Archie had fallen in love while Dotty was away. And they wanted to get married. But Ruth wouldn't go through with it if she didn't have Dotty's blessing.

Of course, Dotty was thrilled. I think she would have relished shouting about her inadvertent matchmaking skills from the rooftop, but Ruth swore her to secrecy. As relieved as she was to have Dotty's approval, I think she was a bit insecure. Perhaps she worried people might think Archie had settled for her. Which, of course, wasn't the case. My parents were wild about each other.

Anyway, all of this is to say that Dotty wasn't just my aunt. She was the person who brought my parents together. If it weren't for her, I wouldn't be here. And neither would you or your brother. Neat, right?

Love,
Dad

From: Rosie Benson
To: Tommy Benson; Lily Lopez-Benson
Subject: Did you know about this???
Date: June 6

So, apparently, our grandfather hooked up with Dotty before he married our grandmother? Our family is so not normal! And how did I not know this??

From: Tommy Benson
To: Rosie Benson; Lily Lopez-Benson

Yeah, Dad mentioned it a while ago. He said Dotty never talked about it out of respect for Grandma Ruth. Pretty weird. But also cool that they were all so adult about it.

From: Rosie Benson
To: Tommy Benson; Lily Lopez-Benson

Cool? Tommy, that would be like if I'd dated Lily before you!

From: Tommy Benson
To: Rosie Benson; Lily Lopez-Benson

You could do a lot worse ;)

From: Lily Lopez-Benson
To: Tommy Benson; Rosie Benson

I think it's sweet! And Rosie, you can take me on a date anytime you'd like. I'm all yours.

From: Rosie Benson
To: Lily Lopez-Benson; Tommy Benson

You guys are weird.

CHAPTER SEVENTEEN

I'd gone straight to my room after getting home from Lily's shower, eager to read Dad's letter. I still wasn't quite sure what to make of it, but by the time I woke up the next morning, I was starting to wonder if maybe Marcia and I could find a way through this. If Donovan could forgive his father and Dotty could forgive her sister, surely I could find a way to forgive Marcia.

But we'd have to have the conversation that I'd been dreading, first. I needed to know everything. Even if I wasn't going to like it.

So, when Marcia attempted to lure me onto our rooftop with a carafe of coffee and a massive box of donuts, I'd relented, my motivations equal parts hunger and hope. Bug sat between us on one of Dotty's old sarapes, occasionally growling at a raven that had perched on a nearby ledge. I'd secretly named her Denise.

"Thanks for agreeing to this," Marcia said, her voice quiet. "Should I go first?"

My fingers tightened around my coffee cup as I nodded. "Sure."

She sighed. "Okay. Well, for starters, I'm sorry for the way everything went down with Raj. And for springing him on you the other night. I totally botched this whole thing. I just didn't know how to tell you."

"You should have just told me."

"I was worried about how you'd react."

That wasn't totally unfair. I did tend to react a little dramatically to bad news. I'd always told myself it was an endearing quality in an *I'm the youngest so I'm allowed to be a little pouty* sort of way. Maybe I was wrong. "That shouldn't have stopped you."

"I know. But by the time I realized he was *that* Raj, I liked him. A lot. I guess I panicked. I didn't know what to do so I decided not to say anything to either of you, which ultimately blew up in my face. As you know."

"When did you figure it out?"

"A couple of months ago. I saw him talking to Gemma after a game and I asked how he knew her. When he said he was her boss I got this instant sinking feeling in my stomach." She flashed a sad, bitter smile. "Of all the people for me to fall for."

"You sure know how to pick them."

Marcia ignored my dig. "He wants to talk things out with you. And to apologize for the way he handled everything."

I would rather suffer through a thousand baby showers than have that talk with Raj. "I don't think I'm ready for that."

She nodded, keeping her eyes fixed on the horizon. "What would help you to feel ready?"

"I think . . ." I looked down at the coffee cup in my hands, as if I would find the answer there. "I think I need to know everything," I said. I hadn't ever been cheated on before, let alone been in a relationship long enough to be cheated on, but according to everything I'd learned from movies and TV, the cheatee often forced the cheater to spill every detail of their indiscretions. It had always seemed masochistic to me, but I think I understood now. I had to know the totality of what I was forgiving Marcia and Raj for before I could move forward. Like sucking venom out of a snake bite.

"Okay." She drew a shaky breath. "What else do you want to know?"

"Did Raj know that you were my best friend when he fired me?"
She winced. "Not exactly."

My left eyebrow spiked involuntarily. "What does that mean?"

"He'd figured out that we knew each other, but he had no idea that you were my roommate, let alone my best friend." Her shoulders sagged. "I hadn't told him yet. I was still trying to sort through my feelings and I didn't want to make things awkward if they didn't need to be."

Something about the way she said it, the uneasy inflection in her tone told me everything I needed to know. Marcia was dancing around the truth. "You told him I was with you at the beach that day, didn't you?"

"Not directly. But yeah, I sent him a selfie from the beach. I didn't realize you were in the background. He recognized you."

I knew it. Somewhere deep down, I'd known it from the moment Raj barged into our bathroom.

I thought back to the day I got fired. I was sure Raj had seen the picture of Marcia and me on my computer and figured it out from there. I'd even told Marcia that. She'd let me believe it was my fault.

"Did you even bother to tell him that *you* were the one who'd dragged *me* there?" I said, my voice rising without my permission. The raven took off abruptly, her inky black wings gleaming in the morning sunlight. She must have sensed that this wasn't a conversation she wanted to witness. I couldn't blame her.

"Of course I did." She shook her head, as if willing things to be different. "When I confronted him, he said he was already going to fire you one way or another. It was only a matter of time. The picture was the last straw. I was so pissed at him. He felt awful, for what it's worth."

The thought of the two of them discussing my job at Driftwood felt like another betrayal. I didn't know what to say, so I didn't say anything.

Marcia pressed her fingertips against her eyes and groaned. "It's all so messed up."

"That's an understatement," I shot back.

Bug whined quietly. She didn't like tension. I placed a reassuring hand on her side.

"I know, *I know*. God, Rosie. Do you think I wanted this to happen? I kept hoping this was just a stupid fling, that my feelings would fade away like they always do. But it's different with him."

"How?"

"I really, really like him." The way her voice sounded, small and sad and pleading, made the ice around my heart thaw ever so slightly.

There was so much I wanted to say—that she could do way better than Raj, that his taste in clothing was abhorrent, that his lame tech bro persona was downright cringey—but I managed to hold my tongue.

I looked out over the rooftop to our neighborhood below. Hungover twentysomethings in search of brunch and health nuts with yoga mats strapped to their backs had started to emerge from their respective apartments. I envied every single one of them. Surely none of their friends were dating their nightmare ex-bosses.

Marcia bounced her feet up and down, her shoulders bobbing along. "I'm mad at you, too, you know. The Donovan thing—it's not ideal. I mean, it'll be fine, but still. Of all the people you could have hooked up with that night?" She stopped, probably recognizing the hypocrisy of her anger. "But I don't really have a leg to stand on after what I did with Raj."

I rolled my shoulders, hoping to loosen the knots that had formed on either side of my shoulder blades. "You know, after I went home with Donovan, I felt so guilty. I knew how hard it had been for you to work with him and I didn't want to screw anything up for you."

"Thanks," she muttered.

"I really am sorry," I said. "I was going to tell you as soon as you woke up that day, but then Raj was there. And what you did to me was so much worse."

"I know," she said quietly. She flexed her fingers open and closed. "I know this is hard for you. It's hard for me, too. It's an incredibly shitty situation. But I'm not going to let you throw away our relationship over this. I still need you."

My chin began to wobble as I blinked back tears. "I still need you, too," I said. "But I'm going to need some time, first."

She leaned over Bug and rested her head on my shoulder. I didn't shrug it off. "Take all the time you need," she said. We sat there for a long time, neither of us acknowledging the heavy boulder that had settled between us.

* * *

When Marcia offered to take Bug for a walk, I didn't refuse. I wanted to be alone anyway.

I didn't know how to process any of this. Marcia's careless decision to text Raj from the beach, knowing full well that I'd lied to him about why I'd skipped work. Her guilt-driven dedication to helping me find a job. The way she'd humored me when I'd rant about how awful Raj was, all the while knowing she'd sneak off to see him later that night.

I knew that I'd messed up at work. I knew that, ultimately, getting fired was my fault. But knowing that my best friend had helped it along . . . I never would have thought Marcia was capable of doing something like that.

But I wasn't willing to get into a long, protracted cold war. Marcia had messed up, but I knew her apology was genuine and I wasn't going to let a lifetime of friendship fade into history that easily. I needed to figure out a way to move forward.

A deft fluttering interrupted my wallowing. Startled, I looked over my shoulder. Denise was back. I watched in amusement as the large black bird took a tentative hop toward the box of half-eaten donuts. I swore I saw hope in her beady blinking eyes.

As a kid, I was terrified of ravens. When I told Dotty that I hated the menacing birds that loitered on the playground at school, she'd scoffed. "They're beautiful, intelligent creatures," she'd said with great conviction. "Maybe you should try to learn more about them before you decide whether to hate them."

A week later, I had gotten a package in the mail. It was an encyclopedia of birds. In the margins, Dotty had written little notes. *Did you know that ravens pick up bits of trash to use as toys? Or that they collect shiny metal objects to impress their friends? Some can mimic human speech better than parrots!* Naturally, Dotty's favorite things about ravens became mine, too.

I slid the cheerful pink box toward the bird. "Knock yourself out."

Dear Dotty,

Dad told me about you and Grandpa Archie. How did I not know about that? What else didn't you tell me?

I miss you so much. There are so many things I wish I could talk to you about. So many things I want to know, want you to know.

Remember how much I hated my boss, Raj? Well, Marcia is dating him. She was dating him when he fired me. Can you believe that? How did you get over Grandma Ruth marrying your ex-boyfriend? Knowing you, you'd probably say you have to love people, warts and mistakes and all. I just wish I knew how to do that. She seems so happy with him. I want to be happy for her, but it's all so complicated.

I'm starting a new job next week. I'm going to be a recruiter. You'd hate the office—it's all modern and minimal. If you were here, you'd tell me to hold out for something better, something more in line with what I really want.

But the thing is, I don't know what I really want.

I know that I want you back. And that I want Marcia to get over this Raj thing. I wish she'd never met him. I want Mom to snap out of her weird midlife crisis and stop breaking Dad's heart. I guess I just want my old life back.

At least I have Bug. Thank you for trusting me with her. She misses you so much. We both do. My new boss said I could bring her to the office with me. She said Bug could be the company mascot. That feels like a sign, right? Like I'm doing the right thing?

I know I need to get it together. I'm dating this new guy, Donovan. He's only a little older than I am, and he's so accomplished. He owns his condo and has his own business, and he irons his clothes. He helped me get this job. And he introduced me to whiskey. I feel very sophisticated when I'm with him.

I wish I could bring him over to your house for martinis.

I don't even know why I'm writing all this to you. You'll never read it.

CHAPTER EIGHTEEN

I tried to ignore the stabbing pain in the balls of my feet as I stepped off the elevator. I finally understood why so many people wore tennis shoes on the bus. I desperately wanted to take my pumps off, but for all I knew, blood was pooling around my toes. I should have broken in these heels around the apartment first.

At least I looked the part. And so did Bug. I'd given her a bath the night before (much to her dismay) and tied a pink bandanna around her collar. As she strutted down the hall toward Le Agency, I wondered if she knew how important my first day at this new job would be.

"Welcome back," Evan said, as Bug and I walked into the lobby, his smile faltering as his eyes landed on Bug. "You brought your dog."

"Nadine said it was okay."

"I thought she was joking."

I squared my hips, digging my heels into the hardwood floor. "She's the best dog ever. You won't even know she's here."

"Is she potty-trained?"

"She's six."

Evan reached for an enormous cup of iced coffee, the cubes sloshing against one another. He took a long, slow sip from an aluminum straw, his eyes never leaving Bug. "Does she bark?"

"Rarely."

"Jump on people?"

"Not unless they want her to."

"Eat shoes?"

"Not that I'm aware of."

He returned the iced coffee to the desk. "If she poops anywhere in this office, we're going to have a problem."

I tucked away the beginnings of a laugh. "I'll be sure to communicate that to her."

Evan shimmied his shoulders as if trying to shake off our ridiculous exchange. "All right, then. Welcome to the team."

* * *

Evan gave us a tour of the office, taking great pains to show me how to get onto the balcony. "In case of emergencies," he said, looking at Bug. She stared back, her tiny underbite looking especially pronounced. I bent to pat her on the head, proud of her for taking Evan's passive-aggressive reaction in stride.

"This will be your desk," Evan said, rolling out a silver armchair with white vinyl cushions. It sat against an exposed brick wall just outside Nadine's office. "You can set up Bug's—" He raised his eyebrows, awaiting confirmation that he'd gotten her name right. I nodded. "You can set up Bug's bed under here." He pointed to the bare floor beneath the glass-topped desk. "Pilar should be in shortly." He gestured to the tidy desk beside mine before flicking his gaze to the final desk in the row and said, "Kate, too."

I peered past Pilar's minimalist setup. Kate's desk was littered with framed photos, brightly colored folders, and an assortment of dirty coffee mugs. Neon Post-it notes covered every inch of her monitor's frame. "They're polar opposites," Evan said, examining his nails.

"You don't say."

He flashed a conspiratorial grin. "Just wait. Never a dull moment with those two." Great. More drama was just what I needed at the moment. "Well, I'll let you get set up." He handed me a piece of heavy white paper. "These are your log-in credentials. We'll go over your benefits enrollment and all that fun stuff later today. Get excited," he said, his voice monotone. In spite of his lukewarm reaction to Bug, I was pretty sure I was going to like Evan.

"Thank you," I said.

"You bet," he replied, casting a final disapproving look at Kate's desk before turning to leave.

* * *

Pilar arrived a few minutes later, dressed in black from head to toe. Her formerly purple ponytail was now bubblegum pink. "I heard there's a pug back here," she said by way of greeting.

"It's true. Hope that's okay."

Her lips parted into a thin smile, her dark eyes brightening behind thick black-rimmed glasses. "This is going to drive Evan crazy," she said.

"That's . . . a good thing?"

"Fantastic. It's fun to see him squirm. He's such a control freak." She dropped a brown leather messenger bag on her chair before jiggling her mouse. The thin white monitor on her desk glowed to life. She turned around to face me. "I'm Pilar, by the way."

"I know," I said. "I'm Rosie."

"I know."

"Do you want to meet Bug?"

"Sure." Bug, hearing her name, emerged from under my desk, tail wagging. Pilar cocked her head to the side. "She's cute," she said, as if she was stating a proven fact. "How long have you had her?"

"About a month. I've known her for years, though." Pilar's face twisted in confusion. "She was my great-aunt's dog. She died a little while ago."

"Damn. I'm sorry."

"Me too," I said, a swell of grief rising in my throat. I swallowed hard.

"You're a nice person," Pilar said, her eyes scanning my face. "I like nice people." She bent down to pat Bug on the head before returning to her chair. "You'll be training with me this afternoon," she said over her shoulder.

I'd forgotten how exhausting the first day at a new job was. I hadn't been in the office for more than an hour before I desperately needed caffeine. Evan was kind enough to show me how to work the shiny silver coffee maker. "We're an espresso family," he said, pointing to a button illuminated with blue light. "But you can make regular coffee, too. I usually put mine over ice on Mondays. Because . . . you know, Mondays."

Bug remained by my side as the espresso machine clinked and clunked. I rotated my lower jaw in circles, trying to relax. I hadn't realized I'd been clenching my teeth all morning.

"Oh. My. God," a high-pitched voice squealed. I looked up to see a girl with long, stick-straight red hair and a splash of matching freckles across her nose and forehead. Her hands were clasped just below her chin. "Is that your dog? Can I pet her?" she said, already reaching for Bug. "I'm Kate."

"I'm Rosie. And that's Bug," I said.

"Buuuuug!" Kate squealed. She dropped down to her knees, arms outstretched toward my little dog. Bug looked to me for ap-proval before crawling into Kate's lap and giving her chin a cautious sniff. "Oh, she's just the cutest thing I've ever seen," Kate cooed, rubbing Bug's velvety ears. My eyes fell to her left hand, which appeared to be missing the middle and ring fingers.

Kate must have noticed me staring. "It's called *small hand*," she said, holding her hand up for me to see. Her nails were all painted red.

"I didn't mean to—"

"Cool, right? And very rare. Have you ever seen a hand like mine before?" I shook my head. "*Exactly*," Kate said proudly.

The espresso machine dinged, signaling that my much-needed caffeine was ready. I pulled it off the tray and cupped the tiny mug between both hands.

"I'm sorry I wasn't here when you got in," Kate said, her eyes still on Bug. "I had to drop some swag off for a *client*," she emphasized the word *client*, in the way I sometimes heard Lily emphasize words like *Louis Vuitton* or *Gucci*.

"All good," I said. "Evan got me set up. And Pilar seems great."

Kate pulled her lips into a tight line, tilting her head to the side. "She can be a bit salty," she said, as if confiding a closely guarded secret. "Evan, too. I think they're still a little bitter about the merger."

"Merger?"

"You don't know?" I shook my head. Kate looked down at Bug, who'd shed about a pound of fur onto her bright red skirt. "Does she like to be held?"

"Loves it," I said, mentally batting away an inkling of possessiveness. I'd become even more protective of Bug since that day in Peter's office.

Kate scooped Bug into her arms, expertly supporting her back paws with one hand and her solid little torso with the other. She now stood eye level with me, in heels that were at least two inches higher than mine. I couldn't help but notice their red soles. "What were we talking about?" Kate's hazel eyes flicked to the ceiling before snapping back to meet mine. "Right, the merger. Nadine had another Le Agency down in *L.A.*," she said, as if I should be impressed. "But when her husband got transferred to San Francisco, she decided to expand. This office used to be called Bell Recruiting Associates or something like that." She shook her head, indicating the name didn't really matter. "When Nadine bought it, the original owner left. But Evan and Pilar stayed. And I think they used to do things a lot differently. That's probably why Candace didn't work out."

Candace. The recruiter I'd replaced. "How long have you been here?"

"A little over a year. I'm one of Nadine's hires. Like you." She tossed a sheet of red hair over her shoulder. "You're going to love working with Nadine. She's trained me so well. I almost feel bad for Evan and Pilar, you know? They've had to relearn a whole new style of recruiting."

I didn't know how to respond, so I sipped my espresso instead.

"You worked at Driftwood before this, right?" Kate asked. Her tone was light, innocent. I wondered if Nadine had told anyone else on the team about my being fired. If she had, Kate was hiding it well. I nodded. "That's so cool," Kate said, her approval appearing genuine. Then she stepped toward me and lowered her voice. "Nadine hates them."

My shoulders tensed reflexively. "Why?"

Kate shook her head. "Something to do with an old contract, I think. Nadine thought she had an exclusive deal, but they screwed her over when the company went public. That's probably why she hired you. For revenge or something." Kate stopped, catching herself. "I mean, it's probably just one of the reasons she hired you.

You seem great." She bit her lip. "Well, I really should get to my email." She set Bug down on the floor, giving her head a final pet before standing. She walked over to the refrigerator, also shiny and new, and pulled out a bottle of kombucha. "Let me know if you have any questions at all," she said with a wave.

I stood there, alone in the kitchen, in my new clothes, with my new dog, clutching a lukewarm cup of espresso, feeling almost certain that I couldn't trust Kate.

* * *

By the time Nadine breezed into the office, I was on my second espresso and shaking like a leaf. She greeted me warmly, complimenting Bug on her manners as I willed my hands to stop jittering. She wore a crisp white top that fell just below her rib cage and looked like it cost more than my annual salary. I did my best not to stare at the slice of midriff that peered out over her high-waisted sailor pants. "Just give me a moment to get settled," Nadine said, her eyes darting to her office door. "We have so much to do." She wriggled her shoulders, as if learning the ins and outs of recruiting would be a treat.

Minutes later, I sat at Nadine's desk, my third espresso resting on a creamy white saucer. Her private office was even more luxurious than I remembered. I'd somehow missed the wet bar in the corner and the chaise lounge against the window the last time I was there.

"Well," she said, straightening her shoulders, "you've met the team." Her eyes fell to my mug. "And found the espresso maker. So I'd say you're off to a great start. I'm so excited for you to get to know everyone. I think you're just the missing piece this team needs." With that, the shaking in my hands eased. "Now," Nadine said, shifting gears. "Let's get started. You'll be training with me for most of the week, but I've scheduled some time with Pilar, too. Kate's still a bit green, but she's showing a lot of promise. That said, Pilar is our top earner. Even if she does things . . . a little differently." She paused, as if considering whether she wanted to confide more. "You'll see what I mean."

I dipped my chin in response. I'd only been at Le Agency for a couple of hours, and it was already apparent that there were divisions among the ranks. Maybe I should have been worried, but it all felt so . . . civil.

"Quality control is everything," Nadine said, flattening her hands on the desk for emphasis. "If we're sending candidates to subpar employers or sending unqualified applicants out on interviews, the agency looks bad. And we lose business. Make sense?" I nodded. "Good. We're going to start you out on the candidate side for now. Reviewing résumés, doing phone screens, sitting in on interviews, that kind of thing. Once you're comfortable with all that, you can take on a couple client accounts."

Nadine oozed confidence. I could almost feel some of it rubbing off onto me. She swiveled her monitor around for me to see. "I'll walk you through the way I review a résumé, and then you can give it a try. . . . So, at first glance, there are just a couple of things you need to look for: a name, contact information, relevant experience—we only place marketing and administrative candidates, primarily at tech companies and start-ups—limited gaps in employment, and absolutely no typos." She pulled up a résumé and eyed it closely. "At first glance, this person looks good. She has a degree, some experience as a receptionist at a start-up, and I don't see any errors . . ." She minimized the document and pulled up

LinkedIn, typing the person's name into the search bar. A profile popped up, revealing a photo of a woman about my age. She stood against a bright yellow wall, her hair pulled into a smooth ponytail. Nadine nodded in approval. "And she has the look. I'd move her to the next step."

"What's 'the look'?"

Nadine leaned forward. "This is a bit controversial," she said, her husky voice just above a whisper. "But our clients expect a certain type of candidate from Le Agency. They need to be . . . polished. Like Kate." She sat back, taking in my hair—freshly trimmed—and my blouse. "Like you." My cheeks flushed at the compliment. "We can always make exceptions, of course. Like in Pilar's case." Nadine crinkled her nose. "And some candidates are coachable. They just need a little nudge in the right direction. But we can deal with those on a case-by-case basis."

We spent the morning picking through résumés and assessing LinkedIn profiles. Trying to guess who Nadine would like or why she might turn someone down was like a game. A game that I decided I would learn to play very, very well.

* * *

"Forget everything Nadine taught you," Pilar said, her voice flat. She tugged the door to the glass-walled interview room shut and turned on her heel to face me. "She's about as deep as a puddle." My eyes widened with surprise. The left corner of Pilar's mouth twitched upward. "You'll see."

Pilar crossed the room and pulled out a bright white chair. Her nails were painted black and stacks of elastic rubber bands lined her wrist. "Nadine is a one-trick pony," Pilar said, taking a seat

before opening her laptop. "She only likes to hire pretty people"—
her eyes darted to me—"no offense."

"None taken." A jittery laugh escaped my throat. Pilar arched a
pierced eyebrow. "I've had too much caffeine today."

"I can tell." Her mouth barely moved when she talked. "So,
here's the deal," Pilar said, her voice dipping. "Nadine only focuses
on a certain type of candidate, which only works for a certain type
of client. Which is fine. That leaves the best ones for the rest of us."

"How so?"

"She passes on qualified people all the time," Pilar said, rolling
her eyes. "So I scoop them up. And you should, too. If you ever
meet with someone you think is good but Nadine passes on, bring
them to me."

"Doesn't Nadine . . . mind?"

"Nah," Pilar said, pulling the corners of her mouth into a casual
frown. "When Nadine bought Bell—that's what this place used
to be called—I convinced her to let me keep all the old accounts.
Nadine said she didn't care what I did with them as long as they
weren't losing any money. I don't think she expected them to be so
profitable, but a deal's a deal." She leaned forward conspiratorially
and added, "My commission checks are huge."

"So you're basically running your own agency within Le Agency."

"That's about the sum of it. And my clients aren't the shiny
bubblegum start-ups that Nadine is obsessed with. They're good,
normal companies."

"Like what?"

Pilar set a booted foot on top of her knee, holding her shin with
both hands. "Accounting firms, health-care companies, that sort
of thing."

I nodded. "So no fancy tech start-ups?"

"Nope. My clients aren't glamorous. But that's why they're better," she said with conviction. "The best employers aren't always the prettiest."

After my experience at Driftwood, I liked the sound of that. "How long have you been doing this?"

"Since college."

"So, like, five years?"

A sly smile danced across her face. "Are you trying to kiss my ass?"

"What? No. I—"

"I'm forty."

"Oh, wow. You look great. For—"

"For my age?" Pilar asked, clearly amused by the conversation. "Well, you know what they say about us Puerto Ricans."

I shook my head.

Pilar grinned. "Me neither. But we age well. You should see my grandmother. She looks my mom's age. And my mom looks like she could be my sister."

I was pretty sure my mom had kept up her looks with the help of Botox, but I'd never had the guts to ask.

"Anyway, I think my creative hair helps, too." She gestured to her brightly colored ponytail.

"I've always wanted pink hair," I said.

"I'm thinking about dyeing it green next."

"Green like a frog or green like a forest?"

Pilar's eyes danced with amusement. "Is there a difference?"

"Oh yeah," I said, matter-of-factly. "Frog green is brighter. Forest green is darker, more natural."

She grinned. "Frog green it is."

That was the moment Pilar and I became friends.

* * *

"That sounds like a wildly dysfunctional work environment," Donovan said. He pulled a golf club from the wall of putters and winced at the disconcerting stickiness of the yellow rubber handle.

I'd just finished telling him about my first week at Le Agency, about Kate's thinly veiled passive aggression, Nadine's exacting standards, and Evan and Pilar's outright rejection of those standards. "It's really not so bad," I said with a shrug. "It's kind of refreshing how up-front they all are. Even if that means openly disagreeing during every meeting."

"Way to look on the bright side," he said as he produced a pouch of sanitizing wipes from his pocket and handed one to me. "You never know who touched those clubs last."

"Germaphobe."

"I might have just saved you from a staph infection. You should be grateful."

I gave him a playful shove. "Ouch," he said, gamely rubbing his shoulder. "I don't remember golf being a contact sport."

Donovan and his VC partners had rented out an indoor miniature golf course to celebrate the end of another successful quarter. The place was crawling with tech people, all wearing some variation of skinny jeans, tennis shoes, and button-down shirts rumpled in just the right places.

"I'd offer to kiss it better, but I think a lip gloss stain on your shirt would send you over the edge."

Donovan jumped back, holding his club out defensively. "Don't even think about it," he said. His laugh set a round of tiny, charged lightning bolts racing across my stomach.

"I wouldn't dare. I've seen your dry-cleaning bill."

He held my gaze, grinning. "Fair enough. Now let's go sanitize our balls and hit the green."

Donovan was terrible at miniature golf. Like, embarrassingly bad. He shanked his ball off a replica of the Golden Gate Bridge, whiffed more swings than I could count, and nearly decapitated his CFO with an overzealous putt. "Finally, something you're not good at," I said, relishing the opportunity to tease him.

He laughed, revealing the tiny gap between his front teeth that I found to be more adorable every time I saw it. "I'm normal just like you, remember?"

What was decidedly not normal was the after-party. Donovan had somehow managed to reserve a massive table in the VIP section of Sip, a nightclub at the end of a nondescript alley with a line that wrapped around the block. When our car pulled up to the back entrance, we were escorted inside and presented with a towering bottle of vodka with a flaming sparkler poking out the top. I would have felt massively underdressed in jeans and a sweater if everyone else at our table hadn't also been sporting some variation of tennis shoes and ugly fleece vests.

Donovan and I settled into the back of the vinyl booth. "What can I make you?" he asked, gesturing to the spread of bottles at the center of the mirrored table.

I shrugged. "I'll have what you're having."

Donovan mixed up some strong but delicious vodka sodas for us, and before I knew it, a warm buzz was spreading across my chest. Donovan's coworkers stopped by to talk on occasion, all of them perfectly lovely but way too excited about work. The music got louder as the night wore on, making it harder to hear each other. Eventually, everyone else gave up on work talk, opting to hit the dance floor instead.

The crowd beyond our table swayed with indiscernible techno music. I was surprised by how much I enjoyed being tucked away from the action with Donovan, and even more surprised that he hadn't ditched me to hang out with his work friends.

"Did you have fun tonight?" he asked, a lazy smile creeping across his lips.

"I think I really did."

He raised his eyebrows. "You seem surprised."

"I kind of am. I've always considered myself more of a dive bar person." I leaned back against the booth. "But this was a really fun night. Thanks for inviting me."

He dropped his hand on my thigh. "I figured you could use a fun night out after everything you've been through. And from what I hear, Nadine tends to drive people to drink."

I stared at his hand on my thigh, feeling its warmth and weight. My fuzzy brain couldn't quite process what I was feeling, but I knew I wanted more. More of Donovan, more of his kindness, more nights like this.

"Hey," he said, scooting closer so that our arms were pressed together. The neon sign above our heads made his hair glow purple. "I like you."

"I like you, too."

"No," he whined, shaking his head. "I *like* you, like you."

I ignored the fluttering in my heart. "I think you should cool it on the drinks for the rest of the night."

He laughed again before turning his head so that his mouth was next to my ear. "Well, *I think* you should be my girlfriend."

I pulled away so that I could look him in the eye. "Are you serious?"

He smiled. "I'm always serious."

Then he kissed me. It was the best, most romantic kiss I'd ever had. We were drunk and it was late and the music was loud. But something had changed between us.

And I was falling hard for Donovan Ng.

Dearest Rosie,

I apologize for taking so long to respond to your beautiful email. As I'm sure you can understand, I needed some time to gather my thoughts.

How bittersweet for me to meet Dotty's favorite niece under such tragic circumstances. Dotty spoke about you often. She adored you.

I met Dotty many, many years ago on a beach in Hawaii, where I grew up. My brother was teaching a group of tourists to surf and had reluctantly allowed me to tag along. And I'm so glad he did.

I'll never forget the moment I first laid eyes on your aunt. She was dragging a surfboard across the sand in a bright yellow swimsuit, her hair tied up in a ridiculous bandanna. She was the most beautiful thing I'd ever seen. She marched straight up to my brother and asked for a lesson. I was sure she'd fall madly in love with him in no time (all the girls did). But it turned out she only had eyes for me.

Women didn't date each other back then. At least not openly. So we told everyone that we were the best of friends. My brother knew, of course. He'd cover for us when we snuck off to the beach to make love under the stars. Those were some of the best years of my life.

We talked about everything. Our hopes, our fears, our dreams. She wanted to go to college and travel the world.

I wanted to move to the mainland and become a doctor and have a family. And what do you know, we both accomplished our goals. At the time, we thought we might do it all together. But we were so young. And things rarely work out the way you think they will when you're that age.

Did Dotty ever tell you why she moved to Hawaii in the first place? The story may bring you some comfort. She'd been dating a nice young man back in California. And then she'd gotten pregnant. Or at least, she thought she had. She was weeks late, and it absolutely terrified her. Dotty's boyfriend, on the other hand, had been thrilled. So thrilled that he'd proposed marriage. Dotty told me that her whole life had flashed before her eyes in that moment, as this perfect young man was down on one knee offering her all the things she suddenly knew she didn't want.

Dotty wasn't pregnant. Or maybe she was and she lost the baby early on. Either way, she was flooded with relief. She used her connections at the travel agency to book a flight and arrange lodging in Oahu. She'd saved up enough money to live there comfortably while she sorted things out. And that's just what she did.

Eventually, it was time for Dotty to return home. She'd been accepted to a university and was planning to study journalism. My mother had fallen ill with cancer, and I needed to stay behind to care for her. We promised to keep in touch. And I know we'd meant it. But it was much harder to do back then.

Years—decades—later, we ran into each other at a wedding. Life is funny that way. We've been the best of friends ever since.

I must sign off now to have a good cry. How lucky we

were to have Dotty in our lives. I'll miss her more than words
can say.

Sincerely,
Dr. Angela Hokule'a
Veterinarian
Oakland Animal Hospital

From: Rosie Benson
To: Lily Lopez-Benson
Subject: Fwd: Re: Dotty
Date: June 18

Isn't this the sweetest letter you've ever read?

From: Lily Lopez-Benson
To: Rosie Benson
Subject: Re: Fwd: Re: Dotty
Date: June 18

I'm swooning! Dotty's life was like a movie. You have to send this to your dad. I'm sure he's always wondered what Dotty was up to when she went to Hawaii. Have you been getting a lot of responses like this?

From: Rosie Benson
To: Lily Lopez-Benson
Subject: Re: Re: Fwd: Re: Dotty
Date: June 19

A few. Less than I would have thought. I'll forward you what I have, though.

CHAPTER NINETEEN

JULY

I looked up from my menu as a mustached server set a basket of warm bread on the white tablecloth. Pilar wasted no time in grabbing a roll for herself. "Isn't this place great?" she said as she dipped a chunk of bread in a pool of olive oil.

"We like it because we never run into anyone here," Evan added. "Plus, they don't charge extra for the rolls."

Evan and Pilar had invited me to join them for lunch at their favorite restaurant: an old-school steak house complete with cloth napkins and servers in tuxedos. Evan had taken pity on me after watching me eat lunch alone at my desk every day for the last three weeks. "This," he'd said, sweeping his hand in a gesture to include me, my limp caprese sandwich, and the *Forbes* magazine I'd stolen from the lobby, "is sad. You're coming to lunch with us today." And that had been that.

I'd never worked with anyone like Evan or Pilar before. They seemed like they were from a different planet, one where the buzzwords of the tech world didn't exist, where fancy perks were inconsequential, and where being cool simply didn't matter. They were completely unimpressed by the sheen of Silicon Valley.

"We've been coming here every Wednesday for the last six years," Pilar said through a mouthful of bread.

"To reminisce about the good old days and talk shit about Kate and Nadine," Evan added, finishing Pilar's thought. They reminded me a bit of Marcia and me. Before Raj, of course.

Evan and Pilar had met each other at work, back when Le Agency was Bell Recruiting. Pilar had just moved to San Francisco from New York, and Evan had just broken up with his live-in boyfriend. They were both in desperate need of a new friend.

They bonded over a shared love of darts (played exclusively in dive bars, preferably in the Mission District), documentaries about cults and con artists, and the belief that Weezer's Blue album was far superior to the Green one (I disagreed but didn't dare mention it). That, and work. In spite of their indifference toward the tech scene, they both actually liked their jobs.

"You should have seen the office before Nadine. It was straight out of the nineties," Pilar said, her tone almost wistful. "There was Formica everywhere."

Evan shuddered. "It was hideous. I have to hand it to Nadine; the renovations are a huge improvement."

Pilar rolled her eyes. "That's about the only improvement since she took over. Bell was something special, and Nadine wrecked it."

Nadine *was* particular, always looking over our shoulders as we reviewed new applications, listening in on our phone screens, and insisting on meeting every candidate who walked through the door. At the end of each interview, she'd stop by our desks for a debrief, quizzing us on the person's qualifications, salary requirements, and career goals before sharing her assessment—usually that the candidate needed a haircut, a manicure, or a new suit, which inevitably elicited a scoff from Pilar.

When I sheepishly confessed that I didn't think Nadine was

that bad, Pilar eyed me with exaggerated pity from across the table.

"You'll see her true colors eventually. Just give it time," Evan said, drumming his fingertips together in a spot-on impression of Mr. Burns.

I didn't want to see her true colors. I needed Nadine to be the savior I'd built her up to be because I was determined to make this job work. I'd already thrown myself into soaking up every ounce of advice I could from Nadine and Pilar. And I'd even sat in on a couple of Kate's interviews. Not that I'd learned anything. She spent most of the time asking job seekers where they'd gotten their "adorable" shoes.

I'd gotten my first placement that week. It was a minor assignment—a short-term receptionist backfill at a start-up in SoMa—but Nadine had acted as if I'd successfully completed a heart transplant. "I'll take you shopping to celebrate," she'd purred. She was always throwing around prizes and incentives like that: bottles of fancy champagne, dinners at Michelin-starred restaurants, designer purses. Nadine had even gifted Kate with a Gucci wallet that she'd immediately started obviously and obnoxiously leaving out on her desk. I secretly hoped someone would swipe it.

* * *

On Friday, Nadine called a team meeting. She'd ordered lunch from her favorite restaurant, insisting that we all try the house salad. "Isn't the balsamic dressing to die for?" she asked after we'd gathered around the marble table in the conference room.

"Absolutely to die for," Kate said. Pilar rolled her eyes before biting into a tuna melt. Nadine's lip curled, almost imperceptibly.

"Please stop clicking your pen. It's driving me crazy," Pilar chided Evan, who refused to look up from his phone. He elbowed Pilar in response but didn't stop.

"Hey, Pilar," Kate said, tossing her hair over her shoulder. Pilar visibly bristled. "How did your meeting with Tox go? Do they need a receptionist? Because I met this girl Priya yesterday and I think she'd be perfect. She just graduated from fashion school, and her shoes were—"

"I'm not ready to look at candidates for Tox yet," Pilar interrupted. "And please stop pitching candidates based on their outfits."

"Well, it's a *design* firm, so I figured they'd want someone with good taste."

Pilar fished a miniature pickle out of the bottom of a paper bag and eyed it thoughtfully before popping the whole thing into her mouth. Kate crinkled her nose.

"Speaking of your accounts, Pilar," Nadine said, jabbing at a piece of lettuce with her fork, "I wanted to talk about some changes that are in the works. Our account loads are very lopsided." She held one hand higher than the other. "So I've decided that we need to redistribute." She brought her hands level with each other.

"What does that mean?" Pilar's voice was flat, but something flashed behind her eyes.

Nadine's face was the picture of patience. "Great question. I'm reshuffling everyone's accounts. We're going to bring some of the oldest clients in-house and redistribute the rest a little more evenly among the three of you." She looked around the table expectantly.

"What does 'in-house' mean?" Evan asked, his tone accusatory.

Pilar huffed. "It means Nadine wants to take my most successful accounts for herself so that she won't have to pay my commissions anymore."

"Not quite," Nadine replied. "I want to take the more tenured accounts off your plate. They're practically running themselves at this point."

"So all the earnings from the accounts I manage will now go straight to you."

"Straight into the business," Nadine corrected. "I'll be reinvesting the additional funds directly into Le Agency."

"And then you want to take the rest of my accounts—the clients I've managed for years—and give them to Kate and Rosie?"

I made a futile attempt to flatten myself against my chair at the mention of my name. I knew Pilar's anger wasn't personal. Nadine was messing with her income. Evan had told me that Pilar's commissions far outpaced her base salary.

Nadine rested her fork on the side of her plate and reached for a napkin. She held Pilar's gaze as she wiped her hands. "Well, technically, Pilar, they're all Le Agency accounts. And, as the owner of Le Agency, I can do whatever I want with them."

Pilar started to protest but Nadine stopped her. "It's already done. You'll all be getting your new account lists on Monday."

My heart fluttered at the thought of having my own clients, but I refused to let on. I could feel Pilar seething beside me.

"This is bullshit," she muttered under her breath.

Nadine pretended not to notice. "Growing pains are inevitable," she said smoothly. She was in total control. "Especially during the first year after a transition. But I hope you can all use this as a learning opportunity. Rosie, Kate, I want you two to get some practice managing the client side of things. And Pilar"—her tone sharpened—"now that you'll have a lighter workload, you can focus on bringing in new business."

"Thank you for trusting us with this, Nadine," Kate said. "We won't let you down."

Pilar stood abruptly and left without saying a word. I watched through the glass wall as she stomped to the front office and jerked her head toward the door, a signal to Evan to join her in the hall-way. He backed away from behind the table and followed her out. If Nadine was annoyed by Pilar's response, she didn't let on. "Rosie," she said, changing the subject with jarring nonchalance, "are we still on for shopping this afternoon?"

I gulped down a half-chewed crouton and nodded. "Absolutely."

* * *

"I'm so glad we were able to make this work," Nadine said, holding the door open for me. I stepped inside the boutique she'd chosen for my shopping spree and felt instantly frumpy. Every inch of the shop was covered in palm leaf wallpaper, ornate mirrors, and crystal sconces. Sleek satin blouses, cashmere sweaters, and jumpsuits with plunging necklines hung from brass clothing racks. It smelled like expensive coconuts. "Isn't this place fabulous?"

"I didn't even know it was here."

"It's one of my favorite places to—" Nadine stopped midsentence to snap her fingers at the woman behind the counter. I suppressed a wince at the rude gesture. She was giving off serious Miranda Priestly vibes. "We're going to need a fitting room," she called. The woman nodded before ducking behind the counter to grab a key. Nadine returned her attention to me. "You have two hundred and fifty dollars to spend on anything you want."

My eyes swept around the store, uncertain where to start. I could feel Nadine watching me. "Do you have any special events coming up?"

Marcia had invited me to go to another one of her PR parties that weekend, but I'd turned her down. I wasn't ready to hang out with her. I figured she'd rather take Raj, anyway. "Not really."

"Hmm." Nadine pressed the tip of her finger against her chin as if she were puzzling over nuclear physics. "No networking events? Weddings? Trips?"

I shook my head, feeling increasingly lame.

"Dates with a special someone?"

My cheeks warmed at the thought of Donovan. My *boyfriend*, Donovan. "Maybe."

"Ah, young love. Who's the lucky guy?"

I hesitated, weighing whether I should tell Nadine that I was dating Donovan, the person who'd referred me for this very job. I didn't want her to think I was the type of woman who dated successful men just to get ahead. But there wasn't much point in lying, either. "It's Donovan Ng, actually," I said, trying not to cringe.

Nadine flashed a wolfish smile. "Rosie Benson. I'm impressed. Good for you."

I didn't love the way her overly positive reaction made me feel, but I couldn't put my finger on why. "Thanks?"

"I'm going to find you the perfect outfit for your next date!" She proceeded to flit around the boutique, piling skirts, sweaters, shoes, and jewelry on top of a low-slung chaise lounge at the center of the room. She never once glanced at a price tag. After she'd picked her way through the entire store, she ushered me into a dressing room. I obliged, trying on an assortment of high-waisted jeans, hip-hugging pencil skirts, and buttery smooth blouses as Nadine sipped a glass of champagne.

"How do you like Le Agency so far?" Nadine asked, her tone casual. "Better than Driftwood?"

I used to break into a nervous sweat when Raj would ask me

how things were going. But Nadine's question didn't trigger a single drop. I tugged a navy blue dress over my head. "I don't have the words to describe how much better."

I pictured Nadine taking a satisfied sip of champagne on the other side of the door. "I'm so glad to hear that. You're doing a fantastic job."

I beamed at myself in the mirror. I could get used to receiving compliments from my boss. I smoothed the neckline of my dress and stepped out of the fitting room. Nadine crinkled her nose. "We can do better. Try the jumpsuit." I nodded and shut the door.

"How are things with Pilar?"

I hesitated, uncertain words catching in my throat.

"I don't mean to make you uncomfortable," Nadine said. "I'm genuinely curious. And I know you two spend a lot of time together."

I returned the dress to its hanger and weighed my options. I didn't want to betray Pilar, but Nadine was my boss. It wasn't very professional of Nadine to be asking me this, was it? I decided to state the obvious. "I think she is really upset about the new account thing."

Nadine sighed audibly. "I feel terrible about that. What Evan and Pilar don't fully understand is that the business was in shambles when I bought it. It was barely turning a profit after all the bills were paid and commissions were settled."

Evan and Pilar always made it sound like the agency was in its prime before Nadine came along and wasted a bunch of money on office renovations and fancy espresso machines.

"Those two have the former owner on a pedestal," she continued. "I'd rather have them think I'm the bad guy than expose the truth about their old boss. I think it would break their hearts."

I believed Evan and Pilar, but it seemed like Nadine was doing what she thought was right. Even if she was being kind of shady about it. Maybe she didn't always handle everything perfectly, but being an entrepreneur was hard. Regardless, I didn't want to be in the middle of any of it. This job was working for me, and that was all I cared about.

Nadine gasped as I emerged from the dressing room in the jumpsuit she'd insisted I save for last. "It was made for you," she said, rising from the chaise. She placed a gentle hand on each of my shoulders and steered me toward a mirror.

"Donovan won't be able to resist you in this," she said, a mischievous smile tugging at the corners of her mouth.

The thick fabric hugged me in all the right places, from the plunging neckline down to the cropped ankle. I'd never looked this put together before. I felt like a grown-up. A mini-Nadine.

I had to admit, I didn't hate it.

Hey there, Rosie!

I hope you and your family are holding up okay, all things considered. We sure do miss Dotty around here.

Speaking of, I'd love to have you back out for a visit if you're up for it. Barb's been asking about you. And you know how persistent she can be. Any chance you're free next Saturday?

I also have a proposition for you. I don't mean to be cryptic, but I always enjoy having fun chats in person.

Sending a chorus of moos, oinks, and cock-a-doodle-doos to you!

Warmly,
Sonia

CHAPTER TWENTY

Barb was the first to greet me when I arrived at Happy Hooves. I'd barely had time to put the car in park before she pressed her big, mushy nose against the driver's-side window. Apparently she'd missed me.

I crawled into the passenger seat and out the door as Barb looked on, her tail swishing gently. "Morning, Barb," I said before craning my neck around the dirt patch that passed for a parking lot in search of Sonia.

Sonia's email couldn't have come at a better time. Donovan was going to be gone all weekend, so I needed somewhere else to hide from Marcia. Things between us had gone from hostile to tense to unbearably polite. We were treating each other as if we were strangers who'd met on Craigslist, exchanging vague pleasantries over coffee and wearing tight smiles as we passed each other in the hallway.

Barb and I finished saying our hellos (me scratching her snout and her letting me) before making our way over to the barn. There, we found the Flintstones waiting patiently behind the gate. Wilma let out a high-pitched bleat as I got closer. Barb huffed a response. I unhooked the metal latch as the door swung open, much to the goats' delight. They hurried to me, surrounding me like fans at a concert. "Hi, guys. I've missed you," I said, meaning it.

"Morning," Sonia called from one of the stalls. I looked up as she stabbed a pitchfork into a pile of hay. She brushed her hands on her jeans, sending tiny specks of dust and dirt flying. "I see my welcoming committee are taking their jobs seriously."

"I'll say." Fred gave me a nudge. I turned to pet him, scratching right between his curved horns.

Sonia laughed. "Well, we're all thrilled to have you back. Go ahead and finish saying hello. I'll get you some gloves." She clomped away into the barn.

I sensed Barb's jealous gaze as I petted Pebbles and Bamm-Bamm behind their floppy ears and under their little goateed chins. "Better get to work," I said, loud enough for Barb to hear. "Don't want my boss to get mad." Barb swung her head toward the barn, gesturing for me to get a move on. It was official: I loved that cow.

Soon enough, I was scraping soiled hay off the floor of the Flintstones' enclosure and dropping it into a waiting wheelbarrow. Barb looked on, swatting flies away with an occasional swish of her tail. We fell into a rhythm: scrape, swish, drop, scrape, swish, drop. I could hear Rocket crowing in the distance, enveloped in a symphony of chirps and quacks and oinks and grunts. Music to my weary ears.

"Have a minute?" Sonia poked her head around the sliding door. She was barely taller than Barb and almost just as stocky.

I set my shovel perpendicular to the floor and balanced an arm on the handle. "Only if it's okay with you-know-who," I said, shooting a look at Barb.

Sonia turned to the large cow and patted her side. "I think she'll be fine. As long as we work while we talk." As she stepped inside, I could have sworn the enclosure got brighter. There was something about Sonia, a kindness, maybe, that emanated from her. Like a glow.

She jammed a shovel into a mound of yellowed hay. "Have you heard from Peter recently?"

"Peter Simpson, Esquire?"

Sonia grinned. "That's the one."

I shook my head. "Not since he went over Dotty's will with us."

"Ah," Sonia said, dropping a clump of hay into her wheelbarrow. "In that case, you know that Dotty wanted most of her remaining assets to go to charity."

"Yes," I said slowly, the memory of that afternoon crystalizing in my mind. "Peter said that if anything was left after she repaid her debts, it would be donated. And it sounded like there wouldn't be much."

Sonia raised her eyebrows in amusement. "Is that right?"

I nodded.

She laughed to herself. It sounded a bit like Pickles the donkey. "Peter can be a bit of a prankster. Dotty left the sanctuary nearly half a million dollars."

The shovel slipped from my hands, landing on the concrete floor with a metallic thump. "What?"

"Half a million dollars," Sonia repeated. "I guess she'd made some good investments over the years."

"I don't know what to say. That's . . . incredible."

"Dotty was pretty incredible."

"She was."

We stood there, basking in the memory of Dotty's wonderfulness until Barb interrupted us with a loud *moo*. I picked up my shovel in an act of appeasement, but my thoughts lingered on Dotty. "If Dotty had all that money, why was she still working at her age?"

"Dotty loved her job." I could tell from the way Sonia said this—plainly, matter-of-factly—that Sonia loved *her* job, too.

Being in the presence of Sonia's uncomplicated happiness knocked something loose in my heart. I fought the urge to hug her. To thank her for being Dotty's friend, for giving me another missing piece of the Dotty puzzle.

"Speaking of work," Sonia continued, shooting Barb a look. "With this new influx of funds, I can finally afford to hire an assistant manager for the sanctuary. It's going to be something of a catchall job. They'd have to do a little bit of everything—fundraising, planning events, giving tours, managing volunteers, and of course, caring for the animals . . ." She paused, wriggling her eyebrows. "Does that sound like something you might be interested in?"

I paused midshovel. Was Sonia offering me a job? "I don't know," I said, honestly. "Maybe."

"No need to give me an answer just yet," she said quickly. "And no matter what, I hope you'll keep volunteering. The animals adore you." Sonia smiled. So did I. Then she scooped another pile before continuing, "I'd need your help in the office, too. I think your mornings could be spent with the animals, and then we could get you set up with a desk up at the house—if you take the job, that is."

Sonia flipped the shovel over, pressing the broad side into the growing mound in the wheelbarrow before going back for another scoop. "You could start whenever you're ready. But no pressure, of course."

"Wouldn't I need to . . . interview first?"

She raised her arm to her forehead, wiping at a sheen of sweat that had formed above her dark eyebrows. "This was your interview." She jerked her head toward Barb. "If the boss approves, you're okay in my book. Plus, you are so great with all the other animals. I can tell they trust you. That's half the battle."

"I don't know what to say," I managed. "Thank you."

Sonia smiled, her eyes crinkling around the edges. "Don't thank me yet. We haven't talked money. I can't afford much now, but I'll keep working on it. That'll be part of your job, actually. Fundraising. I'd love to expand. More staff, more animals, more land." She looked off into the distance before returning her gaze to me. "Anyway, for now, I can pay you forty-five thousand a year."

I did my best to keep my face neutral. That was a lot less than what I was earning at Le Agency. And there would be no hope of commissions here. I wasn't sure if I could make it work between my loans and increased rent. And I'd be commuting.

"I know it's not much," Sonia continued, sensing my hesitation. I started to protest, but she held up a hand. "I do have a potential solution, although I'm not sure how appealing it would be to a young city dweller like yourself." She leaned her shovel against the wall and gestured for me to do the same. "Come with me."

I followed Sonia around the barn and past the chicken coop to a small stucco bungalow with a wooden door and red, tiled roof. It wasn't much bigger than the shed where Dad stored his tools in the backyard. "This," Sonia said, sweeping her arm toward the little house, "is the groundskeeper's cottage. At least, it was, until he moved out a couple months ago." She turned to face me. "What do you think?"

"It's . . . cute," I said, not sure what she wanted from me.

She turned back to face the cottage. "It needs a bit of work, but it has everything—a full bathroom, kitchen, microwave. Even a little nook for a desk. I'd be happy to lease it to you if you want. Your utilities would be included, of course. So you'd just have to pay rent. We could call it eight hundred a month?"

"You'd want me to . . . live here?"

"Only if you want to," she said quickly. "There's no pressure. I just figured I'd offer, in case cheap rent and no commute might make it worthwhile for you." She stared at the little house, the lower half coated in a thick layer of dirt. "I know it'd be an adjustment. After city life."

That was an understatement. And as idyllic as living in that little house might be, I knew I couldn't leave the city. Not yet. I liked eating out every night, being close to Donovan, working at a fancy agency with blindingly white marble floors. And, I realized, I really did want to get back to a good place with Marcia.

If I took this job, if I moved here, I'd be abandoning everything I'd been working so hard to build.

But this was a dream come true.

Wasn't it?

I knew what Dotty would say. She would tell me to go for it, to live my life the way I'd always wanted to. She'd say that life was short and finding a job you truly loved was rare.

"This means so much to me, Sonia," I said. "I promise I'll think about it."

"Good. And there are no hard feelings either way. Whatever you decide, I'll understand. I was young once, too, you know."

We stood there outside the cottage, Sonia picturing her past and me trying to picture my future until Barb let out a long, leisurely moo, tugging us back to reality. "All right, Miss Bossy," Sonia said, giving Barb a pat on the side before turning to me. "We'll get back to work."

As the three of us walked back toward the barn, Barb leading the way, I could feel my heart breaking a little with every step. Because I was almost positive that I wasn't going to take the job.

From: Vera North
To: Rosie Benson
Subject: Re: Dotty
Date: June 20

Hi Rosie,

My deepest condolences to you and your family. Dotty was an extraordinary lady and will be so missed. Were you planning to hold a funeral service for her? Your email didn't say. It would be nice to get a little closure. I'd love to come if I haven't missed it already.

Your great-aunt and I worked together on a local election back in the '90s. I'm old too, like her. Dotty took a sabbatical from the paper to head up the communications team. I was the campaign manager. We won.

You asked if Dotty had any regrets. I love that question. If you live long enough, you'll have a few. I certainly do! Dotty was a very contented woman, very happy with her life. But I do recall one late-night conversation where she said that she wished she'd "started sooner." When I asked her to clarify, she said something like, "We all waste so much time trying to fit into other people's boxes. I wish I'd started building my own box sooner." Dotty did get a bit of a later start on her career. And there was so much she wanted to do and see in her life. But, to play devil's advocate, our generation wasn't exactly set up for success in that department. Women weren't encouraged to pursue much of anything outside of heteronormative marriage and motherhood back then. And we both know Dotty wanted neither of those things.

I like to think of it like this: Dotty loved the life she built for herself so much that her biggest regret was that she didn't start building it earlier.

I don't know that a gal could hope for much more.

I hope this helps. Let me know about the funeral.

Take care,

Vera

CHAPTER TWENTY-ONE

"G ood morning, roomie," Raj said, with more cheer than was appropriate for a Monday. "Can I pour you a cup?" He held a large pot of coffee in one hand, a mug in the other, an overly enthusiastic smile on his face. It took everything in me not to stare at his striped boxer shorts. Did he have to walk around the apartment like that?

I rubbed my hands up and down my face and grumbled a response. Annoyed or not, I wasn't one to turn down caffeine. "Sure."

"Sugar?" Raj chirped.

I shook my head. "Black's fine."

"Sophisticated." He jabbed the brimming cup in my direction.

Raj's apartment had conveniently flooded over the weekend. He'd be sleeping over for the foreseeable future and, in an apparent attempt to soften the blow, had taken to kissing my ass whenever we bumped into each other. I muttered something that sounded like thank you before shuffling back down the hallway.

"You can't avoid me forever, Rosie," he called after me. The way his voice cracked, ever so slightly, stopped me, but I didn't turn around. "But I think you need to hear this from me first." He paused, maybe gathering courage. "I'm so sorry. For everything. I didn't handle any of this the right way, and I feel terrible."

I eyed the mug of coffee in my hands. There wasn't enough

caffeine in the world to prepare me for this conversation, but I might as well get this over with. I pivoted on my heel to face Raj. "Go on."

"I never should have used Marcia's picture as an excuse to fire you. I should have been straight up with you. I tried to talk to you about how things were going so many times, but I always chickened out. I kept thinking you'd take the hint, but that wasn't fair to you. You didn't deserve that." I couldn't detect even an ounce of the corny Tech Bro persona I was used to seeing from Raj. He was being genuine.

I smiled. "Are you saying I didn't deserve to get fired?"

He smirked in response. "Oh no. You definitely deserved to get fired. But you didn't deserve to be blindsided."

That was fair. Even though it hurt to admit to myself, I knew it was true. "I know," I said. My face twisted into an involuntary wince. "And I'm sorry about that. About the whole being-a-bad-employee thing. That must have been hard for you."

The muscles around his jaw visibly relaxed. He looked relieved. "Thanks. It's forgotten—water under the bridge," he said before glancing at Marcia's door. "We never should have snuck around behind your back. If we could go back in time and do it all over again, we would. In a heartbeat."

There was that *we* again. As much as I hated it, Marcia and Raj were very much a *we*. Despite my efforts to avoid them, I'd glimpsed moments of their blissful coupledom—cooking dinner, washing and drying dishes, giggling in Marcia's bedroom. Even playing with Bug. This was not how I'd expected my best friend to find love. Or the person I ever would have dreamed she'd find it with. But, in spite of myself, I was happy for her. For them.

I allowed my posture to soften. "I appreciate that," I said, forcing myself to meet his eyes. "I probably wouldn't have had the best reaction no matter how I found out. It was kind of a lose-lose situation."

Raj dipped his head with a laugh. "You aren't very subtle about your feelings. Neither is Marcia."

"That's one of my favorite things about her."

"Mine too."

And there it was: we both loved Marcia. And now it was time to find a way to share her, to move forward. I needed to wipe the slate clean.

He sighed. "She really misses you, you know."

I squeezed my lips together. I was not going to cry in front of Raj. I nodded, then said, "I've got to get ready for work. Thanks for the coffee. And the talk."

"You're welcome. Thanks for giving me a chance."

I turned toward my bedroom door as Raj started toward Marcia's. "Hey, Raj?" I said, pausing with my hand on the knob. "Can you just do me one small favor?"

Hope pooled in his eyes, giving me the impression that I could ask him for just about anything, so long as I was willing to call a truce. "Sure."

"Will you burn that ugly vest you always wear?"

He laughed, white teeth flashing. "Only if you light the match."

He was trying. I had to give him that.

* * *

When I got to the office, something was off. At first, I was pretty sure it was me. Sonia's offer had been kicking around my brain all weekend. I felt like I was being ripped in two, pulled by the old Rosie and the new one. And I wasn't sure who I wanted to win.

The office was quiet. And cold. And virtually empty. Only Kate sat at her desk, humming along to whatever song was playing through her earbuds.

"Where is everyone?" I asked as I rolled the chair out from be-hind my desk.

Kate pulled out an earbud. "What?"

I repeated my question, more slowly this time, and she frowned in response. "Not sure. Nadine's door was closed when I got here."

I glanced at Pilar's desk. It looked as neat as ever, but her bag wasn't anywhere in sight. "Did Pilar have a meeting this morning?"

"How should I know?"

"Is Evan in the back?"

Kate attempted to suppress an eye roll. "I haven't seen them." She gestured toward her monitor. "I just got my new account list and I have to introduce myself. It's important."

Kate loved reminding me how important her clients were. I hadn't been at Le Agency long, but I already knew this job wasn't rocket science. She wasn't fooling me. "Don't let me stop you." She flashed me an "okay" sign that seemed more like a "fuck off" and turned back toward her computer. This morning was going to require lots of caffeine.

The kitchen looked untouched, which was odd because Evan was usually on his second iced coffee by now. Had he and Pilar decided to take the day off? It was way too foggy out to justify a beach day. Not that I'd be taking one of those ever again. I fired up the espresso machine and did my best not to salivate as the glorious smell of roasted beans filled the room.

"Bullshit." I jumped at the sound of a muffled, disembodied voice coming from the main office. I peered out from the kitchen. Kate sat at her desk, earbuds in, typing away.

". . . not my problem." This voice was different, but equally muffled. It sounded like it was coming from the wall. The wall the kitchen shared with Nadine's office.

I took a step closer, careful to stay on my toes to avoid making a sound with my new heels. I pressed my ear to the wall.

"You're stealing from me." It was Pilar.

"Running a proper business . . ." That was Nadine.

I heard Evan grumble something, but I couldn't make out what.

". . . doesn't concern you," Nadine said, her tone sharp.

They were fighting about Pilar's accounts again. My heart sank for Pilar. I couldn't blame her for trying to get her clients back. But I also understood why Nadine was doing things this way. The espresso machine beeped, but I ignored it.

"That noncompete is meaningless . . . know it," Pilar said.

"Tell that to my lawyers," Nadine replied.

"What the hell are you doing?" The sharp, unmuffled sound of Kate's voice sent my pulse racing. I spun to face her where she stood, arms crossed, leaning against the entrance to the kitchen. "Are you spying?"

I pressed my hand over my heart in an attempt to slow my breathing. "You scared me."

"You mean I caught you," she said, too loudly.

I shushed her. "Evan and Pilar are in there with Nadine," I whispered. "They're fighting."

Kate scrunched her nose. "About what? The account thing?" I nodded. "But I already sent out my introductions. She can't take them away from me now."

Kate had had her grubby little hands on Pilar's clients for all of fifteen minutes and was already territorial. I shot her a look before pressing my ear back to the wall. She followed suit.

". . . wouldn't dare," Nadine's voice came through the wall.

"Watch me," Pilar said. Evan muttered something in support.

There was a flurry of voices, followed by the sound of chairs scraping against wood. Kate's eyes widened. "They're coming." She darted back toward her desk, heels clicking every step of the way.

I glanced at my waiting espresso and back to my lifeless monitor. I decided the espresso could wait. I slipped off my shoes and sprinted to my chair.

Seconds later, Evan and Pilar emerged from Nadine's office. I plastered a smile on my face as I spun in my chair, hoping to appear casual and oblivious. It didn't matter. No one was paying attention to me.

Evan's typically pale cheeks glowed pink. Pilar's eyes looked puffier than usual. If I didn't know better, I might have assumed she'd been crying. But I was pretty confident that Pilar never cried. Nadine watched from the doorway, arms crossed as Pilar began wordlessly emptying her desk drawers. She tossed business cards, notebooks, a handful of spare change, and what looked like a box of hair dye into a waiting tote bag and slung it over her shoulder. Evan picked up the half-dead fern from the corner of Pilar's desk and cradled it like a baby.

"What's going on?" I asked.

Pilar's eyes darted to mine. "We'll fill you in later," she said quietly.

"Good luck with that one," Evan said, jerking his head toward Nadine. Pilar cast a final cursory glance over her desk before joining him at his side. They walked toward the lobby, never looking back. As they rounded the corner, Evan lifted his hand above his head, middle finger raised. Then they were gone.

Kate and I turned in unison toward Nadine, who remained fixed in the doorway. "Evan and Pilar no longer work for Le Agency," she said. There was an edge to her voice that I'd never heard before. "Kate, can you call that girl you met last week and ask her to cover the front desk today?" Kate nodded. "Good. And can you two divide up Pilar's interviews between yourselves? I'll be in my office, deciding what to do with her remaining accounts." She disappeared behind the frosted glass door without waiting for an answer.

I drooped against the back of my chair, unable to process what had just happened. Had Nadine fired Pilar and Evan? That would be extreme at best. Cruel at worst.

Kate leaned toward my desk, eyes wide. "Do you mind if I take Pilar's TickerTape account?"

Vulture.

*　*　*

Nadine locked herself in her office for the better part of the day, muttering something about damage control. Kate and I soldiered on, divvying up Pilar's appointments and rescheduling meetings. My mind swirled with possibilities. I was dying to know what had happened in that office. But Nadine wasn't interested in talking. And my texts to Evan and Pilar went unreturned.

"What do you mean Pilar isn't available? My assistant just quit, and I need a replacement *now*. Where is she?" I held the phone away from my ear. The CEO of Merkle, Merkle, and Troy sounded like she was about six seconds away from a full-blown meltdown.

I wasn't sure if we were supposed to tell Pilar's clients that she didn't work at Le Agency anymore, but I'd gotten pretty good at artfully dodging uncomfortable lines of questioning. I was terrible at selling things, but I knew how to calm people down. Years of dealing with Mom had prepared me well.

"I'm so sorry about your assistant," I said, infusing as much empathy into my voice as I could. "You must be so stressed out."

There was a sigh on the other end of the phone. "You have no idea."

"Well, don't worry, I can have a replacement for you in no time. Just give me a moment." I pulled up Pilar's client file and gave it a quick scan. According to Pilar's notes, MM&T was a CPA firm, and Corrinne Phelps, CEO, was an "old school badass." That meant I probably couldn't get away with sending any of Nadine's favorites—CPAs didn't really care whether someone had good style. "Do you need someone with a finance background?"

I pictured Corrinne rubbing her temples on the other end of the line. "That would be ideal."

"And will they need to handle any personal errands for you?"

"Just dry cleaning. And maybe an occasional trip to the post office."

"Anything else I should know?"

"I hate it when people are late."

"Me too," I said. She didn't need to know about my propensity for running ten minutes behind to just about everything.

I opened my active candidate folder and scanned the list of names. I'd met with more than a hundred people over the last few weeks, and I didn't have a photographic memory like Pilar. But I knew what I was looking for: someone who wore suits, could handle a hard-nosed boss like Corrinne, and didn't care about fancy perks. That's when I spotted him: Raúl Ramos. Raúl was in his midforties, a former associate at a big four accounting firm who'd pivoted into administrative work after a particularly rough tax season. He'd worn a suit to our interview and had clearly stated that he wouldn't set foot in a start-up.

"Okay, I've got someone. I'll have to call him to make sure he's interested, but I know he can start immediately. I'll send you his résumé now."

I waited as Corrinne read it over. "He's a unicorn," she said. "Do you think he'd take forty-five dollars an hour?"

I knew he'd take forty, but there was no need to tell Corrinne that. Instead, I said, "I'll check with him and get back to you ASAP."

When Raúl answered, I pitched him on Corrinne's job. He was elated—he might have even called me his hero.

I hung up with Raúl and sank back in my chair, relishing the high of another successful placement. I liked this part of my job. I was *good* at this part of my job. I wasn't ready to leave it behind yet—not even for Barb. I was just getting started.

When Nadine finally reappeared, she was clutching an expensive-looking bottle of champagne in one hand and plastic flutes in the other. "I have an announcement," she said brightly, her icy demeanor gone as if this morning had never happened.

Kate and I looked on in bewildered silence as Nadine made quick work of the bottle, twisting the cork off with a well-practiced flourish. She then filled three glasses, passing one to each of us before raising her own. She peeled her red lips into a smile and drew a long breath. "One of you is going to get a promotion."

Kate squealed as her shoulders crept toward her ears. "Really?"

"Really."

"With Pilar gone, we're going to need a new senior recruiter to balance out the team. And I'd love to promote from within. From what I've seen, you both have what it takes to be successful leaders at Le Agency."

Kate's eyes darted in my direction. "But I've been here longer." She leaned forward for effect. "A year longer."

I kept my face neutral. Kate had a point, but I wasn't going to acknowledge that if I didn't have to. Nadine rested her hip against Pilar's old desk. "You know," she said, as if she were about to let us in on a special little secret. "When I first started out in recruiting, I got promoted twice in six months."

Kate sunk back into her chair. She looked a bit like a deflated orange balloon.

"That's amazing," I said, summoning Kate-like enthusiasm.

Nadine fluttered her hand. "I was in the right place at the right time. Plus, I worked my ass off." She took a delicate sip of champagne. Somehow her lips left no mark on the glass. I made a mental note to ask where she got her lipstick. Probably at a store I couldn't afford.

For now.

"I want to give you both a fair shot, so I'll be evaluating your respective performances over the next few weeks. So you'd better bring it."

I felt a case of emotional whiplash coming on, but I pushed it aside. I could grieve Evan and Pilar's departure later. For now, it seemed they'd done me a favor. In a matter of months, I'd gone from woefully unemployed to being on the verge of a promotion.

As Nadine strode back toward her office, I allowed myself to daydream about how it would feel to be a senior recruiter. And how much more money I'd be able to make. I could start to build up my wardrobe again. Maybe I'd even be able to afford an espresso maker.

"Oh," Nadine said, casually pivoting at the entrance to her office. "If Evan and Pilar reach out to you, I'm going to need you to ignore them—politely, of course. I hate to have to ask this of you, but sometimes, when people are desperate, they'll spread all kinds of lies to save face. And I wouldn't want to put either of you in that position." She gave a grave shake of her head before disappearing behind the door.

I swiveled in my chair to find Kate's eyes boring into my forehead. "I hope we can still be friends after I get my promotion."

I stared back, matching her intensity. "*Still* be friends?"

She shot me a smirk before turning back to face her computer.

* * *

Pilar called as I was getting into an Uber headed for Donovan's condo. I answered it as quickly as I could, Nadine's cryptic warning be damned. "What happened today?"

"What happened to hello?"

Leave it to Pilar to keep sarcasm alive at a time like this. "Hello. What happened today?"

I could sense her smirk through the phone. "Nadine didn't tell you? I quit."

Relief rushed through my limbs. If I was going to make things work at Le Agency, I needed Nadine to not be the bad guy. "Why?"

"Well, you know how she took all my biggest accounts and my commissions were going to drop by thousands of dollars overnight?"

"Yeah."

"She claimed that the agency was on the verge of bankruptcy and said that I had to pitch in and take one for the team, but that's a lie."

"How do you know?"

"Evan pulled all the recent financial reports, and the company is more profitable now than ever. The only thing that's changed is Nadine's salary. It's doubled in the last month. She's basically taking money out of my pocket and putting it directly in hers."

The car stopped at a red light. The sun had slipped behind the city skyline, and the sidewalks were crowded with people getting off work or meeting up with friends for happy hour. "What did Nadine say?"

"When Evan confronted her with the info, she went ballistic. She fired him."

"I thought you said you quit?"

"Yeah, *I* quit. In solidarity. I wasn't going to let him take the fall on his own." She huffed. "Plus, I couldn't stand the idea of working for her now that I know the truth."

The Uber lurched forward, making my stomach flip. Nadine had been lying to everyone. Is that why she'd told me not to talk to Evan or Pilar?

"You still there?" I could hear Pilar eating something crunchy on the other end of the call.

"Yeah. Just processing everything," I replied.

"What did Nadine tell you?"

"Nothing, really. Just that you weren't working for Le Agency anymore. And that I shouldn't talk to you."

Pilar barked a laugh. "That's rich. She doesn't want us tipping you off. What a snake."

"What are you going to do?"

"I have some ideas," Pilar said. "I need a few weeks to get my shit together, but I'll be fine."

Pilar's casual tone helped to slow my racing heart. "That's good."

"I'm sorry you're stuck there. Do you want any help finding a new job?"

Traffic slowed as we neared the ballpark. The streets were choked with orange-and-black-clad Giants fans heading for the entrance. "I haven't even thought about it."

"Well, you should. I'd get out of there ASAP if I were you."

"Nadine said she might promote me to senior recruiter."

I heard Pilar blow out a long breath. "Rosie, you're a great recruiter, but Nadine is never going to promote you." Her voice was gentler than I'd ever heard it before.

"You really think she'd pick Kate over me?"

"I think she'll pick herself over everyone else."

* * *

My mind swirled as I approached Donovan's condo. I felt like I'd absorbed the chaos of the city on the drive, its frenetic energy mingling with Pilar's revelation and Nadine's lies.

But when Donovan answered the door, the swirling stopped. He wore a striped button-down shirt, untucked and rolled at the sleeves. His hair was slightly mussed, but in an effortlessly perfect way. It was all I could do not to jump his bones when he smiled at me.

"Hi, Rosie Benson," he said before pulling me in for a kiss. "I just opened a bottle of wine and sushi is on the way."

"Donovan Ng, you are a literal saint," I said. Then I kissed him again.

I'd never been with anyone like Donovan before. He was so grown-up, so confident, so sure about what he wanted. I was starting to think that I wanted those things, too.

Donovan, I realized, had become my escape. When I was with him, I didn't worry about work or my family or Raj. Donovan's pristine condo, with its heated floors, bare white walls, and sleek furniture, was intoxicating. I loved spending most of my evenings there, wrapped in a protective bubble of fancy takeout and wine and sex.

Things with Donovan were blissfully uncomplicated. And I needed uncomplicated.

Dear Dotty,

Sonia offered me a job at Happy Hooves the other day. But I had to turn her down.

I know, I know. It sounds like I've lost my mind.

At first, I thought something must be wrong with me. Why wouldn't I want this job? Wasn't this my dream? But then I talked to Donovan, and he made me feel so much better. He said that I was building a real career at Le Agency, that leaving to work at Happy Hooves would be like hopping off the ladder on the bottom rung. And I have so much room left to climb.

I might even get a promotion soon. It's a long story, but I think it's worth sticking with Le Agency to see if I can do it. I've only been there a couple of months, almost, and I've already learned so much. I'm actually good at this job, Dotty. I've never had that before.

I know you'd probably tell me I'm abandoning my dreams. Maybe I am. Or maybe I'm just making new ones. Either way, I want to make this work. I made a commitment to Nadine, and seeing it through is the right thing to do.

Even if I was going to ignore your advice, I still wish you were here to give it to me.

Love,
Rosie

P.S. I'm going to keep volunteering—as many Saturdays as I can, just like you. I hope that'll make you proud.

CHAPTER TWENTY-TWO

Donovan emerged from his building wearing a fitted black T-shirt, dark gray joggers, and a Giants baseball cap. I fought the urge to let my mouth hang open, instead making a mental note that he looked hot in athleisure, too. I'd only ever seen him in button-down shirts and jeans or, well, naked.

He tossed a bag of Frisbees into the trunk of my car before climbing into the passenger seat. "Ready to get schooled in the art of Frisbee?" he asked, miming a Frisbee toss with a flick of his wrist.

We had plans to play Frisbee golf in Golden Gate Park that day. I didn't have a single ounce of confidence in my Frisbee (or was it Frisbeeing?) skills, but there was sunshine in the forecast and Bug loved exploring the park, so I'd agreed. Donovan's face lit up when I said yes. "You're going to love it," he said. "It's one of my top ten favorite things to do in the city."

The corners of my mouth tugged downward. "I can't do the Frisbee stuff today. There's been an emergency."

Donovan looked at Bug, who was curled up in my lap. She loved sitting as close to me as possible when I drove. It probably wasn't the safest thing in the world, but it was the sweetest. "Is everything okay? Is Bug sick?"

"No, nothing like that. It's Happy Hooves—the animal sanctuary I volunteer at?" Donovan nodded. "The goats escaped their enclosure and chaos ensued. The owner is at the vet with one of the chickens and she wasn't able to get a hold of any of the other volunteers. She asked if I could stop by and try to wrangle the herd."

Sonia had called me in a mild state of panic as I was loading Bug into the car. It had been a couple weeks since I'd broken the news about not taking Sonia's offer. She'd taken my decision in stride, which almost made me feel worse. I was determined to show Sonia that I was serious about volunteering as often as possible, so I'd spent my last two Saturdays at the sanctuary and had plans to go back again next weekend.

In spite of my having plans with Donovan today, I was thrilled that Sonia called me for help. I liked knowing that she felt she could count on me.

Plus, I found the concept of goats running amuck to be downright delightful. What were they doing? Taking joyrides on tractors? Draining the pond? Staging a coup? I figured Sonia wouldn't find any of these scenarios amusing, so I did my best to mask the amusement in my voice when I told her I'd be there as soon as possible.

It was only after I hung up that I realized that I probably should have checked with Donovan first. Now I was holding my breath as I waited for his reaction.

Donovan grinned. "Remember all that stuff I said about you being normal?"

I nodded.

"Yeah, I'm going to have to retract that. This is the most random problem I've ever heard."

I scrunched my face. "Are you mad?"

"Goats escaped and chaos ensued? How could anyone be mad about that?"

"So you'll help me?"

He leaned over and kissed me. I took that as a yes.

* * *

I should have known things weren't going to go well when Bug tried to crawl into Donovan's lap and he asked if he could move her to the back seat. "It's not personal," he'd explained. "I just don't want to get fur all over my black shirt." I didn't have the heart to tell him that a little dog fur would be the least of his problems today.

Barb was standing at the entrance looking annoyed when I pulled in. She was shifting her weight from side to side, the cow equivalent of impatient toe-tapping. She let out a long, exasperated moo as I climbed out of the car. I'd quickly learned that Barb had a moo for just about every situation—happiness, hunger, frustration, sadness, excitement. Animals were excellent communicators if you were paying attention.

I ran my hand along her snout. "Sorry about those unruly goats, boss. I'll get them all back," I said reassuringly. She pressed her nose against my hand in understanding. With that settled, I turned to Donovan. "Donovan, this is Barb," I said proudly. In that moment, I realized that Barb was the first friend I'd let Donovan meet.

"She's . . . huge," Donovan said, his eyes widening at the sight of her horns.

Barb grunted in response. Then she let out a low moo that loosely translated to *Who the hell is this guy?*

"I'll explain later," I whispered. "Now let's go wrangle those goats."

* * *

Goats are a lot like dogs. They love to play, they relish being petted (they're especially fond of back scratches), they wag their little tails when they're happy, and they are full of mischief.

The Happy Hooves goats were no exception. Especially in the mischief department. I spotted Pebbles and Bamm-Bamm in the distance, taking turns jumping off a pile of discarded tractor wheels at the top of a grassy hill. Betty and Wilma were chasing each other through Sonia's garden, leaving smashed tomatoes and uprooted beets in their wake. Bug had dashed off to join them as soon as we'd arrived and was now hot on Wilma's heels. She was already covered in mud.

Fred had managed to climb onto a narrow post that separated the pig enclosure from Pickles the donkey's paddock. He stood triumphantly surveying the madness as Arthur the pig squealed with joy. I'd always suspected that Arthur was something of an anarchist at heart.

On the other side of the sanctuary, Sprinkles, Happy Hooves's newest goat, had tipped over a bin of chicken feed and was enjoying a private feast and Barney had climbed into Barb's water trough. No wonder Barb was so pissed.

I tugged my hair into an even tighter ponytail. Reining in all this chaos was going to take a while, but I had a plan.

Like dogs, goats are very motivated by treats. After I'd gotten Donovan a pair of boots and a set of gloves, I led him to the barn where I opened a plastic bin to reveal a heap of goat food. "This is how we're going to lure them back," I explained.

"It smells," Donovan said, wrinkling his nose.

Goat food smelled more earthy than stinky. Sort of like muddy hay. "They're just grass pellets."

"That doesn't make it better."

I ignored Donovan and handed him a cone-shaped scooper. "Fill this to the top and approach the goats slowly. They'll recognize the scooper right away and come running."

His forehead creased. "Running?"

I dismissed his nerves with a wave of my hand. "They're not going to headbutt you or anything," I said. "They almost never do that."

"*Almost* never?"

Happy Hooves was laid out in three concentric circles designed to keep the animals contained within the safety of the sanctuary. The innermost ring held the shelters, toys, water troughs, a sizable grassy pasture, and a miniature pond, frequented by pigs and ducks. The second ring enveloped the barn, equipment sheds, and Sonia's home—a cheerful blue farmhouse at the top of a rolling hill and surrounded by acres of open fields. The animals got to roam the outer fields daily, but only with supervision. The third and final circle was where the tractors, trucks, and trailers were stored. It also held the dusty parking lot. Beyond that was the highway. The goal was to never let anyone make it to the highway.

Luckily, the goats had only slipped out of the central circle, probably through a gate that hadn't been properly latched, so all we had to do was bring them in from the outer fields.

"Follow my lead," I said to Donovan before making my way toward Wilma, Betty, and Bug, who were still engrossed in a game of tag. It looked like Bug was "it."

Donovan didn't follow my lead. He approached Pebbles and Bamm-Bamm waving the cup above his head like a trophy. The goats interpreted this as an invitation to play and quickly abandoned their tires, racing toward Donovan, which in turn caused him to run away at a full sprint.

"You don't have to run," I called futilely. But Donovan didn't listen, picking up speed instead. The faster he ran, the faster the goats chased him. In a way it was effective.

He let out what could only be described as a primal wail as he hurtled toward the gate and tossed the cup of feed into the enclosure. Pebbles, Bamm-Bamm, and Betty rushed by without giving him a second thought. Wilma stopped just outside the gate to give Donovan a playful nudge of appreciation before following after her friends. It had all been a game to her.

Donovan nearly fell over, catching himself on the fence.

"Good job!" I yelled. "Now close the gate!"

He hopped to, slamming the gate closed before securing the latch. Then he leaned against a wood post to catch his breath, his chest heaving. Donovan was acting like he'd just been through battle. I hoped he found all this as exhilarating as I did.

After I'd managed to coax Fred down from his perch and convinced Barney to climb out of Barb's trough, I enlisted Donovan's help in luring Sprinkles, who turned out to be the most stubborn of all, away from her private feast.

"She's been eating well," Donovan said as Sprinkles waddled by.

Sprinkles was looking more and more like a horizontal wine barrel by the day, but that wasn't for Donovan to judge. I folded my arms over my chest. "Excuse you. We don't body shame anyone here at Happy Hooves. Especially not when they're pregnant." I shook my head in mock disgust.

"Oh, she's pregnant? Sorry."

"And you call yourself a feminist."

"You're right. Patricia raised me better than that."

I patted Sprinkles on her speckled belly. Her fur was black with tiny white spots, hence the name Sprinkles. She'd probably have her baby soon. I hoped I'd be here to see it because baby goats were among the cutest things in the entire world.

I guess that was true of all baby animals. Even star-nosed moles. They grow up to be pretty scary looking, though. It's best not to google them.

"Doesn't breeding animals kind of go against the whole point of running an animal sanctuary?"

"Definitely. But Sprinkles was pregnant when she got here. They just didn't know it." I was actually the first one to notice. The first time I brushed Sprinkles, I noticed that her belly was especially firm, a telltale sign of early pregnancy. Then I took a peek at her udders, which were noticeably swollen. Another sign. I mentioned it to Sonia and her vet confirmed my suspicion the next day.

"For the record, I don't believe anyone should be breeding animals in this day and age," Sonia confided when she called with the news. "But I'd be lying if I said I wasn't thrilled about Sprinkles."

I told her I felt the same.

Sprinkles looped back around to Donovan and started sniffing at his sweats. He stiffened, but to his credit, he didn't back away. "How long is a goat pregnant before she gives birth?"

"About five months."

Donovan grinned. "It's cool that you know that kind of stuff."

"Thanks," I said. "Want to guess what the shortest gestation period is for any mammal?"

"Sure," he said, crossing his arms and arranging his face into a pensive expression. "Maybe a month?"

"The opossum is only pregnant for twelve days."

"Not much time to put together a nursery," he said.

"Stop by any Walmart during breeding season and you'll see hordes of new opossum dads panic-buying diapers."

"I'd pay to see that. Okay, so twelve days is the shortest. What's the longest?"

"Elephants," I said, not missing a beat. "They're pregnant for twenty-two months."

He let out a long whistle. "Almost two years. That's commitment."

"Yep. And if the calf is a girl, she'll stay with her mom for the rest of her life." That was probably the one bad thing about being an elephant, aside from poachers, of course. I couldn't imagine living with my mom for my entire life. Eighteen years had been plenty.

"You're very cute when you're rattling off fun animal facts."

I held up my hands to frame my face. "Thanks." I liked sharing this part of myself with Donovan. Even though I could tell he wasn't totally comfortable around my barnyard friends, I appreciated that he was trying. "There's a lot more where that came from."

He laughed. "I don't doubt it."

I was so distracted by Donovan's flattery that I almost didn't notice that Sprinkles had moved on from sniffing Donovan's leg to nibbling on the pocket of his sweats. "Sprinkles," I scolded, "don't do that!"

Donovan jumped back, but his sweats remained in Sprinkles's grasp. He pulled on the fabric, unwittingly entering into a tug of war with the goat. Sprinkles eventually won out, prancing off with a piece of gray fabric dangling from her mouth as Donovan stared after her, slack jawed.

If I didn't know any better, I'd say Sprinkles had a little extra pep in her step.

* * *

Once we got the goats settled in, I went to check on the pigs (all happily napping in the sun-warmed hay—Arthur was snoring loudly, apparently tuckered out from the day's excitement), Pickles the donkey (he flicked his ears hello before returning to his true passion: grazing), and finally, the chickens. Rocket greeted me with a hearty cock-a-doodle-doo, which caused Donovan to jump a good foot off the ground. Rocket cocked his head in confusion. He was used to being applauded for his exceptional vocal abilities.

Bug came trotting up to us, caked in dirt. Her tail was wagging and she was panting heavily. It looked like she was smiling, which I'm sure she was, but I could also tell she was a little overheated. It was usually a good fifteen or so degrees warmer in Marin than San Francisco and the sun had reached its peak. "Let's get you some water, Love Bug," I said, reaching down to give her a pet. A puff of dust floated up as I ran my hand down her back. "Maybe a quick bath, too."

I got Bug cleaned up and Donovan and I changed out of our boots and gloves. Then I filled up a pair of glass water bottles and a bowl for Bug, grabbed a bag of presliced carrot sticks from the barn's refrigerator, and led Donovan to my favorite spot: a picnic bench under a big, shady oak tree on a small hill that overlooked the barnyard. The bench was so old and weathered that the edges were slightly rounded and the wood was smooth, splinter free.

Donovan poked his finger through the hole in his pocket.

"Sorry about that," I said. "It's a goat thing."

I spotted Sprinkles peering at Donovan from behind a tree in the distance. It reminded me of the way murderers return to the scene of the crime. Maybe she was feeling guilty. Or more likely, she was hoping to get another piece of Donovan. Either one would have been understandable.

"They're just sweats," he said, attempting to sound chill about the whole thing. I could tell he was upset, though. He was making the same face he made when I dropped a spaghetti noodle on the kitchen floor last week.

Barb lumbered up the small hill to join us in the shade. She'd been jealously guarding her water trough after we'd gotten Barney out, but now seemed satisfied that the naughty goat wouldn't commit the same offense again. Bug wagged her tail as Barb approached. I gave them each a carrot stick.

"You did good today, Rosie Benson," Donovan said, playfully punching my arm. He said it like he was talking to a kid who just scored her first run in Little League. I shot him my best *don't patronize me* look.

He laughed. "Seriously. It was cool to see you in your element. I don't know anyone else who would have known how to handle a bonkers situation like that. It was sexy."

My cheeks warmed. "Thanks."

I breathed in the fresh, hay-tinged air and relished the feeling I always had after a day spent at Happy Hooves: warm, content, and tired. Not a sleepy tired—more of a cozy, satisfied tired. Kind of like the feeling of climbing into a jacuzzi after snowboarding all day.

We fell into an easy silence, sipping water and munching on carrots. Occasionally Donovan would point out one of the goats or pigs and ask about their story. By now, I knew everyone's history, some innocuous—like how Pepper the potbelly pig's family thought she'd stay small forever and had to surrender her when she outgrew their tiny yard. Others more harrowing—like how Barb had been rescued from a veal crate.

The thought of Barb being treated that way made my stomach turn. I reached over to stroke her big, spotted haunch.

If thinking back to her life before Happy Hooves was upsetting, Barb didn't let on. She remained planted on my side of the picnic bench, methodically chomping on a long piece of grass, her tail gently swishing away the bees who strayed from a nearby honeysuckle bush.

When I was about five, Dotty and I were hanging out in the back-yard at my parents' house and a bee landed on her arm. Dotty re-mained perfectly still, observing the tiny creature for several moments before beckoning me to her side. "I appear to have been mistaken for a flower," she whispered. "What a lovely compliment." Dotty's ease enabled me to get a good look at the bee: its delicate wings, its striped abdomen, its fuzzy little legs. It was actually kind of cute. After a few minutes, the bee flew off without incident.

I've loved bees ever since.

My eyes followed a honeybee as it floated past me, then Bug before coming to rest on Donovan's cheek.

"Don't freak out," I said slowly. "But there's a bee on your face."

Donovan, having not attended the Dotty school of peaceful human-bee interaction, totally freaked out.

He jumped off the table and started spinning in circles, shaking his head, and slapping his own face. At some point his Giants hat flew off, landing in a muddy puddle. Bug jumped up to join him, barking and jumping by his side in a show of support. Barb con-tinued chomping on grass, completely unbothered.

"Ouch! Dammit! It got me!" Donovan yelled, pressing his hand to the side of his face.

I rushed a yelping Donovan into the barn where I knew we'd find a first-aid kit. As we stepped inside, I caught a glimpse of Sprinkles trotting off with Donovan's hat hanging from her mouth. I thought it best not to say anything.

The bee left a dime-size welt on his cheek, but I didn't see a stinger anywhere, which was good news for Donovan because pulling out a barbed, venom-filled stinger was pretty painful. It meant that the bee might live, too, which was a relief to me. It wasn't fair that a honeybee's only means of defense usually led to certain death.

I wiped the wound with an antiseptic patch from the barn's first-aid kit and then dabbed it with cortisone. He winced but didn't complain. Then I snapped an instant cold ice pack in half and pressed it against his cheek. "Hold this over the sting for as long as you can stand it. It'll help with swelling."

Donovan placed his hand over the ice pack and closed his eyes. The cold seemed to bring him some relief.

"What if I'm allergic?" he asked. His eyes were still closed and there was the subtlest of wobbles in his voice. "Should I go to the emergency room?"

"You don't know if you're allergic to bees?"

"I've never been stung before."

"You're almost thirty and you've never been stung by a bee?"

"You have?"

"Well, yeah. If you spend enough time outside, it's bound to happen eventually."

It was actually a wasp that got me during a softball game when I was nine. I didn't like them quite as much as I liked bees. They were a bit meaner, more aggressive.

Less fuzzy.

Donovan grimaced. He really was more of an indoor person. Lawn sports and hikes along well-maintained trails were about as outdoorsy as he got, but there was no point in making him feel bad about it. I pulled a packet of antihistamines from the first-aid kit and handed them to him. "I think you're fine, but take these. Just in case."

That seemed to satisfy him.

"Thank you for coming with me," I said, squeezing his arm. "I couldn't have done it without you." That wasn't exactly true, but it was still a nice thing to say. And I did appreciate the way he rolled with my unilateral decision to ditch our Frisbee plans.

He laughed, gesturing to the ice pack. "I think I was more of hindrance than help."

"You'll get the hang of it."

Donovan sucked in a sharp breath before letting out a long, slow exhale. He shifted so that he could look at me with his unobscured eye. "It's probably better if I don't come with you next time. I don't think I'm much of an animal person. Is that okay?"

Dotty didn't trust people who didn't like animals and generally speaking, neither did I. But I wouldn't say that Donovan didn't *like* animals. He genuinely cared about their well-being. He was just a little uneasy around them. Between the bee sting and Sprinkles ruining what was surely a pricey pair of sweatpants, I couldn't really blame him.

I figured that if Dotty were here, she'd let Donovan off on a technicality.

Besides, people can change.

Hi Rosie,

I'm sorry to hear about your aunt. She and I used to work together at *Travel Times Magazine*. Dotty was my editor.

I'd long admired her articles and was beside myself when she actually responded to my application. I was a lowly intern at the *Chronicle* at the time, and I desperately wanted to write about something more glamourous than community food drives or elementary-school spelling bees. So, landing a job at *Travel Times* was a dream come true.

Or so I thought. I was a miserable travel writer. Spectacularly unhappy. Working with Dotty was kind of a nightmare (she was a ruthless editor), the hours were ungodly, and some of the hotels I had to stay in . . . let's just say I'm lucky I never contracted a case of bed bugs. But I'd worked so hard to get there that I couldn't fathom doing anything else. Then Dotty told me that I should quit. "It's dulling your spark," she'd said, "and it shows in your writing." She was, of course, right. But I didn't listen. So she fired me.

It took me a while to get over it. But ultimately, I understood. And even though I wasn't meant to be a travel writer, I still loved reading her articles.

I don't know if this is what you're looking for, but I hope it helps.

Jordan Barnes

Senior Business Editor

Forbes Inc.

CHAPTER TWENTY-THREE

AUGUST

Daniel Lemon is here to see you." Priya, our temporary office manager, towered over my desk. She was model tall and had the cheekbones to match. Nadine loved her.

I minimized my Dotty emails. I'd developed a habit of reading them whenever I needed a little extra support. Each served a purpose: Tommy's gave me confidence; Lily's gave me strength. Angela's always broke my heart a little, but in the best way.

And I was hoping Jordan's less-than-glowing response (Dotty wasn't exactly known for her bedside manner) would help me get through my next meeting.

Priya popped her gum, snapping me back to reality. "I'll meet him in the conference room," I said.

"K," she said, turning on her very high heels. I allowed myself a melodramatic sigh as she sashayed back to the front desk.

I'd never fired anyone before. But when Nadine had called me into her office to ask me to handle Daniel's termination, I knew I couldn't say no. Not with a promotion on the line.

Daniel Lemon had been at TickerTape—a small digital advertising agency—for less than two weeks, and he'd already shown up late four times, broken the copy machine, lied about breaking the copy machine, hung up on the founder, and pretended to be sick so he could leave early only to post a selfie from the Celine Dion concert later that night.

I snatched an "End of Assignment" agreement from the corner of my desk and started toward the conference room, walking myself through everything Nadine had instructed me to say. "Don't go off script," she'd reminded me. "And don't make it personal." I hadn't bothered to tell her that getting fired was always personal.

Daniel sat against the far wall, his reddish-brown hair almost blending in with the brick facade. This was going to suck. Maybe I should have taken Sonia up on her offer after all. I'd much rather shovel poop under Barb's watchful eye than have this conversation.

"Thanks for coming in this morning," I said, pulling out a chair from under the gleaming white conference table. Daniel's green eyes darted to the stack of papers I was holding against my chest. I lowered them into my lap as I sat down. "How are things going at TickerTape?"

Daniel eyed me pensively but didn't respond. I was about to repeat the question when he said, "It's been a little rocky."

I pulled my lips into a straight line and nodded.

"So you've heard."

"I have."

Daniel fidgeted in his seat. He wore a striped blue-and-white button-down shirt, rolled at the sleeves. I could have sworn I saw the top of Celine's pointy head on his white undershirt. "They work crazy hours over there," he said, as if confiding in an old friend. "Do you think you could talk to them about my schedule?"

I blew out a long slow breath and reminded myself to stay on script. "Your manager has expressed some concerns about your performance," I said, attempting to keep my tone neutral.

He looked genuinely surprised. "It's my first real job. I'm still figuring it out."

"Did you lie about being sick so you could leave early on Tuesday?"

"I was feeling sick."

"But not sick enough to miss Celine Dion?"

Daniel's green eyes widened. "What are you, stalking me or something?"

"All your social media accounts are public."

He sat back in his chair and threw his hands up in mock surrender. "Fine. I lied. I just really wanted to go to the concert, and I knew they wouldn't give me the time off."

"That's because they need someone to sit at the front desk until the office closes." Daniel's hands tightened around the armrests of his chair.

"That's the job," I said, my voice gentler than I'd expected.

He didn't reply. I probably wouldn't have known what to say if I were him either. As I watched Daniel stare down at his hands, surrendering to the reality that he'd royally screwed up, I tried to ignore the flood of sympathy I felt for him. I pressed on. "It's also my understanding that you've been showing up late."

He sighed. "I have to take two different buses to get to the office. So I've been late a few times."

I took the bus most days, too. It wasn't a pleasant experience. A part of me wanted to tell Daniel that I got it. But instead, I said, "You still need to show up on time. Even if that means catching an earlier bus."

"It's just so far."

"Then maybe you shouldn't have taken this assignment."

"I needed a job."

This wasn't going to get us anywhere. "We're going to have to end your assignment," I blurted, ripping off the Band-Aid with one swift pull.

His already pale face grew even paler. "What does that mean? I'm . . . fired?" He looked like he was about to cry.

"Yes. I'm sorry."

"But I'm still new." It sounded like a plea.

"Exactly," I said gently. "That's when you should be on your best behavior. You have to prove yourself first."

"This sucks," Daniel said, crossing his arms over his chest and slumping back into his chair, defeated.

I walked him through the paperwork and handed him a pen. He sat expressionless, nodding here and there to let me know he understood. He wasn't to go back to the office today, we'd mail him his things, he was welcome to file for unemployment, here was his final paycheck, and no, I wouldn't be able to find him a new assignment. He was shell-shocked, I knew. That had been me not so long ago. And even though I knew Daniel deserved to be fired, I still felt absolutely terrible.

* * *

"How'd it go?" Nadine asked after I'd walked a catatonic Daniel Lemon out the door. She was leaning against the marble wall in the lobby, arms crossed over her chest.

"I think I need a drink."

Nadine nodded knowingly before ducking behind the front desk. She reemerged, holding a small white envelope. "I figured you might need a little stress relief after that," she said, extending the envelope. Inside was a gift card to a fancy French spa with a name I couldn't pronounce. "I know it's not easy, but you get used to it. Senior recruiters need to be able to handle the tough conversations." She pressed her lips together into a coy, knowing smile.

She's a snake.

Pilar's warning echoed in the back of my mind. My trust in Nadine had been shaken, but she'd always been kind and supportive toward me. Case in point: she'd gone out of her way to make sure everything with Daniel went well. Not exactly snakelike behavior.

There had to be something I was missing, something lost in translation.

Whatever had happened between Nadine and Evan and Pilar, I'd decided that I had to try to make it work at Le Agency. I wanted that promotion.

Plus, she gave really great gifts.

I didn't waste any time booking my massage—I'd never had a fancy massage before!—but in spite of my excitement about receiving a proper pampering, poor Daniel Lemon haunted my thoughts all morning. I now understood what Raj had gone through when he'd fired me—how he must have felt that day, why he'd been so awkward and fidgety. I almost pitied him.

I decided that the next time Marcia asked me to have dinner with her and Raj, I would say yes.

* * *

I was still turning my chat with Daniel over in my head as I slinked out of the office for a clandestine meeting with Evan and Pilar. I'd planned to meet them under the guise of a bathroom break for Bug. I would have preferred to spend my lunch break with them, but with Kate and I locked in a battle for Hardest Working Recruiter, neither of us dared eat away from our desks.

Bug and I rounded the corner, and there stood Evan and Pilar—

her waving enthusiastically, him leaning against a gaudy gold pillar, arms crossed.

Bug broke into a full-blown run at the sight of her old friends. One of these days she was going to dislocate my arm. She scrambled toward Pilar first, who dropped to her knees to greet the wiggly ball of fur that was my dog.

Evan glanced at his phone. "You're late. Everything okay up there?"

"Just the usual," I said, pushing thoughts of Daniel from my mind. "Superbusy."

"That great, huh?" Pilar asked. She'd dyed her hair again—today it was turquoise.

"Yeah, no need to lie. We know the place is probably falling apart without us," Evan said, nudging me with an elbow.

Pilar smirked. "I think we all need some coffee. Just thinking about Nadine makes me tired."

Seeing them again made me realize how much I'd missed them. I dug my phone out of my pocket to check the time. "I have twenty minutes."

Pilar stood up, cradling Bug in her arms. "That's all we need."

A couple blocks later, we were tucked away at a corner table in a noisy Starbucks, Pilar vigorously sweeping a clump of napkins across the sticky table, Bug curled in my lap, Evan squinting at the menu.

"Quadruple espresso?" Evan asked, pointing at me.

"Just a double."

He pretended to clutch an invisible strand of pearls around his neck. "You've changed."

Pilar waved him off. "Good for you. You used to shake like a Chihuahua by the end of the day."

"Well, I already had a triple this morning."

Evan jokingly placed a hand on my wrist. "That's called an addiction, Rosie. And there's help out there."

When Evan returned with two mugs full of coffee and a smaller-than-usual espresso for me, Pilar didn't waste any time cutting to the chase. "We're starting our own agency," she announced. "I'm going to be president; Evan will be VP—he's going to handle all the business stuff that I don't want to do."

"Luckiest guy in the world," Evan quipped.

"It's going to be a grind for a while," Pilar said, ignoring Evan. "We're going to work out of my apartment until we can afford to rent an office space. So we'll be meeting with candidates at coffee shops or in the lobby of my building."

"Pilar has verbal confirmation from most of her old accounts that they'll give her their business once we're up and running," Evan added before taking a sip of his coffee. "They all hate Nadine."

"Can't say I blame them," Pilar cracked. She returned her attention to me. "So what do you think?"

"I think we should be drinking champagne instead of coffee," I said, jiggling my espresso. "That's amazing, you guys, congrats." What I didn't say is that I wasn't thrilled I'd have to keep this from Nadine. Evan and Pilar were coming for her business, and I couldn't imagine she'd take that lightly.

What would she do if she found out I knew and didn't tell her?

"Obviously you can't tell anyone," Pilar said, reading my thoughts.

"Obviously."

"And once we're up and running, we'd love to hire you."

My eyes widened involuntarily. How many big life decisions was I going to be forced into making this year? I should have been flattered, but all I felt was panic.

"I know this might sound scary," Pilar said, her tone softening. "But I know what I'm doing. And so does Evan. He's more than just a pretty face."

Evan cupped his cheeks in his hands and batted his eyelashes.

"Picture it," Pilar continued, holding her hands up to tick off fingers. "No more Kate. No more Nadine. No crazy pressure or ridiculous incentives. Just three friends, building a new agency from the ground up."

That *did* sound idyllic, but I didn't want any more change. Not right now. No matter how annoyed I was at Nadine, things at Le Agency were going well. Turning down Happy Hooves had been hard enough.

"I . . . I'm really happy for you guys. And I'm honored that you'd want to hire me. I wasn't even sure you liked me very much."

Evan shrugged. "I take great joy in keeping people on their toes."

Pilar squeezed my arm. "You're a great recruiter, Rosie. You're smart, you're kind, you're thoughtful. You look at the people you interview as human beings, not products. And you have a knack for knowing who will fit in where. You can't really teach that stuff."

No one had ever said that to me before. Nadine's praise had always been vague and sweeping. "Thank you," I said, my voice cracking.

"You're not going to cry, are you?" Evan asked. Pilar smacked his shoulder.

"No," I said, forcing a laugh, even though I felt like I could cry.

"You don't have to decide anything right away," Pilar said gently. "We're nowhere near being ready to hire anyone. It'll be at least a couple of months."

"Starting a new agency is a nightmare." Evan sighed.

Pilar shook her head, her turquoise ponytail swishing side to side. "Anyway, we can work out the details later. But one thing is for sure—you'll be able to bring Bug to work with you," Pilar said. Evan huffed in response, but then he reached over to pat Bug's head. She gave his hand a grateful lick in return.

It felt like a flock of hummingbirds were thrumming around in my brain. I knew I should say *something*, but when I opened my mouth, the words caught in my throat.

"We did it, Pilar," Evan said, grinning. "She's finally speechless."

CHAPTER TWENTY-FOUR

I invited Marcia to come with me to Lily's for some Raj-free bonding time. She enthusiastically accepted, which meant more to me than she knew. Because, as much as I appreciated Lily leaning into this whole sister-in-law thing, I needed a friend buffer. Decorating a nursery sounded mind-numbingly boring, but I figured I could blend in with the stuffed animals and let Marcia do all the talking whenever diaper cream weaseled its way into the conversation. She'd nannied every summer when we were in college, so she spoke baby.

Now the three of us were sitting in the freshly painted nursery, Marcia squinting at a surprisingly thick crib assembly manual, Lily in a rocking chair, using her belly as a folding table, and me, placing portraits of baby animals into thick gray frames. I held up the latest, a picture of a fawn with gigantic brown eyes and white spots on its forehead. "Look at this one!" I squealed. Lily and Marcia muttered absent-minded replies without even looking up.

"When does your maternity leave start?" Marcia asked.

Lily sat back and wrapped her hands around her bulging stomach. "At the end of the month. It can't come soon enough."

"Do you think you'll want to go back to work?"

"Probably," Lily said. "I'll have to see how I feel. And if we can find a day care that doesn't cost more than our monthly mortgage payment."

"Can't Mom watch the baby for you?" I asked.

The rocking chair creaked as Lily shifted. She was exceptionally fidgety these days, like she couldn't ever get comfortable. "We were hoping she would. That's why we bought a house so close to them. But she's . . . doing her own thing these days."

That was an understatement. My mother had decided to throw herself a midlife crisis, complete with a new apartment, new hobbies, and virtually no contact with the rest of the family. "Has Dad been around at all?"

Lily cracked a half smile. "Almost every day after work. It's sweet, really. I can tell he's lonely. It probably doesn't help that he's been spending every weekend at Dotty's."

I winced at the mention of Dotty's house. I hated the thought of it sitting empty.

Bug whined quietly at Lily's feet, perhaps sensing that we were talking about Dotty. Lily leaned over to scratch her head. "He says he's sorting through her things, but the last time I was there, it didn't look like he'd done much." Lily had offered to manage the sale of Dotty's house but it needed some work before it was ready to hit the market. I guess Dad wasn't in a rush.

"What do you think he's really doing?"

"Being sad." She said it with so much certainty that I knew she was speaking from experience. "I slept in my mom's bed for weeks after she died."

"Oh" was all I could think to say as a thin layer of gloom settled over the room, making the bright white walls feel almost vulgar. The hollow sound of wood slats knocking against one another as Marcia sorted them into piles filled the space. I knew that Dad's depression wasn't my fault. But I still felt guilty, somehow.

"Found it!" Marcia said, triumphantly holding up a wooden slat. Her enthusiasm seemed to dissipate the cloud that had gathered above Lily and me. "I thought we were missing a part. But it was just in the bottom of the box."

"You're a lifesaver," Lily said. "Really, I can't thank you two enough." She pushed herself up and stretched. Bug wasted no time jumping into Lily's empty seat and making herself comfortable. Lily didn't seem to notice as she started stacking tiny onesies in a dresser drawer.

"You didn't want Tommy's help with any of this?" I asked, doing my best not to sound judgmental.

Lily wrinkled her forehead. "Have you ever seen Tommy build anything?"

I flashed to the coffee table Tommy had assembled for me when Marcia and I had moved out of the dorms sophomore year. It'd only lasted a week before collapsing under the weight of four cans of beer and a handle of cheap vodka. "Good point."

Lily gave me a knowing look. "Plus, it'll be so special to tell the baby that her auntie Rosie helped put her room together."

"Auntie Rosie," Marcia cooed. "I can't believe my best friend is going to have a niece soon."

"Me either," I said, feeling some of Marcia's enthusiasm rubbing off on me. It *was* pretty cool.

Marcia turned her attention back to Lily. "Are you nervous about labor?"

"Terrified. But I've been promised drugs. And I'll have Tommy and Rosie—" She stopped midsentence as her hand fluttered to the right side of her stomach. I could see a small egglike bulge through her fitted T-shirt. "Do you want to feel the baby kick?"

I nodded, rising from my spot on the floor. When I pressed my hand against Lily's stomach, I was surprised at how firm it felt. I don't know why I'd expected it to feel like a bowl full of jelly. She wasn't Santa. Marcia appeared by my side and put her hand next to mine, her pinkie touching my thumb. Sure enough, we felt a distinct jab, as if the baby was trying to elbow us out of her space.

"Does that hurt?" Marcia asked.

"Not right now," Lily said. "But at night, she jabs me in the ribs. *That* hurts."

Marcia pulled her hand away and sighed. "I think I want one." She sounded so uncharacteristically wistful I wondered if I should look into exorcisms when we got home.

I shot her my best side-eye. "We aren't even twenty-five yet, why are you talking about babies?"

"Well, I didn't say I wanted one *tomorrow*."

That was a relief.

"It's just kind of fun to think about," Marcia said. She looked all glowy.

"You'll make a great mom *someday*," I offered. "In the very, very distant future."

She playfully twirled one of her curls between her fingers. "I know, right? I'm really fun and I have lots of wisdom."

"The most wisdom," I agreed.

She laughed to herself. "Wouldn't Raj be *such* a dad?"

I flashed to all of Raj's lame jokes, his abundant enthusiasm for coaching and development, and his enduring fondness of vests. I couldn't help but agree.

"You and this Raj guy seem pretty serious," Lily said.

Marcia sank back down to the floor and pretended to return her attention to the half-assembled crib. "I think we are," she said. I picked up a photo to hang on the wall. In true Lily fashion, she'd stayed up half the night getting the spacing of each nail just right. She said she didn't sleep much these days anyway.

"Don't hold out on me," Lily said. "Tell me everything."

Marcia slid another crib piece into place before sitting back on her heels, hands in her lap. "I don't know . . . Raj is just different. He's smart and funny and kind of nerdy—in an endearing way. And he's so supportive. When I told him that I wanted to start my own PR agency someday, he stayed up most of the night asking me a bunch of questions. He was so into it."

I didn't know any of that. Except for the part about Raj being a huge nerd, of course. It occurred to me that I didn't know Marcia and Raj's anniversary or who made the first move or what they did on their first date, either. My stomach knotted with regret. I'd missed those exciting early days of Marcia's new relationship. I never got the chance to help her obsess over a cryptic text or pick out the perfect outfit for a date or dissect every moment of said date over morning-after mimosas. I hadn't opted out of those moments voluntarily—at least not at first—but that didn't help me to feel like any less of a bad friend.

"It's so nice to have a partner who supports your career," Lily said, in a way that made me think she was actually talking about my brother.

With the exception of a brief but intense boy-obsessed phase in middle school, I'd never really placed much importance on finding a boyfriend, let alone a life partner. Aside from the fun parts (flirting and sex), I just didn't get the appeal. The rest seemed like so much work. I always figured that I'd come around eventually—like in my thirties. Probably my late thirties. But I couldn't deny that Marcia and Lily seemed genuinely happy.

I couldn't quite put my finger on why, but I felt like I was falling behind. My career was finally starting to catch up to everyone else's, but they'd leapt ahead to committed relationships and babies. It was like I was constantly missing the memo about what we should all be doing and when we should be doing it.

I started to wonder if I should be taking things with Donovan more seriously.

I bent down to pick up the ostrich photo and placed it under a picture of a cheetah cub. The three of us worked in silence, Marcia finishing the crib, Lily fussing with decorations, each of us lost in our own thoughts about our respective futures, theirs seemingly much brighter than mine. When I hung the last animal picture (a portrait of a scruffy wolf pup) on the wall opposite the baby's crib, I took a step back to admire my work. Two rows of furry little faces stared back at me. I could have sworn I saw pity in their big brown eyes.

CHAPTER TWENTY-FIVE

My phone chimed loudly as I reached into my bag to switch it to silent. Evan and Pilar had been texting me nonstop since our secret coffee meeting. First to ask what I thought about their agency name ideas (I'd already vetoed EvLar, PiEv, and Nay Agency), then to get my opinion on their logo, and finally, to see if I'd be willing to send Nadine's rejects their way. I was going to have to start charging them for my consulting services.

I sent the call to voice mail and returned to my notes.

Buzz, buzz, buzz.

I ignored another call.

Buzz!

Bug grumbled from under my desk, seemingly irritated by the interruption. The early afternoon was her prime naptime. I picked up the phone, intending to switch it to airplane mode, but the sheer volume of missed calls and text messages caught my eye. My heart sank at the memory of the last time I'd had this many unread messages on my phone. It had been the beginning of the worst day of my life.

But today was going to be something else entirely.

Lily was in labor.

I set my phone on the desk and took a breath. With Evan and Pilar gone, Le Agency had been busier than ever. I was booked solid with interviews until the end of the day. This was terrible timing. Not that Lily could do anything about it. But still.

My phone buzzed again. This time it was a text from Lily.

Where r u?

What was I doing? I had to go. Work could wait.

I typed out a quick response assuring Lily that I'd be on my way soon. Then I texted Marcia to ask if she could come to pick up Bug from the office. Hopefully Nadine wouldn't mind if I left her sleeping under my desk until then. I headed toward her office, half walking, half running, and knocked on Nadine's door. I took a step back and waited, anxiously drumming my fingertips against my thighs.

"Come in," came Nadine's husky voice. I straightened my back, and stepped inside. "How's my favorite recruiter?" she purred. I had been so thrilled the first time she called me her favorite. But I quickly realized she said that to everyone. *How's my favorite client? How's my favorite executive assistant? How's my favorite husband?* I'd heard it all.

"I'm great," I replied. "My sister-in-law is in labor." Nadine's face remained neutral, save for a blink-and-you'll-miss-it curl of her upper lip. "And she wants me there. In the delivery room."

"You're asking to leave early."

My chest tightened. "Yes," I said, attempting to keep my tone neutral. "I can reschedule my candidates for the day—unless you or Kate want to take them?"

I hadn't taken any time off since Nadine has raised the prospect of a promotion. I'd even had to turn down Sonia's request for last-minute help twice. First when she needed an extra person to pick up a sick piglet from a local rancher and the second was when

Sprinkles the goat delivered her kid. An adorable, fuzzy, wobbly-legged girl they named Cupcake.

Sonia had sent me the video of Cupcake's birth after the fact and it was . . . something. I just kept thinking, *Poor Sprinkles. Poor Lily. Poor women!* Trauma aside, I chalked my viewing experience up to good preparation for being in the delivery room with Lily.

Nadine placed her hands on the desk and leaned forward. "We're down two team members, we have thirty open job orders, your calendar is full, and you want to take the afternoon off?"

When she put it that way, it didn't sound so great. But Lily needed me. And I *wanted* to be there for her. "I know it's not the best timing."

"That's an understatement."

"My family's counting on me."

"So am I." Nadine said this gently, as if she were speaking to a child, but I could sense a sharp edge lurking beneath her cool restraint. "I need to be sure that I can rely on you." She didn't mention the promotion. She didn't have to.

"I could come in early tomorrow?" I offered, appalled by the pathetic pitch of my voice.

Nadine leaned back in her chair. It swiveled gently in response. "Well, let's think about this. Is this your sister-in-law's first baby?"

"Yes," I said, sensing an opening. Maybe Nadine would make an exception since this was Lily's first time.

Nadine nodded. "And when did she start having contractions?"

I blinked. "Umm . . ." I said, trying to remember what time all the texts started coming through. "Maybe a half hour ago?"

"Ah," Nadine said, as if we were a pair of detectives who'd just stumbled upon an important clue. "Well then, we don't have a problem. Labor progresses very slowly the first time. I was in labor for thirty-seven hours with Toby."

I wasn't following.

"Did she mention whether her water had broken yet?"

"No."

"Even better!" Nadine stuck out her arm, tugging at a silk sleeve to reveal a delicate gold watch on her wrist. "It's almost one, so you can work through the day and still make it to the hospital by six."

"You want me to *stay*?"

Nadine gave a casual shrug. "It's your choice. But if I were you, I would honor my commitment and work through the day." So it wasn't up to me. Not really.

I wish I'd been brave enough to challenge Nadine, but I was too caught off guard. And if what she said was true, I guess it wouldn't hurt to compromise. "Can I leave right after my four o'clock?"

"Sure."

"Okay." I stood up and started toward the door, feeling like I'd shrunk an inch or two since the start of our conversation.

"Rosie?" I paused with my hand on the doorknob. She flashed me a controlled smile. "Please congratulate your family for me when you see them tonight."

"Thanks, Nadine," I said. But I didn't really mean it.

When I got back to my desk, I had a new text from Tommy. It said:

All checked in. Docs said it'll be a while now. No big rush.

I nearly burst into tears with relief.

* * *

Lily had the baby at 4:07 that afternoon. I was in the middle of an interview when Mom's text came through telling me that

Lily had to have an emergency C-section, but she didn't mention why.

They named the baby Lucía after Lily's mom. Her middle name was Rose. After me.

I ran out of the office as soon as I saw all the missed messages, scribbling Marcia's number on Kate's strawberry-scented notepad on my way out the door. I had to trust Kate of all people to watch Bug until Marcia could come and pick her up. To her credit, she'd been uncharacteristically nice about the whole thing.

As I rushed through the sliding doors of the hospital, I realized I'd never actually been inside one before. At least not since I was a kid, after the car accident with Dotty. It was surprisingly quiet. I don't know why I'd been expecting to walk into a chaotic scene from *Grey's Anatomy*.

I found my parents in the waiting room on the third floor. Mom was biting her nails and Dad was frowning at a paper cup, presumably filled with undrinkable coffee. It looked like they were taking great pains to ignore each other. Mom noticed me first. "There you are." She gave me a limp hug. "What took you so long?"

"We were crazy busy at work." It was a pitiful excuse. But it was also the truth.

"Didn't you tell your boss what was going on?"

"She said it would be hours before Lily was even close to having the baby. I thought I'd have enough time."

Mom pursed her lips. "Babies don't care about work schedules."

"Yeah, I know."

"It sounds like you need to get your priorities straight."

Which one was it? Was I supposed to have a big, important job or was I supposed to be at my family's beck and call? It didn't seem possible to do both.

Dad appeared behind me, dropping a heavy hand on my shoulder.

"You're here now," he said. "Why don't you go meet baby Lucía?" Mom arched an eyebrow but didn't protest. Dad gave me directions to Lily's room. I gave him a grateful wave before hurrying down the hall. I could have sworn I heard my parents bickering as I walked away, but I didn't dare look back.

I slowed my pace as I approached Lily's room—my stomach was in knots. So were my fists. I shook them out before wiping my palms on my thighs. "Are you lost?" a nurse with spiky hair and glasses that hung from a beaded string around her neck called out to me from behind a desk. I shook my head and hurried into room 4A.

Lily sat propped up in a bed with railings on either side. She looked like she'd been through a battle. I suppose she had. "Lily," I said, not bothering to fight back tears. "I'm so sorry—"

She pressed a finger to her lips. There was a plastic hospital bracelet around her wrist. I stopped in the center of the room, my surroundings finally registering: Tommy asleep in an uncomfortable-looking plastic chair, the IV that hung from a pole next to Lily's bed, and the tiny bundle of blankets she cradled in her arms. Lily didn't need theatrics right now. She needed me to be calm. There would be time for apologies later. "Are you ready to meet your niece?" she asked, her voice soft, warm.

I gulped down my tears and nodded. Lily tilted her elbow as I approached the side of her bed. And there was Lucía, all pink and peaceful, with a shock of black hair that stuck out in every direction. Even with her eyes closed, I could tell she looked like Tommy. And me, a little. We had the same chin.

"She's so tiny," I breathed, placing my hand on the top of her head.

"She looks like a little alien," Lily attempted a joke, but her voice was filled with so much love that it made my heart ache.

"A beautiful little alien."

"Yeah."

"Are you okay?"

"I am now."

"I'm so sorry, Lily."

"I know."

"I wish I'd been here."

"Me too."

There wasn't anything else to say. The only thing that would fix this was a time machine.

"Do you want to hold her?" Lily asked.

I couldn't remember if I'd ever held a baby before, let alone a newborn. But I nodded all the same, holding my breath as Lily placed her daughter in my arms.

Lucía was a warm little squish. She practically melted into me. I pulled back a corner of her blanket so I could see her whole face. Then her eyes fluttered, and she let out a sweet little yawn and I knew I loved her, knew I loved being her aunt. "Do I need to rock her?"

Lily tugged on the top of her messy ponytail. "Nah, I think she's just happy to snuggle."

"Okay," I said, forcing myself to stand still. "Is your dad on his way?"

"He'll be here in the morning." Lily's dad still lived in San Antonio, where she'd grown up. He had a better excuse than I did, but at least I wasn't the only one late to the party. I wasn't sure if that made my absence better or worse.

"That's good."

Lily made an *mmm* sound. I didn't know what else to say after that, so I just stood there holding Lucía as Lily let her head drop onto the pillow behind her. She kept her eyes on us the whole time.

There was something calming about watching Lucía breathe. Even if it didn't make me feel any less guilty.

Tommy jerked awake across the room, causing his chair to scrape loudly against the tile floor. My heart leapt at the sound. Then Lucía started to cry, her face turning even pinker. Tommy stared at me, blinking hard as if he couldn't quite process what he was seeing.

"I'll take her," Lily said.

Tommy yawned. "I guess the baby's pissed at you, too."

"Tommy," Lily warned. He opened his mouth like he was going to say something else, but instead he rose from his chair and stretched his arms high above his head.

"Do you want anything to drink, babe?"

"I'd kill for ice water."

"You got it." He crossed the room and kissed her on the forehead. "Rosie, want to come with me?" He said it like it was a question, but I knew it wasn't.

As soon as we rounded the corner and were safely out of earshot, he turned to face me. "Where the hell were you?"

"At work," I said. Unhelpfully.

Tommy pulled a hand through his hair. "Why didn't you have your phone on you?"

"I'm not allowed to bring them into interviews."

"Jesus, Rosie. You couldn't make an exception this one time?"

"I didn't think—"

He huffed. "Exactly. You didn't think."

"But your text said—"

"It said no big rush. Not feel free to stop by whenever it suits you."

My stomach did a sharp flip. I willed myself not to throw up on his loafers. "I feel terrible."

My brother dragged his hands down his face, his gold wedding ring catching the fluorescent lights. His eyes were red and puffy, like he'd been crying. "It was so scary, Ro." Tommy let out a long breath, shaky and ragged. "Everything was fine and then . . ." His voice trailed off. I noticed his hands were trembling. Then he told me the story in fragmented sentences, the knot in my throat swelling with every detail.

First, the baby's heart rate had dropped. Then Lily's blood pressure had skyrocketed. There was a long stretch of time when they couldn't figure out what was wrong. It turned out to be a prolapsed umbilical cord, which meant Lucía wasn't getting enough oxygen. That's why the doctor had to do an emergency C-section. It only took four minutes to get the baby out.

Tommy and I weren't big huggers. Aside from the occasional elbow to the ribs, we barely ever touched. But I'd never seen him like this before. I pushed off the wall, closing the space between us, and squeezed his arm. "You must have been terrified."

Tommy stared at my hand as if it were a UFO that had just touched down on his front lawn. Then he shook it away, his eyes turning cold. "*Lily* was terrified. She could have died, Rosie. Do you get that? She could have died and you weren't there."

"I'm sor—"

"Sorry?" His eyes widened in exasperation. He shook his head. "No. Sorry isn't going to cut it. I almost lost my wife and my daughter today. This was supposed to be the best day of our lives and instead . . ." He blinked back tears. "It's going to take more than an apology to fix this one, Ro."

My brother pushed past me and disappeared into the cafeteria, leaving me alone in the hallway, listening to the distant clinking of silverware and the hum of vending machines, wishing I could disappear.

* * *

Mom and Dad were in Lily's room when Tommy and I got back with the ice water. We'd walked in silence, save for the gentle sloshing of ice against plastic. Mom was holding Lucía. Dad was standing with his arms glued to his sides, staring at Mom. It looked like he was actively resisting the urge to hug her. Lily lit up when we walked in. She must have been really thirsty.

Mom offered to let me hold Lucía and didn't bother to mask her surprise when I said yes.

"You're a natural, sweetheart," Dad said.

"Best aunt ever," Lily said.

"Not better than Dotty," Tommy replied.

It was a jab. But it was true.

Dad came up beside me and peered down at Lucía, who'd fallen asleep again. "I wish Dotty were here for this."

"Me too," I said. The room fell silent. I think we were all imagining what today would have been like if Dotty had been here. She probably would have said something ridiculous about Lucía's mushy little face or snuck in a contraband martini for Lily.

"So, who wants to babysit first?" Tommy asked. He said it like he was making a joke, but he was staring at Mom.

Dad answered instead. "You can call me anytime, day or night. I'm just down the street."

"Just make sure you don't call after one of your father's wine tastings," Mom said.

Dad's jaw slackened and his shoulders slumped. He looked genuinely hurt. "There are only a handful of things that bring me joy these days, Claire. Wine is one of them," he said, his voice quiet.

"What about you, Mom? Are you going to be around to see your granddaughter grow up, or will you be too busy with your new life?" My brother was looking for a fight. I was just glad it wasn't with me. I took a step toward Lily.

"God forbid I finally do something for myself." Mom's tone was sharper than I'd ever heard it. "How many lunches did I make for you kids? How many baseball practices did I drive you to? How many years did I spend pouring myself into your life at the expense of my own?"

At that, we all went quiet. It had never occurred to me that Mom had even an ounce of resentment about raising us. The thought made my rib cage feel like it was splintering.

"Please don't do this now," Lily said. She had her fingertips pressed against her temples. "Not tonight."

Tommy's whole body drooped. He looked so pale. "You're right. I'll drop it." He looked at Mom. "I'm sorry."

Mom rearranged her stricken expression into a forced smile. Lily's head dropped back into her pillow. I'd never seen her look so frail.

We managed to play nice until the nurse with the spiky hair kicked us out. Dad offered to walk me out. Tommy seized on the opportunity to ask Dad to bring him some sweatpants so he could spend the night with Lily and the new baby at the hospital.

Mom disappeared quickly and quietly, muttering something about a long drive. I think I saw Tommy roll his eyes, but I couldn't be sure. He might have just been tired.

* * *

"Quite a day," Dad said as we fell into our usual easy stride down the long, stark hallway.

I let out a long, whooshing exhale. "Yeah."

"Moments like this make me miss her more than usual." He

didn't need to say Dotty's name. We both knew. I nodded my agreement.

"You know what I always admired about my aunt?" Dad asked before immediately answering his own question. "She was unapologetically independent, never afraid to do her own thing."

I loved that about Dotty, too. But I sensed Dad was going somewhere with this so I didn't reply.

"My aunt wasn't around as often as I would have liked. She missed a lot of our family's little moments in favor of chasing her own. She was a family unit unto herself, in a way. But she always showed up when she knew we needed her. When Grandma Ruth got sick, Dotty dropped everything—even her Parisian girlfriend—to be by her sister's side. And she went out of her way to be in the waiting room when both you and your brother were born." He paused, then laughed softly. "She even insisted on cooking us dinner every night for two weeks after we brought you home from the hospital. All vegan meals, of course. Your mother hated it."

In spite of the heaviness I was feeling, I couldn't help but smile at the thought of Mom begrudgingly choking down one of Dotty's famous cauliflower steaks.

Dad stopped short of the big glass entry doors and turned to look at me. There was a look in his eyes that I didn't quite recognize. "What I'm trying to say is, that as often as Dotty chose herself, she was never selfish. She knew when to sacrifice her own needs for the sake of the people she loved. She was there when it really counted." His eyes were now boring into mine. "Do you understand what I'm getting at?"

I was afraid that I did. If I was right, I didn't like it. "I think so," I said tentatively. "I know I should have been here today."

"You let us all down."

I replayed the events of the day, reexamining every decision, considering it from every possible angle. If I'd told Nadine I'd had to leave right away, I would have made it to the hospital in time. But then I almost certainly wouldn't be getting the promotion I wanted so badly. And what would my family have to say about that?

If I'd agreed to stay but had taken my phone into an interview with me, I might have been able to run out just in time. But then I would have gone back on my word and broken Nadine's no phone rule. She'd probably fire me for that.

From where I was sitting, there was no winning.

"I know," I said lamely.

His nostrils flared. "I'm not sure that you do."

I flinched at the sharp edge in Dad's voice. He never talked to me this way. Not when he'd caught me sneaking out of the house or stealing money from Tommy's dumb Hot Wheels piggy bank. Not even when I'd landed myself on academic probation after my first semester of college. I opened my mouth to respond but Dad interrupted me.

"Sometimes I wonder if you realize that simply existing within our family isn't enough. You need to be an active participant. Like it or not, you aren't a kid anymore. You're an adult. It's time to start acting like it."

Then Dad hugged me, told me he loved me, and walked out the door.

From: Rosie Benson
To: Dotty Polk
Subject: No subject
Date: August 17

Dear Dotty,

I keep ruining everything.

Lily had her baby today—a perfect little smoosh named Lucía Rose—and I missed it. I missed it because I was trying to do the right thing. But how do you know what the right thing is when you're trying to serve two competing parts of yourself?

I feel like every time I fix one problem, another one pops up. Is that how life works?

Please tell me that isn't how life works.

Dad said I need to start acting like an adult, that I should be more like you. Doesn't he know that if I knew how to do either of those things, I would be doing them already?

The only thing that made this horrible night bearable was Lucía. I wish you could have been there to meet her. Holding Lucía made me feel like I belonged. With you gone, I usually feel like an awkward, unneeded appendage. If you were the heart of the family, I'm the appendix.

I just wish you were here to tell me that it's all going to be okay.

CHAPTER TWENTY-SIX

I watched as Kate dropped another pod into the espresso maker and pressed start. She took a step back, resting one hand on the counter and the other on her hip as the machine whirred to life. "What are you staring at?" she said, snapping me out of my trance. She wore a black-and-white polka-dot blouse that tied at the neck and her hair was swept back into a low bun. She looked so put together. I found it terribly irritating.

"I wasn't staring," I lied. "I was thinking." About yesterday. About Lily and Lucía. About how we almost lost them. About how I may have damaged my relationship with my brother beyond repair.

She rolled her eyes. "Do you want me to make you a cup or something?"

"I already had a cup." Another lie. I'd completely lost my appetite after last night. After Dad told me that I'd let our entire family down, that I was nothing like Dotty. That he was disappointed in me.

There was nothing worse than disappointing your most undisappointable parent. Mom was one thing—she was chronically disappointed in me. But Dad? That stung more than I ever imagined.

"Just one cup today? But how will you function?" Kate smirked.

I honestly wasn't sure. Concentrating on work was getting harder by the minute. At least today was Friday. I couldn't wait to get home, crawl under the covers with Bug, and not come out until Monday.

Or maybe ever.

"Rosie!" Priya called from the lobby, startling Bug from her nap. "Your ten o'clock is here."

"Be right there!" I called back, not bothering to mask my irritation. "Does Priya have to yell?" I whispered to Kate.

Kate shook her head. "She says her shoes make her feet hurt when she walks in them too much."

"It's ten steps."

Kate shrugged. "They're really cute shoes."

I spent the rest of the morning plowing through interviews, taking half-hearted notes and making empty promises along the way. *We'll give you a call if something comes up* meant you'll never hear from me again. *I'll submit your résumé and see if the hiring manager thinks you might be a fit* meant you're definitely not a fit. With Nadine's guidance, I'd grown accustomed to finessing these conversations. And with Pilar gone, I was uttering these phrases more often than not. I knew exactly the type of candidate Nadine wanted us to focus on: young, pretty, polished, bland.

Not that I felt good about it.

"Thank you so much for coming in today," I said to Gene, a graying middle-aged man in a pilled sweater. He'd been a personal assistant to an insanely wealthy spinster for the last twenty years—right up until the day she died. He was sharp and irreverent, kind of like Dotty. Pilar would've loved him, but Nadine would say he was out of touch. I stood, signaling him to do the same. "We'll give you a call if anything opens up. Personal assistant jobs can be few and far between, unfortunately."

He rose, returning my smile. "I understand. And I'll work on getting my references to you. Except for the dead one, obviously."

"Obviously," I said solemnly, just as the corners of his mouth twitched into a small smile. I couldn't help but appreciate Gene's dry wit.

I walked him out and stood by the lobby door to listen for the telltale chime of the elevator. There was nothing worse than getting stuck on the twenty-four-floor ride down to the lobby with someone you'd just interviewed, except maybe running into them in the bathroom. Satisfied that Gene was safely in the elevator, I rushed back to my desk to take Bug out for her afternoon walk. She sat waiting expectantly beside my chair, her tail wagging as I approached.

"Sorry to make you hold it," I whispered, scratching behind her little ear. Bug closed her eyes as she leaned her head into my hand. I slid my desk drawer open and pulled out her leash.

I slipped off my heels and stepped into my tennis shoes before attaching Bug's leash. She sniffed at it as if she'd never seen it before. I loved how she approached even the most mundane activities as if they were brand new.

As we started toward the lobby, Nadine's office door swung open. I turned to wave goodbye, but she gestured for me to stay, holding up a manicured finger. I stopped in the middle of the room, but Bug kept walking. She grunted when the length of her leash ran out.

"I'm glad I caught both of you," Nadine said, swishing a pointed finger from me to Kate, who had just returned to her desk clutching a stack of résumés. Nadine was accompanied by a man in a tailored suit with no tie. His honey-colored hair was slicked back like an old-school politician, and he looked about Tommy's age. I could almost make out the cloud of cologne that hovered around his body.

Nadine gestured toward the man, who looked so smug that I

half expected him to flash me finger guns. "I want to introduce you to Tyler." The man smirked at the introduction, deep lines appearing on either side of his mouth.

Kate sprung up from her seat, arm outstretched. "Nice to meet you, *Ty*," she said, shaking his hand. "I'm Kate."

He winced when Kate called him Ty. I made a mental note.

"Kate is one of our top recruiters," Nadine said. Kate practically glowed at the compliment. "And this . . ." Nadine turned her attention to me, her smile slipping as her eyes fell to my beat-up tennis shoes. "This is Rosie."

"I'm about to walk my dog," I said flatly. Normally, I'd blush at my own awkwardness, but the past twenty-four hours had stripped me of my ability to care about something so minuscule.

Tyler nodded. "Good to meet you, Rose."

"Nobody calls me that."

He grimaced. "My apologies. It's terribly irritating when someone butchers your name, isn't it?" He cast a sideways glance in Kate's direction. If he'd meant it as a dig, Kate didn't pick up on it. "What an unusual-looking dog," he said, turning his attention to Bug.

My eyes narrowed at the way he said *unusual*.

"She's a pug. Isn't she perfect?" Kate cooed.

Tyler's lips sputtered. "I wouldn't—"

"Bug is something of a mascot at Le Agency," Nadine said, rescuing Tyler from sticking his foot further into his big mouth. "The candidates all love her."

"How wonderful." It didn't sound like he meant it.

Nadine clasped her hands in front of her waist. Her nails bore a fresh coat of ruby red polish. "So, ladies. You may or may not know this, but Tyler is a pretty big deal in the recruiting space." Tyler held up his hands as if to say *guilty as charged*. It was almost as bad as if he'd done the finger gun thing. "He's been a freelance headhunter for years," Nadine continued. "And he's filled countless high-level positions at some of the top companies in Silicon Valley." I wondered if he knew Donovan. "And lucky for us, he's agreed to join our team."

Kate bobbed with delight. "How exciting!" Nadine nodded in approval.

The thought of working with this greaseball didn't sit right with me. "What does that mean?" I asked.

Nadine cleared her throat. "Tyler is going to be our director of recruiting."

"Not a senior recruiter, though?" The beginnings of a headache prickled at my temples.

Nadine and Tyler turned to face each other and laughed in unison. "Tyler is too qualified for that role."

"So you're still going to promote one of us, right?" Kate pressed.

"Well, it would be a bit silly at this point."

Kate furrowed her eyebrows in confusion. "What do you mean?"

Nadine pretended to pick a piece of lint off her spotless cashmere sweater. "Having Tyler onboard will be like having two senior recruiters."

"Two for the price of one," Tyler interjected, looking way too impressed with his own joke.

An eerie paralysis seized my limbs, my breath, my voice. I wanted to scream, to yell, to ball my fists and shoot daggers from my eyes. But I was frozen in place, stuck in some weird state of suspended animation.

I remember learning about the way animals respond to perceived threats in my Behavioral Ecology class (ironically the only veterinary-adjacent class that I did okay in). The professor said that we often talk about fight-or-flight response, but that there is another, lesser known response called freeze. "Think of a deer in headlights," she'd said, doing her best impression of a panicked deer.

That's how I felt now. Like a helpless, panicked deer.

I had broken the most important promise I'd ever made because I thought I was actually building a career here, with Nadine. And while Lily and her baby were fighting for their lives, I was in a conference room talking about calendaring skills and how to dress for an interview out of a misguided sense of loyalty. Meanwhile, Nadine knew all along that I never had a chance at that promotion.

Now it was all crumbling before my very eyes and I couldn't do anything but watch, utterly defeated.

"Are you kidding me?" The words burst out of Kate's mouth like a missile. Her voice shook with anger. "Yesterday you said Rosie couldn't leave to be with her sister-in-law in the delivery room. She missed it because she didn't want to let you down." I'd caved and told Kate about Lily after she asked me for the millionth time why I was being "weirder than usual." She'd been surprisingly sympathetic. "Rosie's been working her ass off to get that promotion and this is how you repay her?"

Kate turned to look at me and something passed between us, a silent truce. Were we allies now? Was this one of those "the enemy of my enemy is my friend" kind of things? Nadine had played both of us. She'd probably been looking for someone like Tyler this whole time.

I could see Nadine's wheels turning behind her amber eyes. Those conniving amber eyes. She was weighing her options.

Nadine let her hands drop to her sides and cocked her head in faux sympathy. "That's terrible. I'm very sorry to hear about your sister-in-law, Rosie." She shook her head. "I know you've both been working very hard. Admittedly, I've asked you to perform at a level beyond your capabilities so, Kate, I'm going to chalk this outburst up to stress." She turned to Tyler, lowering her voice. "I've never seen her like this." She turned back to Kate and me. "Why don't you two take off early today? After you've wrapped up the last of your interviews? You've earned it." Her voice dripped with condescension.

So *now* it was okay to leave early?

I couldn't feel my fingers. I looked down, realizing I'd somehow wrapped Bug's leash around my hand so tightly that I'd almost cut off my circulation. I loosened my grip and flexed my hand.

"I hope my coming aboard won't cause any issues," Tyler said to Nadine.

"Not at all," Nadine said, flicking her wrist dismissively. "We're thrilled to have you. Aren't we, ladies?" She stared at Kate, then me, daring us to defy her.

Kate crossed her arms over her chest. "Our bonuses better be big."

"Oh, Kate," Nadine demurred, forcing a fake laugh. She turned to Tyler, who chuckled along politely. "Isn't she great?"

"So great," he agreed.

"Whatever," Kate said. "I have a candidate waiting." She flashed me a sympathetic look before snatching a folder off her desk and disappearing into the lobby.

"Come on," Nadine said, taking Tyler by the arm. "I'll introduce you to Priya." She glided past me without so much as a glance. "See you tomorrow, Rosie," she said over her shoulder. "I hope your sister-in-law feels better soon."

It sounded like a threat.

"See you later, Rose," Tyler said as he strutted by.

"It's Rosie," I replied, even though I knew he wasn't listening.

As Tyler and Nadine disappeared into the lobby, I could have sworn I heard Bug growl.

* * *

When I somehow managed to drag myself into the office on Monday (thanks to a pep talk from Donovan, who encouraged me to stick things out for as long as I could stand it in order to avoid developing a "choppy work history" or worse, looking like a "job hopper"), I was greeted by a smug-looking Kate and bouquet of white roses on my desk. A petal-pink envelope rested against the gold-flecked vase. Kate looked on as I opened the card gingerly, as though it might be laced with anthrax. Inside, there was a note from Nadine thanking me for my hard work and a check for $2,500.

"Hush money," Kate said matter-of-factly. "And I think we can get more out of her. She needs us. If we both quit now, she'd be stuck with Ty." She flashed a devilish grin.

I couldn't help but laugh. I liked seeing Kate use her evil powers for good.

I looked back down at the note, written in Nadine's perfect, looping cursive. Pilar was right—I should have known something like this would happen. But I was in too deep now. I'd already sacrificed too much for this job. What would my family say if they knew that I wasn't willing to risk my employment to keep my promise to Lily but would walk away when I lost out on a nonexistent promotion? No. Leaving now wasn't an option. I needed to stick this out.

At least I now knew exactly who I was dealing with.

And I would gladly take her money.

CHAPTER TWENTY-SEVEN

SEPTEMBER

I ambled, zombielike through the rest of the week and the next.

When I got home from work on the first Friday night in September, there was a dried grass skirt hanging from the doorway of my bedroom. I called out for Marcia, then Raj, but got no response. When I stepped into my room, I found a loud floral print dress draped across my bed. There was a bright red hibiscus flower and a puka shell necklace resting alongside it. On my nightstand, I spotted a coconut with a yellow crazy straw and a riot of multicolored umbrellas sticking out of the top. A note rested against it that simply read, *drink me*.

I called out for Marcia again. Silence. Bug jumped up onto the bed and arranged herself on my pillows.

As I took a sip from the umbrella-laden beverage (it tasted like rum and coconuts) tropical music began to play. I turned to find Marcia standing in my doorway, wearing a bright pink ruffled off-the-shoulder top and matching skirt. Both were covered in tiny palm trees. She had a yellow flower tucked behind her ear.

My reaction was involuntary, a reflex. I beamed at her. "What is all this?"

"We're going out," she said, in the matter-of-fact way she used to tell me we were going to Alcatraz for a nighttime scavenger hunt or that we'd be watching the Giants game from a boat in McCovey Cove.

It had been months since Marcia insisted that I join her on one of her ridiculous, over-the-top outings. I assumed she'd been saving them all for Raj. Or worse, that she'd stopped cooking them up altogether. I figured that maybe she was a different person now, a proper grown-up who watched documentaries about mountain climbers and had no time for frivolous, impromptu adventures.

Much to my delight, I had been wrong.

I grabbed the flowery eyesore off the bed and shook it at her. "Where on earth are we going dressed like this?"

Marcia grinned. "Just trust me."

* * *

Dotty had told Marcia and me about the Tonga Room when we'd first moved to San Francisco. "It's a real hoot," she'd said. "And you absolutely have to try a Scorpion cocktail. But only one. If you have two, you'll probably end up in the pool." I'd almost completely forgotten about it. But apparently, Marcia hadn't.

The famous tiki bar was tucked away in the basement of the iconic Fairmont hotel. I'd only ever visited the life-size gingerbread house at Christmastime with my family, all the while completely unaware of what lay below.

My eyes widened as I took in the restaurant in its entirety. Lava rocks lined the entrance, giving way to a pirate ship, complete with a deck that served as a dance floor and a soaring mast that held a skull and crossbones flag. Beyond the ship was the dining area, with tables nestled under thatched roofs punctuated with tiki torches.

At the center of the room was a large pool with a small boat floating at the center, home to a yacht rock cover band. "Margaritaville" blared from the speakers.

"What do you think?" Marcia asked, her face illuminated by a flickering battery-powered candle. "Pretty cool, right?"

I took a sip of the Scorpion we'd ordered to share. It had arrived in a large bowl with two long straws. The server had to carry it slowly, with both hands. I was already feeling buzzed and giddy. I hadn't felt this carefree in months.

"The coolest. It kind of makes me want to run away to a tropical island," I said, thinking of Dotty. Maybe that's why she liked it here so much. It probably reminded her of the time she spent with Angela.

"I know," Marcia agreed. "Sometimes when work feels like it's going to swallow me whole, I daydream about moving to Hawaii and opening a snorkel rental shack."

"Same," I agreed emphatically.

Marcia rearranged her face into a sympathetic expression. "I'm sorry things have been so rough at work."

The mention of Le Agency called for another drink from the Scorpion bowl. Marcia followed suit.

My numbness toward work and specifically Nadine had yet to subside. Maybe I'd maxed out on big feelings for the year. I'd certainly gone through more than my share since Dotty died. Or maybe the extra money and my newfound alliance with Kate had softened the blow. Whatever the reason, I welcomed the indifference, even if it was masking latent rage.

Maybe I was a dormant volcano waiting to blow.

Donovan had been traveling for work (this time he was trying to close a deal with a start-up that had built a machine that could convert ocean waves to energy), which meant that I'd been playing third wheel to Marcia and Raj all week. They'd been surprisingly supportive, letting me vent about Nadine (Raj was appropriately horrified and even joked that he'd officially lost the title of Rosie's Most Hated Boss). I'd decided that having Raj around the apartment all the time wasn't so bad.

He'd even agreed to hang out with Bug tonight. When we'd left, decked out in our ridiculously loud outfits, Bug had settled onto Raj's lap and hadn't even bothered to lift her head to say goodbye.

"Let's not talk about work," I said.

"Agreed," Marcia said. "Work talk is banned for the rest of the night."

The band started playing "Take Me Home," which made me think of Dad. Phil Collins was his favorite singer because, of course he was. I'd gone two weeks without talking to my dad. And Lily and I had only exchanged a few simple texts, mostly pictures of the baby. I was pretty sure Tommy wasn't speaking to me.

I silently decided talking about my family was banned for the night, too.

A server appeared with a platter of spring rolls and a bowl of pineapple fried rice. Marcia promptly dunked a spring roll in chili sauce. "I think we're going to need another order of these," she said in between bites. "They're so good."

"Shouldn't we save room for that chocolate banana tart thing?"

She nodded. "And the mango panna cotta."

"I've missed this," I said, not meaning the bar or our plan to overorder tropical-themed desserts.

Marcia smiled in understanding. "Me too," she said. "Now dig into the spring rolls before I finish the whole platter myself."

* * *

By the time we finished devouring dinner and polishing off both plates of dessert, the dance floor had filled with people. Mostly tourists. No one else was wearing anything remotely on theme, except for the people who worked here.

"So dinner's on me," Marcia said, waving her hands before I could even protest. "And that's because I have something I want to tell you."

A bright flash of lightning accompanied by a loud clap of thunder boomed overhead. A sheet of rain began falling from the ceiling and into the pool. The band played on as if nothing was happening.

It all felt appropriately ominous.

The chocolate and mango and rum in my stomach rearranged themselves into a sugary whirlpool of dread. "What is it?"

"It's nothing bad," Marcia said quickly. "It's just—you know how I promised not to keep anything from you? After all the Raj stuff?"

How could I forget? I nodded.

"Well, I wanted to tell you that Raj asked me to move in with him . . . and I said yes."

The way she visibly braced herself for my reaction caused the swirling in my stomach to stop. It was replaced by a guilty ache in my heart. I did not want to be the person who made Marcia make that face.

I looked down at my dress, then up at Marcia's. She'd gone to so much trouble to make this night special, to soften the blow of her news. But my best friend shouldn't be afraid to share huge life events like this with me. Especially since, much to my surprise, I was *happy* for her.

"Marcia," I said, my hands flying to my heart. "That's so exciting!"

Her reply was tentative, as if she were waiting for the other shoe to drop. "Really?"

I bobbed my head vigorously, the rum animating my over-the-top movements. "Yes, really. This is huge! I'm so happy for you guys."

Tears welled in her eyes. She swiped at her cheeks. "Are you sure?"

"One hundred and ten percent," I reassured her. "I see how happy you make each other and that's all that matters."

"He does make me really happy," she agreed.

"I know."

She reached across the table to take my hand. "But what are you going to do? Where are you going to live?"

I had absolutely no clue, but that didn't matter right now. There'd be plenty of time to process what all this meant for me later. "I'll figure it out," I said. "But I do have to tell you that you're setting a very bad precedent here."

"What do you mean?"

I gestured around the restaurant. "If you take me out on a magical tropical date to tell me that you're moving in with your boyfriend, you're going to have to figure out something even bigger when you get engaged."

She laughed, a big, relieved laugh.

"And I think you'll probably have to fly me to Hawaii when you tell me you're pregnant."

"Done," she said. "You're aware that you're completely unhinged, right?"

I shimmied my shoulders. "Well aware. Now, we have to celebrate. Let's break Dotty's rule and get another Scorpion."

* * *

Marcia and I didn't end up in the pool as Dotty had predicted, but we were asked to leave the premises after Marcia tried to scale the mast of the pirate ship. It was just as well, since I'd already lost my voice singing along to the piña colada song and Marcia had lost her shoes.

When we finally made it home, Raj was asleep in Marcia's room. He'd tucked Bug in on the couch under a warm blanket. I carried her into my room and got her settled in her usual spot on my bed. She barely opened an eye.

I was about to change out of my hibiscus flower dress (which, I had to admit, had grown on me by the end of the night) when there was a knock at my door. I swung it open, expecting Marcia.

But it was Raj. His hair stuck up on one side and his eyes were heavy with sleep.

He held up a bag of cheese puffs. "I remembered that you liked these and I thought you might want some comfort food. I hope I got the right brand."

I was touched by the gesture. I was also pretty drunk so I snatched the bag from his hands and tore it open. "Thank you," I said, through a mouth full of puffs.

He dipped his chin. "Marcia said you were super supportive tonight. You're a good friend."

"So is she."

He rubbed his eyes. "Yeah."

I popped another puff into my mouth and chewed, hoping that my loud crunching wouldn't wake Bug. "Congrats by the way. I'm excited for you two. I just hope you know that Bug and I will be coming over for dinner at least once a week." I'd gotten used to enjoying Raj's cooking, in spite of myself.

He grinned. "I wouldn't have it any other way." Then he shifted his weight from one foot to the other. "So, I talked to Marcia and I'm going to start sleeping at my old apartment again until the move."

"Why?"

"Well, that busted pipe has been fixed for weeks now and, more importantly, I thought it might be nice for the two of you to have the apartment to yourselves until then. Sort of like a last hurrah?"

I started to protest, but Raj held up his hands to stop me. "I'm happy to do it," he said. "I mean, it's the end of an era. We should treat it accordingly."

It *was* the end of an era. Tears pricked at the corners of my eyes. I blinked in a futile attempt to fight them off.

Before I knew it, I was hugging Raj. If he was startled by my sudden display of affection, he didn't show it. "Thank you, Raj."

He patted my back. "You're welcome, Rosie."

I'd worked hard to stop thinking of Raj as my old boss and to start thinking of him as Marcia's new boyfriend.

But that night, he became my friend.

CHAPTER TWENTY-EIGHT

Donovan pried the top off a bottle of Jarritos soda and passed it to me. "How long have Marcia and this Raj guy been together?"

I took a grateful sip. "Seven or eight months. Give or take."

Donovan whistled. "I guess when you know, you know," he said before cutting into a fat yellow onion with what appeared to be a very sharp, very new-looking knife. He'd invested in a meal kit subscription after I'd mentioned that it might be fun to cook together. Tonight was our first attempt.

I shrugged. "I guess."

After the rum-fueled glow of my night with Marcia had worn off, the stark reality of my situation had set in. Marcia and Raj were going to be moving out at the end of the month and I didn't know what Bug and I were going to do. I'd ruled out getting a new roommate to replace Marcia because (a) I was pretty confident I could find cheaper rent elsewhere and (b) I couldn't imagine living there without her. So my best bet was to find a studio as soon as possible, since I obviously wasn't going to move back home.

I looked down at the potato peeler I was holding. Its pristine silver blades gleamed up at me. "Donovan?"

He didn't look up from the onion. "Yeah?"

"Have you ever cooked?"

"Like in my life?"

"Like in this apartment."

He set the knife on the cutting board, his face twisting into mock offense. "What are you trying to say?"

"Well, have you?"

"*Well*, I never had anyone to cook for. But now I have you." He smiled that irresistible Donovan smile.

I nudged my hip against his. "So that's a no."

He reached to take the peeler and a half-skinned potato out of my hands and set them on the cutting board. I turned to face him as he wrapped his arms around my waist. "I'm cooking now, aren't I?" he said. Then he kissed me. And suddenly, I didn't care about cooking or apartment searches anymore.

"Now," he said, pulling away to reach for the recipe card, "if you could just keep your hands off me, I'd really like to get back to making these crispy potato tacos."

I kissed him one more time before prying myself away.

"So unprofessional," he said, shaking his head.

We went on like that, chopping vegetables and sneaking kisses and pretending to take the whole endeavor very seriously. Eventually, we turned on some music (Donovan had a killer Motown playlist) and he sweetly pretended not to panic when I spilled a few drops of salsa on the white countertops but moved faster than lightning to wipe them up.

Then we sat, perched atop barstools at the island in the center of the kitchen, and clinked our bottles together to celebrate our accomplishment, the first dinner we'd ever made together.

It was surprisingly tasty. Although it was probably pretty hard to mess up tacos.

"I'm having dinner with my mom tomorrow night," Donovan said casually. "She says she wants to meet you." He cracked a mischievous smile. "But don't worry, I'll protect you from her for as long as I can."

Panic fluttered in my throat. Donovan's mom wanted to meet me? My family barely knew he existed. The thought of coming face-to-face with The Patricia Ng terrified me. Her portrait, the one the city had used when she was the mayor, stared at me from a bookshelf in his living room. She had a dazzling smile and piercing brown eyes. I could tell she wasn't the type to suffer fools.

Things with Donovan had been so easy these past few months—our relationship was light and uncomplicated. We hung out in his condo, drank fancy wine, had a lot of sex. We existed in a bubble. Seeing Marcia and Raj together had made me realize how separate I'd kept every part of my life: work, friends, family, Donovan. What would it look like if I allowed the edges of my worlds to bleed together?

Probably not very pretty, if the disastrous day Donovan and I had spent at Happy Hooves was any indication. He'd worn an unnecessary Band-Aid on his cheek for more than a week (he wasn't allergic, just dramatic) and he hadn't asked to go back since—nor had I dared to invite him. Not that I'd had much time to volunteer lately, thanks to Nadine.

"I'll protect you from my parents, too," I said. "They're a mess. I wouldn't want them to scare you off."

Donovan reached for my hand. "Nothing could scare me off."

That scared *me* a little, but I had no idea why. "You're sweet."

He cleared his throat. "So we agree that we're not involving parents yet," he said. I didn't love the use of the word *yet*. "But what if we tried living together?"

I swallowed a bite of my taco without chewing, the hard edges of the shell scraped down my esophagus. "What?" I asked through coughs.

"Move in with me."

I swallowed a big gulp of fruity soda. "Are you serious?" I asked, my voice scratchy.

"I know it's fast, but I'm crazy about you."

That sent my heart racing. I was really into Donovan, too, but I wasn't ready to *live* with him. That was like expert-level adulting. I'd barely gotten comfortable playing in the amateur league.

"What about Bug?" I said, grasping for practicality. I'd only brought her over a few times, and Donovan hadn't exactly warmed to her. Or Barb, for that matter. But lucky for Donovan, Barb didn't live with me.

That would be fun, though.

"You and Bug are a package deal," he said, holding my gaze. "So you bring her."

This was all making me dizzy. "You're serious, aren't you?"

"Of course I'm serious. I— Well, I can see a future with you, so I don't see why we wouldn't, you know, move forward. Take that next step."

A future with Donovan. That was the dream, wasn't it? Suddenly my brain was mapping out the next decade of our lives. First, I'd move into his condo. Living together wouldn't be that different from the way things were now. Instead of dropping Bug off at the apartment with Marcia, the two of us would go straight to Donovan's after work. We'd cook dinner together and stay up late watching movies and brush our teeth side by side every morning.

Eventually, we'd get married. Probably somewhere cool and iconic, like the Ferry Building or the de Young Museum. I'd wear a sleek white dress and our wedding would be written up in the *Chronicle* with a headline celebrating the former mayor's son's matrimonial bliss.

Maybe we'd honeymoon in the Maldives.

Surely Donovan would want to have kids.

Did *I* want to have kids?

I hadn't thought about having children in terms of wanting them. It always seemed like a given, a mandatory stop on the journey through adulthood.

But was that what I wanted? Not now, that was for sure.

Maybe not ever.

I was spiraling. I grabbed the edge of the countertop to steady myself. The base of my skull ached, a dull nagging pain.

I wasn't ready for the next decade of my life to be all planned out. Not yet.

But Donovan hadn't proposed marriage and babies and growing old together. He'd just asked if I wanted to live with him. Nothing more, nothing less.

I needed to get a grip.

"I don't know," I said. I shook my head, trying to clear away the fog. "It's just that everything is changing all at once. I'm a little overwhelmed."

He reached over to cup my cheek in his hand. "I totally get it. Just think about it," he said, tucking a strand of hair behind my ear. "It's not like you have to move in tomorrow."

Donovan was so sweet, so stable. So reassuring. I was lucky to have him.

I brushed my lips against his. "You really are the best boyfriend. Even if you barely know how to cook."

I spent the next few days wrapping my mind around what it would be like to live with Donovan, to call that gorgeous, wildly expensive condo home. Despite my initial panic, the idea started to grow on me.

It was certainly the practical choice. It might even be fun. Plus, like Dad said, it was time for me to start acting my age. What could be more adult than having a live-in boyfriend?

By the time the weekend rolled around, I'd decided to give it a try. At least until I found a place of my own.

* * *

Our final weekend in our first real apartment came too quickly. The closer my looming goodbye to Marcia got, the more unbearable it seemed. But, in spite of myself, I was feeling optimistic.

Nadine had deposited another $2,500 bonus into my checking account as a thank-you for all my extra work (a result of Kate dropping tons of not-so-subtle hints; it wasn't exactly blackmail, but it was blackmail adjacent; we didn't care), and thanks to Donovan, Bug and I weren't going to end up on the street.

Now I just had to figure out how to fix things with my family. Especially Lily.

"When are you going to go see the baby?" Marcia asked as she stretched a strip of packing tape across a large cardboard box.

I wrapped a half-melted candle in a piece of old newspaper. "Tommy said I could come over anytime, but that there's not much to do. Lucía has colic so none of them are sleeping."

Marcia gave an understanding nod. "You could offer to watch her for a couple hours."

"Me? Alone with a newborn? I don't think that's a good idea."

"It's not that hard."

"I think they're still mad at me."

"And your plan to make them unmad at you is to disappear?"

I dropped the candle into a waiting box. "You know it's not like that."

"All *I know* is, when I messed up and hurt the person I love the most, I didn't ghost her. I stuck around and kept trying to make things better."

I knew she was talking about us. And she was right. Our relationship hadn't been the same since Raj had barged into the picture, but things were good again. She was still my best friend.

We'd been through so many phases of life together, from our awkward middle-school years to getting grounded for stealing gin from her grandpa's liquor cabinet, to graduating from college and moving into an apartment we couldn't really afford in a city where we believed all our dreams would come true. We'd grown up together. And we'd always been there for each other—through heartbreaks and family drama and first kisses and huge, life-altering mistakes. And now she was leaving. We were never going to be the same again. Everything was changing.

I set down an unwieldly wad of packing tape and wrapped her in a tight hug. "It's the end of an era," I said.

She hugged me back even tighter. "I know. Am I crazy for moving in with a boy?"

"Yes."

"But he's so cute."

"Oh god. You're going to marry him, aren't you?"

Marcia laughed as she dropped her arms. I saw her wipe away a tear. "I think so. Isn't that insane?" she said, crinkling her nose.

"Clinically insane," I said. "But I'm really, really happy for you two loonies."

"How do you feel about playing house with Donovan?"

I hesitated. "Good, I think. I stay over all the time, so it won't be that different. Plus, it's only temporary."

She stared at me, unblinking. "Okay."

"What?"

"Nothing."

The front door creaked open, sending Bug flying from her bed in the corner. "Who wants coffee?" Raj called as Bug bolted toward him, tail whirring. I stifled a laugh as she almost made him drop the tray full of paper cups.

The three of us spent the rest of our last weekend together packing up the apartment until all that was left was a bare mattress, six suitcases stuffed to capacity, an inordinate number of hangers, and a pile of cardboard boxes. I insisted that Marcia and Raj take all our kitchen supplies and living room furniture since I wouldn't have anywhere to store it. And I figured I could use Nadine's bonus to help furnish my new studio (which was probably all I'd be able to afford) when the time came. Marcia begged me to let her pay for everything, but it was all so old and mismatched that I would have felt guilty taking her money. The truth was, they'd be doing me a favor by taking everything off my hands. I needed to travel light until I knew where Bug and I were going to land long term.

"Is Donovan going to help you with any of this stuff?" Marcia asked out the side of her mouth. She only talked out of one side of her mouth when she had a strong opinion about the subject. She still hadn't fully warmed to the idea of Donovan and me. The fact that I hadn't once invited him over and kept him separate from the rest of my life didn't help.

"He's busy with work," I said. The truth was he had offered to help. But I didn't want him to. And I couldn't tell my best friend why.

Because I didn't know.

CHAPTER TWENTY-NINE

OCTOBER

Bug and I officially moved into Donovan's condo on Sunday night. By Thursday morning, I'd realized that sleeping over a couple nights a week and living together full-time were *not* the same thing. Guests didn't have any responsibilities. Roommates, on the other hand, were supposed to know which sponge to use for the dishes and which to use for the counters. There was a difference, apparently.

"Hey, Rosie?" Donovan asked, peeking his head out from the bathroom, an electric toothbrush in one hand and a mangled tube of toothpaste in the other. "Would you mind squeezing this from the bottom up from now on?" He shook the tube for effect.

I was still in bed and bleary-eyed from sleep. Donovan had the most comfortable mattress in the entire world—it was like memory foam and a cloud had had a baby. "Sure," I grumbled, wrapping my arms around Bug, who lay curled up by my side. Donovan hadn't been thrilled about her sleeping in the bed, but where else was she supposed to sleep?

"And can you make sure that Bug doesn't use my pillow?" There was a tinge of anxiety in his voice.

"She's not going to use your pillow."

"It had a weird indent in it yesterday, like she'd been lying on it."

"She has an alibi for that. I was with her all day. I'd swear to it under oath." I patted her little head. "My client might have the means and motive, but she didn't have the opportunity."

That got him to laugh. He was so cute when he laughed. "You should be an attorney."

I pulled Bug closer to me and squeezed her little tummy. She sighed but refused to open her eyes. She wasn't a morning person. "Bug has me on retainer."

He shook his head, undoubtedly finding me irresistibly charming. Hopefully that would make up for my toothpaste faux pas. I reminded myself that Donovan was an only child who hadn't had a roommate since his freshman year of college. After a harrowing experience in the dorms (something about filthy communal showers), his mom had sprung for a studio off-campus.

"How does Thai food sound for tonight? A new place just opened up next to the office and everyone's raving about it."

Now we were talking. "I can't believe you even had to ask."

"Cool. I'll pick it up on my way home." He paused, seeming to remember something else. "Also, would you mind putting all your laundry in the hamper before you leave for work today?"

"Sure thing," I said, flopping back down onto my pillow, trying not to miss the comfortable messiness of my old room.

* * *

Being at the office had once been a welcome escape. But now, it was more of a necessary evil. With my hopes of a promotion vaporized, I'd resigned myself to tolerating Nadine and her antics for the foreseeable future. Granted, she'd been on her best behavior since

Tyler came onboard, but I knew it was only a matter of time before she pulled something else.

Tyler, on the other hand, didn't bother with good behavior. He was just as awful as I thought he would be.

Maybe even a little worse.

Just this week, he'd asked Kate to bring him an espresso in the middle of a team meeting, hit on Priya, who to her credit appeared entirely disinterested, and name-dropped Elon Musk so many times that I'd lost count. It was definitely more than thirty.

I'd successfully avoided him most days, filling my schedule with back-to-back interviews. Today was no exception.

"When was your last job?" I asked, eyeing the résumé of a woman whom I guessed to be in her midthirties, with a stylish black bob and nearly concealed circles under her eyes. She folded her hands in front of her, revealing a deep purple—almost black—manicure.

"Three years ago." Her voice carried an almost imperceptible tremor. "I was a social media manager at a FinTech start-up. And while I was on maternity leave, it got acquired by a larger company and my position became redundant." She unclasped her hands, splaying her fingers. "It made the decision to stay home with my son a lot easier."

I nodded, looking at her résumé again. I'd developed a bad habit of not memorizing an interviewee's name before we sat down. This woman's name was Parker Kim. I liked her. "And you want to get back into social media?"

"Yes," Parker replied with an exaggerated breath, "I'm dying to get back to work. I miss going into an office and having adult conversations and creating something besides Lego castles and finger paintings." She pressed her hands into the table and leaned forward conspiratorially. "This interview is the most thrilling thing

I've done all year." I smiled in appreciation of her candor. Then I drew a tiny star next to her name, shorthand for *this one's a keeper*.

She bit her lip. "Do you think I'll have a hard time finding a new job since I've been out of work for so long?"

"That can make things a little more challenging," I said. "But you have great experience and you interview really well. If we can get your résumé in shape, I think I can line up a few interviews for you next week."

She brightened at that. "Thank you. I wasn't sure what to expect. Some people can be sort of judgmental . . ." Her voice trailed off, a painful and unspoken story hanging between us. I wondered if that would happen to Lily if she didn't go back to her job right away. I hoped not.

A new sense of purpose bloomed in my chest. If I was going to stick it out with Nadine for the time being, at least I could help people like Parker.

"There are plenty of hiring managers who won't bat an eye at a little time off. We just have to find them." I flashed my most encouraging smile and stood. "I want to introduce you to our president before you go. She likes to meet all our new candidates in person."

Nadine perked up as Parker entered her office. She was polished and pretty. And not too old. Nadine's favorite. I made my introductions and handed Parker's résumé to Nadine, who remained seated at her desk. She pinched the sheet in her left hand, her emerald ring glistening in the bright office lighting. We stood in silence as she read it over. I felt like a kid waiting for a discerning teacher to grade my test.

Nadine dropped the résumé onto her desk with a flick of the wrist before leaning back in her chair. She eyed Parker up and down. "Your last job was three years ago," she said. It wasn't a question.

Parker clasped her hands in front of her. "Yes, I took a little time off after we adopted my son."

"Three years is more than a little time."

"I suppose," Parker said quietly.

"Tech and social media evolve almost weekly. Three years might as well be a decade."

Parker's mouth fell open as she turned toward me, a panicked look in her eyes.

"Parker's been managing her community center's Twitter account and she built their Instagram profile from scratch," I said, jumping in to help Parker. "They got five thousand new followers in the last year. We're going to add it to her résumé to fill in the gap." I could feel the back of my neck getting hot. "And she's fluent in Korean," I added, pointedly. "So she'd be perfect for that marketing agency that's based in Seoul."

Nadine made a clicking noise with her tongue, apparently unimpressed. I noticed she was fiddling with her ring—never a good sign. "I don't know," she said slowly, looking from Parker to me. "I just don't think she's going to be a fit." She said it as if Parker weren't even in the room. My face twisted into a scowl. Nadine pretended not to notice. "I'm sorry"—she cast an obvious glance at Parker's résumé—"Parker. But I don't think we'll be able to help you." She flashed a tight, red-lipped smile as the words *bitch bitch bitch* flashed through my head. Parker wrapped her arms around her waist, looking like she was about to throw up. "And Rosie?" Nadine said as I turned to leave with Parker. "We need to talk."

Parker was out the door before I even had a chance to react. I started after her, but Nadine stopped me. "Do I need to remind you that we aren't a charity?" she said, pushing Parker's résumé to the edge of her desk.

I balled my fists. "She was hardly a charity case."

"Her shoes said otherwise."

A couple months ago, I might have thought that was funny. But now I knew that Nadine didn't have a funny bone in her body. She was all mean. "What the hell is your problem, Nadine?" I said, surprising myself. I'd never talked to an authority figure that way before. Come to think of it, I hadn't talked to anyone that way before. Except maybe Mom.

"Have a seat."

I hesitated, wanting to rebel. But then I remembered that Dotty had once told me never to be the only person standing during an argument. "It gives the other person the upper hand, makes them feel superior." I obeyed begrudgingly, plopping myself down into an overly stuffed chair—the same one I'd sat in when I'd interviewed all those months ago.

"I'm not saying Parker isn't employable," Nadine began. She spoke slowly, careful not to sound condescending. "She's just not the right fit for Le Agency. We have a reputation to uphold." She shrugged as if to suggest that this was out of her hands. I hated her for being so calm.

"You didn't have to be so rude."

"Blunt and rude are two different things."

I rolled my eyes, sending an uncharacteristic flash of anger streaking across Nadine's face. She recovered with a sigh. Then she said, "I've let you down, haven't I?"

I crossed my arms over my chest and narrowed my eyes, unsure how to respond.

"I have." Nadine shook her head sadly. "I blame myself. I asked you to do too much too quickly. You've only been here a few months, and here I was putting ideas in your head about taking on a more senior role when you clearly weren't ready."

I scoffed. "So now I'm bad at my job?"

Nadine leaned back in her chair, placing her elbows on the armrest. "It's not your fault. I shouldn't have said anything about a promotion. It made you overly confident."

Nadine's words sucked the air right out of my lungs. I inhaled sharply, trying to catch my breath as memories of the last few months flashed before my eyes. All the placements I'd made. How quickly I'd learned to play Nadine's little games. The ridiculous amount of overtime I'd worked. The countless Saturdays I'd missed at Happy Hooves, too exhausted to get out of bed. The sheer number of people I'd turned away because they didn't meet Nadine's ridiculous standards. "You've been using me," I said.

"Asking you to do your job is hardly using you."

"You never even considered promoting me."

"I may have been overly optimistic about your potential—"

"You lied."

"Is that how you want to talk to the person who just gave you not one, but two performance bonuses?"

"That was a bribe. I'm not stupid. Also, if I'm so terrible at my job, why did you give me two bonuses?"

Nadine smirked. "You think I don't know about Evan and Pilar's little agency?"

It took everything in me to keep the shock from registering on my face.

"I know they're trying to recruit you," she said. "They'll probably go after Kate soon, too, if they haven't already. I was just protecting my interests. I don't need the two of you running off with our clients, do I?" She fixed me in her icy glare.

I gripped the armrests of the chair so tightly I half expected my bones to poke out from under my skin. I felt the breath in my lungs and the blood in my veins and a new, deep certainty in my gut.

And suddenly, I knew.

When I thought about the major, controllable circumstances of my life, I'd more or less fallen into all of them. I'd accidentally met my boyfriend in a bathroom at my friend's party. And he'd gotten me this job. I moved in with Donovan because Marcia had decided to move out. Even adopting Bug had been happenstance. It's not that any of these things were bad—least of all Bug—but I hadn't actively pursued them.

It was time to make a choice, to make something happen.

"I don't want to work for you anymore," I said, my voice strong and clear.

"Careful," Nadine warned.

"I don't need to be careful," I said, coolly. "I don't want to work here anymore." I leaned forward. "I quit."

"I won't give you a good reference," she said through curling red lips.

I smiled. "That's fine."

"You'll need to leave the office immediately."

"Then I'll get my stuff," I said, snatching Parker's résumé off the edge of Nadine's desk as I stood. Then I stormed out of her office.

I'd never felt more certain, more powerful.

I could get used to this.

"Is everything okay?" Kate asked as I stomped toward my desk and started indiscriminately shoving the contents of it—an expensive-looking gold stapler, a plastic cup full of mint green pens, a Le Agency branded notepad—into Bug's backpack. "What happened?" she whispered, casting a glance back at Nadine's office door as it slammed shut.

I gave her the highlights, and when I finished, Kate grabbed my arm and said, "You're a badass, Rosie. I didn't know you had it in you."

I laughed; leave it to Kate to insult me while complimenting me.

"What are you going to do now?"

I shrugged. I definitely hadn't thought this out. "Evan and Pilar are hiring. Maybe I'll go work for them."

Kate's eyes widened. "Can I come with you?"

That would take some convincing. Evan and Pilar weren't Kate's biggest fans. But before I had a chance to respond, Tyler emerged from an interview room with a candidate who looked just like him. "Hey, ladies," he said, oozing faux charm. "I want you to meet Charlie—"

"Can you give us a minute?" Kate snapped. Tyler jerked his head back at Kate's words, but his hair didn't move.

"No prob," he said, recovering quickly. "We'll go talk to Nadine first." Kate nodded at Tyler as he steered his doppelgänger toward Nadine's office.

"He's so annoying," she whispered, shaking her head. "You should go before he comes back. We can catch up later."

She squeezed my arm as a silent understanding passed between us. "I know we haven't been close, but I am going to miss you. Bug, especially." She pulled me into a rushed hug, my arms dangling by my sides. "And I won't tell Nadine that you stole that stapler."

CHAPTER THIRTY

When Donovan got home that night, bags of takeout dangling from his arms, I was still buzzing with energy. I paced the kitchen as he arranged containers of spring rolls, gyoza, edamame, and pad kee mao on the counter. My hands shook as he passed me a glass of wine, but he didn't seem to notice. I waited until we were seated at the table before I broke the news. I wanted his full attention. "I quit my job today," I said as Donovan took his first sip. He stopped midgulp before carefully returning his glass to the table.

"You're joking."

"I'm the opposite of joking."

He blinked. "What happened?"

I told him the story in vivid detail. How rude Nadine had been to Parker. How I'd finally stood up for myself when Nadine had tried to make me feel small. And how I'd called Parker as soon as I'd left the office to give her Pilar's number. Donovan listened intently, brow furrowed, elbows on the table, hands folded beneath his chin. "Wow," he said when I finished, pressing his clasped hands against his mouth.

"Right?" I said, beaming. "Your girlfriend is a badass."

"Are you going to try to smooth things over with her?"

"Why would I do that? She's a nightmare."

"Nadine's pretty well known. And kind of vindictive."

"So?"

"So she could really hurt your career if she wanted to. If you've pissed her off enough."

"Didn't you hear what she said to me?" I asked, my voice cracking. Bug pawed at my shin, anxious that I was upset. I hoisted her up onto my lap. Donovan grimaced as she leaned forward to sniff at a piece of broccoli on my plate.

"I don't blame you for quitting," he said evenly. "Nadine was acting like a monster. But don't you think you were a little impulsive?"

"I mean, yes. But what I did also took guts. I was terrified, but I did it anyway."

"True," he said before taking another swig of wine. It didn't feel like a compliment. "Have Evan and Pilar figured out their funding yet?"

I coaxed a noodle onto my fork. "I'm not sure."

"Have you tried calling them?"

"Yes," I said between bites. "But that's not what we talked about." That was only partially true. I'd, of course, told them everything about my epic exit, basking in their celebratory whoops of joy. But when they'd mentioned potentially being able to hire me within the next few weeks, I told them I'd need more time.

He squeezed the back of his neck with his left hand. He usually only did that when he was stressed about work. "How was that not what you talked about?"

I wrapped my arms around Bug, who remained fixated on my plate. "I just need a minute to think. I don't want to keep taking jobs that I don't even like."

"How are you going to pay rent? You can't just live here for free forever. You have to take this seriously."

"I have some money saved," I said, wounded. I'd never asked Donovan for anything like that. "And I do take my career seriously. Why aren't you being supportive?"

"Supportive?" he repeated, shaking his head. "You want to talk about being supportive?"

I nodded, feeling wary about where this was going.

"You called *Pilar* after everything went down with Nadine today. I offered to help you pack up your apartment, but you insisted on doing it yourself. You wouldn't even let me help you carry a single box upstairs." He sighed as his face softened. "And now, we're living together and I haven't even met any of your friends— let alone your family."

"You know Marcia."

"You know what I mean."

"I guess."

"Why are you like that?"

I shrugged, keeping my eyes fixed out the window. I knew Donovan was right. The truth was that I was afraid of what would happen if I let my worlds collide. I'd worked hard to be a functional, pulled-together person (or to at least look like one) since Dotty died, but it always felt like I was one misstep away from falling apart all over again. I think I was scared that if I let anyone see the whole me, see the state of my life in its entirety, they'd realize that I'd been faking it all along.

I didn't feel like I could say any of that to Donovan, though. I knew he wouldn't get it. "I don't know," I said instead. "I've never had a boyfriend before."

Donovan bit into a bulging edamame shell, squeezing a bean out with his teeth. I watched as he chewed, jaw flexing. That's when Bug made her move, putting her front paws on the table and nabbing a chunk of tofu before I could stop her. "Bug, no!" I said, pulling her back. She lunged for another bite, sending my wine-glass flying. It shattered on the floor, oozing deep red liquid onto Donovan's snow-white rug.

I pried Bug free of the table and carried her over to the couch, careful to avoid the broken glass. "Don't move," I said through gritted teeth, feeling instantly guilty as she tucked her tail between her legs. I gave her a reassuring pat on the head before turning to face Donovan. "I'm so sorry," I said, feeling the high I'd been riding all afternoon slipping away.

He passed me paper towels and set a bottle of sparkling water on the table before sinking back into his chair. I could hear his foot tapping nervously against the hardwood floor. It drove him crazy when I forgot to load the dishwasher. A red wine stain was probably going to send him over the edge. "I'm really sorry," I said again.

"Can we not have the dog at the table?" His hand was over his eyes, fingers splayed.

"It was an accident."

"A preventable one."

I didn't say anything else. But as I sat on the floor, blotting wine out of a rug that probably cost more than any commission I could have ever hoped to earn at Le Agency, I started to think that I might have made a huge mistake.

Bug slept on the floor that night.

To: Dotty Polk
From: Rosie Benson
Subject: I get it now
Date: October 15

Dear Dotty,

I get it now.

I get why you turned Grandpa Archie down. And why you ran off to Hawaii after your pregnancy scare. I get how someone can offer you the world, but if it's not the world you're meant to live in, it can feel like you're being escorted into a cage.

But I don't get how you dealt with the guilt. Or how you can break a perfectly wonderful person's heart when they haven't done anything to deserve it.

I want to feel what you had with Angela. I thought I'd found that, but I was wrong. It was something else.

I don't know what to do next. I've blown up my whole life, Dotty. And I don't know how to fix it.

CHAPTER THIRTY-ONE

Donovan and I broke up a couple of days later. "You're not happy," he'd said, his tone flat. I didn't even try to argue with him. "Is there anything I can do?" he'd asked, even though he already knew the answer.

There was nothing wrong with Donovan. And plenty wrong with me. But I didn't have the energy to try to change, in order to be what he needed. So I packed my bag, gathered Bug's toys, and bid Donovan a numb goodbye. I think we promised to talk soon. But, aside from figuring out how to get the rest of my stuff out of Donovan's spare bedroom, what was there to talk about?

I'd quit a perfectly good job without a second thought. Now I was leaving a perfectly good guy. He was kind and funny and successful. But he didn't love Bug. And I didn't love him. Dotty always said love wasn't logical.

I debated calling Marcia to ask if I could stay with her and Raj, but they hadn't even been in their new place for a month. And I wasn't in the mood to be around a happy couple anyway.

Staying with my family was out of the question. I couldn't bear the thought of telling them I was unemployed. Again.

There was only one place I could think to go. I just hoped no one had changed the locks.

As I carried Bug up the steps toward Dotty's front door, I was greeted by a familiar pang of sadness, one that I'd been trying to ignore since Dotty died. Once inside, Bug scrambled out of my arms and sprinted toward Dotty's bedroom. Her naive hope that Dotty might still be here, that these past months were just a terrible misunderstanding, brought my own heartache rushing back in a violent, paralyzing wave. I stood motionless in her front room, feeling like an intruder.

Everything looked exactly the same, save for a few scattered boxes and a light layer of dust: walls packed with a nonsensical array of artwork and framed photos, books stacked high on end tables, an ancient floral rug stretching across the worn hardwood floors. But it felt entirely different. It was as if nothing and everything had changed.

Bug stood outside Dotty's bedroom door scratching at the base, her tail whirring at a blinding speed. I knew what I had to do, and I felt terrible about it. But I couldn't protect Bug from the reality of Dotty being gone forever. And I couldn't blame her for holding out hope, either. I moved to open the door, pausing with my hand on the knob. Maybe there was a part of me that expected to see her ghost on the other side. The door creaked open and Bug rushed in. I switched on the light as Bug began sniffing every corner with increasing urgency, her tail no longer wagging.

Dotty's bed sat bare and empty. Someone—Dad, probably—had stripped the sheets and stacked her pillows and comforter in a neat pile at the foot of the bed. Her purple glasses sat on top of her nightstand, next to a book about the kama sutra. The room still smelled like her perfume. A lump gathered mass in my throat. I'd forced my grief over Dotty's death to the far corners of my mind, using Nadine and Donovan and Marcia and Raj as distractions. But now it was back, front and center, and heavier than ever before.

Bug eventually gave up on her fruitless search and stood in the center of the room, looking lost, her soft whimpers tearing at my heart. "I think we'd better sleep on the couch tonight," I said, switching off the light and pulling the door shut.

We camped out in Dotty's living room for the rest of the day while I did my best not to drown in a puddle of grief and anger and shame. Somehow, I'd found myself back where I was months ago: a single, jobless failure. Only this time, I was homeless, too. I'd been so confident that I was doing the right thing in the moment, but in the quiet stillness of Dotty's empty house, things didn't seem quite as clear.

I didn't call Marcia. I ignored Evan's and Pilar's texts. I didn't even want to think about what Mom would say when she found out about all this. The one person who wouldn't make me feel like the world's biggest failure was Dotty. And she wasn't here anymore.

* * *

Bug barked at the doorbell, startling me out of my pity party. I wiped my eyes with the sleeves of my sweatshirt and hurried to the door. The pizza delivery guy eyed me suspiciously when I answered. I'd watched enough *Dateline* to know that it should really be the other way around. He was a stranger on my doorstep, after all. I snatched the pizza box out of his hands and set it on an end table. Bug sniffed it eagerly. "How much do I owe you?"

"Do you live here?" He wore a faded black Amici's hat, and upon closer inspection, was cute—handsome even—in a skater boy kind of way. He reminded me of Breckin Meyer's character in *Clueless*.

"Obviously," I said, subconsciously attempting to smooth the sides of my ragged ponytail. His eyes fell to Bug, who continued to sniff at the box. "Where's Dotty?"

"You knew Dotty?" His face fell at my use of the past tense. "She died a few months ago," I said. "I'm her niece."

"Damn. I really liked her."

"Me too."

"She's ordered the exact same pizza every Wednesday for as long as I can remember," he said. "Same as you—medium with bell peppers, onions, and black olives. No cheese. Extra sauce. We called it the *Dotty Special*. When she hadn't ordered it in a while, I just figured she was traveling again . . ." His voice trailed off. We stood there in uneasy silence, him holding an empty pizza bag, me holding the screen. "It's on me tonight," he said, straightening his shoulders. I started to protest, but he interrupted me. "It's the least I can do."

"She'd want me to tip you."

He laughed. "You're probably right." I gave him a twenty. Not that I had it to spare, but he was nice, and he liked Dotty. He stuffed it in his pocket and turned to walk back down the stairs. "Have a good night, Dotty's niece."

"You, too, Dotty's pizza guy."

* * *

I ordered the *Dotty Special* again the next night, and the night after that. The one after that, too. Patrick, Dotty's pizza guy, kindly pretended that this was perfectly normal. I even started looking forward to our little visits. He was the only human I'd interacted with since Donovan and I broke up, and he was surprisingly easy to talk to. He'd always hang around for a few minutes, asking questions about Dotty or telling me about his day. I showed him pictures of Barb and a video of Sprinkles and Cupcake playing on a large wooden teeter-totter as Cupcake bleated with delight.

Patrick even brought me free breadsticks when he found out he'd been accepted to culinary school. He said he wished Dotty were here so he could thank her. She was the one who'd introduced him to the head of admissions.

After I paid Patrick, I'd devour half the pizza, washing it down with a big glass of wine. I was always sure to save some crust for Bug, who would gobble it up gratefully. When we were done with our respective dinners, I'd pick up my glass, careful not to slosh any wine onto the floor, and wander over to Dotty's bookcase, where I'd pull photo after photo off the shelf: Dotty standing next to an attractive woman in a gauzy blue dress with hair that fell past her elbows. Dotty on a boat next to a man who looked like the guy on the box of frozen fish sticks Mom used to buy when I was a kid. Dotty surrounded by a group of people about her age, all covered in dirt, arms wrapped around one another, grinning from ear to ear.

I'd scrutinize their faces, pressing my nose against the glass. But no matter how hard I tried, I didn't recognize a single person.

Had she surrounded herself with pictures of these strangers to create the illusion of a full and happy home? Did she think these people actually cared about her? Because I'd only heard from a handful of them after she died.

Tears came more easily now. I'd become so comfortable with crying that I didn't even register my own sobs until my cheeks were slick and salty. I cried for myself. I cried for Dotty. I cried because I couldn't stop crying.

* * *

Loneliness crept up on me. Staying at Dotty's probably wasn't the healthiest choice. It was so quiet at night. I knew my family or

Marcia or even Raj were just a text away. But I couldn't bring myself to pick up the phone.

When Sonia called, I sent her to voice mail. I thought a lot about Mom after the divorce, the way she'd disappeared from our family. At the time, I thought she'd been selfish, but now I understood. She'd been drowning in shame.

It might have been a Thursday when I heard the scrape of a key turning in the front door. I bolted upright from the couch, startling Bug, who leapt off my lap and scrambled toward the door, eager to greet whoever was behind it. I grabbed a dolphin statue off Dotty's coffee table.

Lily jumped at the sight of me, recovering in time to greet a wiggling Bug. Her dark hair was piled on top of her head and Lucía was strapped to her chest. "Rosie," she breathed. "What are you doing here? Are you okay?" She placed an overly stuffed diaper bag on the floor. I pretended not to notice the way she looked at my greasy ponytail and stained sweatpants. "Why aren't you at work?"

"Why are you here?"

Lily shut the door and took a step closer, concern etched in the delicate lines of her face. "You look terrible."

"I quit my job."

Her expression remained fixed. Maybe this wasn't a surprise. "Why aren't you at your boyfriend's place?"

"We broke up."

A nod. "Okay . . . you don't look well. Have you had anything to eat today?" Her eyes drifted over my sunken cheeks. I'd been surviving on takeout since I'd left Donovan's. It had been days since I looked in the mirror.

"I quit caffeine cold turkey." Dotty didn't have any coffee in the house and I hadn't been able to bring myself to go outside, let alone into a grocery store.

A fellow caffeine addict, Lily nodded gravely. "Why didn't you tell me things were this bad?" It looked like she was about to cry. I barely mustered a shrug before I started crying myself.

Lily got me a glass of water and force-fed me a granola bar from her purse. Eventually, I calmed down enough to tell her every last detail. It felt good to finally talk to someone, to get it out. I don't know why I hadn't reached out to Lily sooner. I hadn't been fair to her. She'd decided to trust me a long time ago, asking me to be by her side during the most important moments of her life. But I'd withheld so much from her. I knew I needed to let her in. I had to stop fighting to keep my life so compartmentalized. Even if I wanted to, I didn't have the energy anymore.

"I can't believe you were dealing with all this on your own," she said quietly after I finished.

I wiped my nose with the sleeve of my sweatshirt. It smelled like Bug. "I was trying to grow up."

"Grown-ups are allowed to ask for help," she said, rubbing my back. "God knows I've had to."

I dropped my face into my hands and let out a moan. I'd been a terrible sister to Lily—so selfish and immature. I'd chosen my commitment to a stupid job, my goal of getting a fictitious promotion, over the promise I'd made to Lily. I would probably spend the rest of my life making it up to her. "I'm the worst. I'm so sorry, Lily."

She let out a gentle laugh. "Well, I *was* mad at you, but now that I know how bad things were, you're forgiven." She unhooked the straps at her shoulders and pulled Lucía out of her carrier. She'd grown so much since the day I'd met her. Her hair still stuck out in every direction, but her cheeks had gotten rounder, chubbier. So had her little tummy. "Can you hold her for a minute?"

"Of course," I said, extending my arms. Lily passed Lucía to me with practiced ease, reminding me to watch her head. I tried to ignore the ball of guilt in the pit of my stomach as I cradled my niece. I should have gone to visit sooner. Even if I was scared.

Lily stood and stretched her arms overhead before removing the carrier from her chest and dropping it to the floor. "Has it been hard?" I asked as Lily rooted around in Lucía's diaper bag.

She pulled out a bottle of milk and started shaking it. "Yes," she said emphatically. "So hard and so wonderful." She returned to her seat beside me on the couch. "Tommy's been amazing. And so have your parents. They're actually getting along pretty well if you can believe it." I gave Lily a look that said, *I'll believe it when I see it.* She smiled. "It shocked me, too. Have you talked to your mom at all?"

"Nope."

Lily looked like she was about to say more, but then her attention went to Bug, who'd slowly been edging her way closer to me as I held Lucía. She was now just inches away from the baby's head, wagging her tail in nervous, methodical swishes. Bug gave Lucía's head a sniff, then looked from me to Lily. "This is your cousin," Lily said. "You'll be best friends someday." Bug thumped her tail, apparently liking the idea. I loved that Lily called them cousins. "Are you okay to feed her while I take a look around?" she asked, extending the bottle in my direction.

I'd forgotten that Lily had been tasked with selling Dotty's house once the baby was born. I beat back another pang of guilt as I realized I never offered to help, opting to forget all about Dotty's place until I'd needed it for myself.

Lily spent a good half hour roaming the house, opening and closing cabinets, turning on faucets, flicking light switches, and jotting down notes along the way. "This place is going to need some work," she said when she reappeared in the living room. "I'm going to have to get a contractor out here. And a painter. And a stager."

"Your job sounds hard."

"It's just a lot to keep track of," she said, not looking up from her phone. "Especially now that my brain feels like a scrambled egg."

"Are you even supposed to be working right now?"

"Not really. But I need to get this off my plate. And there's no point in letting the house sit like this." She looked around, taking in the cluttered bookshelves, mismatched furniture, and crooked picture frames. "It almost feels like she's still here, doesn't it?"

"Almost," I said. My eyes drifted to Dotty's old bar cart. It appeared to be sagging under the weight of highball glasses, cocktail shakers, and a clunky ice bucket. I flashed on the first time Dotty had taught me how to make a proper martini in that very spot. "The secret is in the shake," she'd said. "Shaking things up isn't a bad thing. Remember that." The memory sent a pang of grief straight through my heart.

"Lily, can I ask you something?"

"Of course."

"Have I ruined everything?"

Lily looked startled by my question, as if I'd unexpectedly lobbed a football at her head. "Of course not," she said, setting her hand on my shoulder. "You're going to be fine."

I didn't realize how much I'd needed to hear that until she said it. I really wanted to believe her.

Lily's stomach growled loudly, breaking the spell of the moment. "Sorry," she said. "I've got to eat something. I'm starving. But I want to talk about this—just let me get some food in me first."

I settled back into my spot on the couch with Lucía still in my arms as Lily wasted no time unwrapping a massive sub. She sat on the floor so she wouldn't have to hunch over the coffee table. "Want my pickle?"

I took it gratefully, surprised by the sudden return of my appetite.

"Sorry I didn't get you one. I would have if I'd known you'd be here." She bit into the sandwich without waiting for my response.

"It's fine," I said. "I have leftovers in the fridge."

"I bet you do." She eyed me warily as she chewed, like she knew that whatever my leftovers were, they probably didn't hold any nutritional value.

"Hey," she said, dropping the sandwich. "I have an idea."

"What?"

"Well," Lily said, growing increasingly animated. "I have my hands full with Lucía and you're not exactly busy at the moment." She gestured toward the couch, which had started to develop a Rosie-shaped imprint.

"So?"

"*So* I was thinking you could help me out with Dotty's house."

"Help out how?"

"You can pick up where your dad left off," she said, looking around at the remnants of Dad's half-hearted attempts to clean out Dotty's place. Apparently he'd abandoned the project shortly after Lucía was born. "You can sort through all Dotty's things and manage the repairs. You're here all the time, anyway, so it'll give you something to do. You'll be like my assistant."

"I don't know anything about houses. Or real estate."

"I'll walk you through everything. And you can always call me if you have questions. It'll be fun."

The thought of weeding out all of Dotty's crap sounded like the opposite of fun. "I don't know, Lily."

"It's not like you're doing anything else right now."

She had me there. But I didn't have to tell her that. "I'm looking for jobs."

"This is a job."

"What are you going to pay me?"

"Your payment is that you get to keep living here rent-free."

"And if I say no?"

"I'll have to tell your family that there's a squatter living here."

For the first time, I understood how Lily was able to stay married to Tommy. She was an even better arguer than he was. And she wasn't afraid to play dirty. In spite of myself, it made me love her even more. "Well, I guess I don't have a choice," I grumbled.

Lily rubbed her hands together, sending crumbs flying. "You guessed right," she said, grinning.

From: Peter Simpson Esq.
To: Rosie Benson
Subject: Re: Dotty
Date: October 30

Hello Rosie,

Please accept my apologies for this severely delayed response! It appears your email got lost in the shuffle of my perpetually full inbox.

I want to start by thanking you for this thoughtful message. It brings me great joy to know that my dear friend was so loved by you. Now, regarding Dotty's outlook on how her life turned out, I think I may be able to help here, as I once asked Dotty that very question.

I'll never forget that day. It was a few years ago. And it was September. We'd decided to forgo our usual piano bar and martini night for an afternoon at the beach. The weather was simply too beautiful to ignore.

Dotty packed us the loveliest picnic—complete with real silverware and prosecco!—and we lay sprawled on a checkered blanket with Bug napping in the sun and waves crashing distantly onshore. It was one of those perfect days, the kind you only get a few times a year.

I'd needed a day like that. My kids were driving me crazy, and my (now ex) wife and I had just gotten into a huge fight over something stupid and I was teetering on the edge of quitting my practice altogether after a particularly devastating setback in court. "Life has you on the spin cycle," Dotty had said in her wry way.

I must have quipped that she was lucky not to have to worry about all of it—kids, marriage, feeling stuck in an unfulfilling job. "You're smart to keep it simple," I'd said.

"Life is never simple," she'd replied. It then occurred to me that maybe she'd wanted all those things but hadn't been able to attain them. Maybe Dotty was unattached by circumstance rather than by choice. I felt like an ass. I'd never even asked. So, I did. And her response will always stick with me.

She said, "There have been moments throughout my life where I thought it might be nice. I've seen how happy getting married or having children made my friends and family. But I spent a lot of time reflecting on what I wanted for myself—not on what I'd been told I wanted—there's a big difference. And I knew in my gut that it simply wasn't meant for me. Nothing is for everyone." Then she took a long, luxuriant sip of prosecco and said, "I've lived the most wonderful life I could. And I wouldn't change a damn thing."

So there you have it, my dear. If given the chance, Dotty wouldn't have changed a damn thing.

Sincerely,
Peter S. Simpson, Esquire

CHAPTER THIRTY-TWO

NOVEMBER

The shelves in Dotty's living room seemed as good a place as any to start. The woman had an absolute riot of miniature statues and beaded bracelets, lanterns, ornaments, and books. So many books. The ones in her office appeared to have been limited to the sciences, but she had volumes of novels crammed onto rows of shelves in the living room. I had no way of knowing whether any of her stuff was valuable, so I boxed it all up, setting aside the things that reminded me of Dotty the most (a heart-shaped piece of coral from Stinson Beach, a *World's Greatest Aunt* pin, and a dinosaur fossil for Tommy).

Bug sat on the couch, her big brown eyes following my every move. "I'm sorry about packing up your house," I said. She whined in response, her little brow furrowing. "I know you made lots of great memories here. But I promise to take you to visit some of Dotty's favorite spots soon." I'd spent my morning reading and rereading Peter Simpson, Esquire's email about Dotty, longing for one last day at the beach with her. One last picnic. One last moment. Making vague plans to take Bug back to Baker Beach was at least a small consolation.

I was admiring a tiny carving of a frog that I'd found behind a vase filled with peacock feathers, next to a troll doll with a green gem in its belly button, when the doorbell rang. I hopped down from the shelf I was balanced on and made my way to the door, clutching the smooth wooden statue in my fist.

Bug joined me at my heels as I opened the door, expecting to find Lily on the other side. But my hands went limp at the sight of Mom standing on Dotty's doorstep. The frog carving slipped, clattering onto the floor. "Mom," I breathed, surprised at how good it felt to say. "What are you doing here?"

"I thought you might need some help," she said, peering over my shoulder. "Can I come in?" At the rate I was going, I'd be as old as Dotty was before I finished cleaning out her house. And Mom was an organizing savant. But was she going to want to talk? I didn't have the energy for a lecture. I started to shake my head, but Mom interrupted. "I'm sorry I didn't call first. But I brought coffee." She held up a carafe.

I bounced in place, fighting with myself. Retreating into the safety of Dotty's house alone was tempting. But something about the look on Mom's face—concern tinged with hope—won me over. "Come in," I said, stepping aside. Her face softened at my invitation. I think she was relieved.

She politely picked her way around the maze of boxes and stacks of books. I had a reason for every pile, but I'm sure it looked like a disaster zone to Mom. "You can set the coffee here," I said, pushing a stack of magazines to the edge of Dotty's counter. She swept her hand across the freshly cleared patch of laminate. I could see her fighting the urge to sanitize it with one of the antibacterial wipes she always kept in her purse. To her credit, she didn't.

"How are you?" Mom asked as I pulled a pair of mugs out of the dishwasher. She sounded nervous.

I passed her a mug. "I'm fine."

"Lily told me you quit your job."

My nostrils flared. "She promised not to say anything."

"I got it out of her. I know about the boyfriend, too. And Marcia moving out. She didn't give it up easily."

I felt like I'd been punched in the gut. But I couldn't blame Lily. I knew all too well how persistent Mom could be. I squeezed the coffee mug so tightly the tips of my fingers turned white. "That's none of your business," I said. "She had no right to tell you any of that."

"She was worried about you, sweetie. We all are."

"We? Dad knows?" I asked, panic rising in my chest. Mom nodded; her blue eyes were rimmed with red. Like she'd been crying. "Tommy, too?"

"I don't think those two keep things from each other."

I hated the idea of my family talking behind my back, thinking they could solve all my problems for me when I wasn't even in the room. "Did she say anything else?"

Mom shook her head. "Just that you're staying here until you figure out what to do next."

I blew out a long breath. Mom reached for my mug. It took me a second to realize I needed to loosen my grip. I handed it over. "I didn't come here to yell at you if that's what you're thinking," she said. I watched as she unscrewed the cap of the carafe and filled my mug to the brim.

"So why are you here?" I asked. I think part of me was still expecting a gotcha moment. Mom was the reigning champion of the bait and switch.

She passed my mug back before filling her own. "Can we sit?"

"Okay," I said, gesturing toward the sofa where Bug lay sprawled on the center cushion, blissfully unaware of our human problems.

We settled in on either side of her, Mom still clutching her mug. I set mine on top of a small pile of paperbacks on the coffee table.

"I owe you an apology."

My eyebrows ticked up. "For what?"

"For so much. I'm not even sure where to start." She stared down into her cup as her shoulders started to shake.

"Mom, don't cry."

She waved me off. "I'm fine," she said, her voice catching. "I just need to get this out." She looked up from her coffee, meeting my eyes. "After your dad and I decided to file, I started seeing a therapist. And I realized, among other things, that I haven't been the mother you've needed for a very long time."

I'd never seen Mom like this before. She looked smaller, almost frail. "What are you talking about?"

"Maybe I should back up," she said, straightening her shoulders. "Your grandmother—my mother—wasn't exactly a stable parent. I'm not sure she even wanted to be a mom. My childhood was very . . . uncertain. We didn't always have food in the house or clean clothes to wear to school. It wasn't like that all the time, but she never had a steady job. And your grandpa was never in the picture, so he was no help. There were a lot of ups and downs is what I'm trying to say."

Mom never talked about her childhood or my grandparents. They'd both passed away before I was born. I guess I'd just assumed her life had always been so easy, so perfect. "I had no idea."

"That's because I never told you." She mustered a weary smile. "Anyway, when I met your father, he felt so safe. So stable. He was an honest, straightforward man with a kind heart and a good job. How could I not fall in love with him?" She shrugged. "And then when I found out I was pregnant with your brother, it all felt meant to be. I promised myself I was going to be the best mom ever. You kids were always going to have everything you needed."

"We did. Maybe more than we needed."

"Maybe. But as you got older, I got scared."

"Why?"

"Because you reminded me of my mother. And of Dotty."

"Because I'm irresponsible?"

"Because you're a free spirit."

"You didn't want me to turn out like them."

"I thought if I could push you in a different direction, you'd be happier. I wanted you to have all the things I didn't. I wanted you to have stability. I thought I was helping you. But I didn't stop to ask you what you wanted, and I'm so sorry."

My mind flashed to all the little moments when Mom had nudged me into things I didn't want to do. Softball. Dance class. Buying the pink prom dress instead of the green one. Changing my major. "What does all this have to do with you and Dad?"

"Your dad is a wonderful man," Mom said. "And he was a wonderful husband. But I lost myself in our marriage by trying to be the perfect wife and mother. We built a really nice life together. But it didn't feel much like life anymore."

"And now?"

"I'm happy. Or working on being happy. I'm trying to let go and see where life takes me." She lifted her gaze. "And I want that for you, too. I don't want you to end up like me, realizing you spent decades of your life chasing the wrong things."

"I don't even know what I'm chasing anymore. My life is a mess right now."

"You're brave. And you're young. And you're being true to yourself. That's far from a mess."

I didn't know what to say. Here was my mom, pouring out her

heart to me in the middle of Dotty's disaster zone of a living room. I think it was the most honest conversation we'd ever had. I liked this version of Mom. I reached past Bug to squeeze her knee. She placed her hand over mine. "I want you to know that I'm proud of you," she said. "No matter what."

Something let go in my chest, a knot I didn't know was there. "Even if I quit a hundred more jobs and couch surf with Bug for the rest of my life?"

"Let's try to cap the job count at fifty." She patted my hand.

"That's fair," I said. It was nice to joke with her. "Why didn't you tell me any of this sooner?"

Something in her face shifted like I'd hurt her feelings. "You never said anything about my email. I figured you weren't ready."

"What email?"

"The one about Dotty."

"I never got it."

Her expression softened. "Well, it doesn't matter now. It's probably better that we talked in person anyway."

"Yeah," I said, mentally flipping through the list of emails I'd received. Tommy, Lily, Dad, Peter, Angela, a couple of coworkers, and a handful of friends from other countries. One from a guy who was mad about an unflattering article Dotty had written about his hotel. But definitely nothing from Mom.

* * *

Mom stayed most of the day, doing her best to help me make sense of Dotty's treasures. By the time we were done, we'd stuffed two garbage bags with old magazines—each filled with an assortment of dog-eared recipes, hotel reviews, and ads for brightly colored pashminas. A part of me hated to throw them away, knowing

Dotty had held them in her hands, creased the pages with her fingers. The donation boxes were easier. It made me happy to imagine Dotty's crystal vases and collection of nesting dolls finding a home with someone new. I kept her cocktail shaker, though. I knew she'd want me to have it.

I'd been missing Mom without even knowing it. It was nice to have her around. Comforting, even. She was actually kind of fun to talk to when she wasn't constantly telling me what to do. I even got her to tell me what happened the night she'd decided to end things with Dad.

"It sounds so silly in hindsight," she said, tucking a strand of hair behind her ear.

"I still want to know."

"He suggested we hire a house cleaner."

I attempted to keep my mouth from falling open but failed miserably.

"But it wasn't about the house cleaner," Mom said hurriedly. "That just happened to be the moment I realized how lost I was."

I'd had lots of moments like that recently. "So what happened?"

Mom's face softened. "Well, I mentioned something to your father about how I was feeling like all I was good for these days was cooking and cleaning and folding laundry. It had been so much more fulfilling when you kids were home. I felt so needed." She smiled, but her eyes were sad. "Then your father said we could hire someone to 'take care of all that' if I wanted. And suddenly, I felt like I'd spent my life doing things that were so insignificant that they could be outsourced with the snap of a finger. At least in the eyes of your father. The thought made me feel lost. So utterly lost."

I'd never thought of Mom that way. She was the one who'd held us all together, kept us on track. Things would have fallen apart without her.

"I tried to make it through dinner, but before I knew it, I just blurted out that I wanted a divorce. Your dad was shocked. So was I, honestly."

I thought back to my breakup with Donovan. That moment when we both just knew it was over. I couldn't imagine how awful that would feel after thirty years. It was bad enough after a few months.

"You're a lot more than a house cleaner to all of us. Everything you did for us mattered. You know that, right?"

Mom smiled, for real this time. "I do."

* * *

I practically had to shove Mom out the door when it was time to leave. "Are you sure you don't want me to stay the night?" she asked for the fifth time.

I shook my head. "Bug and I have been here for weeks. We'll be fine."

As I watched Mom reluctantly making her way down Dotty's front steps, I couldn't stop thinking about her missing email. What if hers wasn't the only one I'd missed? "Hey, Mom?" I called.

"Yes, sweetheart?"

"Where did you send your Dotty email?"

She scrunched her face in confusion. "What do you mean?"

"Did you send it to my address or to Dotty's?"

She shook her head, trying to remember. "I just hit reply. So I guess it went to Dotty. Did I mess something up?"

I smiled. Beamed, actually. "No," I said. "Not at all. Thanks, Mom."

As soon as Mom drove away, I sprinted toward the back of the house, my footsteps becoming more urgent as Dotty's office came into view. The room remained unchanged: jewel-toned pillows were piled haphazardly in the corner, thirsty-looking houseplants crowded Dotty's desk, and a dusty old laptop lay askew on the floor, its charging cable plugged into the wall. I plopped down, flipped open the computer, and pulled up Dotty's email browser.

I found my email in Dotty's outbox. It had been 184 days. One hundred eighty-four days since we'd sat in Peter's office, each of us falling apart in our own way.

My heart fluttered with hope as I clicked Dotty's inbox. She had hundreds of unread emails, most of them news alerts or promotional offers. I typed the subject of my email into the search bar and hit submit. My search returned thirty-three unread messages.

How had I not thought of this before? I'd asked everyone to reply to me, but of course some people would miss it. People were terrible at reading directions—especially in the throes of grief.

"Bug," I called, my voice shaking. "You're going to want to see this," I said when she poked her head into the office. She looked at me like I was crazy, but that didn't stop her from climbing into my lap.

I read Mom's email first.

From: Claire Benson
To: Dotty Polk
Subject: Re: Dotty
Date: June 10

Hi honey,

I'm very proud of you for the way you're handling all this. I know how much you looked up to Dotty.

I'd be lying if I said it didn't bother me. I think all mothers hope their daughters will look up to them. You did for a while, at least. Until you were about twelve. You were never disrespectful. Even as a teenager. But it was as if we suddenly started speaking different languages and never found our way back to each other. I really hope we can change that.

So you want to know about Dotty. Well, the first time I met her was right after your dad and I had gotten engaged. Your grandparents hosted a dinner party to celebrate, and then Dotty breezed in, fresh off an airplane from Greece. (Greece! I'd never even left the state.) She was tanned and tall and beautiful. And so gregarious! She walked right up to me, grabbed me by the shoulders, and said, "You're gorgeous. Our David is lucky to have you," before kissing me on both cheeks. She then proceeded to spend the rest of the evening peppering me with questions as she sipped a dirty martini. I felt like I was being interrogated.

I told myself I loved Dotty. I wanted to love Dotty. Your father adored her. Archie adored her. Ruth had her on a pedestal.

But something about Dotty always scared me. We were just so different. I couldn't understand the choices she made. Never settling down. Never having children. Jet-setting all over the world. Because of that, she often missed out on the most precious of moments. You know she never came to a single one of your plays? Or Tommy's baseball games? She also missed many Thanksgivings and Christmases and birthday parties. And she was so blunt. Always blurting out whatever came to mind. It all felt so irresponsible, as though she was refusing to grow up.

She reminded me of my mother. And my mother was not someone to be admired.

I'm starting to realize, though, that maybe the difference between Dotty and my mother is that Dotty stayed true to herself while my mother didn't. Dotty didn't chase things she knew wouldn't make her happy. She followed her heart, even if it didn't make sense to anyone else. If Dotty had forced herself into the box I'd wanted to put her in, maybe she would have turned out like my mother. A bitter, self-involved woman who pushed away her only daughter.

Dotty was anything but bitter or self-involved. She was unflappably happy, incredibly generous, and in her own way, she was an essential part of this family—even if she insisted on questioning my every decision. Especially when it came to you. I think she saw herself in you.

I think I did, too.

And I know I didn't handle that well. Sweetheart, I was so afraid you'd turn out like Dotty that I discouraged you from pursuing the things you wanted for yourself. I think I pushed you too hard. I think that's why we aren't as close as I'd like us to be.

For what it's worth, I've pushed myself in the wrong direction, too. I sacrificed the parts of myself that didn't fit into my idea of how a perfect life should look. And I'm trying to remedy that now. That's why your dad and I are splitting up. I know it's hard to understand. But I'd love to talk to you about it when you're ready. I hope you'll give me a chance to explain.

I'm so sorry about Dotty. I hope you know that she loved you very, very much.

And so do I.

Love,
Mom

If the day I'd spent with Mom had shifted my perspective, her email shattered it. She was right; we'd been speaking different languages for years. And neither of us had tried hard enough to understand the other. But Dotty had finally changed that.

After reading Mom's email a dozen more times, I moved on to the rest, each holding its own revelation about Dotty—big and small.

There was an email from a guy named Stuart who said Dotty inspired him to quit his medical practice and become an outdoor adventure guide. Stuart had written his email from a yurt in Cambodia. Dr. Richard Burmeister, an entomologist who claimed he was the inspiration for Bug's name, responded with a story about a time he and Dotty had gotten so high, they'd decided to spend the night in a tree in hopes of befriending some local macaws.

A woman named Meredith, who grew up down the street from Dotty and Ruth, said Dotty was her idol because she'd had the guts to leave their little town. Meredith's sister, Jane, responded, too. She and Dotty had worked at an ice cream shop every summer when they were teenagers. Dotty had claimed the owner, a sweet old man with a genuine passion for ice cream, was a fascist. But she'd softened on him when he'd recommended her for a job at the local paper.

There was an email from one of Dotty's old college friends who hadn't spoken to her in years because of some dumb fight. And another from a man she'd hooked up with in a hotel pool while on a trip to Miami just last year.

I even learned where Dotty had gotten her name. Dotty's friend Sandra, a woman she'd met in college, said that one of Dotty's professors—a sexist pig, according to Dotty—had a habit of refusing to learn the names of the women in his class. On the rare occasion that he called on them, he'd make up names based on their appearance or what they were wearing, like Blondie or Scarf. Apparently, Dotty had a pension for polka dots back then, so he'd called her Dotty. The following semester, Dotty wrote an article for the school paper exposing the professor for having lied about his writing credentials and forging his journalism degree. She'd wanted to be sure he'd know she was the one who'd gotten him fired, but she also knew he wouldn't remember her name. So she used the name Dotty in the byline. The article was the most-talked-about thing on campus for months. Dotty was a hero. And the name just stuck.

The sun went down long before I finished reading every last message. By the time I was done, my neck ached from hunching over on the floor with my nose practically touching the screen. I sat up tall and stretched my arms. I should have been tired, but I was buzzing with energy. I couldn't believe I'd spent months thinking that only a handful of Dotty's friends cared enough to respond to my email when that was the furthest thing from the truth. Dotty had been loved by so many people. I hadn't realized I'd been shar-ing her. She'd always done such a good job of making me feel special.

* * *

I stayed up the rest of the night, piecing Dotty's life together one email at a time.

Dotty had grown up in a small beach town in Southern Califor-nia, the oldest daughter of an attorney and a homemaker. Her little sister, my grandma, was her best friend despite their differences. While Grandma Ruth had dreamed of getting married and raising children, Dotty had dreamed of going to college and traveling the world.

When she returned from Hawaii, Dotty enrolled in the journalism program at a local university. After graduation, she'd gotten a job at a San Francisco newspaper where she worked for the next fifteen years. She'd protested the Vietnam War. She'd followed a woman named Iris to France. She'd come home without Iris when Grandma Ruth had gotten sick. It sounded like a bad breakup. Iris said it was her greatest regret.

When she was in her sixties, Dotty had become a freelance travel writer. Not because she'd had to, but because she'd wanted to. She'd hiked breathtaking trails in Patagonia. She'd slept under the stars on a safari through Kenya. She'd watched the northern lights with a Norwegian man named Mathias. And she'd saved up enough money to buy her house from an old artist with paint-splattered hands who'd wanted his home to go to a fellow free spirit.

She'd volunteered at Happy Hooves and had taken mixology classes and had even helped get her friend Patricia Ng—as in *Donovan's mom*—elected mayor of San Francisco. That was the campaign she and Vera had worked on together.

And somewhere in between all her adventures, she'd found time for me. And for my family. And Bug.

Dotty had lived an incredible life. She'd traveled. She'd fought with friends. She'd lost jobs and quit jobs and fallen in love and made mistakes and tried new things. And she'd had a family. She'd built it to suit her, lovingly pulling one person after another into her orbit and making them hers. And she'd done it all with such love and grace and flair. Dotty had lived life exactly the way she wanted.

She'd been happy.

She'd been free.

She'd been true to herself.

Maybe I could too.

CHAPTER THIRTY-THREE

This place is so cool," Marcia said, running her hand along a now empty bookshelf. "How long did Dotty live here?"

I'd been avoiding Marcia since quitting my job and breaking up with Donovan, too embarrassed to admit to yet another failure. But talking to Mom and reading all of Dotty's emails had me seeing things differently. And there was no point in pushing my friend away when I needed her most. So I called Marcia the following day and told her everything. She'd insisted on coming over right away.

"She was here for more than twenty years," I said.

Marcia nodded. "It feels lived in, in a good way." I couldn't believe she'd never been inside Dotty's house. The way she looked around with such warm admiration for Dotty's home had me brimming with pride.

I led Marcia around the house, pointing out Dotty's beloved avocado green refrigerator and the ridiculously ornate chandelier in her bedroom. We ended the tour in Dotty's office, where Marcia instantly fell in love with her collection of jewel-toned pillows and heavy emerald drapes.

"She has so many cool pictures," Marcia said, slowly walking along the far wall, taking each one in as she went. She pulled a picture off its nail and motioned for me to come closer. It was a photo of Dotty, donning a bright blue beanie and a massive puffy jacket. A strikingly handsome man at least ten years her junior had his arm draped over Dotty's shoulders. His hair was so blond it was almost white. "Where was this taken?" Marcia asked.

I rested my head on her shoulder, squinting my eyes. "I don't know. Somewhere cold?"

"Helpful," Marcia said with a laugh. She flipped the picture over. "Have you taken any of these out of their frames?"

"I haven't started packing the office up yet. Why?"

Marcia set the frame face down on Dotty's desk and pried the clasps upward. "What are you doing?" I asked.

"I have a feeling . . ." she muttered. She plucked the photo from the frame. "I knew it."

"Knew what?"

She passed the photo to me. Dotty's handwriting was scrawled across the back and read Mathias in Tromso — 1999.

"No way . . ." I said, sinking down onto an orange pouf. "This is the guy from Dotty's emails."

"This guy responded?"

I nodded. I could see Marcia's wheels turning as she cast a glance around the room. Every wall was packed with mismatched frames, each containing a picture of Dotty grinning next to people I'd never seen before. "Pull up the emails," Marcia said, crossing the room and pulling picture after picture from the wall. "I want to see if any of the others match." She laid the frames out on the floor and began removing the backs. Then she started reading Dotty's notes aloud—Jane from the old neighborhood, Matilda from book club, Dr. Burmeister at the Tambopata Research Center. I recognized almost every name.

"What about Angela in Hawaii?" Marcia asked, holding up a picture of a young Dotty next to a Hawaiian woman with long dark hair, each holding one end of a massive yellow surfboard.

"That's Angela?" I said, rising from my pouf. I took the photo from Marcia and ran my thumb over Dotty's smiling face. "This was her first girlfriend."

"That's so cute," Marcia said dreamily. "They look so happy together."

"They were. For a while, at least."

"What happened?"

I shrugged. "Life."

Marcia put her arm around my shoulder. We stood there in silence, both lost in the snapshot of Dotty's past. "Dotty was kind of a babe," Marcia said eventually. I'd never thought about Dotty like that. She'd always been my kooky old aunt. But there was something special about her, a beauty that radiated from within.

"Yeah," I agreed. "She was."

"Let's see who else we can find," she said, gently removing the photo from my hands and placing it on top of the pile of matches we'd already found.

When we were done, Dotty's walls were bare, and frames were scattered across the worn wood floor. But we'd matched a photo to almost every one of the replies in Dotty's inbox and mine, forty-four in total. And that filled a hole in my heart I hadn't realized was there.

Marcia stayed for dinner because I wanted to introduce her to Dotty's pizza guy. If she thought it was weird that I'd developed a meaningful relationship with my pizza delivery guy, she didn't say anything about it. And for his part, Patrick seemed relieved to find that I finally had company.

It was an unseasonably mild night, so we decided to eat on

Dotty's deck. Marcia filled a pair of mismatched goblets with wine. We ate pizza straight from the box, with Bug looking on, eager for her usual piece of crust.

"The pizza guy seems nice," Marcia said. It sounded like a question.

I nodded as I chewed. "He is," I said. "He was friends with Dotty. Bug, too."

"Uh-huh. And the fact that he looks like he could star in an Avril Lavigne music video is totally lost on you?"

I gulped down another bite, an involuntary grin spreading across my face. "Patrick?" I attempted a casual shrug. "I mean, I guess he's cute but it's completely platonic. He's seen me at my absolute worst—unshowered, bleary-eyed, drunk . . ." My voice trailed off as I shuddered at how terrible his first impression of me must have been. "Besides, I'm not ready to date anyone yet. Not after the whole Donovan thing."

"Well, I never said you needed to date him." She wriggled her eyebrows. "If you know what I mean."

I tossed my napkin at her. "Very subtle."

She laughed. "Just a suggestion."

"I'll take it under consideration," I said, just to shut her up. I wasn't ready to admit that I might have developed a bit of a crush on Patrick.

"Good," she said, turning her face toward the sky. I followed her gaze. The moon was nearly full.

"I can't believe you didn't think to check Dotty's email sooner," Marcia said. Her curls bounced as she shook her head.

I slapped my hand to my forehead. "Neither can I."

"This changes things, right?"

"How?"

Marcia dipped her chin, her nonverbal signal for *come on*. "You've been trying to prove yourself to everyone for so long. And it only got worse after Dotty died."

"What do you mean?"

Marcia tilted her head. "Sticking it out at Driftwood for way too long, taking that job at *Le Agency*." She said the name of my former employer with exaggerated affectation. "Always trying to impress your mom, dating Donovan." She paused. "*Moving in* with Donovan."

"I'm well aware of all my misadventures in adulting, thanks."

"It's just that you were trying to be this other person, this impressive, successful techie robot. As if being you wasn't good enough."

My throat tightened. "And why are things different now?"

Marcia shot me a look that said, *Rosie, you're dense*. "Dotty's life is like a blueprint for all of us. She did what she wanted; she didn't get hung up on what it might have looked like from the outside or what other people thought of her. And her life turned out great."

My thoughts drifted to my memories of Dotty. How happy she'd always been. How free. The way she'd always told stories about interesting friends who were scattered across the globe. The way she'd pushed me to quit my start-up job, even though she'd known it would piss Mom off.

Dotty had given me the greatest gift she could: permission to live my life the way I wanted to live it. And I'd crumpled it up and thrown it away. I wondered if it was too late to dig it out of the wastebasket and smooth out the edges.

"You're right," I said, my voice sounding distant.

"I know. So that should give you something to think about." Marcia took a long drink of wine. "Are you going to respond to the rest of the emails?"

I hadn't thought that far ahead. But of course I would. I had to. "Maybe I can send them Dotty's pictures."

"I bet they'd love that," Marcia said.

"Yeah." We sat in comfortable silence, listening to the distant sound of crickets in the trees behind Dotty's house.

Marcia's snort interrupted the momentary peace. "Remember when we ran into Dotty at the beach . . ." She started breaking into a fit of laughter. "Naked?"

"Don't remind me," I pleaded.

"Do you think she got sand stuck in her . . . bush?"

"Marcia!"

She laughed even harder at my reaction. Which made me giggle. "I was more traumatized by her friend's floppy penis."

Marcia hunched over in her chair, grabbing her side. "It was so floppy!"

"Do you think he responded to my email?"

Marcia's laughter subsided enough for her to wipe a stray tear. "God, I hope so."

"I don't know if I'd recognize his face, but I'd know those droopy balls anywhere."

That sent both of us into another round of giggles. I couldn't believe how good it felt to laugh. It had been so long. When had my life gotten so heavy?

As we sat under the stars on Dotty's old deck, eating pizza and drinking wine and laughing about genitalia, I knew this would have made Dotty happy. Wherever she was, I hoped she could see us.

CHAPTER THIRTY-FOUR

The Dotty Emails, as they would come to be known in my family, were a revelation. Learning about Dotty's life—her whole
life—was the push I'd needed to take charge of my own. I finally
knew what I wanted. And for once, I was going to be brave enough
to go after it.

But first I needed to get Dotty's house in shape.

So I decided to call in reinforcements. I enlisted Mom's help
gathering boxes and told Dad to bring sandwiches. They'd shown
up on time but in separate cars. I wasn't sure if I'd ever get used
to that.

Lily had been right, though. Something about becoming grandparents had eased the tension between them. As they worked in
Dotty's office, Dad sifting through paperwork and Mom thumb-
ing through photo albums, I saw a flash of the couple they'd once
been. My heart ached for what our family would never get back.

"David," Mom called over her shoulder. "Remember that trip
we took to the Caribbean?"

Dad set a stack of papers on Dotty's desk and straightened them
before rising from the chair. "The one with all the jellyfish?"

Mom plucked a photo from Dotty's album and held it up for
Dad to see. "That's the one."

Dad took the photo, holding it gently between his fingers. "We didn't even dip our toes in the water."

"I didn't want to get stung."

Light broke through the cracks in Dad's wrinkled face as he smiled down at Mom. It had been weeks since he'd last shaved. And even longer since he'd cut his hair. But for a moment, I saw the old Dad lurking beneath his sad, tired facade. "We found other things to do," he said, grinning. Mom smacked Dad's arm, her cheeks flushing.

"Hey, Rosie," Dad said without looking up. "Want to see a picture of your mom and me on the day you were conceived?"

"David!" Mom pretended to be horrified, but she was laughing. I didn't have to pretend. I *was* horrified. "Nope."

Dad turned back to Mom. "Why didn't we ever go back?"

"You wanted to wait until after you retired," she said gently.

I flashed on the morning Mom and I had spent in Dotty's living room, clutching mugs of rapidly cooling coffee as Mom had poured her heart out, desperate for me to understand why she'd left. And I finally did. Mom felt stifled by the life she and Dad had built, while Dad had grown increasingly content.

Mom pulled the picture out of Dad's hand and placed it back in the album. "We had a lot of good, happy years together, David. We just wanted different things in the end."

"Right." Dad's lips tightened. "Well, we'll be at this all day and night at this rate. I'll get back to it." He settled back in at Dotty's desk as a weighty silence fell over the room. Awkward as it was, this was progress. My parents were talking, even laughing, as we worked our way through Dotty's possessions. But it was clear that Dad hadn't moved on yet, not in the way Mom had. At least they didn't hate each other.

We went on like that for hours, asking one another questions, half listening to the absent-minded responses. Dad carted garbage bags full of old papers off to the shredder and Mom organized piles of albums for Dad to store at the house. We donated the poufs and pillows to a vintage rug shop. I finally got around to watering Dotty's neglected houseplants. Somehow, I'd kept Bug alive for months but had nearly killed three ferns and an orchid. Mom agreed to take them off my hands. It was best for everyone.

I tackled the books on Dotty's office shelves, combing through rows and rows of titles about Russian history, astrophysics, rare birds, and the mysteries of Easter Island, taking care to set aside the books in which Dotty had scribbled notes on the title pages or along the margins. I couldn't bear to hand them over to Tommy and Lily. I felt closer to her as I ran my fingers over her handwriting.

"What do you say we do the kitchen next?" Dad said as the three of us stood in the doorway of Dotty's office, surveying our progress. The room was nearly empty, except for Dotty's now tidy, spotless desk, a faded red rug, and a solitary floor lamp. The space looked smaller without all her stuff packed inside.

"I've got to get going soon," Mom said. "My art classes start up again next week and I have a long drive ahead of me."

"Lily and I can handle it. She's going to come by with Lucía on Monday."

Dad squeezed my shoulder. "You're doing a great job, sweetheart."

"Do you want us to stay for dinner?" Mom asked. The crease between her eyebrows had deepened over the years. I couldn't tell if she was worried or just tired.

I shook my head. "I have leftovers." I sensed my parents exchanging a look behind my head. "I'm fine. I promise."

"It's just a little concerning, knowing you're here all by yourself," Dad said.

There was a time, not too long ago, when I would have been annoyed that my parents were worrying about me. I would have interpreted it as doubt when really it was well-intentioned concern. But as I reflexively reached for that old reaction, I couldn't find a trace of irritation. Instead, I felt loved.

"You both live by yourselves."

"But Dotty—"

"Died here?" I turned to face them. "That's why I don't sleep in her room," I said gently, hoping to strike a reassuring tone.

Dad looked at the ceiling. I think he was trying not to cry. Mom placed a gentle hand on Dad's arm. "We're all living with the ghost of something, David."

He covered her hand with his. "Yes, I suppose we are."

* * *

That night, as I was polishing off a day-old container of fried rice, I got a text from Tommy.

Can you send me the emails you got about Dotty? I want to read them.

My brother hadn't shown much of an interest in Dotty's life, not in the way Lily and I had. But seeing Dotty through the eyes of her friends had changed me. Maybe it would be good for Tommy, too.

He cared more than I realized. It just looked different.

I stayed up late compiling Dotty's emails into a single document, arranged in chronological order. I think a part of me wanted to be sure that Tommy got the full picture. That he got *her*.

Sitting on Dotty's familiar velvet couch with her dog by my side and her old computer balanced on my lap, I realized that my relationship with Dotty wasn't over. She'd given so much of herself to so many people without ever asking for anything in return. I owed so much to her.

I owed her a proper goodbye. We all did.

That was the night that my plan to honor Dotty in the way she deserved started to take shape.

CHAPTER THIRTY-FIVE

DECEMBER

It had been just over a month since Lily had first found me squatting at Dotty's. Since then the house had evolved from a quirky hideaway, stuffed with furniture, dripping in jewel tones, and peppered with knickknacks, into something much prettier and more modern. The walls bore fresh coats of thick, white paint, all the light switches worked, the faucets no longer leaked. The wall that once housed a robust collection of books and treasures was bare, replaced with a marble-topped bistro set.

I should have been sad about it. I'd even considered asking my family if we could keep it, if I could just live there forever. But it was time to move on. And I was in no position to take on a mortgage.

Lily handled the finishing touches, expertly directing the stagers, hanging abstract artwork, arranging candles, fluffing pillows. In a matter of hours, the remainder of Dotty's furniture had been removed and replaced with sleek modern pieces (a crisp gray love seat in place of Dotty's green velvet sofa, a glass-topped desk swapped for her old oak monstrosity). When she was finished, the place was unrecognizable. "This," Lily said, crossing her arms over her chest, "is going to sell quickly."

It sold in less than a week to a sculptor named Rufus who had a cat called Pineapple. He wasn't the highest bidder by a long shot, but I knew he was who Dotty would have chosen. Mom and Dad balked at first, but to my utter shock, Tommy and Lily sided with me. I now had a decent chunk of money coming my way, thanks to Dotty. In true grown-up fashion, I planned to put most of it into savings. But first, I was going to make a sizable donation to a pro-choice fund in Dotty's name.

Lily managed to negotiate a longer close to give me and Bug time to find a new place. Things were changing again, the ground shifting beneath my feet just as it had been for so many months now. But I was finally starting to feel at peace with the uncertainty of it all.

* * *

I ordered one last pizza from Patrick before Bug and I moved out for good. When I answered the door in my best sundress, hair blown dry, lips glossed to perfection, his eyes widened with surprise. "Wow," he said, "you look—"

"Do you want to hang out sometime?"

Patrick blinked. Then he started to laugh.

My stomach dropped. I was an idiot. He probably already had a girlfriend. Or a boyfriend. I'd never thought to ask. All those times I thought he might have—maybe?—been flirting with me, he was probably just being nice as a favor to Dotty.

But did he have to *laugh* at me? I wrapped my arms around my stomach. "Sorry—I . . . never mind," I mumbled.

But Patrick wasn't listening to me. He'd pulled my pizza out of the insulated bag and was holding the box in front of him, like a present. Now he was grinning, smirking actually. At least he wasn't laughing anymore. He lifted the lid of the box. "Great minds think alike, I guess."

There was a message scrawled in black marker on the inside of the lid. It read: **Do you want to hang out some time?** A phone number was written below. I looked back up at Patrick, who was now chewing on his bottom lip. His remarkably kissable-looking bottom lip. "You're braver than me," he said. "I was going to sprint back down these stairs before you had a chance to notice my note."

I reached for the pizza, my fingertips tingling as they brushed his. I held the box away from my body, admiring the message. "This is the cutest note I've ever gotten."

Patrick blushed at the compliment. "Good," he said, before letting out a huge sigh. "This went way better than I expected."

I closed the lid and set the box on the table, unsure of what to do next. Pay him? Wish him a good night? Invite him in?

"So . . ." Patrick said, rubbing the back of his neck.

"So?"

"I guess . . . we'll hang out soon then?"

"I think that's what we've established here."

Patrick nodded, his cheeks still flushed. "Cool. The pizza is on me tonight. It's the cute customer discount."

My stomach did a thrilling flip. How had I not noticed how utterly adorable he was sooner? I took a step toward the door and looked up at Patrick. "Well, you should at least let me thank you," I said, standing on my toes. He dipped his head down and brushed his lips against mine. He tasted like mint and smelled like soap.

He was an excellent kisser.

As I stood there on my great-aunt's doorstep, making out with a sweet man I never would have met if it weren't for her, I knew I'd always remember this moment. Someday, if I was lucky, I'd regale my own niece with my quirky story about the time a hot pizza guy wrote his number on the inside of a to-go box. She'd humor me or act horrified or maybe even want my advice. Then she'd tell me what was going on in her life, and I'd listen intently, knowing full well how precious and fleeting our time together was. Hopefully this would all happen over a round of filthy martinis.

But until then, I was going to enjoy kissing a new person, and collecting as many stories and experiences as I possibly could.

I knew Dotty would approve.

* * *

"I can't work for you," I blurted as soon as Pilar's face appeared on-screen. I'd been putting off this video call for too long, afraid of what her reaction might be, of what this decision said about me.

She blew out a long exhale. "That sucks."

"I know."

"Is there anything I can do to change your mind?"

"If there was, I'd tell you."

"I blame Nadine."

Evan poked his head into the frame, looking as smug as ever. "What are we blaming Nadine for now?"

"Rosie's not taking the job," Pilar said. When she turned to look at Evan, I noticed she'd gotten a new nose piercing. It suited her.

Evan rolled his eyes. "You suck."

"I know," I said. "But I hope we can still be friends?" My voice cracked on the last word. I felt weirdly vulnerable, like a girl on the playground asking the cool kids if she could join them on the monkey bars.

"Of course we'll still be friends, you weirdo," Pilar said in a way that made my heart swell.

"But no more disappearing for weeks on end," Evan said, eyeing me pointedly through the screen.

"I promise. I'm done with disappearing acts. Can we go out for drinks next week? I have a lot to tell you. And I want to hear all about the agency, too."

"I'll check my calendar," Evan said. "But I think I can make that work." He winced, probably because Pilar had just pinched him.

My shoulders loosened. I didn't know why I'd been so afraid to be honest with them. "Awesome," I said. "I'd love that."

"Us too," Pilar said.

There was one more thing I needed to tell them, but I wasn't sure how they were going to take it. "I think you should hire Kate." Their eyebrows shot up in unison. "She's way more normal than we realized. And she hates Nadine, too."

"Interesting," Evan replied.

"Think about it."

"We will," Pilar promised. "See you next week."

Within seconds of hanging up, I got a text from Evan:

Didn't get to ask. What are you going to do now?

Thanks to Dotty, for the first time in a long time, I had a plan. I was finally going to follow my heart. I replied:

What I should have done a long time ago.

And then I called Sonia.

CHAPTER THIRTY-SIX

FEBRUARY

Dotty had insisted she didn't want a funeral. We'd all taken it at face value, chalked it up to Dotty being Dotty. But getting to know my great-aunt in a way I hadn't known was possible when she was alive had made me see things differently. And it occurred to me that Dotty never said we couldn't throw her a going-away party. When I called Peter to tell him my idea, he'd agreed. He also said he knew just the place for such a shindig (his words).

Peter managed to secure the entire piano bar he and Dotty used to frequent every month. He'd saved the owner from some legal trouble a few years back and said she owed him a favor. So there we were, in a dimly lit bar covered in dark, nearly iridescent wallpaper and dripping in red velvet. A massive, gleaming piano sat in the corner of a small stage with a crystal chandelier above. The polished wood bar stretched the length of the room, with three tuxedoed bartenders pouring champagne into tall, skinny flutes.

Peter was right. This place was perfect.

"How are we on time?" I asked Lily, who was cradling Bug in her arms like a baby. I'd dressed her in a red cable-knit sweater, one of Dotty's favorites.

She glanced at her watch. "Five minutes 'til six."

I gulped down a nervous lump in my throat. Everyone would be here soon; people I'd spent the last two months getting to know over email. And now I was going to meet them in person. I plucked a glass of champagne off the bar and took a long sip.

"You did an amazing job," Lily said, looking around. "Dotty would have loved this."

My eyes landed on the gold-and-black *Bon Voyage, Dotty* banner I'd had made at a print shop down the street. "It feels like she's going to be here," I said. "Like she's going to walk through the door any minute."

"Tommy says that all the time," Lily said.

I tried to ignore the fuzzy warmth enveloping my heart. I still wasn't used to feeling that way about my brother. "Speak of the devil," Lily said as Tommy approached, holding Lucía. She had a big green bow in her hair and looked so cute that my arms were reaching for her before I even knew what I was doing. Tommy passed her to me gladly. Then he ruffled my hair. I pretended to hate it.

"Happy birthday, sis," he said. "How does it feel to be a quarter of a century old?"

I'd insisted on throwing Dotty's party on my birthday, which, lucky for me, fell on a Saturday this year. When Dotty died, the thought of turning twenty-five without her by my side was unbearable. This wasn't the same—not even close—but it felt right. I wouldn't have wanted to spend today any other way.

I cast a glance around the room. "It feels . . . lucky."

Tommy nodded in understanding. "You've done an awesome job with all of this, Ro," he said, sounding more sincere than I'd ever heard him. "You should be really proud of yourself."

"He means he's proud of you," Lily interjected. "We both are."

I blinked in rapid succession, trying to keep tears at bay. It had taken Marcia forever to glue my fake eyelashes on straight. She'd insisted that I'd want to look extrahot for Patrick-the-Pizza-Guy who was now just Patrick. We weren't exactly dating, but we weren't just friends either. Dotty would probably call him my lover. Whatever Patrick and I were, we had fun together—going for hikes with Bug, trivia nights at his favorite dive bar, and, unsurprisingly, ordering pizza and watching *Top Chef*—and that was enough for me. Marcia was convinced we'd get married someday, but Patrick was heading to culinary school on the East Coast in a couple of months and I wasn't interested in anything long distance. Regardless, Marcia would kill me if I cried her handiwork off before the party even started.

"I've been looking up Dotty's travel articles, reading about all her trips," Tommy said, shifting his weight back and forth. "She went all over the place. It's really inspiring."

Something about Tommy was different, softer. I couldn't put my finger on it, but I liked it. "Yeah," I said, resting my head on Lucía's. "It was."

"Lily and I have been talking about taking more trips. We think Dotty would have wanted Lucía to see more of the world than either of us have."

Neither Tommy nor I had ever left the country. Dotty must have been horrified, but she'd never made us feel bad about it. "That's great."

"We were thinking about starting small since this one's still so young." He squeezed Lucía's chubby little thigh. "Maybe Costa Rica for her birthday?"

I did my best to mask my disappointment that I wouldn't get to spend Lucía's first birthday with her. I'd already started looking forward to the part where she'd smear cake all over her cute little face. But then Tommy said, "We were wondering if you'd want to come with us?"

"You'd have your own room," Lily said quickly. "We found a great little house right on the beach."

"You want me to go with you on your family vacation?"

"Only if you want to," Lily said.

I didn't have to think about it. "I'd love to."

Lily squeezed her shoulders up to her ears. "I was hoping you'd say that." She was beaming.

"You'll have to buy your own plane ticket, though. We aren't going to pay for *everything*," Tommy said. Lily slapped his shoulder. "But I'm really glad you said yes."

I was, too.

* * *

I greeted my parents with hugs, feeling extrasparkly in light of Tommy and Lily's invitation. Marcia and I had always talked about backpacking around Southeast Asia together. But then we'd moved to the city, and she met Raj, and that was that. I'd never expected to find travel companions in my brother and sister-in-law. The thought made me happier than I ever could have imagined.

"You look beautiful, sweetie," Mom said, wrapping me into one of her too-tight hugs. "You're glowing." I hugged her back, tighter than usual this time. Lucía cooed her approval. She loved group hugs.

"And this place is incredible," Dad said, taking in the old-fashioned crown molding. "Well done, birthday girl."

"Can we help with anything?" Mom asked.

I shook my head. "Just grab a glass of champagne and enjoy yourselves."

Something funny happened to Mom's face. "Tell me, Rosie. When exactly did you become such a grown-up?"

I shrugged casually, secretly basking in the compliment.

"I'm going to go say hello to Mary from the old neighborhood," Dad said. "I'll find you two later?"

Mom watched Dad leave, affection flitting across her face. When he was safely out of earshot, she turned to me. "Is Peter here?"

"Yeah, he's in the back talking to the pianist," I said slowly, sensing a questionable thread that I didn't dare tug on.

Mom pulled a compact out of her purse and checked her reflection. Her makeup was flawless as always. "Well, I'd better go thank him for helping you with all this."

"You do that."

She squeezed my arm and disappeared toward the back of the bar. Mom could do a lot worse than Peter Simpson, Esquire. But if those two started dating, Tommy's head was sure to explode. I hoped I'd be there to see it.

I moved Lucía to my other hip. "Grandma is on the prowl," I said. She blew a raspberry in response. "My thoughts exactly."

* * *

I set my now-empty glass of champagne on the bar as I sensed someone approaching behind me. A familiar feeling tingled at the base of my skull. I knew it was Donovan before I even turned around.

"Hi, Rosie Benson," he said, grinning. He stood with his hands dug into his pockets.

"Hey, stranger." An involuntary smile stretched across my face. "Thanks for coming."

"Thanks for inviting us."

Us. That's right. The person I was most nervous about meeting today was Patricia Ng.

"Who's this?" Donovan asked, pointing to Lucía. She flashed him a gummy grin.

"This is my niece, Lucía," I said, bouncing her on my hip.

"She's cute," he said. "What's it like being an aunt?"

"It's pretty awesome," I said. "I think Dotty was onto something. Being an aunt is kind of the best of both worlds." As if to drive the point home, Lucía tugged on my earring. "I can give this one back whenever I'm ready," I said, through a wince.

Donovan laughed as my eyes drifted toward his Adam's apple and down to his chest. His shirt was unbuttoned one button too many. Just like the night I met him. "It's good to see you," I said, meaning it.

"You too." His smile melted me—just a little. I guess you don't stop being attracted to someone just because you don't want to date them anymore. "Sorry again for . . . everything."

"Me too," I said. "But I've been thinking. My aunt stayed friends with almost all her exes. And it seemed to make her really happy. Maybe we could give it a try?"

He pressed his lips into a smile, revealing the dimple that used to drive me wild. "I'd like that. Maybe someday this little one will be friends with one of my kids. Like a generational friendship thing."

I made a mental note to warn Lucía about Donovan Jr. when the time came. But the idea was sweet. "That would be adorable."

He playfully nudged me with his elbow. "Well, now that we're friends again, I can give you this." He held up a cotton-candy-pink gift bag with yellow tissue paper sticking out the top.

"You didn't need to bring me anything—"

"It's not for you," he interjected. "It's for Sprinkles the goat." He pulled out a pair of gray sweatpants, the same ones he'd worn that day at Happy Hooves. "Think of them as a belated baby shower present."

My heart swelled at the gesture. Just because Donovan wasn't *my* person didn't mean he wasn't a good person. "Goats don't have baby showers," I said, laughing.

"Oh really? But opossums buy diapers at Walmart?"

"You're something else, Donovan Ng."

"Back at you, Rosie Benson." I hadn't realized how much I'd missed this. Missed him.

Donovan's gaze drifted over my shoulder. "Hey," he said, eyes fixed on whatever was behind me. "I want you to meet my mom."

I turned to see a petite woman in a burgundy power suit striding toward us. She had a blunt, black bob and held a glass of amber liquid with a single square cube in the center.

"You must be Rosie," she said without pausing for me to respond. "What a fabulous party. Dotty would have been absolutely tickled."

"Thank y—"

"You know, your aunt and I knew each other for more than thirty years. She helped run my first mayoral campaign."

"Yes, I—"

"She was brilliant. An excellent writer. And honest as can be. I don't think I ever saw her lie. I wish I could say the same for myself."

"Mom," Donovan grumbled.

Mayor Ng flashed her son a practiced smile before turning back to me. "My son says I talk too much."

"You do talk too much," Donovan said.

She laughed. "It's a gift, I guess. So tell me, Rosie, what do you do?"

"I actually just started a new job. At Happy Hooves. It's a—"

"Farmed animal sanctuary," Patricia said. "I'm familiar. Sonia is doing great work there."

I nodded. "She is."

"What are you doing for them?"

"A little bit of everything. Administrative stuff. Taking care of the animals. And . . ." I looked at Donovan. "Fundraising."

His forehead wrinkled as he raised his eyebrows. "Looking for investors, huh?"

"Maybe," I said, keeping my tone casual. "You might be hearing from Barb soon."

"I like this one," Patricia said to Donovan. "She's got a little shark in her."

"Just like my aunt," I said.

"Just like her," Patricia said. She started to say something else, but Dad's voice interrupted her. "Rosie!" he called from the bar. "I want you to meet Dr. Burmeister."

"I'm so sorry, my dad needs me," I said.

"No problem, dear. Hosting duties call. Come find me later." I gave Patricia a nod. Donovan mouthed an apology as he passed me the sweatpants. I waved him off. I understood all too well what it was like to have an overbearing mom.

* * *

Richard Burmeister was just as eccentric as I'd expected. He was short, with rich brown skin, a silver Afro, and a slightly receding hairline. He wore a grasshopper tie and a beetle pin on the lapel of his blazer. "So this is the famous Rosie," he said as I approached. His voice was nasally but in an endearing way.

"Professor Burmeister, I presume," I replied. Something about him reminded me so much of Dotty. I liked him right away.

"In the flesh," he said, spreading his arms and revealing a pair of suspenders beneath his suit jacket. Lucía reached for Dad. I passed her to him.

"Have you seen Bug?" I asked Dad. "I want her to meet her namesake."

"I'll have Lily bring her over," he said before disappearing into the crowd.

I proceeded to pepper Dr. Burmeister with questions about his work in the Amazon jungle. Bugs weren't exactly my thing, but his life was more similar to Jane Goodall's than anyone I'd ever met. He was currently entrenched in a tiger moth census and invited me to join him as a citizen scientist if I ever found myself in the area. "Your aunt described you perfectly," Dr. Burmeister said, looping his thumbs into his suspenders. "I admire your inquisitive spirit." He looked over his shoulder as if concerned that someone might be eavesdropping. "You were her favorite, you know."

My cheeks warmed at the compliment. "She was my favorite, too."

Dr. Burmeister grinned. "What a gift, to end up in the same family."

I hadn't thought of it that way. But he was right.

Bug, seeming to sense the presence of a new friend, appeared at Dr. Burmeister's feet, eagerly sniffing at his shoes. "I take it this is Bug," he said, bending to greet her. She grunted her enthusiastic hello. Before I knew it, Dr. Burmeister was seated cross-legged on the floor with Bug in his lap. "I never had any children or pets of my own," he said, not taking his eyes off Bug. "Dotty naming her in my honor was the greatest compliment I could have imagined."

"You're welcome to visit her anytime you want."

"I'd like that very much," he said. Bug licked his cheek. I wished Dotty were here to see it.

* * *

One by one, they all showed up. Stuart and Meredith and Mathias. Marcia and Raj. Patrick, looking dapper in a blazer-T-shirt tennis-shoes combo that only he could pull off. Sean from college and Cara from the *Marin Journal* and Sonia from Happy Hooves. I met old friends, new friends, coworkers, travel companions, and lovers. Iris came all the way from France. She was lovely and teary and hugged me for what felt like an hour.

And then there was Angela. She was just as radiant as her picture, with long gray hair and high cheekbones and deep brown eyes that sparkled when she smiled. It was no wonder Dotty had fallen so hard for her all those years ago. After that summer, Angela had gone to veterinary school on a small island in the Caribbean before moving to New Mexico, where she met her wife, Gina. They had two kids and four grandkids. She and Dotty had reconnected ten years ago when Angela had taken a job in Oakland. "She was my dearest friend," Angela said.

It wasn't that Dotty hadn't mentioned Angela. When I thought about it, I'd heard her name in passing all the time. But I never thought to ask who she was to Dotty. I wished with all my heart that I had. Meeting her was a gift.

"Dotty told me that you wanted to be a veterinarian when you were younger," Angela said.

This topic of conversation used to send bolts of shame coursing up and down my body. But not anymore. "I did, but it wasn't meant to be."

"Dotty said that, too."

My heart warmed at the thought. Dotty had a way of knowing what was best for a person before they even knew it themselves. "Your aunt was an old soul," Angela said as if reading my mind. "She was very observant and very wise. But not always so tactful."

"That was one of my favorite things about her."

"Mine, too," Angela said. I liked the way the corners of her eyes crinkled when she smiled. "Dotty had another dream for you, though. And I heard it may have come to pass. Is it true that you're working for Sonia now?"

"Yes," I said. "I started a few weeks ago."

"That would have made Dotty so happy, my dear," she said, pulling me into a warm hug. I squeezed her back. My heart felt a little more whole.

* * *

When it was time to eat, my family gathered around a large circular table. Mom was beside Dad, Lucía in my lap. Tommy sat to my left and Lily to my right, cradling Bug in her arms. Dotty's absence was palpable, but I couldn't shake the feeling that she was close by. There had been moments like that in the months since she'd died when I was sure that if I just turned around, I'd catch her sneaking up behind me, a mischievous glint in her eye.

That was the thing about people like Dotty. They kind of live on forever.

It didn't take long for Dad to raise a glass, just as he'd done at so many family dinners before. "To our dear Dotty and all the gifts she's left behind." It was the first of many toasts that night, peppered with stories and memories and laughs. As I sat there, at my dead aunt's party, with my own niece on my lap, surrounded by the family I'd once thought to be perfect, I finally saw them for who they really were. They were flawed but happy, and they were mine.

There was a time when I would have been terrified to fill a room with people from disparate corners of my life. I think I was worried they'd compare notes and uncover some terrible secret I didn't even know I was hiding. Now I understood that I was afraid of letting everyone see how flawed, how human I was. The thought now seemed ridiculous. I think learning about Dotty's life—warts and all—helped me to let that go. It was yet another gift from my wonderfully imperfect aunt.

As dinner began to wind down, Peter swept through the room, dropping stacks of paper in the center of every table. "I put together a little surprise send-off for Dotty," he said, handing me the sheet. It was the lyrics to "Hello, Dolly!," but Peter had changed the words to *So long, Dotty*. "This was one of her favorites."

We all gathered around the piano as Peter took the stage, microphone in hand. He flashed a thumbs-up to the pianist, a barrel-chested man with a thick mustache, who began to play. As the familiar, old-timey melody filled the room, everyone started to sing along with Peter:

So long, Dotty
Well, farewell, Dotty
We'd love to have you back where you belong
But it's been swell, Dotty
You can tell, Dotty
You're still glowing, you're still crowin', you're still goin' strong
We feel the room swayin'
For the band's playin'
One of your old favorite songs from way back when . . .

Soon everyone was arm in arm, a tangle of limbs swaying with the music. It was cheesy and wonderful and so beautiful that tears began streaming down my face. I knew Dotty would have loved this. I could almost picture her up onstage next to Peter, wearing an impish grin and singing at the top of her lungs.

I wanted to remember this moment forever. Mom and Dad reading from the same sheet of paper, looking like a pair of good old friends. Tommy dancing with Lucía in the corner. And Lily, wrapping me in a tight hug, singing loudly and off-key, and feeling like the sister I never knew I needed.

We stayed well into the night, people taking turns making requests of the mustached piano player—everything from "Piano Man" to "Luck Be a Lady" to "Ice Ice Baby." We danced and drank and laughed and cried. And when it was time to say goodbye, I felt more at peace than I had in a very long time.

EPILOGUE

Sweat was starting to pool in the small of my back. It wasn't even nine A.M. yet, but the sun loomed large in the sky. I could have sworn it was bigger than normal.

"Are you ready?" Sonia asked, her hand above her forehead to protect her eyes from the glare.

"Ready," I said as a jolt of excitement coursed through my body. I was nervous. But good nervous. Something nudged me from behind, forcing me to take a step forward. I turned to see Barb, eagerness flashing in her big brown eyes. I scratched her nose. "You ready to go make some new friends?"

The three of us made our way past the chicken coop and through the paddock, where pigs and goats and Pickles the donkey lazily grazed at their communal trough.

"Where's Bug?" Sonia asked.

"Playing with Cupcake." As if on cue, Bug darted in front of us with the baby goat hot on her heels. She was covered in dirt. But I would be, too, soon enough.

"I think Bug thinks she's a goat."

"Or Cupcake thinks she's a dog."

"A dog who can climb trees," Sonia cracked. And fences. I'd spent the better part of the afternoon yesterday coaxing the mischievous kid down from a post.

Sonia wrapped her hand around the fence handle and braced her feet. "I'm going to have you take the lead," she said before sliding the gate open. "This was your baby, and you should run with it."

"Okay," I said, doing my best to ignore the nervous flutter in my stomach.

A group of volunteers, all my recruits, stood in the dusty parking lot. They ranged in age from sixteen to seventy-two and wore sunglasses and ponytails and flannel shirts tied around their waists. And they collectively lit up at the sight of Barb lumbering toward them. Marcia and Raj stood off to the side, next to Evan and Pilar, all waving eagerly as I approached—except for Raj, who was frowning at his white shoes.

"Welcome to Happy Hooves," I said, my voice steady, confident. "I'm Rosie, the sanctuary manager, this is Sonia, the founder, and this is Barb. She's our boss."

Rocket the rooster crowed in the distance. A ripple of giggles worked its way through the group. "Thanks for coming today," I continued. "I'm really excited to meet all of you in person and for all of you to meet our residents. We'll be dividing up into small groups today; some of you will be mucking stalls, others will be cleaning the chicken coop, and I'll also need a couple of volunteers to keep the animals occupied. They like to help us clean, but they're actually not very helpful at all." Barb grunted in protest. "Except for Barb, of course," I said, patting her side. "She'll be supervising your work."

The group smiled and nodded in response. Pilar bounced on her heels, looking like she was about to jump out of her skin with excitement. Raj, on the other hand, looked terrified at the thought of such a large animal following him around.

"We'll get you all set up with boots and gloves and then we can get started," I said. "But first, does anyone have any questions?"

Everyone shook their heads, seemingly eager to get started. "All right," I said, clapping my hands together. "Follow me."

I dared myself to look at Sonia, who flashed me a thumbs-up and mouthed, *Great job*. I sighed with relief. I *had* done a great job. It felt better than I'd ever imagined.

Marcia jogged to catch up with me, Raj trailing behind her. "This is amazing, Ro," she said, grabbing my arm and giving it an enthusiastic shake. "I'm so proud of you."

"I shouldn't have worn white shoes," Raj said.

"You only own white shoes," Marcia said.

"We have boots for you," I assured Raj. He seemed to relax at that. "I'll put you two with the chickens," I continued. "They're smaller and easier to manage. Plus, Barb isn't allowed in their enclosure."

"Oh, thank god," Raj breathed dramatically.

"Where's your cottage?" Marcia asked. "I want to see where you live."

I pointed toward the back of the property. "It's just past those stalls."

"I can't believe you live here."

"Me neither," I said. I'd never imagined that I would live next door to my boss. Or that my job would require work boots over heels. Or that I would come home invariably covered in some form of poop. But I'd never been happier. "You're staying for lunch, right? I made dolmas and muddled mint lemonade."

"Of course," Marcia said, giving my hand another squeeze. "Has your family been out here yet?"

"They're coming next week." I couldn't wait to introduce Lucía to all the animals. Or to make Tommy shovel goat poop.

"They're going to love it," she said, her head swiveling back and forth, taking it all in.

I nodded. "I hope so."

"And what about Patrick?" she asked, nudging me with her elbow.

I shook my head in amusement. Marcia had turned into such a love pusher ever since meeting Raj. I knew she was going to be even worse soon, because Raj was planning to propose. I'd gone with him to help pick out the ring. Keeping this secret from her was among the hardest things I'd ever had to do. "Patrick's coming by later tonight to help me tuck the chickens in."

"Is that what you kids call it these days?"

I started to remind Marcia that Patrick was leaving soon, but I knew it was futile. She just wanted me to be happy. It was sweet. I *was* going to miss Patrick, but one of the many things Dotty taught me was that you never knew how big or small a role someone would play in your life. Maybe Patrick and I were destined to end up together. Maybe he'd be a rebound-turned-old-friend. Or maybe he'd become nothing more than a fleeting memory of a happy moment in time. No matter what happened, I wasn't afraid of the idea of being single again. I liked being independent. Plus, between Barb and Bug and the Flintstones, I was never really alone.

I would miss the sex, though. And the free pizza.

We gathered in the barn and I began distributing gear to the volunteers. Bug came running in to greet her old pals Evan and Pilar. To his credit, Evan didn't even flinch when she got mud all over his jeans. I scooped her into my arms and gave her a squeeze. She smelled like sunshine and hay.

"Before we get started, I want to share a quick story with all of you," Sonia said. "This barn"—she gestured around the space, her eyes sweeping over the bins of feed and racks full of shovels and rakes and pitchforks—"is named for my dear old friend, Dotty Polk. Without her, none of this would be possible. Dotty volunteered here every Saturday for almost a decade, up until the ripe old age of eighty-one. She passed away about a year ago, and she left Happy Hooves a large sum of money in her will. That money enabled us to hire a full-time sanctuary manager." She waved her hand in my direction. "Rosie has thrown herself into recruiting wonderful volunteers like you to help us care for our residents and hopefully rescue more animals in need. Thanks to Rosie, you can now volunteer here every Saturday—rain or shine. She's also helped us secure a grant to cover veterinary expenses and finally got me on Instagram." I glanced at Marcia, who'd helped me with that part. She mouthed, *You're welcome.*

"Rosie also happens to be Dotty's great-niece." There was a muted murmur of excitement from the group. "And Bug was Dotty's dog." Bug perked up at the sound of her name. "Rosie took Bug in after Dotty died. She's obviously wonderful with animals." I blushed at the compliment. "And she's doing a great job with the sanctuary. I'm very lucky to have her."

I felt lucky to have this job. And Bug. I couldn't bear to imagine what my life would have looked like without Dotty. I owed her everything. "Thank you," I said, trying unsuccessfully to choke back the emotion in my voice. I looked at the group of volunteers. "Now let's go make Dotty proud."

Dear Dotty,

You were so much more than my great-aunt. You were also my teacher, my mentor, my protector, and my friend. You were the person I could always turn to for advice. And you never lied to me.

You showed me what it means to be unapologetically yourself. You taught me that you can be honest while also being kind. You saw me for who I was, flawed and insecure and immature, and you loved me for it. You encouraged me to follow my heart, even when everyone else wanted me to do the opposite. And, perhaps most importantly, you taught me how to make a mean dirty martini.

When you died, my world turned upside down. I didn't understand how this larger-than-life woman, this force of nature could suddenly just slip away. It made me doubt everything. Myself. My goals. My decisions. But worst of all, it made me doubt you.

I started to worry that maybe your life hadn't been as incredible as it appeared. What if you'd been sad or lonely or riddled with regrets? I can see now that you weren't done teaching me.

Losing and then rediscovering you was the push I'd needed to finally grow up and take ownership of my life. To go after the things I wanted. I wouldn't be where I am without you. And I wouldn't be here without all of your friends, either.

Their stories brought you back to life. They helped me to see you as a whole person for the first time. I'm sorry that's what it took for me to really see you.

Dotty, you were nuts. You were brash and wild and over the top. And you were happy. And smart and loving and kind.

You were my hero. You are my hero.

I don't know what kind of life I'm going to live yet. But I do know that you will always be with me. You left me with more gifts than I can count. I wouldn't be me without you.

Love you always,
Rosie

ACKNOWLEDGMENTS

I'm overflowing with gratitude for all the people (and animals!) who made this book happen, so trying to find the words to adequately thank them is more than a little daunting. But here goes.

Thank you a billion times over to my editor, Asanté Simons, for loving this book, these characters, and especially for *getting* our girl, Barb. I'm so grateful for her dedication, perspective, and insightful edits, all of which helped me to add dimension to this story and, most importantly, gave me an excuse to write more scenes with Barb. Asanté, thank you for being so supportive, thoughtful, collaborative, and amazing to work with. I couldn't have chosen a more perfect editor for *Dear Dotty*.

A huge, over-the-top thank-you to my agent, Rachel Beck, for believing in this book, for her spot-on revisions, for helping me realize that Rosie wanted to make out with Patrick the Pizza Guy, and for making my dream of becoming a published author come true! Rachel, you are the best—kind, patient, insightful, knowledgeable, and just all-around wonderful. Someday we'll have that celebratory martini together.

Thank you to Lynn Wu, Liza Dawson, and Havis Dawson for helping with my contract and for answering so many of my questions!

Thank you to Laurie McGee for your copyedits and for making my timeline make sense, and to Rachel Weinick for your careful review. I can't tell you how much I appreciate your time and attention to detail.

A huge thank-you to the amazing team at Avon/Morrow, especially Erika Tsang, DJ Desmyter, Mary Interdonati, Jennifer Hart, Kelly Rudolph, and Liate Stehlik.

To Kerry Rubenstein and Sarah Horgan: thank you for the beautiful cover design. I love it so much.

I wouldn't have made it through the first draft of *Dear Dotty* without the Stanford Continuing Studies Online Novel Writing Certificate program. Thank you to the staff, the instructors, and my fellow students (especially Kelly Caiazzo, who is lovely and talented and so supportive) for helping me to figure out how to write a book.

An extra special thank-you to Stacey Swann, who started as my teacher, became my mentor, and finally, my friend. Stacey, thank you for all the time, thought, and care you put into helping me write this novel. I'll always cherish our cathartic pandemic-era Zoom calls. I can't wait to hang out in person someday.

To the talented Marla Daniels (and NY Book Editors), whose developmental edits helped me to get *Dear Dotty* into querying shape. I wouldn't have gotten this book over the finish line without her. Marla, you are a true delight, and I feel like I could talk to you for hours and hours. Thank you for all your wisdom and support.

A massive thank-you to Heather Lazare and the Northern California Writers' Retreat, where I learned so much about writing, querying, and the publishing industry (all wildly different pieces of the puzzle and all equally perplexing to a newbie like me). Heather has built the most wonderful community of writers, and I'm so grateful to be part of it.

A special thank-you to my fellow NCWR alums Sarah Chamberlain, Angela Christianson, Eileen Conway, and Sasha Rives for their help with my second draft of *Dear Dotty*, and Jessica

Leibe for being so wonderful, knowledgeable, and supportive. I can't wait to hold your books in my hands!

Thanks to the Women's Fiction Writers Association and the dedicated writers who keep it all running. You're the best.

Thank you to Rancho Compasión, an incredible farmed animal sanctuary in Marin County, California. Organizations like this one, along with the Gentle Barn, Farm Sanctuary, and Goatlandia (just to name a few), make this world a better, kinder, and more compassionate place. If you live near a sanctuary like this, I highly recommend paying them a visit!

To The Muse, the home of my first paid writing job, and especially to my editors, Stacey Lastoe, Alyse Kalish, Stav Ziv, and Regina Borselino: thank you for making me look good and for helping me to become a better writer in the process.

Thank you to Susan Coleman and David Meyer for being such fantastic employers (and people!). Your flexibility, patience, and generosity as I worked through this novel writing process was more helpful than you know.

To my parents, Rick and Nancy Raggio. Thank you for sharing your love of books with me, for reading to me before I could even talk, for letting me hole up in my room with a stack of Goosebumps or Little House on the Prairie books for hours on end, and for saving so many of the unhinged little essays I wrote in elementary school. Thank you for believing that I could do this. I wouldn't be here (literally or figuratively!) without you.

To my in-laws, Carol and Wally Westlake. Thank you for your support and enthusiasm for my writing! Your encouragement means the world to me, and I'm so happy that I get to share this experience with you.

To my grandparents: Norma Jones-Hodson, Bob Hodson, Jack

Jones, and Dianne and Lou Raggio. I wish you were here to see this. Actually, I just wish you were here. The way Rosie misses Dotty doesn't even come close to how much I miss all of you.

To my extended family (hi! love you!) and to my aunts and uncles, Cathy and Rick, Bob and Barbara, Dot, Wilma and Cal, who always make me feel like their most special niece (even though I know you love us all the same), and especially to my great-uncle, Raymond Raggio. Uncle Ray was a proud Italian American, a WWII veteran, and a lifelong resident of Lombard Street in San Francisco. Truly one-of-a-kind, I never saw Uncle Ray wearing anything other than a suit or smoking jacket; he commissioned an artist to paint a mural on the ceiling of his hallway depicting each of his great-nieces as cherubs; he had a literal throne installed in his backyard; and the doors to his eclectic home (complete with imported Italian fabric on the walls) were always open to his beloved siblings, nieces, and nephews. Uncle Ray never married or had children, but he had the richest family life of just about anybody I know. I suspect he and Dotty would have gotten along famously.

To my amazing friends: thank you for your support, your enthusiasm, your words of encouragement, your celebratory toasts, and your patience with me as I disappear into my writing cave for months on end. I love you all. You're my family, too.

To Kirk: you're so much more than a brother-in-law to me. You're one of my best friends. Thank you for spending hours (and hours) talking book stuff with me. I love being a part of The Three Best Friends That Anyone Could Have.

To my nieces and nephews: thank you for letting me be your auntie. I know I'm biased, but I'm pretty sure it's a scientific fact that you're the cutest, smartest, funnest kids on the planet. I'm so excited to watch you all grow up. I promise that I'll always have lemonade (or martinis when you're old enough) and that you'll never bump into me at a nude beach.

To Brian, my husband, my best friend, the sweetest dog dad, and my biggest supporter. I'll never stop marveling at the fact that you didn't even bat an eye when I told you I wanted to write a novel. You are a much mellower, more stable person than I am. You amaze me every day with your kindness, your creativity, your ingenuity, your sense of humor, and your chill vibes. Thank you for all of the long, drawn-out book conversations you gamely participated in, for being my sales job fact-checker, for always believing in me, and for being so damn handsome. This book wouldn't exist without you! I love you way more than any words could say. Thank you for being my person.

To my little dog, Indiana Jones: Indy, you're so wonderfully weird and bossy and mischievous and loving and cuddly and adorable and long-bodied. I'd say don't ever change, but at fifteen years old, you've made it abundantly clear that you never will. I love you so much.

And finally, to you! Thank you for reading my book. I hope you liked it. I hope you find your chosen family, and I also hope that you get to adopt a pet or befriend a cow someday. If you already have a dog (or a cat or a chicken or a lizard), please give them my regards.